THE
LAST
WAGON
TRAIN

LOOK FOR THESE EXCITING WESTERN SERIES
FROM BEST-SELLING AUTHORS
WILLIAM W. JOHNSTONE AND J.A. JOHNSTONE

The Mountain Man

Luke Jensen: Bounty Hunter

Brannigan's Land

The Jensen Brand

Smoke Jensen: The Early Years

Preacher and MacCallister

Fort Misery

The Fighting O'Neils

Perley Gates

MacCoole and Boone

Guns of the Vigilantes

Shotgun Johnny

The Chuckwagon Trail

The Jackals

The Slash and Pecos Westerns

The Texas Moonshiners

Stoneface Finnegan Westerns

Ben Savage, Saloon Ranger

The Buck Trammel Westerns

The Death and Texas Westerns

The Hunter Buchanon Westerns

Will Tanner, U.S. Deputy Marshal

Old Cowboys Never Die

Go West, Young Man

Published by Kensington Publishing Corp.

THE LAST WAGON TRAIN

WILLIAM W. JOHNSTONE

AND J.A. JOHNSTONE

PINNACLE BOOKS
Kensington Publishing Corp.
www.kensingtonbooks.com

PINNACLE BOOKS are published by

Kensington Publishing Corp.
900 Third Avenue
New York, NY 10022

All Kensington titles, imprints, and distributed lines are available at special quantity discounts for bulk purchases for sales promotion, premiums, fund-raising, and educational or institutional use.

Special book excerpts or customized printings can also be created to fit specific needs. For details, write or phone the office of the Kensington Sales Manager: Kensington Publishing Corp., 900 Third Avenue, New York, NY 10022. Attn. Sales Department. Phone: 1-800-221-2647.

First Printing: November 2024
ISBN-13: 978-0-7860-5128-1
ISBN-13: 978-0-7860-5129-8 (eBook)

10 9 8 7 6 5 4 3 2 1

Printed in the United States of America

CHAPTER 1

They would have just let the Indians go if not for the prospector.

A team of mule skinners out of Deadwood and angling northwest to Montana had found him along a creek when they'd stopped to water the animals. He was a mess, all beat up, shoes gone, and scalped, which was how they'd known it was Indians. One of the freight drivers recognized the prospector as Henry Jakes. A mule and the man's Spencer rifle were missing. The mule skinners took the body to the nearest marshal, who sent a telegram to the blue coats at Fort Keogh.

Lieutenant W. P. Clark hadn't been happy. The Northern Cheyenne trouble was supposed to be over, but there were always rogue groups, and a murdered white man wasn't something he could ignore. A green second lieutenant named Foster and a dozen equally green troopers were all he could spare.

After careful consideration, Clark couldn't in good conscience send out all those inexperienced men without somebody who actually knew what he was doing.

He called Master Sergeant Isaiah Parks into his

office. Parks snapped to attention, throwing out his barrel chest. He was a beefy, florid-faced man with red hair now streaked with gray, forty-five years old, twenty-two of which had been spent in the army. He'd taken a Confederate bayonet to his left buttock at Bull Run and had only in recent years developed a sense of humor about the scar. He sported new stripes on his blue sleeve, three up and three down.

"At ease, Sergeant," Clark said. "How would you like to escort our young Mr. Foster on a little nature walk?"

"My pleasure, sir."

"You understand what's expected?"

"Noses wiped and diapers changed," Parks said. "Bring the lieutenant back relatively undamaged."

Clark hid a smile. "That's not how I'd put it if Mr. Foster's in earshot, but yes, you have the basic idea. I suppose I should send an experienced scout with you. Is Mort Whittaker still in camp?"

"Beggin' your pardon, sir, but Tom would be my suggestion," Parks said. "He's at that saloon he likes so much, and it's on the way. If we leave early enough, we can pick him up before he gets started."

Tom referred to Luke Callahan. Tom was short for Tomahawk, which was what all the men called him. Lieutenant Clark had never worked with the man, but he trusted the sergeant's judgment.

"Okay, then," Clark said. "You know what to do. Get started."

* * *

Luke "Tomahawk" Callahan sat at a corner table in Shakey's Place, a low-ceilinged, ramshackle saloon inside a squat log structure along a muddy road between Fort Keogh and the rest of the world. A traveler wouldn't have known it was called Shakey's Place if he just happened by. One either knew Gil Shakey, or one didn't. The shutters were closed against the cold, what with winter clinging and spring slow to develop in the first week of April. The only light in the place came from three lanterns and a modest blaze in the stone fireplace.

Callahan tossed two cards on the table and kept three. The two horse soldiers, a lanky corporal and a short private with a bushy mustache, had already thrown their cards down in disgust, wishing they could have their antes back.

That left the slicker.

Or, at least, *slicker* was how Tomahawk Callahan thought of the man. He had *back East* written all over him, talked educated. He wore a dark suit with a red waistcoat, some kind of tight pattern in the fabric that was hard to make out in the saloon's dim light. A gold chain disappeared into the waistcoat pocket, and presumably there was an expensive watch in there. Gold cufflinks. Bowler hat cocked at a jaunty angle. He smoked a thin cigar. Callahan was no expert on fine tobacco, but the cigar smelled good, so it was probably expensive, too. Mustache and beard well trimmed. No dirt under his fingernails. He told everyone he'd recently been let go from the railroad and was on his way to anywhere else.

The slicker's eyes flicked back and forth between his cards and Callahan. He licked his lips. Nervous.

Or maybe just *pretending* to be nervous. Callahan had learned early on you played the man as much as you played the cards.

He wondered how he must look to the slicker. Tall and rangy, five days of black stubble on his square jaw, beat-up buckskin jacket, battered old brown hat hanging on the back of his chair. A Colt Peacemaker hung on his right hip.

Luke didn't see a gun on the slicker's hip. The man was either too trusting or hadn't been West long enough.

The slicker looked at his cards again and then at the pot. A lot of money there, a sizable pot for so early in the day. It wasn't quite lunchtime.

"I seem to be facing a conundrum." The slicker looked at Callahan. "I beg your pardon, *conundrum* means—"

"A confusing or difficult problem," Callahan said. "I know."

"See, you've only taken two cards, so I'm forced to infer the three you have left are good ones," the slicker mused. "Whereas, I'd planned to take three cards."

A child could see the man was stalling, running his mouth just to see if Callahan would blink or flinch or give anything away.

"I didn't mean to *imply* anything specific about my cards," Callahan said. "You are, of course, welcome to *infer* as you like."

The man laughed. "Sorry. I guess that was pretty

clumsy. I noticed you haven't looked at your new cards yet."

"I don't have to yet." Callahan had learned he couldn't give away anything about his cards if he didn't know what they were. If the slicker folded, then it wouldn't matter. If Callahan had to bet, he'd look at his cards then.

The slicker grinned as if amused. "Not even curious?"

Callahan shrugged. He could wait all day.

The slicker threw down two cards. The corporal dealt him two new ones. The slicker looked at them, face blank.

Callahan picked up his cards, forcing himself not to hurry. He held them low and squeezed them out one at a time, seeing his original cards first—three nines. He squeezed the next one. Jack of spades. No help.

He scooted the final card out from behind the rest with his thumb.

The fourth nine.

It was difficult to keep his mouth from quirking into a smile, but Callahan managed to maintain a blank expression. Luck was on his side. Callahan had won a few hands, small amounts of money, but he'd just gotten the best hand of the day right when the pot was the biggest. A bet too big would scare the man off.

Callahan tossed his chips onto the pile, not enough to confirm to the slicker he had a winning hand, but enough to make him pause and think.

"Well." The slicker pushed his bowler back on his head and wiped his forehead. "I can't legitimately claim to have a very strong hand. Having said that, it chagrins to let that sizable pot go without a look at your cards."

Callahan smiled. "It's a conundrum."

The slicker laughed and tossed in his chips. "Call."

Callahan laid down his cards.

The corporal whistled.

The slicker leaned over the cards and frowned. "Four nines. That figures."

He tossed in his cards.

Callahan scooped the chips toward him, allowing his poker face to finally drop in favor of a pleased grin.

The corporal pushed away from the table and motioned for the private to follow him. "That's all for me. Come on, Del, let's get a beer."

The slicker said, "I'd love a chance back at all that money I just lost, but I suppose I'd better not dig my hole any deeper."

A shrug from Callahan, not quite apologetic. "Some days you get the cards. Other days, the other fella has the luck."

"Well, I'd like to prove I'm not a poor sport at least. Let me buy you a whiskey."

"I'll buy you *two* whiskeys if I can get one of them cigars," Callahan said. "Smells good."

"That seems a fair trade." The slicker stuck out his hand. "Ronald Parsons."

Callahan shook. "Tomahawk Callahan."

"Tomahawk?"

"Long story."

Parsons patted his jacket pocket, a thoughtful look crossing his face. "You know what. I don't have any cigars on me. I'm pretty sure I have more in my saddlebags.

Follow me. I'll set you up. I need some air, anyway. It's too close in here with all the shutters closed. My horse is out back."

Callahan stood, and then gathered the chips. "Let me cash these in. I'll meet you out there."

He took the chips to the man behind the bar, Gil Shakey, a man barely as tall as he was wide with a bald head and a drooping mustache that looked like he was letting a squirrel live rent free on his face.

Callahan cashed in his chips and pocketed the money, then stepped out the back door, and a cold wind hit him at once. He grumbled. Tomahawk Callahan had already had his fill of winter. Spring was taking its own sweet time getting here. He went to where Parsons had his horse tied and stood politely, waiting. They were the only two out back. Most people tied their horses out front. Probably, Parsons had come up from the southern trail, and he'd seen the back door first.

Parsons went from one saddlebag to another. "Apologies. I'm sure I have a few more of those stogies stashed somewhere."

"It's okay if you don't. I'll still stand you a whiskey for good intentions." Callahan wasn't keen to linger any longer in the biting wind. The cigar was rapidly losing its attraction.

"No, no. Just a moment."

It was a bit early in the day to start on the whiskey, but now Callahan figured he'd need it just to warm up.

"*Voila!*" Parsons came out of the saddlebag with a small, wooden box in his hand. He opened it and fished out one of the cigars, then handed it to Callahan.

Callahan stuck it in his mouth. "Obliged. I'll light it inside, and we'll get our drinks."

"Thank you, but I'll need to drink quickly," Parsons said. "I should have been on my way to Bozeman long before now." He pointed. "Is that the best way to go?"

Callahan turned to look where he was pointing. "You can go that way, but it's not the fastest route. If you angle south a bit—"

Pain exploded at the base of Callahan's skull, white lights and stars flashing in his eyes a brief moment before everything went dark.

CHAPTER 2

Callahan came awake with a start, sputtering and spitting and freezing cold. He wiped water from his eyes, looking around, trying to remember where he was and how he'd gotten there.

He looked up into the grinning face of Isaiah Parks. The sergeant held a bucket in his hands. "Looks like you started on the whiskey a bit early even for you."

Callahan checked his pockets. All of his money—including the poker winnings—was gone. He stood, spitting a string of curses.

Parks frowned. "Problem?"

"I've been robbed." Callahan touched the sore spot at the base of his skull with three fingertips. Tender, but he'd be okay. "He hit me."

"Who did?"

"Ronald Parsons . . . if that's even his name."

Callahan squinted up at the sun. He'd been out at least an hour. He cursed again, scanning the ground. Too many hoofprints. People came and went all the time to the saloon. Parsons had said he was headed to Bozeman, but, of course, that was a lie. If Callahan followed the wrong trail for half a day, that would only increase the slicker's head start.

He went back inside Shakey's Saloon, asked everyone within if they knew anything about Ronald Parsons or where he might be headed, but nobody had any useful information.

"Some bad luck," Sergeant Parks said. "Sorry, Tom."

"Dirty son of a . . . If I ever see him again, there'll be nothing left of him, I can tell you that. He didn't take my six-gun and knife, at least," Callahan said.

"Good, because you'll need 'em," Parks said. "That's why I come looking for you." Parks briefly explained the expedition with Lieutenant Foster to find the rogue Cheyenne.

"Huh." Callahan scratched his head, thinking it over. "I guess I'm in no position now to turn down a paying job. Okay, Sarge, just let me change into some dry clothes."

They angled southeast toward the spot where the prospector had been found. Callahan rode his painted horse next to Parks, the dozen cavalrymen riding two-by-two behind them. They were traveling known roads, so Callahan's skill as a scout wouldn't be needed yet. Foster rode out front, and Callahan sized up the man.

He was the worst possible combination of everything that made for a rotten officer. He was fresh out of West Point, which meant he probably thought he already knew everything, even though he'd been west of the Mississippi for less than a month. He was appallingly young, which didn't make him a bad person or stupid, but experience counted for a lot out here, and Lieutenant Horace Foster didn't have any. What he did have was a perfectly clean and pressed uniform and the shiniest buttons Callahan had ever seen.

We'll see how long that lasts.

Callahan chastised himself. His opinion was based on young officers he'd met before. Every man deserved a chance to be a blank page. Let Foster write his own story, then Callahan would judge.

They spent the night on a knoll overlooking the road. The troopers were green, according to Parks, but they went about the business of making camp, hobbling the horses, preparing dinner, and setting sentries in a professional manner.

Later that evening, Foster approached Callahan near the campfire, a folded newspaper under one arm. "Callahan? We left Fort Keogh in a hurry and haven't had a chance to meet officially. I'm Second Lieutenant Horace Foster."

"Lieutenant." Callahan shook his hand. "I usually answer to Tom or Tomahawk, but Callahan works, too."

"I understand you have people back in Missouri." He handed Callahan the newspaper. "That issue of the *Post-Dispatch* is only a week old. I've finished it, if you'd like a look."

"Obliged for that." He took the paper and angled it to catch the firelight. A headline caught his eye. THE LAST WAGON TRAIN? Curious, he folded the newspaper and stashed it inside his jacket. "I'll read it when I have better light. Thanks again."

"Well, I'm going to sleep," Foster said. "Early day tomorrow."

They set out the next morning just as dawn was humping up red-orange from the horizon. It warmed soon after, and Callahan wondered if spring had finally made an appearance. By midafternoon, they'd made it to the place where the mule skinners had found the dead prospector.

Callahan dismounted next to Foster. "Lieutenant, keep the men back, will you?"

Foster twisted in the saddle. "You men hold position."

Callahan approached the creek, taking it slow and stepping carefully. He knew the area, knew the little trickle was called Gibson's Creek, although he had no idea who Gibson was. The mule skinners who'd found the body had made Callahan's job harder, both men and horses tromping all over the scene. At least it hadn't snowed or rained. He found a churned up piece of ground on the other side that he suspected as the location of the murder—lots of boot prints and moccasin prints, both in all different directions, like maybe the prospector had put up a fight, and of course, why wouldn't he? Callahan tried to imagine them pushing and shoving and stepping every which way.

He slowly made an ever-widening circle from the spot until he found what he was looking for, a trail made by moccasined feet, trudging single file away from the creek, going north. They'd gone single file, which made it tougher to determine how many.

"Wait here!" he called back to the troopers.

He followed the trail a quarter mile to see if the

Indians continued on foot or if they'd tied horses somewhere. No hoofprints, but he spotted a muddy patch of ground that gave him pause. Tracks came in from another direction to intersect the trail he'd been following. He examined the ground for a while and drew a conclusion.

Callahan guessed maybe two or three Cheyenne had ambushed the prospector. They left the scene of the crime and had met another group, a little larger. Then all of them left together, the trail going north.

Callahan went back to the blue coats and took his horse by the reins. "We'll need to walk a ways. I don't want to lose the trail."

"Sergeant, have the men dismount," Foster said.

Parks shouted the order back to the troops.

"How many?" Foster asked.

"Can't be certain," Callahan told him. "A half dozen at least. More maybe."

"More like maybe eight or ten? Or more like fifty?"

Callahan chuckled. "Not fifty. Not a war party. And they're not mounted."

"That's something at least."

They crossed the creek and followed Callahan into the forest, staying back about ten yards to give him room to work. Callahan kept his eyes on the ground, but his mind worked as he followed the trail. It had been his experience that Indians were like anyone else in most respects. Some were good, others bad. Some smart and some stupid.

Callahan wondered if these were stupid Indians. Why kill the prospector? For a mule and a rifle? They surely knew that would bring the blue coats. And they were on foot, so they didn't have the option of a quick getaway. Something wasn't adding up, but there was only so much a man could glean from footprints in the mud.

The forest thinned, then cleared, and Callahan found himself looking across open ground. His attention was drawn east to a rocky formation atop a low hill. A thin tendril of smoke rose from the top. He followed the trail another half mile to confirm it angled toward the hill.

Callahan waited for Foster to catch up and pointed out the smoke.

Foster grinned. "They're making it easy for us."

"They're probably cooking the prospector's mule," Isaiah Parks commented offhandedly.

The lieutenant found the notion distasteful, if his expression was any indication.

Callahan mounted his horse. "Well, we found them. Now the hard part."

"I suppose we go up and get them," Foster said.

Callahan shook his head. "Nope."

Foster frowned. "What is it you suppose we're doing out here, Mr. Callahan?"

"I know we've got a job to do, Lieutenant. I just mean we can't go charging up that hill," Callahan said.

"Explain."

"First, they're going to see us coming, maybe have seen us already," Callahan said. "That means they'll have time to decide. Fight or run. Except they can't run, and they know it. They can sneak down the other side of the hill, but on foot, we'd ride them down easy. That means they have no choice but to dig in, shooting down on us from good cover."

"They might wait until nightfall," Parks said. "Then try to sneak away. They might even scatter."

"They might," Callahan agreed.

"Then what are we supposed to do?" Foster asked.

"Let's get closer," Callahan said. "Make *sure* they see us, so they know they're in it deep."

"And then?"

"Then I go up there," Callahan said.

He spurred his horse forward, and the others followed.

They called a halt just out of rifle range, and Callahan dismounted to search his saddlebags. He came out with an Indian tomahawk and stuck it in his belt. He checked the load on his Peacemaker, then dropped it back in the holster. He pulled his Henry rifle from the saddle sheath and checked it, fifteen .44 rimfire shells and one in the chamber.

He mounted again and put the Henry across the saddle in front of him. "Wait here. Keep your eyes open. Everything I said might be wrong. They might try to run, so be ready."

"What do you figure to do up there all by yourself?" Foster asked.

"I guess we'll see." Callahan spurred his horse to a gallop.

He reached the foot of the hill without getting shot and dismounted. He didn't bother tying the horse to anything. It was a good animal and wouldn't wander off. He took his time looking for the best way up and soon found the path the Indians had used. He put his rifle on his shoulder, holding it casually, hoping he was conveying the right demeanor. *I'm ready for trouble, but not looking for it.*

Callahan headed up the hill.

He kept his eyes and ears open but also turned his thoughts back to the two groups of Indians. Callahan had a hunch. If he was wrong, it might get him killed.

About halfway up, the path took him through a cluster of boulders. Some instinct put Callahan on alert, and he crouched through, rifle up and ready. He came out the other side of the cluster, paused, looked left and right. Nothing to see.

He lowered the rifle and let out the breath he'd been holding.

Callahan heard the all-too-familiar sound of a lever action sliding a shell into a rifle chamber. He muttered a curse under his breath. *Caught like some fool greenhorn.*

He turned slowly, eyes going up. Four Indians in buckskin stood on the big boulder above, three pointing rifles down at him. The fourth was older, gray streaks in his braided hair. He held his rifle in the crook of his arm, a dour expression on his face.

"Looks like you got the drop on me," Callahan said.

The older Indian's eyes fell to the tomahawk in Callahan's belt. "Where did you get that, white man? Did you take it off a dead brave?" His English was good.

"It was given to me by Dull Knife," Callahan said.

The Indians stirred, shooting glances at each other. They recognized the name as Callahan had hoped.

"Why?" asked the one in charge.

"I saved his nephew's life."

The Indians exchanged words, then the one with gray in his hair said, "So you saved Laughing Otter's life?"

"His name's Walks with the Wind," Callahan said. "And he's got big ears."

A sly smile. "Perhaps you speak the truth after all."

"Where are the others?" Callahan asked.

The Indian's smile faded. "There are no others."

Callahan considered his next words carefully. "You left a trail, and the trail told a story. Some Indians killed a prospector along Gibson's Creek. These Indians met some others and then they traveled together to this hill. I seek the end to the story. You've seen the blue coats below?"

"We've seen them."

"The story ends one of two ways," Callahan explained. "The blue coats take all the Cheyenne here, and all are punished for the murder. Or the blue coats take only the killer. Help me write the best ending to this story."

"Why did you come up here alone?"

"What would happen if all the blue coats came at once?"

The Indian thought about it. "A bad ending to the story for all."

Callahan nodded. "My name's Callahan."

"I am called Slow River," the Indian said.

"And those at the top of the hill?" Callahan asked.

"Tall Elk. He is the one who killed the prospector," Slow River said. "His brother Bright Pony is with him."

"Dull Knife has already made peace," Callahan said. "There's talk your people won't be sent south again. Some of the Cheyenne like Little Wolf have even started working as scouts for the blue coats. There's no reason to begin trouble anew. Give the blue coats Tall Elk for the prospector."

Slow River thought long about it but shook his head. "I warned Tall Elk it was foolish to kill the prospector. It would bring the blue coats. And now that very thing has come to pass. But I am Cheyenne. Tall Elk is Cheyenne. It goes against my heart to give him to the blue coats. Still, I know the blue coats will not rest until there is justice for the dead prospector. Fetch him yourself, if you will, Callahan. We will not stand in your way."

Callahan looked up the mountain, then back at Slow River. "Can I call up the troopers to help me?"

"There is not trust for that yet," Slow River said. "You must go alone, Callahan. The story is in your hands. Write the best ending you can."

CHAPTER 3

Callahan headed up the hill slowly, a tight grip on the Henry. It hadn't gone so bad with Slow River. He'd started with a six Indian problem, which was now down to two Indians. He considered trying to signal Lieutenant Foster. Maybe he could bring the troops up the other side of the hill and they could close in on Tall Elk from there.

No, it was a bad move. Slow River wasn't a fool. If he saw the blue coats coming, he'd think Callahan had pulled some trick. Callahan had to face facts. He'd made his bed when he'd started up the hill alone. Now he had to lie in it.

The smell of meat cooking increased as Callahan approached the top of the hill, and he wondered if it was the mule, as Isaiah Parks had suggested. Men had eaten a lot worse in the deep winter when game was scarce. He paused, listened, thought maybe he heard voices. Or maybe it was a trick of the wind.

It didn't matter. There was nowhere to go but up.

The crown of the hill was ringed by huge boulders. It would have been the perfect place to hole up if they hadn't given themselves away with the cookfire. The path led him to a crack between two boulders just large enough to squeeze through. It would take him into the clearing at the top of the hill, but Callahan wasn't keen to be caught flat-footed again.

He moved around the outside of the boulder ring, found some smaller rocks to use as stepping stones and scrambled up on top of a large flat boulder. From his new vantage, Callahan could look down into the clearing where an Indian sat by the cookfire, tending a big mule haunch on a spit over the flames.

The Indian looked up, saw Callahan, and quickly reached for a bow and a quiver of arrows, three feet from him.

Callahan lifted the Henry rifle. "Don't!"

Maybe the Indian knew English, or maybe he didn't, but Callahan's message was simple enough. The Indian froze halfway to the bow and quiver, his hard, dark eyes never leaving Callahan's.

"Where's the other one?" Callahan asked.

"Right here, white man," came a voice to his right.

Callahan's eyes shifted while keeping his rifle trained on the first one. The other one had a Spencer rifle trained on him, probably the one he'd taken off the prospector. This Indian was a bigger version of the one below, wide shoulders, muscles bulging under his buckskin, his glossy black hair in braids, showing a single eagle feather. *I've had about enough of Indians sneaking up on me.*

"Tall Elk?"

The Indian nodded slowly, appraising him. "I am called Tall Elk."

"I got a bead on your brother," Callahan said. "You shoot, and I shoot, and I never miss. So we can all start shooting, or we can all start talking."

Callahan's eyes bounced back and forth between the two brothers. Tall Elk's eyes were shifting back and forth, too, between Callahan and back down the hill. Callahan could guess what Tall Elk was thinking. How had Callahan made it up the hill past Slow River and the other braves?

"They're not going to help you," Callahan said.

Tall Elk's face made an annoyed twitch. "And where are your blue coat friends?"

Well, I guess they're not going to help me neither.

The other one—Bright Pony—was still frozen halfway, reaching for the bow and quiver.

"Go ahead and get comfortable," Callahan said. "This might take a minute."

Bright Pony backed away from the bow and quiver and sat cross-legged.

"Those blue coats below don't need to take you alive. They got no problem dragging a dead Cheyenne back to Fort Keogh," Callahan said. "But if you come with me, you get a fair trial. Maybe the prospector pulled his gun on you, and you had to defend yourself."

Tall Elk shook his head. "You know these are lies. They will hang me by the neck until I am dead."

"Then what do you suggest?"

"We put down our guns and fight like men. Knives." Tall Elk gestured to the tomahawk tucked in Callahan's belt. "Tomahawks, if you wish. If you kill me, then it is a better death than the rope. If I kill you, then at least my brother and I have a chance to escape."

"Putting my gun down seems like a bad idea," Callahan said.

"We both will," Tall Elk said. "First your gun belt. Then we will both set our rifles aside. I am Cheyenne and proud. I give you my word we will fight man-to-man without guns."

They stood a moment in silence, Callahan's rifle trained on Bright Pony, Tall Elk pointing his gun at Callahan. There were no good options. He could try to whip the Henry around and take a shot at Tall Elk. Maybe Callahan would be fast enough. Maybe not. Callahan sighed, unfastened his belt, and let it drop.

"Now the rifles," Tall Elk said. "Together."

They watched each other as they slowly lowered the rifles, then just as slowly bent to lay them on the boulder. They jumped down to the clearing within the ring of boulders. Tall Elk took off his buckskin shirt. He was all hard muscle. Bright Pony looked at Callahan and grinned.

Callahan kept his face neutral and shrugged out of his jacket. He rolled up his shirtsleeves and drew his knife, holding the tomahawk in the other hand.

Tall Elk said something to his brother, and Bright Pony tossed him a tomahawk. Now both Tall Elk and Callahan were armed exactly the same.

Callahan eased into a fighter's crouch, weapons up. He had no desire to kill Tall Elk. Yes, the man had to pay for the prospector's death, but that was the army's job and a judge's. It was no easy thing to kill a man, especially up close with a knife. Maybe Callahan could wound the Indian or knock him out.

But that would mean Tall Elk, holding a knife now, would be fighting all out while Callahan was fighting halfway. That kind of thinking could get a man killed. Killing didn't appeal to Callahan, but getting killed appealed even less. He reminded himself he was fighting for his life. If he didn't pay full attention to what he was—

Tall Elk sprang forward, swiping his knife across Callahan's line of sight. Callahan stepped back but kept his weapons up and ready. It hadn't been a serious attack. Tall Elk was testing Callahan's nerve.

They circled each other.

Tall Elk lunged again, knife thrusting for Callahan's gut. Callahan caught the Indian's blade on his tomahawk, sweeping it aside and clearing the way for his own thrust, knife driving toward Tall Elk's chest. The Indian's eyes went wide, and he took five rapid steps backward. Both men reoriented themselves, circling.

Callahan felt sweat down his back despite the cold weather. His heart hammered in his chest.

A moment of tension and then both men flung themselves at each other, tomahawks and knives whirling and clashing, thrusts and blocks, the ring of steel on steel echoing off the surrounding boulders. Callahan faked a thrust, and Tall Elk swung his tomahawk to block, leaving himself open. Callahan stepped in close. A backhand slash with his knife caught Tall Elk on the forearm, a deep five-inch gash.

Tall Elk hissed in pain, flinched, and dropped the tomahawk. He stepped back, holding his wounded arm against his torso, knife coming up fast to show he wasn't out of it yet.

"Give it up," Callahan said. "You're bleeding, and you've lost your tomahawk. It's not too late to come quietly."

"I won't hang," Tall Elk said defiantly. "You'll have to kill me!"

Tall Elk threw himself at Callahan, feigning high then going low.

Callahan went over the thrust, crossing his knife and tomahawk to trap Tall Elk's blade and keep it from coming up again. Callahan leaned his weight into it, forcing the Indian to stumble forward. Callahan lowered his head and bull-charged, smashing Tall Elk's nose flat. The Indian dropped the knife and stumbled back, blinking stars, blood flowing freely from both nostrils.

Tall Elk staggered on wobbly legs. He tried to turn and put some distance between himself and Callahan, but that's when Callahan pounced. He spun his knife around in his hand, holding it by the blade, and smacked the hilt across the base of Tall Elk's skull.

The Indian staggered again, then went to his knees. He was working hard to get back up.

Callahan hit him again.

Tall Elk's eyes rolled up, and he went down in the dust. He hit the ground hard and stayed there. Callahan stood over him, panting. He sheathed his knife and stuck the tomahawk back into his belt. He bent over Tall Elk, touched two fingers to his throat. The Indian was breathing fine.

Callahan straightened and blew out a sigh. "Sorry,

Tall Elk. I know you don't want to face the rope, but I don't want to kill a man if I don't have to. I would have killed you if it was the only way, if it came down to me or you, but that's not how I prefer—"

A hiss sounded through the air, and Callahan felt white-hot pain explode in his left shoulder. The world blurred as he stepped back, his legs going, then he was on the ground. He propped himself up on one elbow and saw the arrow sticking from his shoulder. His eyes shifted to where Bright Pony stood by the campfire.

Bright Pony grinned wickedly. He slowly drew another arrow from the quiver and lifted his bow. He nocked the arrow and drew it back.

Callahan raised a hand in a *hold on a minute* gesture. "I could have killed him, Bright Pony. Let's be reasonable."

Bright Pony spat some words in Cheyenne. Callahan didn't catch much of it. Nothing flattering.

Bright Pony aimed the arrow at a spot between Callahan's eyes, his grin widening.

The crack of a rifle shot.

A spot just above Bright Pony's left ear exploded red. He spun away, loosing the arrow harmlessly to the side, stumbled back, kicked the cookfire apart, and tripped over the spit with the mule haunch. He hit the ground and didn't move, eyes frozen open in death, lines of blood dribbling down his face.

Callahan looked up, saw Slow River standing with his rifle in his hand. A moment later, the gray-haired Indian had scrambled down and helped Callahan to sit up, examining the wound.

"It could be better," Slow River said. "It could be worse, too."

"Why'd you shoot him?" Callahan asked.

"I came up the hill to watch what transpired between you and Tall Elk," Slow River said. "I kept quiet and hidden. You fought well and with mercy. I found it . . . surprising."

"You disapprove?"

Slow River thought about it. "I don't know. None of the Cheyenne wishes to face death by the rope. You might have done Tall Elk a better favor by killing him. On the other hand, there is a kind of strength in restraint. I will have to think long on it. Bright Pony had no right to interfere. The fight was between you and his brother Tall Elk. I no longer consider Bright Pony Cheyenne. In the meantime, I have sent my braves down the hill to fetch the blue coats. They will help you and take Tall Elk away. As for me . . . I am not sure. Perhaps I will be a scout. There is much to think about."

Soon the hill swarmed with Lieutenant Foster's troops. They put Tall Elk in shackles. Isaiah Parks gently removed the arrow and put a bandage on Callahan's shoulder. "You'll need a proper doctor. Closest one is in Spearfish, maybe. Can you ride?"

"I can ride."

Parks helped Callahan stand He felt weak. *That's how it goes,* Callahan thought. *A man's blood gets up in the heat of battle. Then everything drains away when it's over. I could sleep for a week.*

"My guns." Callahan's eyes drifted up to the top of the big boulder in front of him.

"I'll send a trooper to fetch them," Parks said. "You just go easy. You already did your bit for today, although I'm not sure what picking a fight with the biggest Indian here says about your smarts."

"How do I look?" he asked Parks.

The beefy sergeant shook his head. "Like ten miles of bad road."

"I never been shot with an arrow before," Callahan said. "I don't recommend it. They got a saloon in Spearfish?"

"Doctor first, then saloon," Parks said. "First one's on me."

CHAPTER 4

The doctor told Callahan the saloon would have to wait. He'd had a shock to the system. The doctor cleaned the wound and stitched it up. Callahan was ordered to get a good night's sleep. The doc would be back in the morning, and if nothing was infected nor amiss in any fashion, then Callahan could be on his way.

Sleep came easy. He'd been wounded and then had a long ride to Spearfish, so when his head hit the pillow, he closed his eyes. They didn't open again until morning light streamed through the bedroom of the doctor's home window. His shoulder hurt like the dickens. But more than anything, he was starving, having skipped dinner the night before. A matronly woman with a caring way about her brought him ham and eggs and biscuits with coffee. He remembered the newspaper Foster had given him and decided it would be pleasant to read while he ate.

He sipped the coffee and unfolded the paper. The same headline again caught his attention. *The Last Wagon Train?*

Callahan's Uncle Howard had been in the wagon train business for years, taking groups from Missouri west to California and Oregon. He wondered if the article mentioned his uncle at all. He sipped more coffee and was just starting to read when the doc came in.

"You seem to have had a good night's rest," the doctor observed. "Any pain?"

"Plenty."

The doctor chuckled. "Well, that'll teach you to jump in front of arrows."

He took Callahan's arm and gently twisted it one way and then the other, extending it and prodding at the stitches. "I'm guessing you won't have any permanent loss of motion, but no heavy lifting for a while. Go ahead and finish your breakfast and get dressed. We'll fix up a sling for the arm."

The doc left, and Callahan bit into a biscuit. He went back to reading the newspaper article. As he read, he slowly lost his appetite. He'd wondered if the article would mention his uncle. Turned out the entire article was about his Uncle Howard, the wagon train business, and the railroads. It was such a bewildering story, Callahan had to read it twice to make sure he understood. He gulped coffee and quickly got dressed, wincing occasionally as pain flared in his arm.

The doctor came back into the room and fixed his arm up with a sling. "I sense your mood has changed, Mr. Callahan. Everything okay?"

"Something with my family. Nothing you did, Doc. I appreciate you stitching me up," Callahan said. "Have you seen the cavalry folks I arrived with?"

"Down to the stables, saddling up," the doctor told

him. "I think they're just waiting on you before starting back to the fort."

"Obliged again, Doc." Callahan snugged his hat down on his head and was out the door ten seconds later.

The troopers were at the stables just as the doc had said they'd be, men packing saddlebags and preparing to ride. Tall Elk rode between two serious-looking troopers, his hands manacled behind his back.

Callahan went straight to Lieutenant Foster and came right to the point. He was set for Missouri and wouldn't be going back to Fort Keogh.

Foster pushed his hat back on his head and scratched behind one ear. "I suppose that's fine. Mission's complete, and you need time to heal up, anyway. I'll let Clark know you had a family matter."

"Thanks, Lieutenant."

The two men shook hands.

Next, Callahan went to Sergeant Parks. He pitched his voice low, so only Parks could hear. "Isaiah, can we talk a second?"

They stepped out of earshot of the other troopers. Callahan explained why he wasn't returning to Fort Keogh.

"And if I'm not going back to the fort, then I guess I won't be seeing the paymaster, either," Callahan said.

Parks rolled his eyes. "You know what sergeants get paid?"

"I wouldn't ask, but you know I got rolled by that slicker. I don't have a dang nickel."

Parks grumbled and searched his pockets. "I got three dollars. You're welcome to it."

Callahan grinned and took the money. "You know I'm good for it."

"Stop picking fights with Indians then," Parks said. "You've got to live long enough to pay me back."

Sergeant Parks helped Callahan saddle his horse, and the men clasped hands.

"Good luck," Parks told him.

Two minutes later, Tomahawk Callahan rode his painted horse out of Spearfish, headed for Missouri.

Callahan was grateful for the three dollars Isaiah Parks had given him, but it wouldn't mean soft beds in fine hotels all the way to Kansas City. Not that it mattered. He was used to camping out, and he didn't smell rain coming. It would be fine.

But making and breaking camp one-armed was a test. Building a campfire. Unsaddling his horse at night and then saddling it again in the morning. Even taking off his boots.

He'd manage.

Callahan had stretched the three dollars as far as humanly possible. Buying flour and living off biscuits. He bought two pounds of coffee, an indulgence in his mind, but he didn't replenish it when it finally ran out. Beans. He tried to supplement his supplies by hunting, but it was difficult to hold a rifle. He set snares and caught a few rabbits. He set lines and pulled a few trout out of the Platte.

The days grew warmer as he lost elevation coming out of South Dakota and heading across Nebraska.

Turned out spring had been here all along, it had just gone out of its way to avoid Montana. All told, he was twenty-five days getting to Kansas City. The city had grown in the five years he'd been away. Hopefully, the location of Callahan Bros. Outfitters hadn't changed or Callahan would be obliged to ask around. Most of the wagon trains originated from Independence, but Callahan's uncle had moved his location closer to the new train station in an attempt to stand out. It had seemed to work, although things might have changed while Callahan was out West.

Callahan had been gone for five years, prospecting until he found he was bad at it and then trapping, which he wasn't much good at, either. But all that bad prospecting and bad trapping had taken him every which way, crisscrossing Montana, the Dakotas, Idaho, and Oregon. He knew the land, the roads, the rivers and streams, every mountain and hill. So when he ended up scouting for the army, he'd finally found something he was good at.

There'd only been a handful of letters in those five years. Everything had seemed fine until he'd read the newspaper article, so Callahan figured it was finally time to come home, but not to stay. No, the frontier was in his blood, but a visit? Sure. It was time.

He found Callahan Bros. Outfitters right where he remembered and was hit with a wave of nostalgia. His father and uncle led wagon trains, to California occasionally but mostly to Oregon. One year, his father hadn't come back. He still remembered his Uncle Howard telling him that his father had lost his life to a

Shoshoni raiding party, but it could have been anything, sooner or later. The Oregon Trail was fraught with danger—Indian raids, bandits, rattlesnake bites, sudden blizzards in the high passes, flooded rivers, wolves, disease, and on and on.

His uncle had wanted to bring Callahan into the wagon train business as a matter of course, but in the way of young, independent men, Callahan had wanted to carve his own place in history, make his own way. His uncle had understood and wished him well.

Callahan dismounted in front of the outfitters' office and looped the reins of his horse around the hitching post. There was a glass window in the front door that hadn't been there before—CALLAHAN BROS. OUTFITTERS AND TRAIL MASTERS in arching red letters trimmed in gold. The shade behind the glass had been pulled down. A CLOSED sign told the world to go away.

Callahan knocked. No answer. He knocked again. Still nothing.

He turned the knob. The door was unlocked. He pushed it open and entered, shutting the door behind him again. He looked around. A large room yet somehow smaller than he remembered, filled with various ropes and lanterns and packs and sacks of feed and all the dull miscellany that went into a wagon train. If they were still doing it like before, then this was all overflow. Much more of the stuff would be in a warehouse out back next to the animal pen. Many people arrived already outfitted, wagon and animals and supplies ready to go. Others arrived needing the works—a wagon, a team of mules, and everything else right down to proper boots.

Callahan Bros. prided themselves on handling everything from soup to nuts if that's what the customer needed.

"Anyone here?" Callahan called.

He heard a body stir in the back, a small office, if he recalled correctly.

"Hello?" he called again.

"Can't you read?" A woman's voice. "We're closed."

Callahan went to the doorway and stood there. She sat behind a tiny desk cluttered with papers. She'd be sixty, Callahan remembered, but had always seemed both younger and older. Younger because of her energy, the strength in her limbs, her unfailing ability to keep going even when Uncle Howard was pooped. Older because of the lines in her face. She'd seen a lot, been through so much. She was thinner than he remembered but still a sturdy woman, more gray in her black hair. She wore a man's trousers and striped shirt.

The woman looked at him hard, tired, and in no mood. "Mister, if you don't have some life-or-death emergency, just go ahead and turn yourself right around and go."

Callahan grinned. "Aunt Clara, don't you recognize your own nephew?"

She stood slowly, eyes widening. Then she laughed. Hard.

Clara came around the desk and threw her arms around her nephew. They hugged tight.

She backed away, still holding onto his hands. "Well, no wonder I didn't recognize you, covered in all that

Nebraska dust, and don't take this the wrong way, boy, but you could use about ten baths."

Callahan chuckled. "And a shave thrown into the bargain."

"What happened to your arm?"

He briefly related the story of his fight with Tall Elk.

Clara whistled in appreciation. "Sounds like you've been off on an adventure. Any chance you could use a drink?"

"I thought you'd never ask."

She went to the bottom drawer of the desk and came out with a half-full bottle and two glasses. She filled them and slid one across the desk to Callahan. "Take a load off."

He sat. They drank.

"I don't know how long you're in town, but you'll stay with me, of course," Clara told him. "About two years after you left, we bought a bigger place on a nice quiet street, and, yes, there's a bathtub, so you can turn yourself back into a human being again instead of the wilderness creature sitting before me."

He laughed. "I'll take you up on that generous offer."

She refilled both the glasses, and they drank, lapsing into a short silence.

Finally, she said, "I guess you've heard. That's why you're here, I take it."

He nodded. "Yes, ma'am."

Clara sipped her whiskey and sighed. "News travels fast."

Callahan took the newspaper from inside his buckskin jacket and set it on the desk between them. "I read it, but I'd like to hear it from you if you don't mind, start to finish. I just want to make sure I'm understanding correctly, and sometimes a newspaper article can be long on excitement and short on important details."

"Right." She looked down at the newspaper, and all the wind seemed to go out of her sails. "Well, that's a story and a half for certain." She refilled her own glass and tossed down the whiskey, closing her eyes, feeling its pleasant burn down her throat, maybe working up the intestinal fortitude to tell the tale.

"If Howard had just been there an hour later or an hour earlier," she said. "If he hadn't heard what the railroad man had said, hadn't let himself be goaded . . . I'm going too fast. I need to slow down and tell it proper, don't I?"

Clara refilled both glasses again. "There was a family just off the train from New Jersey. No wagon. No mules. What they did have was money to spend."

CHAPTER 5

Howard Callahan had two of the boys pull the wagon around to show the family from New Jersey. They'd been impressed. The Conestoga was bigger than they thought it would be.

"Consider you're moving your whole family—your whole *life*—all the way across the country. I count three kids and a wife. Plus anything else you want to take . . . equipment?"

Howard asked the man what business he was in. Kosher butcher was the reply. Apparently, Trenton was lousy with kosher butchers, but in Oregon, maybe the man could corner the market. He'd saved and saved, and when the time had come, he sold the shop—lock, stock, and barrel. They'd been frugal. They wanted the best nest egg possible for setting up shop out West. They'd come all the way by train with nothing but four suitcases, their clothes, and a few family keepsakes.

"I'll buy whatever I need for a proper butcher's shop here in Kansas City and take it with me," he said. "The wagon is more than large enough."

They dickered.

"That price includes the mules?" the man said.

Howard made a face as if alarmed by the prospect. "Certainly not, sir, not at that price."

Dickering began anew.

Finally, the man from New Jersey said, "I think we can agree on that price. However, I'd like to come back in a few hours. I need to see how much I'm paying for new knives and other butcher equipment."

Howard *tsked*. "It's a fine wagon at a good price. I don't think I could pass on another offer since there's no guarantee you'll be back. Now, if you put down a deposit—"

The shrill cry of a train whistle drew their attention. The station was right across the square from the Callahan Bros. office, so Howard practically knew the schedule by heart. There wasn't a train due, not at this hour.

A huge locomotive pulled into the station, belching steam, the whistle screeching again. Howard knew little about trains, but this locomotive seemed a bit bigger and sleeker than others he'd seen. The tender was larger, too, and there was only a single car.

People hurried across the square to the station. There was some sort of excitement involved in the unscheduled train's arrival. Howard noticed a small stage had been built on the platform. People gathered around it.

Howard and the man from New Jersey looked at each other. By unspoken agreement, they both walked toward the station, crossing the square. It was for dang sure *something* was happening, and the two men wanted to know. They gathered with the rest of the crowd just off the platform. Men in suits crowded the stage.

The locomotive had pulled forward enough to align

the train's only car with the stage. A group of men in very expensive suits came out of the train car. Mutters from those assembled. One of the men came and took the stage, and people applauded.

The man held up both hands, a big grin across his face. "Thank you. Thank you all. You're too kind."

He was slick looking, black hair greased flat. He had a lived-in-looking face and a well-trimmed mustache, maybe in his late forties, if Howard had to guess. A man with an air of importance.

"Ladies and gentlemen," he said, voice projecting as if he were no stranger to public speaking. "I appreciate this warm welcome to Kansas City. I've always said that the people here are some of the finest people in the world!"

Redoubled applause.

Howard frowned. It was a cheap way to get people to clap, but he supposed it worked well enough.

"And, of course, it's always good to see the esteemed members of the press." He gestured to the men around the stage. "For those who don't know, my name's Kent Arbuckle, and I'm a railroad man! And we all know that the railroad has been a big part of what makes Kansas City the success it is today!"

More applause. Howard was beginning to wonder if the man was running for something.

"And let me tell you folks, it doesn't stop at Kansas City," Arbuckle continued. "Because the railroad has and will continue to make America great!"

Now even Howard found himself clapping along. *Sure. Why not?*

Still, I do wonder if he'll ever get to the point.

"And that's why I'm here," Arbuckle said. "To boast? You're darn right! When it comes to America, I'm happy to boast. I'm proud of my part in our country's progress and proud to be an executive for Gladstone Railways!"

Now that rang a bell. Howard remembered reading about Gladstone in the paper recently. They were an offshoot of Gladstone Shipping out of Boston and were trying to expand into railroads. They'd recently contracted with Union Pacific to do some branch lines. *So this was some sort of publicity thing? Had Gladstone wired ahead to arrange the newspaper reporters? Must be a slow day for news.*

"The West is the future," Arbuckle said. "And the future means progress! Advancements! Parts of this great nation are considered remote, nearly unreachable . . . Well, going to these places won't be any more difficult than visiting your old Aunt Petunia in St. Louis."

Polite laughter rippled through the crowd.

"Think about those who've gone West before us," Arbuckle said. "How many months did it take them? Why not make the trip in days instead of months? Why expose your families to the harsh perils of a wagon train?"

Howard flinched inwardly, purposely not looking at the man from Trenton standing next to him.

"Dangerous wild animals! Red Indians! Floods! Landslides!" Arbuckle shouted. "Not only can we now cut the time it takes to get to the West Coast, but we can also do it in comfort and style. Behold the Pullman Palace Car behind me!" He gestured to the railcar. "This one has been modified for my special needs, but other such cars, nearly as luxurious, wait for those with the means and the fortitude to go west as modern man was meant to. Why take your loved ones into danger, when you can take them in comfort?"

The man from New Jersey leaned close to Howard and whispered, "I think I need to sleep on it. The wagon, I mean. I . . . uh . . . I don't want to rush into anything."

Howard cursed inwardly. He turned to tell the man there was no guarantee the wagon would still be available tomorrow at the same price, but he was already walking away.

Blast it!

"In a few short days, I'll take my special locomotive and train car to the very end of the Gladstone line in Hansen's Bend," Arbuckle announced grandly. "Now, I'll just wager that nobody here has actually heard of Hansen's Bend."

Howard, in fact, had not, and he'd taken plenty of wagon trains west. If he hadn't heard of it, then he pretty much figured there was nothing worth hearing. Mumbles in the crowd indicated nobody else had heard of the place either.

"Ah, but my friends, you *will* hear of it!" Arbuckle insisted. "For when I get there, it will be my duty to personally explore the territory and select the route which will take us all the way to Oregon!"

More applause, but a little tamer this time. He did better when he mentioned Kansas City.

"I predict that in two years' time—maybe sooner—Hansen's Bend will be known throughout America as the gateway to the Northwest," Arbuckle claimed. "And all of you will be able to say you heard it here first!"

Applause, but only a smattering. The novelty of the shiny new locomotive and the special Pullman car had worn off. Now Arbuckle was talking about a faraway place that had nothing to do with them. Reporters scribbled in their notebooks with little enthusiasm.

The railroad man must have sensed he was losing the crowd and groped for something to recapture their attention. He scanned the crowd and the square . . . and smiled.

"Just look at that old prairie schooner over there." Arbuckle gestured at the Conestoga wagon across the square.

Howard's Conestoga wagon.

"Imagine that's your home for six months," he said. "A tent on wheels?"

The crowd laughed.

Howard frowned. He didn't take kindly to the railroad man using *his* wagon to try to win back the crowd. The railroad had taken a big bite out of Howard's business in the last few years, but Arbuckle didn't have to rub it in.

"But there is one advantage," Arbuckle went on. "When you travel by covered wagon, the entire prairie is your privy."

More laughter.

Arbuckle pointed at the wagon, shaking his head and chuckling. "People in the future will someday look back and wonder what fools would cross America in that thing!"

Laughter and applause.

Howard felt his face go hot with anger.

Arbuckle beamed, pleased to have won back the crowd. Apparently, he was going to quit while he was ahead because he raised his hands again and said, "Thank you, thank you, one and all. If any of the newspapermen have a specific question, they should feel free to approach me. Now, I have a meeting to get to, just one of the many things I do to make Gladstone Railways a success."

A final bit of polite applause as Arbuckle left the stage. A few of the reporters went up to ask questions, but most began drifting away, scribbling final details in their notebooks.

Howard went to the edge of the train platform. "I don't think those comments were very respectful."

Arbuckle looked down at Howard. "What?"

"I don't think calling folks you never even met *fools* is very generous," Howard said. "I appreciate you're obliged to stir up some attention for your railroad enterprise, but I feel moved to speak my mind."

Arbuckle blinked down at him. "Who in the blazes are you?"

"Howard Callahan," he said heatedly, pointing across the square. "And that's *my* wagon you've decided to make the object of your ridicule."

Some of the newspapermen who were drifting away paused, taking an interest in the exchange. Howard saw that Arbuckle had noticed, too, for the railroad man raised his voice and said, "Surely, Mr. Callahan, you do not deny progress. The railroad is the future. Your wagon trains will very soon be a thing of the past. A blind man can see it coming."

Howard's frown deepened. "I'm not a fool, sir. I do not deny progress, and I realize wagon trains may be a thing of the past . . . although that day has not yet come. Merely, I point out that your tone is not respectful. There are brave men and women who've died on those trails, hoping a wagon train might take them to a better life. I suggest it's possible to tout modern rail travel without belittling those who have come before."

But while Arbuckle faced Howard, it was clear that it was the newspapermen to whom he was really speaking. "Men and women sacrificing their lives. From your own mouth, you remind us that these journeys are fraught with peril. Why should the fine people of this country risk their necks just to create a future for their families? Why should they endure months of misery and hardship when our railroads can take them in safety and comfort? Do you realize how slow wagon trains truly are? I could go to the end of the line, pick my route, organize the labor, lay the tracks, and still be in Oregon with my feet up, drinking a cold beer before you and your wagons can get there."

Howard knew he should just call the man a blowhard and walk away, but he couldn't. "That is a wild and arrogant boast, sir. I acknowledge the locomotive is faster. Obviously. But you've not even lain the tracks of the final leg. You're talking utter nonsense for the benefit of these newspapermen."

"I'm willing to put my money where my mouth is,"

Arbuckle insisted. "I've got ten thousand dollars that says my train gets to Oregon before your wagons."

The newspapermen scribbled furiously in their notebooks.

Howard was truly angry now. Was Arbuckle trying to embarrass him? Surely, the railroad man must have suspected Howard didn't have that kind of money. "Not all of us are so fortunate to have such deep pockets."

"Then put up your wagon train business," Arbuckle suggested. "Never mind if it equals ten thousand or not."

Howard hesitated. He felt a lot of eyes on him.

"What would any of this prove?" Howard asked.

"That I mean exactly what I say," Arbuckle insisted. "That Gladstone Railways can accomplish exactly what we claim, and for the entire world to know it. If you think my boast is outrageous, then it's easy money, isn't it? I take it you're organizing a wagon train even now?"

"Well . . . yeah."

"Then it's easy money."

Howard thought about it. *Could it really be that simple? The man's claim was nonsense, wasn't it? It would basically be free money.*

"I see that you hesitate, sir," Arbuckle said mildly. "I don't blame you. Not everyone has the backbone for such a wager. You claim I talk nonsense, but backing up words with action is a very different kettle of fish. That you timidly back away from your hasty words is understandable."

"I'll take your dang wager, Arbuckle!"

Excited muttering among the newspapermen.

Howard cursed himself. He'd blurted it without thinking, a hotheaded reflex. "But there must be certain rules," he added quickly, hoping to mitigate the damage. "I won't lose this bet because of some trick or technicality!"

"Agreed!" Arbuckle pointed to a saloon down the street. "Let us repair to yon establishment and hammer out the details of our historic wager!"

A crowd followed them, not just the newspaper-men but also people who'd caught wind of the wager. Howard and Arbuckle sat at a table, drinking whiskey. If Howard had hoped to keep the bet a private matter, he was out of luck. There was standing room only in the saloon as people crowded around the table to hear and see what transpired. Arbuckle was, of course, delighted by all the attention.

Pen and paper appeared, and conditions of the wager were put into writing.

Arbuckle insisted Howard Callahan lead a normal wagon train that would go about its routine in the normal, expected way. "I don't want you setting off with a single wagon and a fast team of horses and claiming it's the world's smallest wagon train."

People in the saloon laughed, but to Arbuckle it was a serious point. "You must arrive in Oregon with all the wagons you had when you left Missouri."

Now it was Howard's turn to object. "There's always the risk of some loss. You pointed out yourself it's a hazardous journey."

They finally agreed that some wagons might be lost along the way, but such losses must be kept within expected parameters. No fair leaving ninety percent of the wagon train in Kansas and claiming them "lost."

"By the same token, your train must have cars with paying passengers," Howard insisted. "Sending only your fastest, most modern locomotive violates the spirit of the wager."

Arbuckle agreed, but very reluctantly, and Howard suspected the railroad man had been thinking along those exact lines. It was a victory, but a minor one. Howard was mostly counting on the fact there simply wasn't enough time to lay seven hundred miles of track. That's where Howard was hanging his hopes.

Numerous other small details were written into the agreement. Howard noticed a few of the newspapermen were writing the details of the wager word for word. *I suppose that's good,* Howard thought. *With the details of the wager public knowledge, nobody will later be able to claim what they did or didn't know. It's all out in the open.*

"Nothing left but to sign," Arbuckle said. "Allow me." The railroad man signed his name at the bottom of the page.

Howard signed next.

One of the newspaper reporters and the saloon owner both signed as witnesses.

Howard and Arbuckle pushed away from the table and stood.

"Signed paper or not, where I'm from, a deal isn't a deal until both parties shake hands," Howard said.

"I heartily agree," Arbuckle said.

Both men spit into their hands and shook. A cheer went up in the saloon.

Howard stumbled out of the saloon, back into the daylight, feeling lightheaded. He'd just bet Callahan Bros.—a business he'd built from scratch with his brother—on the outcome of the next wagon train, maybe the last wagon train he'd ever captain.

Good Lord, Clara's going to kill me.

"And I almost did." Clara refilled both the shot glasses, and she and her nephew drank again.

Callahan shook his head, wanting to laugh but knowing it wasn't funny, not really.

"It does sound like Uncle Howard," Callahan said.

"It surely does," Clara agreed. "And like your father, too, God rest his soul, and I hope you don't mind, Luke, but it sounds a bit like you, too. All you Callahan men hate to back down, stubborn as mules."

"When I read about the bet in the paper . . . well, it just seemed like a joke."

"I wish it was." Clara sighed, suddenly seeming so tired, the weight of the world on her weary shoulders.

"I'll talk to him," Callahan said. "Maybe we can figure a way out of it."

"Talk to him?" Clara looked confused.

"Uncle Howard," Callahan said. "Have you talked to an attorney? I wonder if a bet like that is even legally binding."

A deep sadness crossed Clara's face. "I thought you'd said you heard the news."

"I did," Callahan said. "Like I told you. I read all about the wager in the newspaper."

"I meant . . . well, there's other news, too, Luke. I'm sorry. It's just so awful." Clara drew in a breath and let it out again in a ragged sigh. She tried to keep her voice steady and almost succeeded. "Your Uncle Howard's dead, Luke. Killed three nights ago."

CHAPTER 6

Kent Arbuckle was losing time.

He'd lingered in Kansas City after making the wager with Howard Callahan. He had several meetings with banks. Financing, making sure tools and equipment made it west in a timely fashion. The paperwork was endless.

He was excited. This was why he'd signed on with Gladstone in the first place. The thrill and the adventure. Was the money good? Of course. He liked nice things and expected to maintain a certain lifestyle, but if money was all he was after, he could have stayed on with one of the big houses back East.

Kent Arbuckle wanted risk.

And the West offered plenty of that. But the wager—ah, the wager!—that added the extra element of excitement that sent hot blood shooting through his veins. As soon as he'd finished his business in Kansas City, he'd want nothing more than to hop aboard his custom locomotive and head west.

But then the telegram had arrived.

"Wait in KC. Take no further action. Horace is coming."

The short message had spoken volumes. When one of the brothers took a personal interest, it meant one of two things. The first was that Horace was coming to congratulate him.

As Arbuckle had yet to achieve anything, he found that scenario unlikely.

The other possibility was that Kent Arbuckle was in the doghouse, and Horace Gladstone didn't come out from behind his polished oak fortress of a desk for any mere scolding. He was one of the *brothers*, for Pete's sake, yes, the youngest of the three, but still one of the mighty Gladstones and no one to be trifled with.

So Arbuckle had been obliged to *waste* six days in Kansas City, waiting for the man. He hadn't been idle. He'd sent the survey crews ahead. They'd have reports for him to read upon his arrival. He'd bought supplies and tools in bulk and sent them west.

On the sixth day, Arbuckle had found a note waiting for him at his hotel. He'd been summoned to a nearby café for coffee.

Coffee in and of itself was something of a message. Champagne for celebrations. Beer and whiskey for fellowship.

Coffee said, "This is serious."

Arbuckle had entered the café at the appointed time. He was immediately stopped by a man in a brown plaid suit and a bowler hat.

"Do you mind?" Arbuckle said. "I'm expected."

The man put a hand on Arbuckle's chest. "I understand, but I'll just have a look first, sir."

Arbuckle's eyes darted around the interior of the café. A half dozen men, all similarly dressed, stood at various spots in the room. Horace's men, Arbuckle realized.

The man who'd stopped Arbuckle patted him down, checking inside his jacket. Arbuckle had, in fact, recently purchased a Smith & Wesson Schofield revolver for his trip west but had yet to wear the thing. Found to be unarmed, Arbuckle was allowed to enter and pass through the main part of the café to a private room.

Horace Gladstone waited for him in a plush, high-backed chair, coffee service for two on the small table next to him. He gestured to the empty chair on the other side of the table.

Arbuckle sat. The two men did not shake hands, nor did they exchange bland pleasantries.

Horace Gladstone wore an expensive blue suit, a pin with a large diamond in his red tie. Expensive shoes. He was in his midfifties, a hint of gray at his temples, hair otherwise a uniform black. Mustache thin and neatly trimmed. Eyes a keen and alert blue.

Horace poured his coffee and stirred in a splash of cream.

Arbuckle took his black.

Horace sipped and nodded approval. "Why have you brought me to Kansas City, Kent?"

It was hardly my idea, he thought, seemed a poor choice for an answer. He sipped his own coffee to buy himself a second to think. "Obviously, I regret causing you any inconvenience, Mr. Gladstone."

"And yet, here I am. Inconvenienced."

"I suppose you saw the article in the paper," Arbuckle said.

"Papers. Plural. New York, Boston, Baltimore, Philadelphia, Chicago. It's been picked up all over."

"Well, you did say I should gin up some publicity for the enterprise."

Horace frowned. "Is that some sort of joke, Kent? Is this funny to you?"

Arbuckle swallowed hard. "I wasn't being flip, sir. I'm sure you've seen that Gladstone stock has ticked up the last few days, not significantly, but up is better than down."

"And you believe this to be some sort of accomplishment?" Horace asked. "Such temporary gains are not uncommon whenever there is some bit of excitement. They seldom translate into a long-term win. Your wager with this Callahan person might indicate a high level of confidence, and there's some minor benefit in that, I admit, but what happens if you lose?"

"I assure you, sir, that I would not carelessly wager Gladstone's money," Arbuckle said. "The ten thousand dollars would come from my personal funds. There would be no risk to—"

"No one will care about or even remember your measly ten thousand dollars, Kent." Horace spoke as if he was losing patience with an especially dimwitted child. "Ten thousand dollars is nothing compared to Gladstone's good name. When you make such a wager, Kent, people might speculate you have a reason to be confident, but when you lose such a bet, we are no longer in the realm of speculation. The failure is very real. The unmet goal is cold, hard reality. We are no longer guessing what Gladstone might be capable of but instead know with absolute certainty what Gladstone *can't* do. Our shortcomings are exposed for all the world to see. Our deal with Union Pacific to build and run their branch lines goes up in smoke. Have you even stopped to consider how many miles of track you need to lay in a day?"

"Yes, sir, I have," Arbuckle said, trying to sound confident. "I figure three miles a day. I asked around, and Callahan's a good wagon train captain. He'll likely make it in four to five months and plans to head out the first week in May. Three miles a day makes us competitive."

"The average is two miles a day, and there will be rough terrain," Horace said. "I don't have a map in front of me, but even conceding three miles a day, Hansen's Bend to our station in Salem is . . . what? Seven hundred miles? Three miles a day only gets you halfway by September."

"Yes, sir, your math is right on the money," Arbuckle said. "And halfway is about right. That's why I'm thinking we need two crews. One in Hansen's Bend working west. The other starting in Salem and coming back east to meet us."

"This all costs money, you understand."

Arbuckle leaned forward, trying to appear as earnest as possible. He considered his next words carefully. First . . . contrition.

"Mr. Gladstone, let me start by saying that you're absolutely right. I should never have made that wager. In the heat of the moment, I thought only to grab some headlines. I've risked tarnishing the Gladstone name, and for that I accept full responsibility. I would certainly not expect to continue in your employ should I fail."

Horace sipped his coffee and made a face. "It's gone cold." He poured hot coffee on top of the cold, mixed in the cream. "Go on, Kent. Obviously, there's more."

"It seems to me, the way forward is clear," Arbuckle said. "My only choice is to make good on my boast. The milk has been spilt. If Gladstone were to withdraw from the wager, it would be an admission that we cannot accomplish what we claim."

"What *you* claim," Horace corrected.

"Indeed, sir, here in this room, you have the right of it," Arbuckle said. "My claim. My error. But to the world, it will be Gladstone's failure. There is only one acceptable solution. We *must* succeed."

Horace sighed and sipped coffee. "I'm forced to agree."

Relief flooded Arbuckle.

"If it had been up to Woodrow, I wouldn't be here at all," Horace explained. "We simply would have sent someone to deal with you. He's no fan of stunts."

Woodrow was the eldest brother. Arbuckle had never met a more humorless and sour human being.

"Fortunately for you, Casper sided with me," Horace said.

The middle brother Casper was slightly more reasonable but only slightly.

"So here's the long and short of it," Horace said. "If you succeed, then Gladstone takes the credit. If you fail, we will do everything in our power to lay the blame at your feet, but you understand that simply terminating your employment won't be enough. Woodrow is . . . vindictive."

Arbuckle felt cold sweat behind his ears and under his armpits. He cleared his throat nervously. "I understand."

"I hope you do," Horace warned. "One last thing. You're quite right that Gladstone cannot pull out of the wager. We'd look weak. On the other hand, if Howard Callahan would happen to throw himself on our mercy, that would be a different situation altogether. I think it would be an opportunity to look magnanimous, big business lets the little man off the hook, that sort of thing."

"I suppose that's a thought," Arbuckle agreed.

"Then that's Plan A," Horace said. "If we can put all this wager nonsense behind us, then let's do it. If not, then, as you say, Kent, you have no choice. You have to win."

Arbuckle had left the meeting with Horace Gladstone feeling a strange mix of relief and nervousness. It could have gone *much* worse.

And so Arbuckle had gone straight away to Callahan Bros. to give Howard Callahan a chance to back out of the bet as Horace Gladstone had suggested. He'd realize later how badly he'd bungled it. He should have started with an apology. Anyone could see that Howard was a proud man. Instead, Arbuckle had gone in aggressively, insisting he was going to do the poor, dumb slob a favor but letting him beg his way out of the wager.

Howard had spat a string of curses at the railroad man and shown him the door.

Arbuckle's temper had flared. He'd offered that lousy nobody outfitter Howard Callahan a way out, and the man hadn't seen the gift for what it was. Arbuckle had decided to get tough and hired three street ruffians to waylay Howard in the alley behind his favorite saloon one night. They'd been asked only to rough him up and get him to reconsider the wager. It had gotten out of hand. They'd thought Howard unarmed, but when he'd pulled a revolver, one of the ruffians had panicked and stabbed Howard with a hunting knife.

Howard's death had shaken Arbuckle. He'd never meant for it to go so far. He'd paid the ruffians to leave town. *Would the authorities get involved?*

Howard's murder was three days ago. It had been ruled a robbery gone bad. It did not seem as if the police would come looking for Kent Arbuckle.

He blew out a sigh of relief.

He needed a drink.

CHAPTER 7

Tomahawk Callahan needed a drink.

The news of his uncle's death had hit him hard. First his father. Now his Uncle Howard. His head was light from the bottle of whiskey he'd finished with his Aunt Clara, but not light enough.

He entered the saloon down the street from Callahan Bros. Outfitters, the very establishment where his uncle had agreed to the ill-conceived wager. The last place his uncle had been before being murdered in the alley out back.

Callahan had grown used to ramshackle little saloons out West, shacks and cabins with a plank for a bar, whiskey from a jug. The Cattleman's Corner, by contrast, was a proper saloon. A long, polished mahogany bar. Gilded chandelier and fixtures. A wide, carpeted staircase curved up to the second floor, presumably where there were rooms for entertaining. A piano player in a striped shirt and string tie assaulted an upright with more enthusiasm than talent, but the tune was pleasant and almost familiar, the music mixing with lively talk and laughter.

At the moment, Callahan had no use for talk or laughter, but he wasn't ready to go back to his aunt's house, the two of them stewing in mutual gloom. He needed to be alone, and in the middle of a crowd was often the best place to do that.

He headed to the far end of the bar, where there was open space. Callahan was flat broke, but his aunt—bless the woman—had lent him a dollar. He ordered a shot of whiskey and tossed it back. He ordered a second and sipped it more slowly.

Dead. His uncle was dead. Callahan had come a long way . . . to do what exactly? Maybe turn right around and go back to Montana. His Aunt Clara had seemed unsure what her next step would be. Her world had been turned upside down.

Callahan finished his whiskey and ordered another.

"Haven't seen you in here before, stranger." A female voice, too soft and inviting to be sincere.

Callahan wasn't in the mood for some random saloon gal, and he didn't have the money, anyway. He was about to tell her he wanted to be alone when he heard her gasp, a small, startled sound.

"Luke? Luke Callahan?"

His head snapped around.

Callahan didn't recognize her at first, not all dolled up, a gorgeous wad of red hair piled on top of her head, lips stained a deep red, cheeks pink with too much rouge. Somehow the makeup didn't go with the spray of freckles across the bridge of her nose. A lace corset pushed her assets up front and center, stockings rolled below her knees. She must have caught him looking and quickly pulled a knit shawl around herself.

"Becky." Callahan averted his eyes, not wanting to embarrass her.

"Velvet," she said.

"What?"

She lowered her voice and leaned close to whisper. "They call me Velvet here."

Callahan didn't know what to say to that.

He didn't know anyone called Velvet. The girl he'd known as a scrawny, awkward teen had been called Becky Griffith. She'd grown into a woman, but those playful green eyes were still the same. The same tilt of the head when she looked at him. Even when she was a schoolgirl in braids, every boy could glimpse the woman she'd become, and she hadn't disappointed.

But Callahan had never imagined her in a place like this.

He felt her slip something into his hand.

"Sure, I love for you to buy me a drink," she said loudly. Then she whispered, "Just so we can keep talking."

Callahan opened his hand and looked down. She'd slipped him a coin.

He looked back down the bar and saw the bartender eyeing them. He had a pinched face, an unhappy expression, and a dozen strands of black hair strategically combed flat over a glistening pate.

"I'm supposed to move on to someone else if you're not interested," Becky whispered.

Callahan put the coin on the bar, caught the bartender's attention, and held up two fingers. He refilled Callahan's glass and brought one for the lady.

"Thanks." Becky smiled. She still had straight, white teeth, and Callahan still liked the smile as much as he did back then.

They made small talk as if they were drinking tea on somebody's front porch and not sipping hooch in a smoky saloon. Callahan wished that he'd had the money to buy her the drink himself and that she wasn't wearing that distracting outfit and the makeup. He wished a lot of things.

Her folks had passed away from influenza three years back. Callahan said he was sorry to hear it. But Becky herself was in good health. Callahan said he was glad. No, Callahan had never married or started a family. No, he hadn't been back in Kansas City long. No, he wasn't sure what he was doing next.

The small talk exhausted in one breathless gush, they lapsed into awkward silence.

"This isn't really me. This isn't who I am," she said in a small voice, gesturing to herself and then around the saloon, indicating her situation or maybe the whole world. "It's temporary."

"I wouldn't judge you."

"I know. I'm not saying that," Becky assured him. "I just wanted to say it, just wanted you to know."

"Okay."

"I'm saving money," she said. "For the next thing. To get out of here."

Callahan lifted his glass. "To the next thing."

"To the next thing," she echoed.

They drank.

* * *

Kent Arbuckle entered the Cattleman's Corner saloon, knowing a bottle of whiskey wouldn't solve his problems.

But he didn't see how it could hurt.

He squeezed in at the bar. "A bottle of the good stuff."

The bartender set the bottle in front of the railroad man, along with a clean glass.

Arbuckle drank, relished the burn down his throat. He refilled the glass and shot that one back, too. There were two ways to get the Gladstone brothers off his back—win the bet or have it called off in a way that didn't embarrass the company.

Were they really so timid? They'd inherited their great wealth, Arbuckle reminded himself. *They were a generation removed from the spirit of adventure that had built their company in the first place. Surely, men were made for more than sitting in plush mansions and counting money. Had they no appreciation for the frontier? That a man could lay it all on the line and come out the other side of his venture a hero or a goat, that was the stuff of life.*

The Gladstone brothers weren't living life at all. They plodded through some drab existence of numbers and ledgers and bottom lines. The idea of an epic race—the opportunity to leave their mark on history—occurred to them not at all.

Arbuckle drank another shot.

If only those fool ruffians hadn't killed the man.

"Mr. Arbuckle?"

Arbuckle looked up at a man in a brown tweed suit standing next to him at the bar. "Yes?"

"I'd like a few moments of your time if that's possible," he said. "Happy to buy you a drink."

Arbuckle gestured at the bottle. "I'm fixed well enough."

The man pulled a cigar from inside his jacket. "A smoke then."

'You have me at a disadvantage, sir," Arbuckle said flatly. "Who are you?"

"My pardon, sir." The man tipped his hat. "Frederick Dalton. I'm with the *Times*."

Arbuckle sighed. Another blasted newspaperman. "Were you here?"

"In Cattleman's Corner when you struck the wager?" Dalton asked. "Afraid not. My editor put me on a train to Kansas City as soon as he got wind of the story, so I guess I'm playing catch-up. With respect, Mr. Arbuckle, trains are old news. Wagon trains even older news. But this wager . . . well, that's something new, something that will capture a reader's attention. Making history is never dull. I thought maybe I could ask you a question or two, considering Howard Callahan's recent death."

Arbuckle cursed inwardly but did a good job of keeping his annoyance off his face.

"How has Howard Callahan's recent death changed the situation?" Dalton asked.

Arbuckle tossed back yet another shot of whiskey before answering. "We are addressing that situation now. It would be irresponsible to comment until it's resolved." Arbuckle hoped his bland nonanswers would send the reporter away.

"Uh-huh." Dalton pulled out a notebook and scribbled in it.

Arbuckle frowned. What could he have possibly said worth writing down?

"And is that what you're doing here tonight?" Dalton asked. "Trying to resolve the situation?"

"Here in the Cattleman's Corner?" Arbuckle was confused. "I'm here to get a drink. That's all."

"I thought perhaps you'd come to speak with Mr. Callahan about a resolution," Dalton said.

This comment only confused Arbuckle further. "Did we not just say that Callahan was dead?"

"Your pardon, sir," Dalton said. "I was referring to Luke Callahan, the late Howard Callahan's nephew. Is that not him at the other end of the bar in conversation with one of the saloon's sporting ladies?"

Arbuckle stepped back from the bar and looked. A lean and hungry-looking fellow in a dusty buckskin jacket. Battered brown hat back on his head. A revolver slung low on his hip.

"I've never laid eyes on that gentleman before in my life," Arbuckle told the newspaperman.

"But I'm sure you understand my question," Dalton said. "I'm not a big believer in coincidences. Young Luke rides into town just a few days after his uncle's murder? As a newspaper reporter, it's my job to put two and two together. Are you sure you're not here to meet him?"

Arbuckle scowled. "I've told you already, I don't

know him. You've put two and two together and come up with five. Having said that, it's possible I might speak to the young man in the near future. You seem to have some knowledge of the fellow. Is he Howard Callahan's heir?"

Dalton shrugged. "No idea. I was hoping to get more from you. I overheard the young lady mention his name and immediately wondered if there was a family connection. I asked around."

A noncommittal grunt from Arbuckle. "Mr. Dalton, I'm afraid I don't have any more information for you. I wish you luck with your journalism."

Dalton knew a dismissal when he heard one. He shrugged and wandered away.

Arbuckle poured himself another whiskey but took his time with it. He'd intended to get good and drunk, then go back to his hotel and flop into bed. The world and its troubles would still be there in the morning, but now, Arbuckle had other ideas. Maybe Luke Callahan could be useful. He drank slowly and watched.

Callahan and the saloon gal were still talking. If he decided to make a night of it and take the girl upstairs, then there was no point in Arbuckle waiting around.

But that's not what happened. The girl wrapped her shawl tighter around herself and offered a slender hand to Callahan. She seemed businesslike, not come-hither, as Arbuckle would have suspected. Callahan took off his hat and shook her hand. She smiled briefly, then drifted away, thirty seconds later letting the shawl drop to expose white, freckled shoulders as she talked to another man across the room.

It seemed a curious exchange, and Arbuckle wasn't sure what to make of it.

Not that it mattered. The girl didn't interest him. He kept his eyes on Callahan. The dusty cowboy slowly put his hat back on his head, a thoughtful look on his face. He drained his whiskey glass, then turned and headed for the door.

Arbuckle gave the man a few seconds head start, then followed. Outside, Arbuckle realized that if Callahan got on a horse, he would not be able to follow. Arbuckle's hotel was only a few blocks away, but he didn't have a horse of his own.

But apparently, Callahan was on foot. He turned in the opposite direction from Arbuckle's hotel. Callahan didn't walk as if he were in any particular hurry, hands in pockets. Arbuckle followed at a safe distance. He wasn't even sure what he intended—to talk to Callahan, certainly, find out more about his connection with his uncle, if his arriving in town had anything to do with the murder. He didn't try to catch up. He wanted to talk, but not just yet. Arbuckle was at odds with himself over how to approach the man.

They transitioned quickly to a residential neighborhood with tidy, well-built houses, good homes for a certain kind of person, families of modest means. Arbuckle could appreciate these houses. He couldn't see himself living such a drab existence, but he wasn't born into money. He was self-made. If his life had gone differently, he might have lived in a house just like one of these and counted himself lucky.

It occurred to him in a sudden flash that he had ruined the lives of a family in one of these homes, that a simple, hardworking man had been goaded into a wager that would ultimately cost him everything. Arbuckle suddenly felt a wave of respect for Howard Callahan. He had been willing to risk everything he had for his own pride; whereas, the Gladstone brothers wouldn't even risk a temporary smudge on the company's reputation.

Frederick Dalton had said making history was never dull.

Howard Callahan shouldn't have died. Arbuckle had failed the man in this respect. And he might fail the Gladstone brothers, as well. He might even fail himself.

But Kent Arbuckle wouldn't fail history.

Callahan turned up a walkway to a small but well-kept house, climbed the front porch steps, and knocked on the door. The door opened, and Arbuckle glimpsed an older woman inside. Callahan entered and the door shut.

Arbuckle stood for a moment and considered. He squashed an understandable human urge to leave simple people alone. Let the family grieve. Come back another time or not at all.

No. Arbuckle chastised his own softheartedness. The machinery of history chewed up so many average men and women. *What's two more?*

Arbuckle climbed the steps and knocked on the door.

The woman answered, and her face clouded with recognition, her frown deepening into a disapproving glower.

Arbuckle recognized her now. Howard Callahan's wife.

"Mister Arbuckle," she said crisply. "Can I help you with something?"

"I apologize for the hour, but I thought we might talk." Arbuckle took off his hat and held it to his chest. "In light of recent events."

She hesitated, appraising him stone-faced. Then she stepped aside and gestured that he should enter. He walked in, and she shut the door behind him. Across the room, the man who'd been pointed out to Arbuckle as Luke Callahan rose from a chair, a wary expression on his face.

"Luke, this is Kent Arbuckle," Clara Callahan said with cold courtesy.

Arbuckle saw the recognition darken Callahan's features.

They shook hands in a perfunctory manner and without warmth.

Arbuckle felt with certainty that he could put an end to the wager here and now. It was absolutely what the Gladstone brothers preferred and expected. He could simply tell Clara Callahan that he'd heard of her husband's tragic demise and that he was terribly sorry—indeed, as were all at Gladstone Railways—and that under the circumstances, he would not hold Callahan Bros. to the wager should she wish to withdraw. Who could possibly think less of a grieving widow who'd suddenly had her husband so abruptly taken away from her?

But he couldn't risk it. She'd thank him and accept the offer and that would be the end of it.

And that just wouldn't do for Kent Arbuckle.

"I suppose you're going to try to weasel out of our wager," Arbuckle said without preamble.

Clara Callahan blinked, stunned at the audacity.

"I beg your pardon?" she said after a moment.

"Come now, let's not play dumb," Arbuckle said. "It's sad about your husband, but a bet's a bet, yes?"

The woman went pale, not sure what to say.

Luke Callahan's face had gone red with fury. "The woman only just lost her husband a few days ago, and I only found out today my uncle's gone. You've got a lot of nerve pushing your way into somebody's home with that kind of attitude, mister."

"Please. We're all grown up people here," Arbuckle said. "And by the way, I've never laid eyes on you before tonight. Do you have the authority to even have an opinion in this matter?"

"You can leave this house right now under your own steam, Mr. Arbuckle." Callahan's hand fell to his Peacemaker. "Or you can be carried out. That enough authority for you?"

Arbuckle swallowed hard, suddenly wondering if he'd overplayed his hand.

CHAPTER 8

Anger surged in Callahan's veins.

Maybe it was the whiskey in his belly, but Callahan felt he could draw the Peacemaker and start blazing and not feel the least bit bad about it. He'd never taken a dislike to somebody so fast in his life as he had with Arbuckle. It was almost as if the man was asking for it.

"Luke Callahan, you get your hand off that six-shooter right now. There will be no violence in this house." Clara's eyes slid to Arbuckle. "Even if our guest is being rude."

Callahan lifted his hand from his gun, but his eyes still burned fire into the railroad man.

"This wager has been in every newspaper from New York to San Francisco," Arbuckle said. "That means if you don't go through with it, you'll be seen as cowardly in front of the whole country. Look, I don't blame you. If you insist on backing out, I'll even do you a favor. You come stand in front of some newspapermen, and we'll give them a good story. Tell them you never had a chance, anyway, not against such a modern railroad enterprise. I'll step up and magnanimously let you off the hook. It will look good for Gladstone Railways. The big railroad company taking pity on the little people in over their heads. I suggest you take this offer, Mrs. Callahan."

"If we weren't under my aunt's roof right now, I'd scatter you all down the street, Arbuckle," Callahan said. "So be nice to the lady. She'd the only thing standing between you and a fat lip."

Arbuckle rolled his eyes. "Don't be absurd, Mr. Callahan. Fisticuffs might give you a moment of satisfaction, but they won't solve your aunt's problem."

Callahan's hands curled into fists. "Life's short. Sometimes a moment is all you get."

Clara stepped toward Callahan, put a hand on his arm. "Easy, Luke." She shifted her attention to the railroad man. "Mr. Arbuckle, you seem to hate us for some reason. I don't know what call you have to talk to people the way you do, but under all that rudeness, I guess you are offering to let us off the hook. Let me sleep on it, Mr. Arbuckle, and we can talk again in the morning."

"Very well. I'll call on your place of business at nine tomorrow morning, if there's no objection," Arbuckle said.

Clara nodded. "That's fine."

Arbuckle put his hat back on and nodded to Callahan and Clara. "Then I'll show myself out." He departed, pulling the door closed behind him.

Clara and Callahan stood silent a moment.

"What an unpleasant man," Clara finally said.

"You should have let me take a poke at him."

Clara shook her head and sighed. "No, he's right,

Luke. That won't solve anything. I guess . . . well, I suppose I need to take him up on his offer."

Callahan blew out a frustrated sigh. "I hate to give a smug fool like that the satisfaction. But Callahan Bros. is your company now. It's your decision."

"About that." Clara looked at him, obviously something important weighing on her mind. "There's two things I was going to tell you earlier, but I didn't get around to it. The first is that I was going to go to Arbuckle, anyway, and ask to be let out of the bet."

Callahan opened his mouth.

"Now just keep shut a minute and let me talk," Clara told him.

Callahan shut his mouth.

"The fact is there just ain't no Callahan Bros. Outfitters without Howard," Clara explained. "Howard's right-hand man retired a month ago. We were in the middle of training a new man, but then Howard . . . well, you know. A number of the experienced hands have quit to join up with other outfits. Can't say as I blame them. They've got to put food on the table like anyone else. As for me . . . well, I'm a tough old bag if I do say so myself, but I'm not cut out to lead no wagon train. No, Luke, all this race stuff was over before it began. I'm gonna have to swallow my pride and do what Arbuckle wants."

"I hate to give a man like that the satisfaction." A shrug and a sigh from Callahan. He suddenly felt so tired. "I can't tell you what to do, Aunt Clara. It's your call."

"Well, that brings me to the other thing I need to tell you," she said. "It's not just *my* call."

"Well, who else?"

"You."

Callahan shook his head. "Aunt Clara, I'm happy to give you advice or help any way I can, but it's not my place to—"

"It is your place, Luke," she insisted. "When your pa died, his half of the business went to your uncle, but it didn't end there. See, your pa knew you were your own man and wanted to make your own way, so he wasn't going to try to force you into anything. Sure, he would have loved for you to come into the family business, but he respected your independence."

Callahan looked at his aunt, then looked away. "I . . . never knew that. I just thought I disappointed him, running off to do my own thing. Have my own way."

"He respected your independence, but he also thought about leaving behind something for you," Clara told him. "The agreement was always that when Howard died, your pa's half would go to you. If me and Howard had produced any children, well, they'd be partners, too, but we never did. Oh, we tried, but it wasn't the Lord's will, I guess. That just leaves me and you."

"Partners."

Clara nodded. "Exactly. As you can see, you have as much a say in this as anyone."

Callahan spread his hands. "Then that settles it. I'll take the wagon train to Oregon, and Arbuckle can choke on it."

Clara sighed and sank into a chair, putting her face in her hands.

"Aunt Clara?"

She looked up, the lines on her face suddenly seeming much deeper. "I'm tired, Luke. So tired. If I . . . if *we* . . . take Arbuckle's offer to withdraw from the wager, I can still sell off some of the wagons and other equipment. It won't be much, but something for me to live on."

"Aunt Clara, I know every inch of the territory from here to Oregon," Callahan said. "I can do it."

"You've never captained a wagon train, Luke," Clara reminded him. "It crawls along at a snail's pace. People get sick and hurt, or they argue with each other, or wagons get stuck in the mud, or . . . Lord, so many things."

Callahan rubbed his eyes with the heels of his hands. Suddenly, everything seemed impossible. "I just . . . want to help."

"I know you do," Clara said. "I think we need to let this go."

"But—"

"Luke." Clara's tone was the perfect balance of stern and loving. "It's over. Let it rest. You're my partner now. I'm asking you, please. Let it be over. Let me rest."

Callahan could barely contain himself. He felt like a volcano about to erupt.

Clara laughed without mirth. "You Callahan men."

"What's that supposed to mean?"

"Your father and uncle were the same way," she said. "They could both get real hot real fast."

Callahan didn't consider himself a hothead. He'd had to be calm and coolheaded during the Indian wars, scouting for the army, but something different happened inside him when it came to his family. The contempt Arbuckle had obviously had for his uncle and the insulting way he'd spoken to Aunt Clara made Callahan's blood boil.

He took a deep breath and let it out slowly. "I don't know what got into me. Still . . . that was one of the most unpleasant human beings I've ever encountered."

"You won't get an argument out of me," Clara said. "As for having a temper, well, I figure it's just in your blood, same as your pa. Harness that temper and it can give you a little something extra in a tight spot, but if you let it control you . . ." A shrug.

"Aunt Clara, I didn't even know until right now I was part owner of anything. And you're right," he admitted. "I don't know much about wagon trains, certainly not like Uncle Howard. Just tell me what you want to do, and I'll go along with it."

She stood, and Callahan heard her knees click. She stretched. "Right now, I'm dog-tired. Let's sleep on it."

"I guess I should go to bed, too," Callahan said.

"Not on *my* clean sheets you're not." Clara said, grinning. "I got the extra room fixed up for you, but you need a bath first. I heated the water right before you arrived. It's probably cooled a bit, but go on and get clean."

"Yes, ma'am."

"And use *soap*."

It was Callahan's turn to grin. "Yes, ma'am."

"And I'll wash them clothes, too," she told him.

"You smell like horse, whiskey, campfires, and sweat— trust me, it's a snoot full."

Callahan laughed.

The bathwater was still plenty warm. Callahan soaked and scrubbed and felt better, all the aches from sleeping on the ground fading into memory. His aunt had laid out some clean clothes for him—a blue shirt and tan trousers, his uncle's clothes. The shirt fit well. The pants were a bit loose, so he cinched his belt tighter.

Callahan was tired but restless. He went out to the front porch. The night was cool. He stood a while in the quiet darkness. He'd come a long way, not knowing what he'd find. He'd never expected to learn his uncle had been killed and he was now a half owner of a business . . . although that was shaping up to be a short-lived situation. What would his aunt do now? Had she saved enough to live? A whole new list of questions was just now occurring to him, but they'd have to wait until morning. Clara had already gone to bed.

He went up to the room his aunt had prepared for him and draped his new outfit over the back of a chair. Callahan crawled into bed and lay there with his eyes open, sleep elusive. He was exhausted, no doubt about it, but his mind was a swirl of thoughts.

He awoke the next morning with no memory of falling asleep the night before. Dusty sunlight came in through the crack in the curtains. He must have been really worn out because he was usually up before dawn. He dressed and went downstairs, the smell of fresh coffee drawing him on.

"Sleep okay?" Clara asked, handing him a cup.

"Eventually."

"Me, too."

He sipped the coffee. It was good.

Clara had put together a top-notch breakfast. Callahan sat at the small kitchen table and dug into eggs, bacon, and fresh biscuits. He hadn't eaten much the day before and realized he was famished. He ate until his belly was tight.

"Nothing wrong with your appetite," Clara said lightly.

"Your cooking beats army beans any day."

It hit Callahan acutely that he missed homelife. An army fort didn't count. Sleeping out in the wilderness on the cold ground for darn sure didn't count. He missed this. Not just a home-cooked breakfast and a soft, warm bed and a roof over his head, but family. He'd stayed away too long. Aunt Clara was the only family he had left. He promised himself to look after her. Whatever happened with Arbuckle, Callahan would make sure she was properly situated.

"You okay?" he asked.

She sat across from him, stirring a spoonful of sugar into her coffee. "I will be. I guess I need to go down there and do what Arbuckle wants. It'll be hard to swallow, but better to get it done and over with. Then I can get on with my own life again."

Callahan's first instinct was to object. Surely, there was something they could do. But he stopped himself. Aunt Clara had earned the right to decide her own fate.

"I'll go with you," he said.

"Thank you, Luke."

They walked down to the square, and they were both surprised at the crowd waiting for them in front of the

Callahan Bros. Outfitters front door. Arbuckle and a gaggle of newspapermen and the usual gawkers eager for a show. Someone had assembled a makeshift stage from wooden crates, on which had been placed a podium.

Kent Arbuckle stood behind the podium, spreading his arms to silence the crowd. "As promised, gentlemen, here comes Mrs. Callahan now to illuminate us as to the latest development in this exciting story."

"I don't know why I'm surprised," Clara muttered from the side of her mouth to Callahan. "He did say he was going to make a show out of it."

"Best get it over and done with," Callahan said.

"Right." Clara walked toward the little stage.

Newspaper reporters began shouting questions as Arbuckle shifted a bit to allow room for the woman.

"Gentlemen, please," Arbuckle said. "Allow the lady to make her statement."

Clara looked small and frightened behind the podium, and Callahan felt bad for the woman. She wasn't used to having so much attention on her all at once. Callahan shook his head in disgust. There were problems in this world one man could solve by punching another in the nose, but this just wasn't one of them. All he could do was watch while his Aunt Clara endured this brief humiliation, and then, like she said, she could get on with her life.

Clara stepped up to the podium, obviously nervous.

Arbuckle put a hand on her shoulder and leaned in to whisper something in her ear.

Callahan watched as something changed in the woman's expression. The timid look faded as her eyes narrowed, a new and cold determination setting her jaw.

Whatever Arbuckle had said to her must have been the last straw, Callahan guessed, because her eyes shot daggers at the railroad man.

Clara put her hands on the podium and leaned forward. She fixed all the newspaper reporters with a hard stare. "With the unfortunate death of my husband, Howard Callahan, there has been some loose talk about the wager being called off. Well . . . I'm here to tell you . . ."

The newspapermen waited breathlessly, pencils poised over notebooks.

"I'm here to tell you . . . that it's *not true*," Clara stated loudly. "Not a word of it!"

Uproar among the reporters as everyone tried to talk at once.

"Mrs. Callahan!" One of the reporters managed to shout over the others. "With your husband tragically departed, who's going to lead the wagon train?"

"Why, my nephew, of course!" Clara pointed right at Callahan. "Luke 'Tomahawk' Callahan!"

Every head turned to look at him.

Callahan swallowed hard. *Aw hell.*

CHAPTER 9

"What on earth made you change your mind?"

Clara rummaged through her desk drawers. "Dang it, I know there's another bottle in here somewhere."

"Aunt Clara!"

She looked up, fire in her eyes. "What?"

"Are you gonna explain what happened out there?"

Both Callahan and Clara had been swarmed by reporters after her startling announcement. They shouted questions, many concerning Callahan. Who was this mysterious nephew? How had he shown up so suddenly? Where did the nickname Tomahawk come from? All Clara would say was that the wager was still on and that Callahan Bros. Outfitters was, by God, gonna win! Callahan had hustled her into the office, closing and locking the door behind them as the reporters continued to shout questions.

"I thought you were supposed to be the calm one in the family," Callahan said.

"Do you know what that son of a—" Clara took a deep breath and let it out, composing herself. "Do you know what Arbuckle said?"

"I saw him whisper something to you," Callahan said. "You didn't seem to like it much."

"Indeed, I did not." She found the bottle in the bottom drawer and set it on the desk. "He said I was doing the right thing because . . . because a little, unimportant man like Howard never had a chance to win that bet, even if he was alive. He was foolish to make the bet in the first place, and I shouldn't have to suffer for what my fool husband did."

"I'm glad I didn't hear that," Callahan said. "I'd have been up there swinging fists."

"Well, I swung you into a mess, instead," Clara said. "You don't have to do it, obviously. Must have given you a heart attack when you heard me say you'd be leading the wagon train."

"I'll do it."

Clara set two glasses on the desk next to the bottle. "I was just so angry. A woman can only take so much, you know, especially when some weasel is badmouthing her man. I just couldn't take no more of it, and I couldn't give that skunk the satisfaction. I suppose I'll have to go crawling to him now and set things straight. I've only made things worse."

"Aunt Clara."

She opened the bottle and filled the glasses. "What?"

"I said I'd do it."

She looked at him, grateful, but then shook her head. "Oh, Luke, I can't ask you to do that. It's not fair."

"Forget fair," Callahan said. "I want to put Arbuckle in his place just as much as you do. If Callahan family pride's at stake, then I'm your man. Heck, I told you last night I'd do it, didn't I?"

"There's still the fact you've never led a wagon train before," she reminded him.

"You said your best man retired?"

"That's right. Cookie Mayfield."

"Then I best go find him and un-retire the man," Callahan said. "You got a notion where he might be?"

"It's a ways out of town. Cookie likes his privacy." She gave him directions.

"I'd better get a move on then."

"But . . . you're going right now?"

"As a cranky master sergeant pal of mine is fond of saying, we're burning daylight." Callahan snatched up one of the shot glasses and tossed back the whiskey. "Can I count on you to round up the rest of the crew?"

"Consider it done," she said. "I'm glad I didn't send those letters out to the settlers telling them the wagon train was canceled."

Callahan turned and headed for the door. "Save me some of that whiskey. I have a feeling I'll need a good belt later."

"Luke."

He paused, and then looked back at her.

A smile brightened his aunt's face. "Thanks."

Callahan rode north, leaving the town behind, coming to open fields, then a wide creek, which he followed into the woods. The creek widened into a large pond, and across the pond, Callahan spotted the shack, a small but tidy clapboard structure with a slanted tin roof and a crooked stone chimney, a thin tendril of smoke wafting into the sky.

A narrow path circled the pond. Callahan dismounted and led his horse by the reins.

Two shots split the cool, morning air.

Callahan pulled the horse into the trees just off the path, his eyes raking the area across the pond. Pistol shots, no mistake. And then another weapon sounded. A shotgun this time. Callahan knew he had two choices. Climbing back on his horse and riding away was the first. Whatever was going on here was none of Callahan's business. The second choice was more problematic.

Callahan would make it his business.

He looped the reins over a tree branch and headed for the shack.

More shots. Another blast from the shotgun. Callahan estimated the gunplay was coming from the other side of the shack. He broke into a run, and when he reached the shack, he put his back against the clapboards next to a window and chanced a peek inside.

He caught a glimpse of the interior through thin, wispy curtains. Table and chairs. A potbelly stove. A narrow bunk. A shirtless man in his underwear squatted next to the window on the other side of the shack, frantically thumbing fresh shells into a double-barreled twelve-gauge. He looked to be in his midsixties, chest hair matted and gray, beard gray with streaks of black, thinning on top. A bent nose. The ropey, sagging muscles of someone who'd been a powerful figure in his youth. A vague memory stirred from when Callahan was a boy. This was Cookie Mayfield. Callahan remembered him with less gray in his hair and not as stooped, but this was the veteran wagon train hand without a doubt.

"Throw out that scattergun and give us your money, old man," someone shouted from beyond Cookie's window. "Do it now, and maybe we'll let you live."

"You go to the devil!" Cookie shouted back.

"All you're doing is talking yourself into a shallow grave," the man replied. "Now, don't be stupid. We got you surrounded."

Callahan glanced back and forth. There was nobody on his side of the shack but him, so all the talk about Cookie being surrounded was a bunch of hot—

A man came around the corner, six-gun in hand, wearing denim, black shirt, and a leather vest, black mustache and squinty eyes . . . but the eyes widened when he spotted Callahan. The man was momentarily taken aback, not expecting to find anyone behind Cookie's shack, but he recovered and brought his revolver around.

Callahan reacted on pure reflex, the Peacemaker clearing his holster in a heartbeat. He fanned the hammer twice, the Peacemaker belching fire, splotches blooming red across the other man's chest. He went spinning back and hit the ground hard.

The shots set off more gunplay, pistol fire coming through the shack, the tinkle of broken glass in windowpanes. Callahan dove for the ground. Cookie's scattergun thundered twice more. Shouts and a commotion.

"I'll blow your dang head off, old man," someone shouted. "Tell us where you got that money hid!"

Callahan scrambled to his feet, lowered his shoulder, and slammed through the shack's back door. His momentum carried him through faster than expected, and he went flat across the floor. His clumsiness saved him because the man standing over Cookie turned and fired, the shot going high.

Callahan rolled onto his back and fired, catching the other man square in the knee. An explosion of blood, and the man went down screaming. He dropped his revolver, which clattered out of reach. Callahan staggered to his feet, gun trained on the man, but all the fight had gone out of him. He writhed on the floor, clutching the ruined kneecap and screamed and screamed and screamed.

"You dirty . . . son of a . . ." He trailed off into a string of curses, his screams now a series of low, sick moans as he went ashen, the blood pouring out of him and making an ever-widening puddle.

Callahan ignored him, Peacemaker up and ready for whatever happened next as he scanned the room. Cookie was on his hands and knees, a smudge of blood above one ear. A man lay heaped in the corner, blasted with buckshot. Cookie at least had gotten in his licks before someone had bashed him on the side of the head.

"You okay?" Callahan asked.

Cookie lifted his head, blinked, trying to uncross his eyes. "Look . . . look out!"

Callahan glanced back at the open doorway. A shadow falling through it gave him a split second of warning, and he lifted his six-gun and fired just as the man's bulk filled the doorway. The man took the shot in the middle of his barrel chest and stumbled back out the way he'd come.

Callahan turned back just in time to see the knee-shot man pull something from his boot. A glint of metal. Callahan fired again, putting a bullet right between the man's eyes.

The little shack had suddenly gone quiet, filled with gun smoke and the copper stink of fresh blood. Callahan waited, eyes going to every door and window. "Is that all of them?"

Cookie shook his head. "I . . . I dunno. I hope."

Callahan went to the dead man and stepped on his wrist. The hand opened, revealing a single-shot derringer, a .41 short. Callahan bent, plucked the derringer from the man's palm, and tucked it into his pocket.

Cookie staggered to his feet, swaying. He would have fallen over again, but Callahan grabbed his arm and steadied him. Cookie touched three fingers to the side of his head and squinted at the blood.

Callahan examined the wound. "Don't look too bad."

The old man blinked, eyes coming into focus. "Stonewall?"

Cookie jerked his arm away from Callahan and ran for the door. "Stonewall!"

Callahan followed him out of the shack and found him kneeling in the mud next to a stout-looking bloodhound. The dog lay still, a bloody hole in his side. Cookie gathered the dead dog into his arms. "Oh, no . . . no, no, no."

"That ain't right." Callahan looked away, disgusted. "No call to shoot a man's dog."

"Stonewall was barking," Cookie said. "That's how I knew they was coming. I had just enough time to grab the twelve-gauge."

"Is there a shovel?" Callahan asked. "I'll help you bury him."

"Behind the chicken coop." Cookie didn't look up and kept stroking the dog behind the ears.

They found a nice spot between two trees, and Callahan dug the hole. Cookie Mayfield wrapped the hound in an old gray blanket and gently lowered him into the ground. Callahan covered him up with dirt. They stood a moment in silence.

"I need a minute, if you don't mind," Cookie said. "There's coffee inside if you want to help yourself."

"Okay."

Callahan went back to the shack and rummaged around until he found the coffee. There was already water in the pot. He stoked the fire in the cast iron stove. By the time Cookie returned, the coffee was ready. Callahan handed the old man a cup.

Cookie cupped it in both hands and sank into a rickety chair. He blew out a sigh and said, "Mister, you saved my skin and that's for sure, but it only just occurs to me I have no idea who you are."

"My friends call me Tomahawk or Tom for short," Callahan told him. "But my right name is Luke Callahan. I'm Howard's nephew."

Cookie stared at him a long moment and then threw his head back in laughter. "Well, dang, boy, I'd never have guessed it. Last time I saw you, you was only this high." He held his hand down by his knee, and then he sobered suddenly. "I read about your uncle in the paper. A dang shame, and I'm sorry. I was thinking I should look in on Clara, but . . . well, I dunno. Sometimes, people like to be left alone after something like that."

Callahan sipped coffee. "I suppose you read about that other business, too."

"You mean that fool bet with the railroad? Yeah, I read about it." Cookie rolled his eyes. "That's Howard all over. He was a good man but hotheaded. I wasn't surprised he could be goaded into such nonsense. Listen, Luke . . . er, Tomahawk . . . I'm grateful you're here, but why are you here?"

Callahan grinned. "I was hoping you could help me win a fool bet with the railroad."

Cookie groaned. "Not you, too."

"I guess I got caught up in family pride."

"Well, I'm sorry, but I'm retired," Cookie stated flatly. "Has it occurred to you this wager business and Howard's death might be connected?"

"It's occurred to me."

"Well, that's it for me then," Cookie said. "The Oregon Trail kills people all by itself. It's a long, hard path. Throw in cheating railroad men willing to kill to win a bet . . . Well, no thank you. I'm too old. And I aim to get older."

Callahan nodded and set his coffee cup on the table. "Fair enough. I'll get out of your hair. Thanks for the coffee."

"One second. Maybe you can do me a favor." Cookie

crossed the room to his bunk, knelt, and pried up one of the floorboards. He reached through the opening, pulled out a sack, and dropped it on the floor. It hit with a metallic clink. He replaced the floorboard, then brought the bag to Callahan.

"Five hundred dollars," Cookie said. "All I have in the world. I know Clara has a little safe in her office. Maybe you can ask her to put this in there for me."

Callahan took the sack. "You keep it in the floor?"

Cookie shifted his feet, looking sheepish. "It's why them robbers was here. I was running my mouth down at the Riverside Inn, saying how my brother lost all his money in the panic of '73, and that's why I didn't trust banks, preferred to have my money where I could keep my eyes on it. I still don't trust banks, but I suppose I need this money locked up somewhere proper."

"I'm sure Aunt Clara won't mind. Take care, Mr. Mayfield." Callahan turned for the door.

"Just . . . wait."

Callahan paused in the doorway.

Cookie looked at him hard and long, trying to decide something. "You ever lead a wagon train before."

Callahan shook his head. "Nope."

"Oh, for crying out loud." Cookie turned away, rubbing his eyes, and mumbled what sounded like four-letter words under his breath. He turned back. "And you talked Clara into this?"

Callahan grinned again. "It was her idea."

Cookie let loose with a new string of obscenities. "You Callahans are gonna be the death of me. Okay, look, I got dead bodies all over my dang shack. Them boys must have horses around here somewhere. Let's load up these bodies, take them to the marshal, and explain what happened. Then . . . well . . . I guess you need an experienced hand to show you the way to Oregon. You saved me, so it's only fair I save you, even if only from your own stupidity."

CHAPTER 10

"They started gathering two nights ago in the muster area north of town," Clara said.

"All of them?"

"Some dropped out," his aunt said. "But some late-comers joined. It looks like we're actually on schedule, believe it or not."

Callahan nodded, feeling nervous and hopeful at the same time. It was the second of May. Tomorrow at dawn, on the third of May, the wagon train would head west.

With Tomahawk Callahan as the wagon train captain.

How in God's name did I land myself in this mess? Never mind. There's work to be done.

Callahan stood, stretched his arm over his head, and rotated the shoulder, wincing only slightly.

"All better?" Clara asked.

"Mostly," Callahan said. "If you get the chance to have an Indian shoot an arrow into you, take a pass."

Clara laughed. "I think I can figure that one out for myself."

"I'm going to ride past the muster," Callahan said. "Just to make sure everything's okay."

Clara waved him on. "Go on then. You know Cookie's got it handled, but I know you can't sit still."

"Speaking of Cookie, he wanted me to double-check that his five hundred dollars is still in your safe," Callahan said. "He says he don't trust banks, but when it comes to money, it seems like he don't trust hardly anyone at all."

"It's safe." Clara shook her head and laughed.

"What's the joke?"

"I just never thought in a million years Cookie Mayfield would be able to save up five hundred dollars," Clara said. "The man couldn't spend his paycheck fast enough, mostly cards and whiskey. Go on, Luke. You tell Cookie his money's safe."

Callahan rode north of town until he reached the wide, flat field, the muster area used to gather all the wagons that intended to participate in the wagon train. Dusk slid into night just as he arrived, and families gathered around cookfires. The smell of stews and roast chicken and a dozen other aromas mixed and wafted across the field. Small children ran between wagons, laughing and chasing one another, heedless of the hardships ahead.

This is what this is all about, Callahan reminded himself. *Not some wager. Not pride and competition. This is about families going west in search of a better life.* He swore to himself to remember that in the weeks to come.

"I figured you'd be along to have a look." Cookie Mayfield reined in his horse next to Callahan's.

"I am supposed to be in charge of this mess, after all," Callahan said.

"Don't worry, it ain't as chaotic as it looks," Cookie assured him. "There's an open lane right down the middle of the camp, and each wagon's been given a number. They'll fall in one at a time as we move out. It's a system your uncle and I worked out years ago. Circle up each night, move out by the numbers the next morning."

Callahan nodded. "Well, if it ain't broke, don't fix it. Are they still arriving?"

"Not so much," Cookie said. "Anyone going is already here. Or they changed their mind and ain't coming."

"Anything else I should be concerned about?" Callahan asked.

"Well . . . naw, I suppose not."

"Say it if you got something to say."

"I just wish we had some more experienced hands going along with us . . . No reflection on you."

Callahan laughed. "I wish the same thing. That's exactly why I came looking for you."

"Fair enough," Cookie said. "But we got four other fellows as green as grass. Billy Thorndyke made the last wagon train with your uncle. So he at least knows what it tastes like. He brought his little brother Ike. Hopefully, Billy taught him a thing or two. But Clancy Davenport ain't never been west of Kansas. Same with that kid from Little Rock. Both of them are stout lads, but I just wish they had a little more seasoning."

"You'll just have to teach us all as we go, Cookie." But Callahan understood the old veteran's concern. They had nothing but a small crew to herd a bunch of families all the way to Oregon. Each man needed to know his business and pull his weight.

And that includes me, Callahan thought. *I know the terrain, but wagon trains aren't my business.*

He just had to hope it was in his blood. His uncle had been a wagon train man. So had his father.

"Luke! Luke Callahan, over here!"

Callahan looked around to see who was calling his name.

A woman hung out the back of her Conestoga wagon, waving him over. Two red braids hung down, one past each ear. She wore a man's checkered shirt with the sleeves rolled up. Denim trousers. For the second time, it took Callahan an extra moment to recognize her.

"Velvet?"

She laughed. "There's no Velvet anymore. That was for the saloon, and that's all behind me now. It's just Becky."

"Becky, then." And, indeed, she resembled the Becky he'd known, except, of course, grown up. She'd wiped away the abundance of makeup and now looked plainer but better for it, clean-faced with freckles, smile bright and unforced. "Becky, what are you doing here?"

"I told you I been saving my money," Becky said. "So we're heading west to Oregon."

"I didn't know you meant so soon."

"Reading about all the excitement in the paper, the wagon train racing the railroad to Oregon, well, it just caught my attention, you know?" Becky told him. "And then you appearing out of nowhere just, I dunno, sort of seemed like fate. It hit me that now was the time, I guess."

Cookie hid a grin behind his hand. "I see you old friends need to catch up. I'll circle the camp and make sure everything's still in order." He tugged on the reins and urged his horse in the opposite direction.

"Becky, a wagon train is a serious thing," Callahan said. "It's a long, hard trip."

Becky's smile faltered. "Are you saying you don't want me along?"

"It's not that I don't want . . . well, I mean . . ." Callahan suddenly felt awkward, tripping over his own tongue. "I mean, I'm not sure *want* really enters into it. It's just that it can be dangerous. And a woman all alone . . . which is to say . . . you are alone, aren't you?"

It suddenly occurred to Callahan he was a little more interested in the answer to this question than he should be.

"Alone?" She giggled. "No, I brought some company with me."

Callahan should have figured. A girl like Becky would have a beau, maybe even a husband. A good thing, really, he supposed, someone to look after her over all the long miles to come.

"Here's my traveling companion now," Becky said.

A little girl, no more than six years old, popped her head up from the wagon bed, hair the same color as Becky's and braided in a similar way. Freckles all over her face and a front tooth missing, a light dress with a tight floral pattern and lace at the collar.

She grinned and waved. "I'm Lizzy!"

Becky put a hand on top of the girl's head. "Short for Elizabeth."

"Good to meet you, Lizzy." Callahan's eyes bounced between Becky and the little girl. "Is . . . uh . . . your father coming along on the wagon trip?"

Becky's face hardened. "It's just me, Luke. Lizzy's father drowned three years ago."

"Daddy's gone to heaven," Lizzy said.

Callahan summoned a friendly smile. "I'm sure he has."

"Go find your dolly, Lizzy," Becky said.

"Good-bye, Mr. Callahan." Lizzy vanished into the depths of the wagon.

"I'm sorry," Callahan told Becky. "About your husband."

"It's past," she said. "I'm not saying it's been easy, but I do what I need to feed us and keep a roof over our heads. Maybe you don't think a wagon train is the right place for a woman and child alone. Maybe you're even right about that. But I'm here, anyway. It'll be hard, but I'm here and I'm no quitter."

Callahan nodded slowly, taking her measure. "No, ma'am, I don't believe there's any quit in you at all. And I'm glad you haven't deluded yourself into thinking this journey will be easy. And I think you have what it takes to make it. All the same, I think I wouldn't mind checking in on you from time to time. Unless you object."

Becky's expression softened, a tentative smile trying to break through. "To be honest, I was sort of hoping you'd say something like that. Can you keep a secret, Luke?"

"I'll do my best."

"I'm scared to death," she told him. "This is the biggest thing I've ever done, the farthest I'll ever be away from home. A *new* home. Everything new and different. There's nothing but possibilities ahead, and that's exciting . . . and terrifying."

Callahan set his jaw. "Stick with me, Becky Griffith. Hell or high water, I'll get you to Oregon."

Becky brightened, a smile exploding wide with straight, white teeth. Even by the flickering light of the nearby cookfire, Callahan saw the woman was blushing to the ears.

She cleared her throat and looked away awkwardly before looking back at him again. "Luke, I just knew that . . . I mean . . . I had a feeling when you came into the saloon that . . . that . . . well, I'm not sure. That something was going to change and maybe—"

Angry shouts from across the camp spoiled the moment.

"I better look into this." Callahan spurred his horse toward the commotion.

He galloped past other families around their own fires who stood, heads turned toward some altercation a few rows over.

Callahan arrived just in time to see one man punch another square in the face.

The man doing the punching was older, maybe in his late forties, broad shoulders. And a lived-in face. Thinning hair with streaks of gray. He looked more annoyed than angry. Whereas, the man he'd just punched looked furious even as he went sprawling, arms windmilling, scattering the woman and three children who'd been standing beside him.

He went down hard into the dirt but came up fast to one knee, rage flashing in his eyes. He was younger, midtwenties, and the children standing close resembled him strongly—mouse-brown hair, pale complexion, dark eyes, short, and broad. The woman—his wife?— had much darker hair and was skinny. Her face was pretty but worried.

"You're gonna regret that!" snarled the younger man. "I suffer no insult to me nor any of my family, and I generally give twice what I get."

The older man brought his fists up. "You want more of this, then come get it."

The young man sprang up and launched himself at the other one.

But Callahan had already leapt from the saddle and had put himself between the two men, a hand on each chest, shoving them back.

"That's enough! Calm down!"

"Nobody asked you to poke your nose in where it don't belong, stranger," the younger one said.

"The name's Callahan, not *stranger*, and I'm the captain of this wagon train. Who are you?"

The young man took a step back. "I didn't know you were the man in charge. My name's Grainger, Matt Grainger." He jerked a thumb over his shoulder at his family. "My wife and young'uns."

"What's the problem here?"

"He came at me," the older man said. "I was defending myself."

Grainger opened his mouth to object.

"Not now," Callahan said. "You'll get your turn."

Grainger went red but kept his mouth shut.

"My name's Pete Johansen," the older man said. "All I did was tell his children not to get too close to my cookfire, and he went crazy."

"That's not how you said it," snapped Grainger. "You called my kids snotty brats and a few other choice words I won't say in mixed company."

"They've been running around making noise like animals," Johansen said. "Maybe raise 'em right, and they wouldn't be snotty brats."

"You son of a—" Grainger's hand went to the knife on his belt.

"Pull that knife and I'll kick you out of this wagon train so fast, your head will spin," Callahan said with iron in his voice. He glanced around and saw that a crowd had gathered to gawk, so he spoke loud enough for all to hear. "We've got a tough road ahead of us, so if you want problems, we're sure to get our share along the way. There's no need to go out of your way to make new ones. In a group of people this size, I suppose tempers might flare occasionally. Fights like this might happen. But listen to me right now because I'm only saying this once. Anyone in this wagon train pulls a gun or a knife on anyone else, I'll boot you out. No questions asked. No second chances."

Grumbles, but also nods of agreement.

Callahan suddenly wondered if he could actually make good on his promise to kick people out of the wagon train. If they arrived in Oregon without a certain number of families, Callahan would forfeit the wager, wouldn't he? He might need to look the other way if somebody broke a rule.

No. That wouldn't do. These people were here to get to Oregon and start a new life. The bet with the railroad was nothing to them, a curiosity maybe, but not the reason they were here. Callahan was obligated to do his best for them, and hopefully, the wager would come out the right way.

He realized everyone was looking at him, wondering what he was going to say next.

"You." Callahan pointed at Grainger. "Children need to play, but tell them to give other folks a wide berth. We're heading west, and if there's one thing we'll have in plenty, it's space. And you." He turned his attention to Johansen. "Courtesy doesn't cost anything. If you've got a problem, try *please* and *thank you* first."

"Sorry, Mr. Callahan." Grainger's demeanor was coolly polite. "You've made the rules clear. Sorry for any trouble." He herded his wife and children back toward their wagon.

"Show's over, folks," Callahan told the crowd. "Get some rest. We start early tomorrow."

People began wandering away, muttering and discussing what they'd just seen and heard. Callahan was about to go back to his horse when he noticed Pete Johansen still standing there, a cross look on his face.

"Something more to say?" Callahan asked.

"I know how *please* and *thank you* work. I don't like having my courtesy questioned," Johansen said. "I'm more apt to give it if I'm getting it, thank you very much."

Callahan's first instinct was to give the man an earful, but he thought better of it. "I just want us all to make a good start, Mr. Johansen. No disrespect intended."

Johansen grunted, turned, and headed back to his own wagon.

Callahan shook his head and rolled his eyes. Some men were just naturally unpleasant, he supposed. He hoped Johansen wouldn't give him any more trouble.

He went back to his horse and found Cookie Mayfield waiting.

"You catch that?"

"Most of it," Mayfield said. "I thought you handled it pretty good."

"What do you know about this Johansen fellow?"

Mayfield shook his head. "Not much. He was last to arrive, a late addition."

Callahan wasn't sure what he thought of that. Some instinct told him Johansen would bear watching. He mounted his horse. "I'm heading back to Clara's. Might be the last night for a while I get to sleep in a real bed."

"I'll keep you company to the edge of the clearing," Mayfield said.

The two men rode side by side, chatting about last minute details. A few moments later, they spotted a light ahead of them and reined in their horses.

"Who could that be?" Callahan asked.

Cookie Mayfield squinted into the night. "Coming from the road. A wagon with a lantern hanging from the jockey box."

Callahan considered a moment. "Let 'em come. We'll wait."

The wagon wasn't in a rush. They sat for a few minutes

and let it come. It would have gone right past them, fifty feet away in the dark, if Callahan hadn't called out.

"Hello, the covered wagon!"

A woman's startled gasp. Then "whoa" and the team of mules clopping to a halt. "Who's out there?"

"Callahan."

A pause, then she called out, "Tomahawk Callahan?"

"How do you know that name?"

"I read it in the *Herald*," she replied.

Callahan mumbled a mild curse. *Those newspaper reporters sure love that nickname.*

"Anyway, you're the man I'm looking for." She held up a folded piece of paper. "I've got the agreement right here."

"Stay there," Callahan called. "We'll come to you."

They walked the horses to the covered wagon, stopping just inside the circle of light cast by the lantern.

Callahan took a good, hard look at the woman holding the reins. She wore an expensive blue dress and a matching hat perched atop a pile of well-coiffed brown hair. Clear skin, round face, pretty. There was a "back East" look to her, or maybe it was just that she looked out of place, too fancy to be in a Conestoga wagon, holding the reins to a smelly mule team.

"You mentioned an agreement," Callahan said.

She waved the papers again. "I just came from Clara Howard. I'm the final member of your wagon train."

"Ma'am, we're going to Oregon, and I'm sure you know that's not a journey for the fainthearted," Callahan said. "It's no place for a—"

He'd been about to say *no place for a woman alone*, but if he could accept that a girl like Becky could make the trip with a young daughter in tow, then who was he to deny this woman her chance?

"That is to say, it's not a trip for anyone who isn't ready for some hardship," Callahan finished.

"Please don't let my traveling clothes fool you, Mr. Callahan," she said. "I went straight from the railroad station to the outfitters, then came right here as fast as I could. I've got a carpetbag full of sturdy clothes and sensible boots, so don't worry your little head about me. My name's Anna Masters, and I'm here at the expense of the *Baltimore Register*."

Callahan frowned. "A newspaper?"

"Your wager with the railroad has captured the nation's attention, Mr. Callahan," Masters said. "I'm going to Oregon with you, and I'll be letting our readers know what you and the others in your wagon train are doing every step of the way."

CHAPTER 11

"Well, I guess you'll just have to be on your best behavior," Clara said. "If some lady reporter is taking down everything you say, then watch that mouth."

Callahan grunted, looking down at the empty tin cup in his hands that used to contain coffee. He needed more. He sat next to his aunt on the buckboard's bench, rocking with the ruts in the road, the lantern the only beacon of light in the implacable darkness.

"I wanted one more night in a bed, but I should have just stayed with the wagons last night," Callahan said. "You didn't need to come out with me at this ungodly hour, Aunt Clara."

Clara *tsked*. "Are you kidding? I came to see Howard off every time. I was always here to wave him good-bye. Never missed. And I'm not about to miss my nephew's first one."

The flickering blur of cookfires in the distance drew them on. Folks at the mustering point were already awake and pulling breakfasts together. Clara reined in the horses at the edge of the camp. "I'll watch from here. A good out-of-the-way spot. You go do whatever you need to do."

Callahan jumped down from the buckboard and circled behind where he'd tethered his horse. He mounted and headed into camp. Families ate their last biscuits, sipped their final swigs of coffee. Some were already dousing their cookfires and loading their wagons.

"Seems calm enough, doesn't it?"

Callahan looked back to see Cookie Mayfield approaching, his horse clopping along in no particular hurry.

"Don't worry, it'll get real noisy once we get started," Mayfield assured him. "First couple times it was a mess. Things went a lot smoother when we started assigning numbers."

A young rider joined them, reining in his horse next to the other two men. Billy Thorndyke was barely into his twenties, fresh-faced and clean-shaven, eyes a sharp blue, sandy hair under a tan hat with a black band, lean and eager. Callahan hoped the young man knew how to handle the Colt Army revolver hanging on his hip.

Billy grinned like he was having the best time in the world. "Good morning, Mr. Callahan."

"Call me Tomahawk if you like."

The boy's grin widened. "Yes, sir!" He turned to Mayfield. "I know you're senior, Cookie, but is it okay if I take us out?"

Cookie gestured grandly at the collection of Conestoga wagons. "The train is yours, sir!"

"Yeeeeeehaw!" Billy spurred his horse and headed around to the front of the camp at a gallop.

Cookie squinted toward the horizon. "Not long now."

The people of the camp moved with more delibera-
tion now, men hitching mules, checking harnesses,
loading last-minute items into wagons. Women herded
children, many of the younger ones still rubbing sleep
from their eyes.

The morning light was faint, a pink-orange glow in
the distance, the forewarning of a new day. There was
a tension in the air that Callahan couldn't explain—
expectation, readiness. He felt tense with excitement.
His first wagon train. The very edge of the sun broke
orange-red on the horizon, light flooding the camp,
faces all around him looking up to greet it.

At almost the same moment, the *clang clang clang*
rang out across the camp. Callahan couldn't see it from
where he sat in the saddle, but he could imagine the
man banging on an iron triangle, the sound crisp and
clear in the slightly damp morning air. Anyone not yet
in their wagons scrambled fast.

Someone shouted far up ahead, and the shout was
passed down through the line. "Wagon number one!"

About forty yards ahead of Callahan, someone yelled
"Yaw!" and a wagon pulled into the lane that had been
cleared down the length of the camp. Shouts of "Wagon
number two!" followed, and a second Conestoga pulled
in behind the first. Three came next, then four, and it
went on like that. Somewhere up ahead, Billy Thorndyke
led the parade.

It was a plodding sort of enterprise, but organized
and deliberate.

"Good morning, Luke!"

Callahan looked at the wagon passing right in front

of him. Becky leaned out to wave at him, face beaming. The little girl must have been in the back.

"I'll see you in Oregon!" Becky called.

"Looks like you might get there before me," Callahan shouted back.

She laughed and waved again.

The wagons continued to fall into line, heading west, the sun now fully above the horizon. The final wagon squeaked and rocked and inched passed Callahan, a cross-looking Anna Masters clutching the reins of her mule team. She'd changed out of her fancy dress but still looked out of place. The cream-colored work shirt with the sleeves rolled up looking stiff and starched and obviously hadn't been worn before. She wore a flat, black gaucho hat back on her head, strands of rich, brown hair dangling from either side.

Callahan touched the brim of his hat with a forefinger. "Good morning to you, Miss Masters."

"And what's so good about it?" she shot back. "Am I going to eat the dust of the entire wagon train all the way to Oregon?"

Callahan offered an apologetic shrug. "Sorry, ma'am. Numbers are assigned as people arrive to the muster area. You got here dead last."

Masters made a disgusted snort. "I suppose it will amuse my readers to hear about the city girl suffering in the wilds."

"At least you're not behind the animals." Callahan jerked a thumb back down the line.

Masters turned to look, eyes widening as a small herd of sheep approached, followed by a herd of cattle maybe fifty head strong.

"Yes, I think I'd rather stay ahead of that stink. If you'll excuse me." She flicked the reins, and the mules lurched forward.

"She'll be trouble," Cookie said. "You'll be spending all of your time pulling her out of the mud and killing spiders in her wagon."

"Maybe." Callahan watched the wagon go. "Maybe not."

The dust kicked up by the wagons redoubled as the animals passed by, along with their stink and bleating and mooning and the yap of the dogs keeping the sheep in order, the whole circus a big, loud, smelly mess yet magnificent in its own way. That such a mass of humanity should pick up and move across the nation, their animals and all their worldly possessions along with them . . . well, it was a massive undertaking. Howard Callahan was right to be offended by those who belittled such an effort.

But I still wish he hadn't made that fool bet.

"We'll lose some of those animals," Cookie Mayfield said matter-of-factly. "We always do. A few, anyway. Do you lose the bet if the livestock don't make it?"

Callahan shook his head. "Nothing in the agreement about sheep or cattle. We just need to worry about the wagons and the people."

A horse came back down the line of wagons at a full gallop, the rider reining in abruptly when he reached Mayfield and Callahan. Kicking up yet more dust.

Callahan frowned. "That horse has to last you all the way to Oregon, boy."

The young man grinned, and the family resemblance

to Billy was immediate. Ike Thorndyke was cut from the same cloth as his brother but even younger, as if that were possible. If the kid's jaw had ever seen a razor, Callahan would eat his hat. The boy's neckerchief was such an ostentatious shade of purple, Callahan suspected the kid wore it specifically to dare people to comment.

"Fifty-one wagons, not counting our own resupply wagon and the chow wagon," Ike reported. "And a hundred fifty-nine people. Not counting the crew."

"You sure about your count?" Callahan asked.

"Sure, I'm sure." The boy seemed offended anyone might question his math skills.

"Good enough," Callahan said. "Back to work with you."

The boy turned the horse and took off like a shot.

"I better keep an eye on the boys," Cookie said. "You want to let Miss Clara know the final count?"

Callahan nodded. "Okay."

He watched Cookie Mayfield head for the wagons at an easy trot, then turned his horse back toward his Aunt Clara, who was still perched on the bench of the buckboard a safe distance from the noise and stink of animal dung.

Clara looked up at him on the horse, squinting into the dawn light. "Quite a sight, isn't it?"

"One big mass of humanity and animals," Callahan told her. "All together like a big, lumpy creature. Fifty-one wagons and a hundred fifty-nine people."

"That matches my count, too. I guess we're good

to go," Clara said. "I'll wire the information off to Arbuckle. That was part of our agreement."

"Have all your wagon trains been that big?" he asked.

"We had eighty wagons back in '72," she said. "But, yeah, this is a big one for us."

Callahan shook his head. "That just figures."

"You'll manage."

From your lips to God's ears.

"Luke."

Something in her tone gave him pause. "Yes."

"We both want to win that bet. I'd personally love nothing more than to make that mouthy railroad man eat his words," Clara said. "But that's not the most important thing. Get everyone to Oregon in one piece. Then come back the same way. You hear me?"

"I hear you." Callahan doffed his hat. "Keep a pot of coffee warm. I'll be right back."

Callahan wheeled his horse around and galloped after the wagon train.

They used every bit of daylight, leaving just enough to make camp before nightfall.

"I make that about eighteen miles," Cookie Mayfield said.

Callahan took off his hat, wiped his forehead on his sleeve. "I can't believe how slow we're moving."

Cookie cackled laughter. "Hell, son, this is still the easy part. Wait until we're crossing rivers or up in the passes. You'll long for the good old days when we could put eighteen miles behind us."

Callahan briefly understood Kent Arbuckle's bravado.

A steam locomotive racing along at thirty-five miles per hour made the progress of his wagon train seem like a joke.

But he hasn't even put down the tracks yet. He can't possibly win.

Right?

They made eighteen miles the next day and repeated the number the day after. By the end of the week, they'd put at least a hundred and twenty miles behind them.

"We're off to a good start." Cookie Mayfield sat next to Callahan at the evening's cookfire and handed him a plate of beans with a chunk of bacon. "I'm thinking we cross into Nebraska tomorrow by midday maybe."

Callahan spooned beans into his mouth, digesting the older man's words. It had, indeed, been a good start. Callahan swallowed the beans and said, "I guess you're right. No busted axles. No stray cattle. Nobody ill or lost. No more fights. No thunderstorms washing us out. A lot of things could have gone wrong, but they didn't."

"Looks good for your bet."

Callahan laughed.

Cookie gave him the stink eye. "What?"

"The bet," Callahan said. "I haven't thought about it in days. Been too busy worried about all these people."

Cookie nodded. "Good. Keep thinking like that, and all this wager stuff will take care of itself."

Somewhere among the wagons, the clear notes of a harmonica rose into the night sky. It sounded soft and sweet. It sounded like hope.

"I wonder how the railroad man is doing?" Callahan said. "I wonder if he's having good luck or bad."

* * *

Kent Arbuckle looked back down the mountain at the approaching rider. "I suppose he's coming after us. A messenger maybe."

Mycroft Jones leaned in the saddle, looking back down the narrow trail at the single horse and rider clearly following them. "I wouldn't hazard a guess, Mr. Arbuckle, but he's coming fast, and I can't fathom any other reason for coming to such a desolate place in a hurry. Shall we wait for him?"

Jones had been sent by Horace Gladstone to help Arbuckle keep the books and to assist him in all the various minutia of his current endeavor. A slight, fastidious man, bald and well-dressed with a burgundy waistcoat, gray suit, and a bowler hat, Jones was indeed an efficient organizer and overall right-hand man. He was pale, with the tendency to sniff. Arbuckle thought him sickly, but when they'd left the train to travel on horseback, Jones hadn't balked and, in fact, seemed to keep up rather well . . . although he quite obviously preferred the comfort of Arbuckle's personal railcar.

Arbuckle preferred it, too, he had to admit to himself.

But while he acknowledged Jones's skills in keeping his affairs organized, he suspected the real reason for the man's presence. Jones was a spy for the brothers.

No matter. Arbuckle had nothing to hide.

"We won't wait. Every minute counts," Arbuckle said. "He can meet us at the top."

And with that, the railroad man, Mycroft Jones, and the rest of Arbuckle's entourage resumed their trek up the mountain.

The simple fact was that Arbuckle could not be everywhere at once. He was obliged to put men in charge of different teams, all to accomplish tasks that when added together made up a single effort, striving toward the same goal. But when his advance scouts had sent him three choices for getting across the Cascades, instinct had told Arbuckle he'd need to eyeball the situation himself.

Obviously, he'd read the reports. Tunnels, trestles, go around? Opinions varied, and while he trusted the advice of his experts, he valued nobody's opinion more than his own.

The four of them continued up the mountain, Arbuckle, Jones, and two of Arbuckle's henchmen. It amused Arbuckle to use the word *henchmen*, but really, what else were they? Dour men in bland brown suits and bowlers, serious mustaches, double-barreled shotguns and revolvers in shoulder holsters. Arbuckle had found that if there was a breed of men more suited to the job than a Pinkerton, it was a *former* Pinkerton, a man with a slightly more flexible view of which laws to bend and which to break altogether. If Arbuckle told them to do something—no matter how questionable—they'd bloody well do it.

They reached the peak and paused to look down into the valley on the other side. The river below was docile at the moment, a steady trickle but still an impediment to railroad tracks. A trestle would need to be high enough and sturdy enough to withstand the spring thaw, when the river grew more savage. The approaches were good, meaning they could bring the track in without too much trouble. It would be less time-consuming than dynamiting tunnels through the mountains to the north. Skirting the mountains to the south altogether would add too much travel time.

"We're going to build a bridge," Arbuckle announced. "Right here."

Mycroft Jones took out a pencil and notebook.

"I'll need you to wire back to Pendleton and start assembling a crew," Arbuckle told Jones. "I want the bridge complete by the time the tracks get here. If the track crew is standing around waiting for the bridge to be built, I won't be happy."

"We'll have to double the size of the usual crew," Jones said. "Expensive. We should get someone in here immediately to start felling trees. Lumber for the bridge."

"Triple the crew," Arbuckle said. "I don't care as long as they go fast."

Jones scribbled in his notebook.

"Mr. Arbuckle." It was one of the former Pinkertons, the gruffer of the two, a man named Gaspar.

Arbuckle looked to see what he wanted, and Gaspar nodded back down the trail, where the man they'd spotted earlier approached. Gaspar sat easy in his saddle, the short shotgun resting on one shoulder. His eyebrow went up, asking the obvious question. *Want me to do anything about him?*

"Let him come," Arbuckle said.

Gaspar nodded and eased back, letting the newcomer rein his horse in close to Arbuckle's.

The man took off his hat and used it to fan himself. "Mr. Arbuckle?"

"That's me."

"I'm Logan," he said. "Western Union's engaged me to bring you any messages immediately upon arrival."

"I know that," Arbuckle said impatiently. "I'm the one who gave the order."

"Apologies, sir." Logan handed over the two envelopes. "Shall I wait to see if there's a reply?"

"Please do."

Arbuckle opened the first envelope, read the message, and frowned. He had eyes and ears keeping track of Tomahawk Callahan's wagon train, and they were evidently off to a smooth start and covering a good number of miles each day. Well, it was still early. Anything could happen. He folded the message, shoved it in his pocket, and opened the other one.

When Arbuckle read the second message, he cursed so sharply, it made Logan flinch. The crew laying track from Salem had run into trouble. Dysentery in the camp, hundreds of Chinamen sick and idle instead of laying track, instead of racing to meet the other crew coming from the east. Arbuckle would need to take steps, but what those steps might be, he wasn't sure yet.

"I'll be replying to both of these messages," Arbuckle told Logan. "If the Western Union office closes before I get back, tell your man to wait."

"I'm not sure he'll care for that," Logan said.

"He shall be compensated. Or he can risk my displeasure."

Logan swallowed hard. "I'll tell him." He turned his horse and headed back down the mountain.

Arbuckle sighed and shoved the second message into his pocket with the first. Callahan had been lucky. Good weather. No problems. Arbuckle had been unlucky.

Time to flip that around. Time for Arbuckle to arrange some bad luck for that wagon train.

CHAPTER 12

They spent the next two weeks chewing up a good bit of Nebraska. The weather held, and the people behaved. Everything was going so well, Callahan was beginning to wonder what the fuss was about. So far, the worst part of the journey was the plodding tedium.

Callahan relieved the boredom by looking in on Becky and Lizzy at least once every evening.

"Something smells good," Callahan said as he approached their cookfire. "What gourmet miracles are you working tonight?"

Becky grinned. "Well, we had beans last night, and beans the night before that, and beans the night before that, so there's just no telling . . ." She bent over the cookfire to look into the cast iron pot. "Oh, my goodness, what a surprise. Beans!"

Callahan laughed. "Any biscuits to go with that?"

Becky shook her head. "I only got so much flour left. I went hard on beans and didn't get enough flour when buying my supplies."

"In that case, I come bearing gifts." Callahan handed

her a red-and-white-checkered cloth napkin tied up in a bundle.

"What's this?" Becky put the bundle in her lap and untied it, revealing a thick square of corn bread.

"Courtesy of Cookie Mayfield," Callahan said. "To go with your beans."

"Lizzy, come see!" Becky called.

The little girl came running around the wagon, and Becky showed her the corn bread.

Lizzy leaned in and took a good whiff. "That smells delicious, Mr. Callahan!"

"Cookie did all the cooking on cattle drives back in the day," Callahan explained. "That's why people call hm Cookie. He switched to the wagon train business, but the name stuck."

"Won't you join us, Luke?" Becky asked.

Callahan rubbed his belly. "I already ate my own plate of beans and three helpings of Cookie's corn bread. I'm tighter than a tick, but I'll keep you company if you like."

She smiled. "That would be fine."

He made small talk while the girls ate their beans. Callahan noticed Becky give her share of the corn bread to Lizzy, and he pretended not to notice.

When they'd finished eating, Callahan said, "I need to walk the circle." That's what Callahan had come to call his nightly habit of walking around the circled wagons, looking in on folks and generally keeping an eye on things. It had been a good way to turn strange faces into familiar names. "Care to stretch your legs?"

Becky brightened at the notion. She told Lizzy, "Clean these dishes, but don't touch the cook pot. It needs to cool. I'm taking the night air with Mr. Callahan, but I'll be back soon."

"Okay, Mommy."

They walked along the inside of the large circle, families calling out greetings as Callahan passed. Soon people would bed down for the night. Mornings came frightfully early on the Oregon Trail, but at the moment, people ate their dinners, socialized, tended to animals, and so on. The mules were tethered inside the circle. The herd of sheep was tied up outside the circle on one side of the camp, the cattle on the other.

"It's a cool night," Becky said.

Callahan walked next to her, hands clasped behind his back. "Good for sleeping."

"Yes."

Callahan felt suddenly awkward, groping for something to talk about. Becky had been nothing but friendly, but that didn't mean anything, really. Neither did the crush he had on her when they were in school. Many miles and years had passed since then. The girl going west was more appealing to him than the girl she'd been at the Cattleman's Corner saloon, although he didn't hold her time there against her. He had no particular ambitions where she was concerned, no plans to make anything happen when it came to the two of them. All he knew was he'd rather be strolling amiably with her than not, so he satisfied himself with that and didn't try to force the conversation.

He needn't have worried. She was happy to do the talking.

"You were an army scout?" she asked.

"That's right."

"That sounds dangerous," Becky said. "At least more so than leading a wagon train."

"I reckon it is," Callahan replied. "At least so far."

"Will you go back to scouting after this?" she asked. "Or stay in the wagon train business?"

"To be honest, I hadn't thought that far ahead," Callahan admitted. "Leading a wagon train is a bit . . . slow-paced."

"That's a bad thing?"

"Maybe if you're not used to it," Callahan said. "But then when I think about some Indian trying to kill me, a little boredom doesn't seem so bad. But . . . well . . . I'm not sure any of that really matters."

"What do you mean?"

"I mean, whether army scouting or wagon trains is a better line of work isn't how I'm thinking about it, although I must admit I'm only just now thinking about it seriously, so I can put it into words." Callahan paused, making sure he had his words lined up just right. "The thing is, that railroad man—Arbuckle—he's right."

Becky's eyebrows arched in surprise. "Oh?"

"I don't mean he's right about insulting people or treating them rudely," Callahan said quickly. "But he's right about wagon trains. I read a headline in a newspaper. THE LAST WAGON TRAIN. That's what they called us. It's not true, not in a strictly literal sense. But it's true in a more important sense, I guess. Someday, there won't be no more wagon trains. Nor Indian wars or a need for scouts, either. There's always been change, but usually it happens so slowly you don't notice. I don't think we're living in those kind of times. I think we can see the change happening right in front of our faces."

"I think that all adds up to the fact you don't know *what* you're going to do, Luke Callahan," Becky told him. "I think this trip west is going to be a big start over for you as well as everyone else in this wagon train."

Callahan digested that and realized Becky might be on to something.

What in the world are you going to do with yourself, Tomahawk Callahan?

"What about you then?" Callahan asked her. "What are your plans?"

As soon as the question was out of his mouth, Callahan wished he could reel it back in again. There was nothing to stop Becky from taking up her old saloon ways when she reached Oregon. He inferred she'd given up that life but didn't like risking that he might hear he was wrong.

She smiled, eyes narrowing with secrets. "Oh, I have a plan. I have some very specific skills. I'll show you when we get back to my wagon."

Callahan was taken aback. *Show me?*

A glimmer of light in the distance caught Callahan's attention. "What's that?"

"What?" Becky followed his gaze, looking between two wagons at something beyond the circle. "Is that a campfire?"

"I need to have a look."

Callahan headed for the fire, then stopped short when he realized Becky was following him. "Where do you think you're going?"

"Oh, come off it, Luke. What do you think's going

to happen?" Becky said, pinning him with a withering look. "I'm curious. You're not the only one bored with Nebraska, you know. Now let's go check out that fire."

"Fine, but if something bad happens, I'll handle it," Callahan said. "You run."

"Don't worry. I didn't come this far to be eaten by a bear or some stupid thing."

"I doubt bears build campfires," Callahan said. "Come on. Let's have a look."

The campfire was close enough to the wagon circle to be easily spotted, but not close enough to see who might be there or how many or anything else. They advanced slowly, and Callahan realized his hand was resting on the grip of his Peacemaker. He took it away, not wanting to alarm Becky. It was just a precaution. Habit. There was no reason to believe there was anything untoward out there in the darkness.

Still, Becky must have sensed his tension. She moved close to him, unconsciously taking him by the arm.

"Not that I don't appreciate the attention," Callahan said. "But if I have to go for my six-gun, you might slow me up some."

"Oh. Sorry." She let go of him, sounding embarrassed.

As they approached the fire, the scene took shape. A single Conestoga wagon, mules tethered off to the side, the silhouette of a man against the flames.

"Hello, the campfire!" Callahan called.

The silhouette twisted, looking back at them. "Come on then."

Callahan recognized the voice. "That you, Johansen?"

"It's me. Come up next to the fire."

Pete Johansen hadn't caused any more trouble since he'd knocked Grainger flat the first day.

Callahan reached the campfire with Becky in tow. Johansen sat on a stool, whittling a short stick down to nothing.

"What are you doing out here, Mr. Johansen?" Callahan asked.

"Trying to stay out of trouble."

"I think I might need you to explain that a little better."

Johansen sighed. "Well, let's just say I'm not much for people."

"Maybe a wagon train was a bad choice."

Johansen stood, brushing wood shavings from his trousers. "I want to get west same as anybody. Look, Callahan, I apologize for not being sociable. I didn't realize it was a requirement, but I spent a lot of time in the Yukon looking for gold. Didn't find much, just enough to buy my way back East. You know what I found back East? People by the bushel. People everywhere you turned, chattering and chattering about nothing at all. I didn't find a lot of gold in the Yukon, Mr. Callahan, but I sure found a lot of quiet. So I'm going back . . . figured a wagon train was the best way, but . . ." A shrug.

"Go on," Callahan urged. "Get it all out."

"I need a little peace at night," Johansen said, looking back at the circled wagons. "Feels sort of crowded over there, people talking, children playing and laughing."

"Children play and laugh," Becky said, offended. "That's just what they do."

"Look, I know it ain't normal," Johansen told her. "I don't mean to be so cantankerous. My nerves are a bit more raw than the average person's, I reckon. Figured I just needed a little distance."

Callahan pushed his hat back on his head, tugged at an earlobe, and blew out a sigh. "I can't guarantee your safety, Mr. Johansen, not as good as if you were circled up with the others."

"I release you from your obligation and acknowledge that should anything fatal befall me, it was a mishap of my own making," Johansen said. "Furthermore, I shall rise earlier in the morning than the rest of the wagon train so as to ready myself to take my proper place in line. I won't foul things up. I'm not looking to cause trouble."

"I guess I can't ask for more than that," Callahan said. "Truth to tell, it's been a pretty quiet trip so far. I doubt you'll have any trouble out here on your own."

A rifle shot split the night.

All three heads jerked around, looking into the darkness. Then a rapid-fire spattering of shots.

Callahan cursed. *Spoke too soon.*

"That's over by the sheep, isn't it?" Johansen said.

Callahan was already running, sprinting toward the gunfire.

"Get back to Lizzy," he called over his shoulder to Becky. "And stay in your wagon!"

Another shot, followed by angry shouts. Dogs barking. Callahan ran for all he was worth.

Nebraska suddenly wasn't boring anymore.

CHAPTER 13

Callahan arrived in time to see Cookie Mayfield astride his horse, talking to one of the sheepherders, who was holding a rifle. Two more sheepherders stood behind him, one with a rifle, the other with his revolver drawn and a lantern in his other hand. Somewhere beyond the lantern light, dogs barked their heads off.

"Who's shooting at what?" Callahan demanded.

"Somethings been at the sheep," said the leader of the sheepherders, a beefy man named Bart Schultz. Callahan had spoken with him on a few occasions, a simple, straightforward fellow with dull eyes and a drooping mustache.

"What do you mean *something*?" Callahan asked.

"Something big and fast," Schultz said. "First it seemed like it was there, and then I thought I saw something over thataway." He pointed with the rifle.

"If you can't see it well enough to identify it, then you can't see enough to shoot at it," Callahan said. "So let's hold off before you shoot each other."

"Well, dang it, there's *something* out there."

Someone came jogging up behind them. Callahan turned to see it was Pete Johansen.

"Something getting at the sheep?" he asked.

"That's what I've been saying," Shultz said.

Johansen looked past them at the writhing mass of sheep and beyond. "Best call them dogs back."

"They're guarding the dang sheep!"

Johansen looked at Callahan, expression grave.

"Maybe call them back, Mr. Shultz," Callahan said.

"Oh, for corn's sake." Schultz turned to the sheepherder with the rifle. "Go fetch 'em back, Lawrence."

Johansen held his hand out to the sheepherder with the lantern and the revolver, a young boy. "Pass that light over, son."

The boy hesitated.

"Go on," Callahan said.

Johansen took the lantern and headed toward the herd—sheep parting to make way for him, Callahan right behind. Cookie dismounted and followed along with Shultz. Johansen slowed his walk, bending low with the lantern, examining the ground as he went, stopping a few times to examine a particular patch of mud before grunting and moving on.

Callahan pitched his voice low for only Johansen to hear. "You've got a notion what it is?"

"Maybe," Johansen said. "I hope I'm wrong."

Callahan shook his head. *To think I was complaining about being bored. Me and my big mouth.*

Johansen stopped abruptly and went to one knee, looking at a set of tracks in the mud. "You know what they have plenty of in the Yukon, Mr. Callahan?"

"What's that?"

"Wolves."

Then everyone talked at once.

"Okay, okay, pipe down," Callahan said. "Cookie, you ever had trouble with wolves before, coming across this part of Nebraska?"

"No, never," Cookie said. "Not in Nebraska. I mean, I guess it ain't impossible, but . . ." He trailed off, shaking his head.

"Well, for dang sure something made off with one of my sheep," Shultz insisted.

Johansen had moved on, still examining the ground. "Two or three at least. They run in packs, you know."

"Over here!" somebody shouted.

They plunged into the darkness and found the sheepherder named Lawrence. He stood holding a dog in his arms, a mixed breed, Callahan thought, with shaggy black-and-white fur. Patches of fur here and there were matted, wet, and bloodstained. Other than the blood, the dog looked bright-eyed and alert.

"Pepper!" Schultz's concern was obvious. "Is she okay?"

"None of the wounds is too deep," Lawrence said. "But I found a blood trail and a bunch of bloody wool where one of the sheep was dragged off."

"Bring the dog to the chuckwagon," Cookie Mayfield said. "I got some stuff to clean her up."

"What do we do now?" Shultz demanded. "I can't arrive in Oregon with no sheep because I'm feeding wolves all the way there."

"They've got a nice fat sheep to eat," Callahan said.

"So I doubt you'll see any more of them tonight." He glanced at Pete Johansen for a second opinion.

Johansen nodded.

"We'll start early tomorrow and put as many miles behind us as we can," Callahan told the sheepherder. "Once we're out of their territory, I doubt they'll bother us anymore."

"Let's hope it works out that way, but I doubt me and the boys will get any sleep tonight," Shultz said. "We're going to stay up and guard the herd." He took the lantern back from Johansen and stomped away.

"I hope you're right," Johansen said to Callahan.

"About what?"

"Your man said they'd never seen wolves on previous trips, right?"

Callahan nodded. "That's right."

"You said we'd probably be safe once were out of the wolves' territory," Johansen said. "But could be they don't have a territory. If they're new to the area, maybe a stronger pack drove them out of the mountains, and they came across the flatlands looking to eat. If they find they like the taste of sheep, they might follow us all the way to Oregon."

"These are guesses."

"Yeah." Johansen nodded in agreement. "But good guesses. In the Yukon, we tried to figure out their behavior. Just when we had it figured, they'd do something different. So who knows? I'm probably wrong. Probably, they'll let us alone when we leave their territory, like you say. Anyway, have a good night." He turned and walked back toward his wagon.

Callahan walked around the circle of wagons to the

cattle herd that was on the other side. He wanted to give them fair warning.

"We think the excitement's over for tonight," Callahan said. "But you never know."

The cattleman was a man named Ace Franklin. Callahan refused to ask how he got the name Ace because to Callahan, Ace seemed like the sort who loved to be asked, and Callahan was in no mood for a story. The man was lean with a hawkish face. Clean-shaven. He wore a black hat with a band of silver and turquoise, maybe something he'd bought off an Indian.

"Come find me when you're ready to kill them wolves," Ace said. "Me and a couple of my best men will bring our rifles and handle it."

Callahan explained they'd be riding out of the wolves' territory tomorrow and that would likely be the end of it. He bid the cattleman good night and headed back to the wagons.

The night, which had started with quiet promise, now stretched into fatigue and worry. Callahan wanted nothing more than to kick off his boots and lay his head on his saddle, but then he remembered Becky. When he'd last seen her, he was running off into the night toward the sound of gunshots. The courteous thing might be to stop by her wagon and let her know what happened, although it was likely the story of the wolves had already gossiped its way all around the circle of wagons. Anyway, she and Lizzy were probably asleep by now.

And yet Callahan found himself walking toward her wagon, hoping she might still be awake.

He arrived to find a dark wagon and a cold cookfire. *Well, it was worth a try. I'll talk to her tomorrow.*

He turned to go.

"Luke." A whispered voice.

Callahan turned back, peered into the darkness of the Conestoga's interior. Becky leaned forward, her face catching the moonlight. She wore a light nightdress of white cotton, buttoned to the throat, some kind of lacy pattern around the neck, and a shawl pulled tight around her shoulders. It probably wasn't the sort of garment that would have gotten her much attention at the Cattleman's Corner, but Callahan thought she looked good and fresh in the night air, not painted and seen through tobacco smoke and a whiskey haze. She beckoned for Callahan to come closer.

Becky put a finger to her lips in a *shush* gesture. "Lizzy's asleep, so whisper, okay?"

As quietly as possible, Callahan told her about the wolves.

"But don't worry," he whispered quickly when he saw her eyes widen with alarm. "Stay within the circle of wagons and you'll be fine. Lots of people and fires. Wolves won't want any part of that. We'll leave their territory tomorrow."

Callahan hoped that was true. Pete Johansen seemed to believe otherwise.

"Well, I just wanted to let you know," he whispered. "I'll let you get back to sleep."

"Wait," Becky whispered back. "I wanted to show you something, remember?"

"Okay."

She ducked back into the wagon, and Callahan heard scraping sounds, something being moved around. He leaned into the wagon to look. Becky pushed a wooden crate to the edge of the wagon. She swung open the lid on iron hinges, and Callahan squinted into the crate. Some sort of contraption lay in a nest of straw. He looked at it a moment, metal glinting in moonlight, the word SINGER prominent across the smooth surface.

Callahan had never seen one before but felt sure he knew what he was looking at. "A sewing machine."

"It was crazy expensive," Becky whispered. She ran a hand over the smooth surface. "I'm good at making dresses. I've always been nimble with needle and thread. This machine will put me in business. I worked so long to save up for it. And for that." She gestured into the wagon and some large, lumpy item under a tarp. "It's a special table for the Singer. It has a foot pedal to work the machine. I can't tell you how long I worked, how many miserable hours of . . . so much money for the sewing machine, the table, the wagon, the last of the money for beans, just to—" Something caught in her voice, and she dabbed at the corner of one eye with the end of her shawl.

She sniffed then, abruptly, picked her head up, and her smile returned as if it had always been there. "I will make beautiful dresses. That will be my life, me and Lizzy's, making pretty things. People will come for miles around for my work and— Are you laughing at me, Luke Callahan?"

Callahan realized he was grinning. "No, ma'am. It's just that hope looks good on you."

There wasn't enough light to see her blush, but Callahan knew.

"Get some sleep, Becky," he told her. "It's going to be an early day tomorrow."

Callahan was as good as his word. The wagon train rose an hour earlier amid a number of tired groans, setting off into the damp darkness. Soon they were eating up Nebraska again a little chunk at a time. The sun beat down from overhead, and the day dragged on like any other. They pushed on an extra hour after sundown, then finally circled the wagons, everyone grumbling and exhausted.

"That was a twenty-mile day," Cookie Mayfield said. "We'll be to Oregon in no time at this rate."

"I'll be satisfied for now just to be rid of the wolves," Callahan said.

They bedded down for the night. Some instinct told Callahan to leave his boots on.

Sleep came slowly in spite of Callahan's exhaustion, but finally he drifted off. He dreamed of Tall Elk. Callahan and the Indian fought again, everything moving so slowly in that odd way of dreams. Callahan's palms were sticky on the handle of his tomahawk. He looked down to see his hands red with blood. He tried to drop the tomahawk but couldn't. He tried to fling it away, but his grip was sticking to the tomahawk like glue.

Tall Elk came at him, the Indian suddenly ten feet tall, a knife raised, and—

Callahan sat bolt upright. It took him a moment to remember where he was. What had woken him?

Rifle shots rang across the camp.

Callahan grabbed his Henry rifle as he leapt up and sprinted toward the herd of sheep. He knew instinctively what was happening.

He arrived to find Bart Schultz and two more of his sheepherders puffing mad and holding rifles.

"Them wolves followed us, all right," Schultz said. "They just dragged away another one of my sheep. Something's got to be done."

Ace Franklin arrived with four of his cattlemen in tow.

"Let's get after 'em," Ace said. "We're ready to go."

"Yeah, right!" Schultz agreed.

"Settle down a minute," Callahan said. "You really want to chase after wolves in the dead of night? It's pitch dark, and I guarantee you those wolves see better at night than we do."

"I'm not going to stand around doing nothing while them animals pick off my herd one by one," Schultz said. "The longer we wait, the farther they get away. I say we track these creatures and kill them right now."

Cookie Mayfield and Billy Thorndyke arrived at that moment.

"Billy, go back to camp and tell them to stay in their wagons," Callahan said. "I'm sure they've heard the shots and are worried about what's going on. Pass the word we've got men on the job."

"Sure thing, Mr. Callahan!" Billy ran back toward the circle of wagons.

"Are we getting after them wolves or not?" Schultz demanded.

"I'm with the sheepherder," Ace said. "If they eat all his sheep, you better believe my cattle are next. Time to take action!"

Callahan didn't like it. Taking on wolves in the darkness on their own turf . . . No, it seemed like a bad bet.

On the other hand, wasn't it Callahan's job to protect these people and—by extension—their property? But stumbling around in the dark was dangerous. They were just as likely to shoot each other as kill a wolf, especially if things got hectic and confusing. The cattlemen and the sheepherders all seemed like stout men, but Callahan really didn't know them that well. A man could panic when lead started flying in the dark.

To Callahan, all options seemed equally bad.

He turned his head, the flickering of a campfire in the distance catching his attention.

"Cookie, fetch Pete Johansen," Callahan said. "Tell him we've got a job to do."

CHAPTER 14

The blood trail led them into a sparse wood just short
of the river. The wagon train had been paralleling the
Platte for days, often camping close enough to take advantage, watering the animals and taking enough for
laundry and so on. Callahan took slow, careful steps, his
grip sweaty on the Henry. He was nervous and didn't
mind admitting it, at least to himself.

This is a bad idea.

Pete Johansen crept along ten feet to his left, a long-
barreled twelve-gauge in a tight grip. They'd made a
point to spread out, creeping into the tree line in pairs.
Shultz and his sheepherders were off somewhere to
the right, Ace and his cattlemen to the left, Cookie
Mayfield with them.

One cautious step at a time, ears open, moonlight
glinting off foliage, the *crunch-crackle* of dried leaves
under their boots. There was no wind, so it was eerily
quiet, nothing but the sound of Callahan's own heartbeat in his ears. Sweat on his neck and under his arms.

He kept his finger off the rifle's trigger. He didn't
want to risk being abruptly startled, jerking the trigger,

and accidently shooting Johansen or one of the other hunters elsewhere in the darkness. Callahan had hunted before—deer, rabbits, squirrels. Game.

This was his first time hunting a predator.

Unless one counted other human beings. Callahan had tracked men.

Pete Johansen waved a hand, catching his attention. He knelt, pointing at the ground, and then gestured that Callahan should come look. Wolf tracks in the mud, blood, drag marks.

Johansen rose and set off in the direction of the blood trail, Callahan following.

Progress had been excruciatingly slow, but everyone agreed blundering into a pack of hungry wolves was a bad idea. They were an hour into their hunt, more than enough time for the wolves to escape if they dragged the dead sheep far away, but Johnsen had predicted they'd stop before that to feed.

Callahan was beginning to wonder. If they didn't come across the wolves soon, he'd have to call off—

Johansen raised a hand to call a halt just as Callahan heard the sounds, low growls and snarls, the wet ripping sound of predators rending flesh. They peered through the underbrush and saw them, four big wolves digging into a bloody sheep, wool matted with blood, innards spilling out. The snouts and paws of the wolves glistening wet with blood.

Johansen motioned for Callahan to lift his rifle and wait. He understood the man wanted them to fire at once, taking out at least two of the animals. If they were quick about it, they might take out the other two. Callahan wished Billy and Cookie were here so they could hit all four at once. Johansen had suggested earlier if they took out the leader of the pack, the others might scatter, but if they could get them all, that would be even better.

Johansen pointed his shotgun at the wolf closest to him, and Callahan aimed the Henry at one of the others, drew a beath, and began to let it out slowly. Pete Johansen bobbed his head once, twice . . .

A third time, and both men fired. Johansen's twelve-gauge belched fire, buckshot scorching the side of a big gray wolf. The animal was knocked over, rolled once, and never moved again. Callahan's shot caught his wolf in the temple, the head snapping around, blood arcing through the air. The other two animals howled and yelped in panic.

Callahan took a bead on the next wolf, quickly levering a fresh shell into the Henry's—

A great weight slammed into Callahan from the side, a snarling growl in his ear. He staggered and managed to retain his footing, but the Henry rifle went flying. Callahan went for his Peacemaker, but the big wolf was on him again, jumping up, huge jaws snapping shut an inch from his nose. The Peacemaker had just cleared his holster when the wolf's claws dug into his hand. He felt blood flow hot down to his fingertips.

Callahan winced and dropped the six-shooter. The weight of the massive animal bowled him over. Callahan sprawled on his back as the wolf leapt atop him. He pulled the tomahawk from his belt. The wolf's jaws gaped, going for his throat.

He got the tomahawk up just in time. The wolf

snapped on the handle, and Callahan pushed away with both hands.

Callahan got his boot under the wolf's belly and kicked with everything he had. He launched the animal off him, and it went flying back, snarling and twisting through the air. Callahan scrambled to his feet and backed up against a thick tree trunk. The wolf gathered itself and ran at him, leaping.

Then two things happened within a split second of each other.

First, the crack of a rifle shot. Bark splinters flew up from the tree trunk an inch from Callahan's face.

Second, another thunderous blast from Johansen's twelve-gauge shook the world. The wolf contorted in midair and landed dead at Callahan's feet. He looked down at it, eyes wide.

Callahan had always heard a man's life flashed before his eyes when he was about to meet his end. Nothing like that had happened. But now his gut churned, heart beating like a rabbit's, cold sweat over every inch of his body. He leaned against the tree, panting. He'd never been much of a churchgoer, but he sent a brief prayer of thanks toward the sky.

Another smattering of rifle shots drew his attention. The cattlemen and the sheepherders had arrived and were chasing after the remaining wolf. Suddenly, Billy Thorndyke was at his side.

"You okay, boss?" Billy asked.

"Yeah, but it was a close thing," Callahan said. "I'm just glad Mr. Johansen is handy with that scattergun."

Johansen approached, the shotgun under one arm.

"I'm glad you kicked him away. I hesitated when he was on your chest. Didn't want to hit you by mistake."

After chasing the wolf, the cattlemen and the sheep-herders gathered around. Someone had evidently had the foresight to bring a bottle of whiskey, and it was making the rounds. Callahan declined a swig of the hooch. Something was bothering him, but he couldn't quite put his finger on it.

Ace Franklin took a big swallow of the whiskey before passing it to Schultz. "Don't let anyone ever say cattlemen and sheepherders can't work together."

"Dang right!" Shultz took the bottle and drank deeply.

Cookie Mayfield arrived with his rifle resting on his shoulder. "Looks like I missed all the fun."

"Lucky you," Callahan said. "Get back to the wagons and pass the word to anyone awake. Tell them to sleep easy. Our wolf problem is over."

Cookie headed back, taking Billy with him.

"We're going to skin these wolves for the pelts," Ace told Callahan. "You want one for a souvenir?"

Callahan shook his head. "No thanks." He didn't feel any particular pride nor joy at killing the animals. They were just a problem that needed to be dealt with. Callahan was glad it was over.

"I'll see you men back at camp. We head out bright and early like usual." Callahan hiked back toward the wagons.

Once Callahan was back in the circle, Cookie Mayfield put some ointment on his scratched hand and wrapped it in a bandage. "Them wounds ain't deep. You'll live."

Callahan sprawled back and laid his head on his

saddle. He was dead tired, but sleep wouldn't come. Finally, he drifted off into restless slumber. He awoke before dawn to the smell of fresh coffee. Cookie handed him a cup.

Callahan sipped. It was good. "Cookie, take the wagon train out this morning, will you? I'll catch up."

Cookie frowned. "Where you going?"

"Just need to double-check something."

As Callahan saddled his horse, Anna Masters showed up, pencil in one hand, notebook in the other. "I understand we had some excitement last night, Mr. Callahan."

Callahan recalled the wolf's bloody teeth, jaws snapping shut an inch from his nose. "A little too much."

"Well, not too much for my readers," she said. "The first dispatch that all was well with the wagon train was fine, but that's going to get real boring, real fast."

The night the wagon train had camped near Kearney, Anna Masters had borrowed a horse to ride into town and make her report. Cookie Mayfield had volunteered to escort her to the telegraph office and back again. Evidently, she planned her next report to be a little more thrilling than her last.

"No offense to your readers, ma'am, but I'm hoping the rest of this trip is dull as dishwater," Callahan told her.

"Don't misunderstand," she said. "I don't want any harm to come to anyone here. But if something newsworthy happens, I don't intend to let it go to waste."

She scribbled in her notebook as Callahan related the details of the previous night's wolf hunt.

Callahan mounted his horse. "Best get to your wagon, Miss Masters. They'll be lining up soon."

He turned the horse and left at a trot.

"Where you off to, Tomahawk?" the newspaper-woman called after him.

"Nowhere that would interest your readers," he called back over his shoulder.

Callahan entered the familiar patch of woods just as the sun was coming up. By the light of day, the blood trail was even easier to follow than it had been the night before, and he moved more rapidly now. He reached the spot where the wolf had tried to kill him and dismounted. He stepped carefully, looking at the tracks in the ground, trying to mentally re-create last night's events—finding the wolves as they fed on the sheep, then the one that had attacked him, and all of the gunplay.

It took him a moment to find the tree he was looking for, but a spent shell casing that was glinting in the morning light caught his attention. It was from his Henry, the shot that had taken down one of the wolves. He'd tangled with the big one and had backed up against this tree.

Callahan closed his eyes, trying to recall the order of things. First Johansen shot and then Callahan. He levered in another shell but never had the chance to fire before the huge wolf barreled into him.

Then the shot had nearly taken his head off, kicking up tree bark close to his face. It was exactly what Callahan had been worried about, that a bunch of men stumbling about in the night might shoot each other. Had it been Pete Johansen who'd taken the shot, trying to hit the wolf?

No. Callahan was pretty sure he remembered hearing

a rifle shot, and Johansen had carried a twelve-gauge. Anyway, Johansen had specifically mentioned waiting for a clear shot, so he wouldn't hit Callahan by mistake.

He ran his hand over the rough bark and found the spot. He drew his knife and used it to pry out the slug. One of the cattlemen or sheepherders maybe. He strained his memory again. It had all happened so fast. The cattlemen and sheepherders came a few seconds later, and the shooting had been up ahead by the sheep carcass.

Callahan dug the chunk lead out of the tree, squinted at it between his thumb and forefinger. It had been mashed up pretty good, probably a .44-40, but definitely not a buckshot pellet. The shot had definitely not come from Pete Johansen.

Somebody was either a really lousy shot or . . .

Callahan tried not to think what he was thinking, but it was no use. He had no proof, nothing definite, but he felt sure his conclusion was right.

Somebody had tried to kill him.

CHAPTER 15

He'd been told to ride out to the middle of nowhere. And he didn't like it.

Not because Roy Benson was concerned for his own safety. It was the inconvenience that irked him. He'd been up late with a pretty little saloon gal the night before, all giggles and blue eyes, and, of course, there'd been plenty of whiskey. He hunched in the saddle, hungover, the late morning sun beating down on him, head pounding, sweat slicking every part of him.

But the note had mentioned a lucrative opportunity, and painted ladies and whiskey cost money.

Benson spotted the train in the distance, the locomotive, tender, and single car perched on a low rise. No station in sight. Benson figured there was only one reason the railroad man wanted to meet so far away from civilization.

And that was because he didn't want to be seen with a man like Roy Benson.

Fine. Benson didn't take offense. He knew what he was.

When he got closer, Benson spotted the man with the scattergun at the back of the train car. He had a lean and dangerous look about him, suit jacket thrown over the balcony railing, shirtsleeves rolled up, bowler hat back on his head. One thumb hooked into his suspenders, the short double-barreled shotgun on his other shoulder.

Benson reined in his horse and looked up at him.

The man with the scattergun nodded at the door. "He's in there."

"Right." Benson dismounted, tied his horse to the back of the train, then climbed up the ladder. "Do I knock?"

"We saw you coming. Just go in."

"Right."

Benson went in and shut the door behind him.

The interior wasn't like any train car he'd ever been in before. Plush chairs and a couch. Lots of red velvet and gold, thick drapes, ornate light fixtures, a sideboard with bottles of booze and expensive crystal glassware. Across the space was a large cherrywood desk.

A door opened behind the desk, and a man came through, shrugging into a suit jacket, presumably the railroad man Arbuckle.

"You're Benson?" he asked.

Benson nodded. "That's right."

"Sit if you like."

Benson took one of the two plush chairs on his side of the desk. He took off his hat and set it on the other. His eyes slid to the sideboard. Maybe the railroad man would offer him a drink.

No such luck. Arbuckle sat on the other side of the

desk, tugging at his shirt cuffs, then running his hands through his hair. Was he nervous or just naturally fidgety? Benson wondered. No surprise if the man was nervous. Benson had done things that would make anyone nervous. That's why he was here, after all. Sometimes straight-arrow citizens needed a man as crooked as Benson to do some dirty work. As long as the pay was right, Benson was happy to oblige.

"I appreciate your meeting me in this remote location," Arbuckle began. "It goes without saying that I'd prefer we not be seen together. I don't know you, and you don't know me. I'm sure you understand."

"I take no offense," Benson said. "I realize those with delicate sensibilities might find my line of work . . . distasteful."

Since his line of work was thieving and murdering, *distasteful* was an understatement.

"If you'd like to describe your needs, we might come to some agreement as to compensation," Benson suggested.

Benson listened patiently as Arbuckle described the situation with the wagon train. As Arbuckle spoke, Benson realized he'd read about the wager in the paper. The race between the wagon train and the railroad had captured his attention, and he felt a vague sense of disappointment that the railroad intended to cheat.

The feeling lasted only a moment. Of course, the railroad would cheat. The big man always stuck it to the little man. It was just the way of the world.

Which was why a long time ago, Benson had made

the decision not to play by the world's rules anymore. He figured someday that decision would catch up to him.

So far, so good.

"I think you understand my needs," Arbuckle said. "You're welcome to employ whatever methods you think will be most effective, but it must look like an *accident*. If it's obvious you're doing whatever you're doing to specifically delay the wagon train, it will undermine the whole enterprise."

"Delay the wagon train, but make it look like something else," Benson said. "Got it."

"Good. Other than that, I suppose it would be nice if you could keep unnecessary violence to a minimum." Arbuckle shrugged. "But that's at your discretion. What are your expectations as far as compensation?"

Benson considered a good number and then doubled it.

Arbuckle agreed immediately.

Benson cursed inwardly. *Should have asked for more.* "I might need to hire some help."

"You'll be reimbursed," Arbuckle assured him. "But any assistants you hire must not know the true nature of the undertaking."

"Assistants." A funny way to say "thugs." He nodded. "I'll keep it to myself."

Arbuckle stood. "If there are no other questions . . ."

Benson stood, too. He knew when he was being dismissed. "Leave it to me, Mr. Arbuckle."

He put on his hat, offered Arbuckle a curt nod, then left.

As he rode back to town, he considered how he'd go

about it. Arbuckle said it would be nice to keep violence to a minimum.

A suggestion. Not an order.

Not that Roy Benson was very good at taking orders.

Mycroft Jones emerged from the back room. "You've concluded your business with the . . . ah . . ." Jones groped for the right word.

"Hired criminal," Arbuckle said. "But I don't suppose that would sound very nice in your report back to the brothers."

"Perhaps some euphemism."

"Private contractor," Arbuckle suggested.

"Oh, I like that," Jones said. "Very businesslike."

"What do you have for me?"

"We've word that the bridge crew has arrived at the site you picked," Jones said. "They'll begin construction shortly."

"What's the rate of track being laid from Hansen's Bend?"

Jones consulted the piece of paper in his hand. "Two miles a day."

Arbuckle made a little disgusted noise in his throat, walked to the sideboard, and poured himself a tumbler of expensive brandy. He brought the glass to his lips but paused. "Any word from the Salem crew?"

"No, sir."

Arbuckle downed the brandy and stood thinking a moment.

Then he said, "Tell the conductor to get us moving.

I want to get to the next town at top speed. Then you're going to the telegraph office."

Jones sat at the desk and picked up a pencil.

"Tell the foreman of the Hansen's Bend crew to pick up the pace or I'll fire him and get somebody who can do the job," Arbuckle said. "Tell the foreman of the Salem crew that anyone not working can ship out. I don't care who's sick. Word it any way you like as long as it's clear I'm unhappy and not fooling around."

Jones stood. "I'll let the conductor know it's time."

"Tell him to fly," Arbuckle said. "From now on, nobody does anything slowly."

Anna Masters rode toward the two-bit town of Vernon's Dell, Cookie Mayfield trotting along at her side. It wasn't much of a place. Six buildings more or less where a road and the railroad tracks came within a stone's throw of each other. Somebody had thought it an appropriate location for a telegraph office.

She was grateful to the people of the wagon train for accommodating her. Anna had a vague feeling Tomahawk Callahan didn't approve of her as a newspaper reporter, like maybe she was some kind of snoop, telling every little bit of the wagon train's business to her readers back home. But more than that, Callahan was concerned about the safety of everyone in the wagon train—even a nosy reporter—so he was hesitant to let her ride off alone. Cookie Mayfield had cheerfully volunteered himself as escort.

They dismounted in front of the telegraph office,

which doubled as the post office and also sold train tickets.

"If you don't mind, ma'am, I'll leave you to it while I visit the mercantile," Cookie told her. "Might pick up a few necessities. Some more coffee, anyway, if they have it."

"Okay," she said. "See you after."

The little office was thick with gray smoke. The balding man with the clerk's visor sat behind the counter, leaning back in his chair, puffing a pipe so hard he might have been doing his impersonation of a locomotive. Fortunately, there was a large, open window behind him or the room would have been uninhabitable. He watched her over the half-glasses perched at the end of his nose.

"Help you, ma'am?"

"I'd like to send a telegram."

"Just in time," he said. "I was about to pack up for the day."

Anna wrote out the telegram, being careful with each and every word. Even though the newspaper was footing the bill, she was still obliged to send the basic facts of the story only. Telegrams were expensive, and she planned to send them whenever she could all the way to Oregon.

"Wolf attack. Sheep taken. Settlers afraid. Successful wolf hunt led by Tomahawk Callahan." She added some minor details about location and weather. She read over what she'd written. Good enough. A writer on the other end would embellish everything and get it into readable shape for the article. Naturally, she was keeping a more detailed account of her journey, scribbling in a journal each night by firelight. The entries would be serialized into a travelogue upon her return to Baltimore.

The clerk read the telegram back to her. "That's what you want?"

"Yes, please."

He sent the telegram, and she paid him.

Anna left the small office and walked quickly down to the mercantile. It would be dark soon. She wanted to find Cookie and head back, but the woman in the mercantile said she'd seen nobody matching Cookie's description. Anna frowned and walked back to the telegraph office.

Just before entering, she almost ran into Cookie as he came out.

"I was looking for you," she said.

Cookie laughed. "I was looking for you, too. Guess we missed each other somehow."

Anna didn't see how that was possible in a place as tiny as Vernon's Dell, but she wasn't interested in quibbling.

"Let's get back," she said. "I don't want to fix my dinner in the dark."

They mounted and turned their horses back the way they'd come.

"Cookie, can I ask you a question?"

"As many as you like, ma'am," Cookie said. "Can't guarantee the answers will be very interesting."

"Have you ever been attacked before by wolves while running a wagon train?"

"Nope. First time for everything, I guess."

"But you've encountered numerous dangers, I take it."

"Oh, yes, that's for sure," Cookie said. "I could tell you stories."

Which was exactly what Anna had been trying to get at. If the remainder of the trek west failed to live up to the excitement of the wolf episode, she might have to pry some of Cookie's stories out of him. Anna Masters had promised her readers thrills, and, by God, she intended to deliver.

CHAPTER 16

"That looks like rain," Callahan said. "A lot of it."

Billy Thorndyke squinted in the direction Callahan was looking. "And upriver, too."

"Right. Fetch Cookie, will you?"

Billy headed back down the column of wagons in search of the old man and brought him back a few minutes later.

"When do we reach the ford?" Callahan asked.

"Midday, I think," Cookie said.

Just a few hours. Callahan watched the dark patch in the distance and wondered how fast the storm was moving. "If we keep going, is there another place to ford?"

"Sure, but then you got to do it twice," Cookie explained. "You cross the South Platte, then the North."

Callahan slouched in the saddle, considering his options. They'd been more or less paralleling the Platte River as they made their way through Nebraska. They could press on and cross at the ford as planned, but a big downpour upriver could give them trouble. They could keep heading west on this side of the river, but then, as

Cookie mentioned, they'd have to ford twice. They could hold up and wait for the weather to pass, but that would cost time.

"We'll keep going until we reach the ford," Callahan said. "We'll decide when we get there."

When they got close, Callahan rode ahead with Billy and Cookie, reining in their horses at the river's edge.

Callahan blew out a sigh, looking up and down the river. At the ford, the river was only about two hundred yards wide. The Platte was shallow and even shallower at the area selected for crossing. Downriver, the Platte ran straight for several miles. Upriver about a hundred yards, it made a sharp bend into a copse of trees.

"Show us how deep, Billy," Callahan said.

Billy Thorndyke clicked his tongue, and his horse nudged out into the water.

Callahan looked at the sky. Still dark in the distance, but blue skies overhead.

Billy returned and said, "Thigh deep in the middle. Should be easy going for the wagons."

Callahan glanced back upriver. The storm was miles away. He still couldn't quite tell how fast it was moving. "Cookie?"

"I say we start 'em across," he said. "If it gets bad, we can pause."

Callahan nodded. "Do it."

It was a slow and methodical process. They'd wait for a wagon to reach the middle of the river before sending the next one. One of Callahan's men rode alongside each wagon—Billy Thorndyke, his little brother Ike, Clancy Davenport, and the kid from Arkansas everyone just called Little Rock.

"Can we do this any faster?" Callahan asked.

"Slower is safer," Cookie said. "Water ain't deep, but you can't see what's under there."

The sky overhead had begun to darken.

They'd gotten forty-two wagons across when the first fat raindrops started pelting them. Five minutes later it came down so heavy, they could barely see the other side of the river.

"The water's rising," Callahan said. "Should we hold?"

Cookie looked worried. "I don't know. There's only a few left."

Callahan thought about it for only a moment. "Keep going!" He had to shout above the racket of the storm.

The wind had picked up, the rain coming in almost sideways, stinging and cold. It had grown so dark, nobody could have guessed it was the middle of the day. Lightning crackled overhead, jagged and bright and sudden. Thunder shook the world.

Callahan pulled alongside the next wagon to go.

Becky Griffith held the reins of the mule team in a white-knuckled grip. Her hair was matted flat and soaked. She blinked water from her eyes.

"You want me to take it across?" Callahan shouted to be heard over the storm.

Becky shook her head. "I can pull my weight like anyone else," she shouted back.

Callahan didn't like it, but there were still other wagons to see to. "Take her over, Billy!"

Billy and Becky started across. Callahan watched, his gut sick with nerves.

Matt Grainger pulled his wagon up next to the river's edge.

"Hold up," Callahan said. "I'll send you across in a minute."

A crack of thunder right over them almost gave Callahan a heart attack.

Whose blasted idea was this, anyway?

Becky's wagon had made it to the middle. Callahan signaled Grainger to take his wagon into the river. Grainger flicked the reins, and the Conestoga began rolling.

Callahan thought he heard somebody shouting. It was too hard to hear over the downpour. He looked and saw Billy Thorndyke gesturing like mad, waving for his attention. The water had risen to the bed of the wagon, high enough to set it afloat. The wagon drifted sideways with the current.

Callahan spat a curse. "Grainger, hold up!"

Grainger's mules had just put their forelegs into the water.

"Back that thing up!" Callahan barked.

"Back up?" Grainger was incredulous. "You know how hard it is to get these dumb animals to go backwards?"

"Just do it!"

Callahan spurred his horse into the river. The water was rising fast.

He reached Becky's wagon and motioned to her. "Get out of there, you and Lizzy both. Get on my horse. Billy can take Lizzy!"

Becky shook her head. "Help me get it across!"

"You'll be swept away," Callahan shouted. "Let's go!"

Becky looked back into the wagon, then at Callahan again. "I can't just leave it."

Callahan understood immediately. Her sewing machine. Her life savings. A future for her and the little girl.

"Give me Lizzy at least," Callahan shouted. "I'll take her to the far bank and come back."

"Lizzy!" Becky shouted back into the wagon.

The girl came to the front, eyes wide with terror. The storm raged, thunder booming.

Callahan nudged his horse as close to the wagon as he could. It was difficult. The wagon drifted. He reached out a hand. "Pass her over."

Suddenly, Becky's eyes shot wide. She pointed behind him. "Luke!"

Callahan glanced back over his shoulder. A surge of water came around the bend from upriver. Not high, but fast. It slammed into the wagon and sent the back end spinning around. Lizzy screamed.

"Billy, the mules!" Callahan shouted. If the animals got pulled along with the wagon, they'd drown.

Billy leapt from his horse onto the mule team, reaching to unhitch them. Callahan didn't wait to see if he succeeded. He jumped from his own horse to the wagon, clinging to the side. The back end of the Conestoga was still spinning around. One of the back wheels must have caught on something under the water. The wagon tipped violently—

—The sound of wood cracking—

—Lizzy screamed as she was tossed off the wagon and into the water.

"Lizzy!" Becky shouted.

Callahan dove into the water after her.

He went under immediately, coming back up down-river, coughing and sputtering as the swift current carried him after Lizzy.

"Swim for the shore!" he shouted.

She must have heard him, for she angled toward the riverbank. The current was strong, and Callahan doubted she'd last long. He swam toward her, taking long strokes and kicking for all he was worth. Slowly, he gained.

Callahan saw her go under and felt a stab of panic. She came up again almost immediately, but she was turned around and swimming in the wrong direction.

"Swim toward me!" Callahan shouted. "Lizzy, over here!"

She swam toward him but made little headway against the current.

But it was enough to allow Callahan to catch up to her. He reached out, latched onto her thin wrist, and pulled her toward him. She threw her arms around his neck, sobbing against his chest. Callahan found he could stand, the water up to his chest. The fierce current nearly took him away several times, and he and the child would both go under until he could fight his way to the surface again, gasping for air. Doggedly, he put one boot in front of the other, planting his foot solidly before taking his next step.

The rain was already letting up, the water below his knees. And then he was out of the water, and he trudged up the riverbank, the girl clinging to him. Becky ran toward them along the edge of the river, screaming Lizzy's name.

She arrived, and the girl flung herself into her mother's arms, both of them crying like they might never stop. Becky put an arm around Callahan's neck and pulled him close for a kiss on the cheek.

"Thank you, Luke. Oh, God, thank you."

"Any time." He sank down and sat in the mud, utterly exhausted, and let the rain fall on his head. He'd lost his hat somewhere. Probably a mile downriver by now.

When Callahan looked up again, Cookie was there, on his horse. He led Callahan's horse by the reins.

"Anyone hurt?" Callahan asked.

"No, thank goodness," Cookie reported. "The rest of the wagons are still hunkered down on the other side, but the rain's stopping. If the water goes down enough, we might still be able to get them all across before we run out of daylight."

Callahan watched Becky and Lizzy walk back toward the wagons. "I almost killed that little girl, Cookie."

The old man frowned. "What sort of bunk are you talking, boy?"

"We could have waited," Callahan said. "I saw that storm coming, and we could have waited, but I didn't want to lose time. If that girl had drowned, it would have been on me."

"I thought we could make it, too," Cookie reminded him. "You ain't in this alone."

Callahan sat a moment, letting the rain hit him. "You seen my hat?"

"Nope."

Callahan got back on his horse, and they rode together back to the wagons. In less than an hour the water had lowered enough to bring the river down so they could cross the remainder of the wagons safely. Callahan put Cookie in charge and fetched dry clothes from his luggage.

He was surprised to see that Becky's wagon hadn't been washed down the Platte but sat at an awkward angle in the middle of the river. He tasked Billy and Ike and Clancy with taking the mules back out and dragging the thing back to dry land.

"Thank God," Becky said, standing on the riverbank, watching the men bring the wagon in. "Everything I've worked for."

Callahan stood next to her and watched, too. It looked like one of the wheels was badly damaged, and bringing it out of the water was a cumbersome endeavor. Finally, they had the wagon on land, and Becky took Lizzy to inspect the interior to make sure everything was still there.

Billy Thorndyke and Clancy Davenport approached Callahan, stood there dripping, each looking at the other as if neither wanted to be the one to talk first.

Callahan sighed. It had been a long day, and his patience had worn thin. "Something on your mind, boys?"

Clancy nudged Billy.

"Uh . . . Clancy's dad and uncles are wainwrights," Billy said. "Wheelwrights, too. Guess it's the family business, you might say."

"That's interesting," said Callahan, who didn't think it was interesting at all. "But unless they happen to live around here, I'm not sure they'll be much help fixing this wagon."

"Yes, sir. I mean, no, sir, that's not what I'm getting

at," Billy said. "Just that Clancy knows the business and . . ." Billy nodded at Clancy. "Go on. Tell him."

"There was a dead log at the bottom of the river," Clancy said. "The wheel was swept into it. Cracked a bunch of spokes all to pieces. Gonna have to replace that wheel."

Some of the settlers had the foresight to bring spare wheels, but Callahan doubted such a thing was in Becky's budget. Fortunately, the outfitters wagon had spare wheels and spokes and other such items. "Take one of ours. Get that wagon fixed." He began to turn away.

"Sure thing, Mr. Callahan," Clancy said. "But it's just . . . well, there's another thing."

Callahan held on to his last scrap of patience with a firm grip. "Out with it, Clancy."

"Might be easier to show you."

"Show me then."

Clancy led Callahan and Billy to Becky's wagon, where it was perched at an awkward angle on the edge of the river. The rear end on the right side was propped up under the axle with a thick log, the same one that had hung up the wheel in the first place, according to Clancy. The busted wheel leaned against the wagon. Callahan could clearly see the jagged edges in the rough wood where five of the spokes had been broken. Without enough support, the wheel had cracked.

Clancy grabbed one side of the wheel. "Help me turn it around, Billy."

Together, the two men flipped the wheel over.

Clancy knelt and pointed to various spots along the ruined spokes. "From the outside, the breaks look rough."

Then he pointed out two even lines across two of the unbroken spokes. "But look at the cuts from this side. Straight and smooth."

Callahan frowned. "Cuts?"

"From a handsaw, I reckon," Clancy said. "Them spokes was cut ninety percent of the way. Wouldn't take nothing at all for them to bump up against something and crack clean through."

"Like if a swift current swept it into a log underwater," Callahan said.

"That would do it," Clancy said.

"Let me get this straight, and think carefully before answering," Callahan told the boy. "You're saying this was done on purpose."

Clancy's eyes went nervously to Billy before coming back to Callahan. "Well . . . I mean . . . I guess I don't see how anyone cuts through a wagon wheel spoke with a handsaw by accident."

Callahan heard Becky rummaging around inside the wagon. He lowered his voice and said, "Nobody hears about this. You two and me, that's all who need to know for now. I suppose I should tell Cookie, too, but that's it. We don't need these people afraid. You understand?"

Billy and Clancy both nodded.

"But we can't just twiddle thumbs and do nothing, either," Callahan said. "Check all the rest of the wagons. All four wheels, every single one of them. If anyone asks, just say you're making sure there was no damage from crossing the river."

"Okay, Mr. Callahan, but . . . well . . . are you sure we should keep this a secret?" Clancy asked. "Maybe we should put the word out. Maybe somebody saw a fella walking around with a handsaw."

"And we might do just that," Callahan said. "But not yet. Whoever did this probably doesn't know we're onto him. That might be an advantage. Maybe he'll make a mistake and reveal himself. If that don't work, then, yeah, we'll sound the alarm."

Both boys nodded agreement.

"Then get checking those wagons."

Billy and Clancy went away to do as they were told.

Callahan stuck his head inside the wagon. "How we doing in here?"

Becky looked up, a relieved expression on her face. "Nothing broken."

Lizzy clutched a rag doll to her chest. "And Miss Elizabeth is okay, too!"

"Glad to hear it," Callahan said. "Becky, we're gonna get that wheel fixed one way or another. Just sit tight."

"Thank you, Luke."

An hour later, the boys returned to report when they'd found.

"Three other wagons have had spokes sawed the same way," Clancy said. "But they were at the tail end of the wagon train and never made it into the river during the storm. I think they'll probably be okay as long as we keep to smooth roads. But one big rock or deep rut, and all bets are off."

Callahan cursed. He'd been hoping he was wrong, that Becky had just gotten a bad wheel from someone when she bought the wagon, but clearly, there was somebody in the wagon train up to no good.

"How long to make repairs?"

"A couple of the wagons have spare wheels," Clancy said. "Others don't. I'll have to carve new spokes. It'll take time either way."

"I figure we're not going any farther today," Billy chimed in. "Unless you want to leave those wagons behind and let them catch up after the repairs."

"We stick together," Callahan said. "That's the point of a wagon train."

There was no reason to believe danger lurked out there on the Nebraska prairie, but why risk it? A small group of wagons might be a tempting target for bandits. And anyway, Callahan hadn't predicted wolves, either, yet they'd posed a problem and had to be dealt with. It was the unexpected things that caused the most trouble.

"Putting on a new wheel is faster than making new spokes, I take it," Callahan said.

Clancy nodded. "A lot faster. And folks can still repair the old wheels while we're on the move."

"Then start asking around, see who has extra wheels. The company will reimburse them," Callahan told him. "And remember, we're just making repairs. Nobody says nothing about sabotage."

Callahan lapsed into dark thought as the other two went about their business. The last few days, as they'd slowly made their way across Nebraska, Callahan had convinced himself that almost getting shot during the wolf hunt had simply been an accident. One of the cattlemen or sheepherders had panicked and nearly taken Callahan's head off. Clumsy? Stupid? Yes, but not necessarily murder. But there could be no mistaking the wagon wheels. The sabotage had been intentional. Callahan didn't need to be a master wheelwright to see it. The truth was plain and simple. They had a villain among them, somebody willing to wreck a wagon.

Somebody willing to kill.

CHAPTER 17

All five of them came skulking into the Four Queens Saloon as a single group—shifty eyed, road dusty, guns slung low, snarls on their faces like they'd practiced in a mirror. Shaves and baths would have done them all a lot of good.

The Zeke Hawkins Gang came ready-made for what Roy Benson had in mind, but there were good things and bad things about hiring a gang instead of putting one together himself.

The good thing was that all the men knew each other. They knew each other's moves, could work together immediately without wasting a lot of time on *getting to know you*. It would also save time. Benson knew from experience that putting together a solid gang wasn't something that happened overnight. It took a keen eye, the ability to size a man up, to separate a greenhorn from a salty veteran. The Hawkins gang already had a reputation, a lot of it bad but in just the right way. These men would fit the bill.

However, the bad thing was . . . *that all these men*

knew each other. In other words, there was no special reason they'd be loyal to Benson if something went sideways. Handpicking his own crew would at least suggest some small bit of loyalty, gratitude for a paycheck if nothing else. If the job was a bust, Benson could quickly find himself in a five-against-one situation.

And the job *would* go bust because that was part of the plan.

But Roy Benson had a plan for that, too. There was no problem a good plan and a little foresight couldn't fix.

The five men sauntered up to the table, daring everyone in the place to look at them cockeyed. There were two kinds of tough men in the world. Those who always had to prove it and those who didn't care what others thought.

Roy Benson was the second kind, and he looked down on the first sort, but these men were handy, so he'd make use of them. He'd told them he'd be at the farthest corner table, so they stood there waiting for Benson to talk.

"So which one is the boss?" Benson asked.

"That's me," said the short one.

Benson was surprised. He'd expected the big one with the barrel chest to speak up, not the little, wiry fellow. He took some coins out of his pocket and slid them across the table. "Tell your boys to have a drink. I don't want a big group of us to draw eyes."

The others looked at the boss.

"Go on then."

They took the coins and went to the bar.

"You're Hawkins then."

"That's right."

Benson could see it now, how the man might be the gang's leader. There was something tight about him, an intensity. He stood with thumbs hooked into his gun belt, legs apart a little, like he was ready to withstand any strong wind that might blow. Vest buttoned with brass. Hat at a low angle over his eyes. A foot-and-a-half of Arkansas toothpick hung from Hawkins's belt on the opposite side of his six-gun.

"Have a seat, and I'll tell you what you're gonna do," Benson said.

Hawkins sat. "You tell me the job, and I'll say if my boys are doing it or not. That's yet to be decided. You've lured me here with promises of a big score. That's fine. But I'll need to hear details before I stick my neck out."

"Fair enough," Benson said. "How about a drink while I fill you in?"

"That's the only civilized way to do it."

Benson motioned for the barkeep to bring a bottle and two glasses. They arrived, and Benson filled the glasses. The two men drank. Benson filled the glasses again.

Then he lowered his voice. "It's a wagon train."

Hawkins sat back in his chair and snorted derision. "Thanks for the free drink, anyways."

"You don't like it?"

"Hell, no, I don't like it," Hawkins said.

"Tell me why not."

"Happy to." Hawkins leaned forward, lowering his voice to match. "How many people in a wagon train? I once saw one with over a hundred wagons! That's a lot of guns. Yeah, they're just settlers, and many will duck and hide, but plenty more will grab their rifles, looking to be heroes or show off for their womenfolk. What are we supposed to do? Ride up and down the wagon train with a sack telling everyone to empty their wallets? No, sir, it's an ill-conceived enterprise. The result is a belly full of lead for me and my boys. I think my time is worth one last drink, and then I'll bid you good day." He reached across the table, snatched the bottle, and refilled his shot glass.

Benson chuckled and shook his head. "Well, Hawkins, if it was that sort of job, nobody in their right mind would disagree with you."

Hawkins raised an eyebrow. "So you think I'm right?"

"If it was that sort of job, yes," Benson said. "But it's not."

"What sort is it?"

"The sort where you get paid and don't get killed," Benson told him.

"That's a nice fairy story," Hawkins said. "No risk at all."

"There's always risk," Benson admitted. "But not some fool's errand like you described."

"Then if we're not robbing settlers, what are we doing?"

Benson grinned. "Robbing settlers."

"You're lucky my good right hand can't hold a glass of whiskey and a six-gun at the same time, mister."

Benson laughed. "Please don't shoot, and I'll explain. For safekeeping, the settlers have put all their money in some kind of chest, a strongbox maybe. It's in the lead wagon under guard. We handle the guards. A lot easier than taking on an entire wagon train. We hit hard, go in fast, take the chest before anyone knows what's happening, and then skedaddle."

Hawkins sipped his whiskey slowly, eyes narrowing. "Why put all the money together? That just makes it easier for us to grab it."

Benson shrugged. "Maybe they were told it would be secure, sort of like a portable bank."

"How much?"

"Between twenty and twenty-five thousand," Benson said.

Going by the expression on the other outlaw's face, he appreciated the number. "How do you know?"

"A reliable source."

Hawkins shook his head. "I don't like that."

"The world teems with disappointment."

"What source? Who?"

"That's not information I can give out. Terms of the deal. He only told me this information on the condition I keep his name out of it," Benson explained.

"But now you've got the information."

"What do you want me to say? Some name that would mean nothing to you?" Benson asked. "Anyway, if I keep my promise to him, then you'll know I'm the kind of man that keeps promises."

Benson had started to concoct a backstory for his fictitious source, but the key to a good lie was to keep it simple. Better to say it was a secret and was going to stay that way. Arbuckle had offered him money to hire men, but then he'd have to explain what he was doing or make up an even more unlikely lie. The best way to dupe a criminal was to tell him he was doing crime.

"Split evenly amongst all of us?" Hawkins asked.

"I thought maybe I should get something more for setting it up." There was no money, of course, but it was more believable if Benson showed a little greed.

Hawkins looked unhappy but not surprised. "How much more?"

"A thousand off the top."

Hawkins shook his head. "Too much. Five hundred."

Now it was Benson's turn to look pained, but he didn't lay it on too thick. "Fine. But there's another five hundred for my informant. That's nonnegotiable."

Hawkins sighed and looked away as if trying to find something elsewhere in the saloon to catch his interest.

"Tell me the rest of the plan," Hawkins said.

Benson took out a map, unfolded it, and spread it between them on the table. He pointed to a spot and made a little circle with his finger. "I figure we can catch up to the wagon train in this area. It's a ways from any town, so even if they send riders for a marshal, the trail will be long cold by the time he arrives. A couple of us should ride ahead and scout the best place for the ambush." He tapped another spot on the map. "There's an abandoned farm here. We can meet there and hold up until the dust settles."

Hawkins frowned. "Meet?"

"We should ride off in a few different directions after we hit the wagon train," Benson said. "Might help throw off any pursuit."

"Not to put a damper on our potential collaboration," Hawkins said. "But if you think I'll let you ride off with the money, you're laboring under the worst sort of delusion. Likewise, I doubt you'll want us to ride away with the money when you might never see it again. You don't strike me as a fool."

"I appreciate that," Benson said. "Do your men trust you?"

"Of course." Hawkins almost seemed offended by the question. "We've all ridden together a long time, through thick and thin."

"Then there's your answer," Benson said. "Take the cashbox with you as we make our escape, but send your best man with me. Then I'll know you'll be at the rendezvous."

"Huh." Hawkins scratched behind his ear, pondering.

Benson let a few quiet moments slip by, then asked, "So what do you think?"

"I'll tell you what I think," Hawkins said. "I think we should finish this bottle of whiskey. And then maybe one more. And then we should go rob a wagon train."

Chinamen, Negroes, Poles, Czechs, Bavarians, even one man who claimed to be from Siam. Kent Arbuckle didn't care. As long as they had strong backs, they could earn the same money as any other man laying track between Hansen's Bend and Salem, Oregon.

He stood atop a low ridge, looking down at the workers laboring in the hot sun. Arbuckle had been obliged to fire the foreman and to hire as many men as he could find, but just over five weeks into the wager and they were back on track, laying three miles of track a day. The new foreman was tough and experienced and had been cracking the whip—metaphorically, anyway. The wagon train, according to his informant, had just passed Cheyenne, Wyoming. The telegram had been lean on details. The wagons plodded along, Tomahawk Callahan leading the way.

Slow, but not slow enough. What on God's green earth is that snake Roy Benson up to? What does he think I'm paying him for?

He'd gotten a message from Benson a week ago saying he had some scheme in the works, but again, details were hard to come by.

He watched Mycroft Jones climb the ridge with the new foreman in tow, a disagreeable man named Kelso. He had a sinister look, a black widow's peak showing lots of forehead, little eyes dark and alert in a lined face. Lean, ropy muscles. An expression like he'd eaten bad cheese and was looking for a place to spit it out.

Mycroft Jones reached Arbuckle, breathing heavily, his jacket thrown over one arm. He dabbed at the sweat on his face with a pocket handkerchief. "I'm born to ride a desk, I'm afraid. This physical exertion is outside my usual skill set."

Arbuckle laughed. "Stick with us, Mycroft, and when you go back east, you can show everyone what a man looks like."

"If I don't have some sort of stroke first."

Arbuckle turned to the foreman. "Keeping the workers on track, Kelso?"

"Yessir, and they'll stay that way if they know what's good for them," Kelso said. "I've held back a chunk of their pay and told them it was some kind of banking problem. If they quit or get fired for slacking, they'll never see that money."

Arbuckle frowned. "Is that legal?"

Kelso shrugged. "Any man who wants to complain is welcome to do so. As long as they don't mind a cracked skull."

"I don't want to know," Arbuckle said. "Use your best judgment. Just don't tell me."

"I'll need to hire a few extra men," Kelso said. "Not railroad workers. Let's call them . . . specialists."

"To do what?"

"I thought you didn't want to know."

"I withdraw the question."

"We've been calling them independent contractors," Jones said.

Arbuckle shot his assistant a scathing look. "You don't want to know either, Mycroft."

"Sorry, sir."

"I'd best get back," Kelso said. "Them sluggards work faster if they know I'm watching."

"I'll leave you to it then," Arbuckle told him.

Kelso touched the brim of his hat and headed down the ridge.

When the foreman was out of earshot, Arbuckle asked Mycroft, "What are the reports from the other crews?" He'd made it clear to Jones that he wanted at least one report a day from each of the work crews. Two would be better. And blast the cost of the telegrams. The company could afford it, and this was no time to cheap out.

"The rail gang out of Salem is back on track," Jones

said. "I think news the foreman here had been replaced lit a fire under them."

"Good. And the bridge."

Jones hesitated. "The foreman there *thinks* the bridge will be done on time."

"Thinks?" Arbuckle didn't like the sound of that. "Send him another reminder. If my train even has to *slow down* when it reaches that bridge, he's out of a job."

"I'll send the message loud and clear, sir."

"Mycroft."

"Sir?"

"Be honest. Can we win this race?"

"Well." Jones cleared his throat. "Comparing the rates of progress . . . ah. The consensus is that we can, that it's possible. But it's far from a certainty."

Arbuckle nodded to himself, letting that digest. The wagon train had experienced a few setbacks, but so had the railroad. It occurred to Arbuckle—not for the first time—that simply getting to Salem first wasn't the only way to win this race. Tomahawk could get there a day or a week or a month ahead of him, and it wouldn't matter if he didn't arrive with enough wagons.

Or if too many settlers fell by the wayside en route.

It was a dark and underhanded way to go about winning.

But Arbuckle had no intention of losing.

Come on, Benson. If you've got something up your sleeve, then get on with it.

* * *

"When's my next chance to send another telegram?" Anna Masters called out to Callahan.

Callahan nudged his horse alongside her Conestoga. He'd been riding up and down the length of the wagon column, checking to make sure everything was okay but also allowing himself to be seen. The settlers needed to know he was on the job.

They all plodded along, eating up Wyoming a mile at a time. They set a good pace, but it still seemed excruciatingly slow to Callahan. The grassland stretched endless and flat and unchanging. Callahan had caught himself dozing in the saddle more than once.

"Didn't you just send in one of your reports back in Cheyenne?" he asked her.

She gave him a withering look as if he should know better. "I need to send in a report as often as possible. Readers want to know what Tomahawk Callahan is up to."

"Sorry I can't arrange another exciting wolf attack or river flood for you." But he smiled when he said it.

Anna Masters had proved surprisingly resilient. Back in Kansas City, Callahan had taken one look at her and her soft hands and well-coiffed hair and Back-East clothing and wondered if she'd last a day on the trail. But she hadn't complained after that first day, not once, at least not very seriously. She'd been a trooper, and Callahan respected her.

Hell, he even liked her. She had a sly sense of humor, and, well, she wasn't exactly hard to look at.

"Fort Fetterman might be your best bet," Callahan

told her. "But I'm not sure what you'll have to report. Wyoming makes Nebraska look downright thrilling."

Masters laughed. "Don't you worry. A good reporter can always find something to write about. I've started interviewing all the people in the wagon train. Did you know the Andersons had a baby? Delivered it right in the back of the wagon. Didn't even stop."

"I heard," Callahan said. "Ten fingers and ten toes."

"What about you, Tomahawk?"

"I'm boring."

"Oh? You married? Strapping, handsome man like you probably has the ladies swarming like flies." She grinned.

Callahan returned the grin. "You asking for your readers or for yourself?"

She threw her head back and laughed, a deep, throaty, genuine sound. "I'm married to my job. Still, if you have the time to buy a lady a drink . . ." She winked.

"If you see a saloon around here, you just shout."

He was smiling as he spurred his horse back up the column.

A little banter's harmless. Anything to relieve the boredom.

Although now that he thought about it, he could use a drink.

The rest of the day passed without incident. They circled the wagons when the sun got low on the horizon. The settlers went about their evening routine.

Callahan sat across the campfire from Cookie Mayfield, spooning beans into his mouth from a tin plate.

Billy, Clancy, and Little Rock were making the rounds, keeping an eye on things, and would eat later.

"Callahan? Anyone here?" A woman's voice.

"Other side of the wagon," Callahan called.

Anna Masters poked her head around the side of the chuckwagon. "That you, Tomahawk?"

Callahan and Cookie stood immediately. "Over here, ma'am."

"Oh, knock off the *ma'am* stuff," she said. "Relax. We've come too far and have too many miles left to act all stiff and formal. Anyway, Tomahawk, if you can't buy me a drink"—she lifted a full bottle of whiskey—"then I'll buy you one."

Cookie raised an eyebrow. "The lady comes prepared."

"Don't give me too much credit," Masters told him. "If I was truly prepared, I'd have remembered to bring glasses, too. Allow me to get us started."

She pulled the cork, took a big swig, then passed the bottle. Cookie and Callahan accepted the bottle eagerly, each taking a large gulp. It had been a while since Callahan had been able to get a drink of good whiskey, and he was grateful. He felt his saddle aches begin to fade.

They sat around the campfire, swapping jokes and stories, slowly making the bottle disappear.

"Ma'am, you hold your liquor well for a woman," Cookie said.

Masters raised an eyebrow. "For a woman?"

"Oh . . . uh . . . well . . ." Cookie stammered. "That didn't quite come out as the compliment I hoped it would be."

She laughed. "Don't worry. Newspapermen are a hard bunch. Competitive. They don't readily accept a woman in their midst. When the whiskey came out, I was obliged to keep up. I earned their respect in a number of ways. And frankly, I *like* whiskey. I wasn't about to make a journey like this without stashing away a few bottles."

They drank and joked for another hour. Callahan told a funny story, and Masters started laughing so hard, she had to put a hand on Callahan's shoulder to steady herself.

"Luke?"

Callahan looked up at the sound of the voice.

Becky had come around the corner of the chuck-wagon, a bundle of something in her hands wrapped in a red-and-white checkered cloth napkin. Her expression went from warm and open to cold and hard in a heartbeat.

Anna Masters let her hand drop from Callahan's shoulder.

"Usually, you stop by my wagon, so I came looking for you." Becky offered the napkin-wrapped bundle to Cookie. "I been meaning to bring some biscuits to say thanks for that corn bread."

Cookie took the bundle. "Obliged, ma'am. They smell fine."

"I can see you're busy," Becky said. "I won't disturb you any longer."

She turned to go, her back stiff as she strode away.

Callahan stood. "Becky . . ."

"Good night, Mr. Callahan." And a moment later, she'd vanished back into the night.

"I get this feeling I somehow caused that awkward moment." Anna Masters shoved the cork back into the whiskey bottle and stood. "It's late, gentlemen. I'm turning in. Thanks for the company."

The two men wished her a good night.

When she'd gone, Cookie grinned at Callahan. "You're one smooth operator, Tomahawk."

"Oh, shut up, Cookie."

CHAPTER 18

Wyoming did its level best to go on forever.

After the unwanted excitement of the wolf attacks and the Platte River flood, the days traversing the grasslands were mercifully boring. Near Fort Fetterman, Anna Masters broke off from the wagon train, escorted by Cookie Mayfield, and rode to the fort to send her latest report to her newspaper back in Baltimore.

A few days later, Cookie nudged his horse alongside Callahan's. "That new hat working out?"

The day after Callahan had lost his hat in the river, a helpful settler—who'd evidently purchased a new hat to celebrate his trip west—had offered Callahan his old one. It was a drab, droopy gray thing with sweat stains around the band.

Callahan shrugged. "It keeps the sun off."

"I've been thinking about our route," Cookie said.

"Do tell."

"We should angle north," Cookie suggested.

Callahan frowned. "Off the established trail?"

"We can pick it up again after we cross into Idaho," Cookie assured him. "Might lose half a day, but the last couple times through, we had storms come down out of the mountains. They always seem to sweep south."

"I don't like storms," Callahan said. "I don't like losing half a day, either."

Cookie shrugged. "You're the boss."

Callahan considered. "Rocky terrain in those foothills to the north."

Cookie waved the notion away. "Oh, I know a trail through. Don't lose no sleep over that."

"I asked you along for your experience," Callahan said. "I guess I'd be pretty stupid not to accept your advice."

"And are you taking my advice?"

"Yes."

Cookie grinned. "Then you ain't stupid."

"Thanks. I was beginning to wonder."

"For the record, you're doing a good job."

"You think?"

Cookie nodded. "The settlers respect you. They feel safe that you're leading them."

It surprised Callahan how much that meant to him. Cookie Mayfield had been his uncle's right-hand man. High praise, indeed. "I appreciate that, Cookie. Means a lot."

"It didn't hurt that you jumped in the river to save that little girl," Cookie told him. "Everyone loves a hero."

Callahan had no intention of being a hero. He'd jumped into the river after Lizzy without thinking. "Maybe Becky will fall in a river, and I can save her."

"She still giving you the cold shoulder?"

Callahan rolled his eyes. "She's always too busy

when I stop by for a visit. I probably shouldn't bother anymore."

Cookie *tsked*. "Maybe you are stupid after all."

The wagon train rolled on, day fading into night, then dawn reinventing the day over and over again until Cookie signaled it was time to veer north. As they rode, Callahan's eyes kept drifting south. He sometimes saw dark clouds that might have come together into a storm, but so far, no weather bad enough to justify the alternate course.

Well, better safe than sorry, I reckon.

The land got rockier as they went along, hills humping up, the land's attempt to look just a little more interesting to the naked eye. Callahan didn't hate the plains of Nebraska and Wyoming, but his preference was for mountains and soaring evergreens. In a way Callahan couldn't quite explain, the wide-open spaces closed in on him like walls. He supposed it didn't make sense.

But Callahan owed no man an explanation.

The land became hillier and rockier, and Cookie indicated two hills in the distance. "Right between them. An easy path, and then we can get back to the main trail."

They headed toward the two hills, and as they drew closer, Callahan spotted the trail in between. Cookie had been right. The terrain was rough, but the path between the hills looked easy enough.

"Lead us through, boss." Cookie grinned. "Show them what a hero looks like."

"Funny man," Callahan said. "And what will you be doing?"

"I'll head back to the end of the column," Cookie

said. "Make sure all them sheep and cattle don't get lost. They've fallen a bit behind."

"Let's go then."

Callahan trotted to the head of the column and led the wagon train toward the hills.

Roy Benson lay flat on his belly atop the rocky hill and watched the wagon train approach. Still a few miles out, crawling along at a snail's pace. Plenty of time to get into position.

Zeke Hawkins belly-crawled up alongside him. "That them?"

No, it's some other wagon train out in the middle of nowhere, dung-for-brains. "Yeah, that's them."

"I figure back where it gets narrow," Hawkins said.

Benson had figured the same thing. Let the wagons approach and enter the defile. They'd spring the trap at the narrow part. There were six of them, Benson plus Hawkins and his men. Benson considered how to deploy them.

"Who's your best man with a rifle?"

"Vincent."

The big barrel-chested fellow Benson had taken for the leader when they'd all walked into the Four Queens saloon.

"Here's how we'll do it," Benson told the other outlaw. "Me and Vincent will stay up here. You pick a man and send him across to the other hilltop. We'll open up on them when they hit that narrow spot, catch them in a crossfire. We shoot the mules of the lead wagon, then that'll bottle them up good. We'll turn that Conestoga into a roadblock. You and your other two men will come riding down the defile from the other direction."

"Why don't I stay up here and shoot, and you ride down the defile?" Hawkins said, a challenge in his voice.

Benson sighed. "Okay, you stay up here, and I'll—"

"No, no, never mind," Hawkins said. "We'll do it like you said. I'd just prefer to be consulted is all."

Good. My plan works better this way.

"Okay, then," Benson continued. "You guys ride up to the lead wagon, bust in, and grab the chest. Gun anybody that gets in your way. Follow me. I got something for you."

They slid down the hill until they were out of sight of the wagon train, then stood and picked their way down to where the others waited with the horses. Benson opened his saddlebags and showed Hawkins what he had. Four bottles, emptied of whiskey and filled again with kerosene and corked. Rags tied to the tops.

"Toss these after you grab the chest," Benson said. "A few burning wagons will keep them off your backs."

Hawkins grinned. "Good thinking. Can you keep them off us until then?"

"After we shoot the mules, we'll spread some lead up and down the column," Benson said. "We don't especially need to hit anyone. We just need to keep their heads down. All the same, get in and out fast. Don't give them time to get organized."

Hawkins nodded. "Right."

"Best get everyone into position," Benson said. "They'll be along directly."

* * *

Callahan rode alongside the lead wagon as they entered the narrow defile, two rocky hills rising up on either side. This close, he could see more hills humping up behind them. Cookie had told him it went like that for four or five miles before opening up again, wider spaces on the other side but still hilly, and the hills would grow and then gradually get serious about being mountains.

The first two wagons belonged to the outfitter, first a standard Conestoga with all the tools and supplies Callahan and the boys would need for the trek to Oregon. Little Rock held the reins, a huge grin stretching across his face. Apparently, he was still tickled pink to be out front, leading all the wagons. Callahan thought the novelty would have worn off by now, but the kid was all raw enthusiasm. Next came the chuckwagon driven by Billy Thorndyke. Cookie often liked to be in charge of the chuckwagon—maybe because he did most of the cooking—but he was obliged to take turns with the other boys. Third in line was the Conestoga driven by James O'Rourke, a young Irishman who'd been first to sign on with the wagon train. He and his family intended to open and operate a flour mill. Unlike Little Rock, O'Rourke had lost enthusiasm for the trail in the first two weeks. His shoulders slumped and his face sagged.

They entered the defile, the hill blocking the sun somewhat as its shadow fell across them. Callahan disliked it immediately. He'd just been complaining about the wide-open spaces feeling unnatural, but the sudden closeness of the hills, the sun being blotted out . . . Well, it didn't sit well.

Never mind. They'd be through it soon enough.

They rolled along, and the hills closed in on them from both sides.

"Pretty tight squeeze, Mr. Callahan!" Little Rock called. "Look, you can almost touch the sides." He held his hands out left and right.

Of course, the boy's hands were nowhere close to touching the hills. Little Rock's idea of a joke. Still, the kid had a point. If they were to meet another wagon train coming the other way, Callahan doubted there'd be enough room for them to pass each other.

"How are you liking your first wagon train, Little Rock?" Callahan asked.

"It agrees with me," Little Rock said. "I knew this land was big, but it takes a man actually seeing it with his own eyeballs to believe it."

Callahan nodded, knowing just what the kid meant. The sky was big. The mountains were big. It was a big country, and it was a pleasure to be overwhelmed by it, especially that first time coming west, the land opening up in front of a man and seeming to stretch on forever.

"You're in charge here, Little Rock," Callahan said. "I'm going to ride back down the column and make sure nobody's lagging."

"No sweat, boss!" Little Rock saluted. "With me on the job, you got nothing to worry—"

The crack of a rifle shot split the air, one of the mules bucked, the side of its head exploding with a spray of blood. The animal wilted to its knees. The other mule's eyes rolled white as it brayed, a panicked, screeching racket. It tried to pull away but was harnessed to its brother's corpse.

Another spattering of rifle shots silenced the second mule, wet blooms of red along its neck and head. It fell over with a thud onto the other mule.

Little Rock drew his six-shooter and blazed away at the top of the hill, firing blind.

"Get down, you fool!" Callahan shouted. "You're not going to hit anything."

Little Rock didn't listen, emptied his revolver at the hilltop and then just stood there reloading as the rifle shots rained down. That dumb kid was going to get himself shot.

"Damn it, Little Rock, get down you stupid—"

A rifle shot sent Callahan's borrowed hat spinning away. He half fell, half jumped from the saddle, got to his feet, and ran to the chuckwagon, putting his back to it.

Billy Thorndyke took aim at the hilltop, too, but at least had the good sense to try with a rifle. He levered a shell into the chamber but never got a shot off. A rifle shot hit the wagon three inches from Billy's knee, kicking up chunks of wood. Billy dove into the back of the wagon.

Not a complete idiot at least.

Callahan looked back down the column. With the lead wagons stopped, the others had started to bunch up from behind. The constant rifle fire from above sent settlers ducking, many crawling under their wagons.

Callahan leaned out to risk a look. Puffs of smoke

offered a hint of where the shooters might be hidden. *They're on both sides. Three or four of them maybe.*

But what in the blazes did they want?

The sound of pounding hooves drew his attention to the front of the column. Callahan drew his Peacemaker and jogged to the other side of the chuckwagon, doing his best to stay low. He eased forward and stepped aside just enough to see around Little Rock's stalled wagon.

Three horsemen rode toward the wagons at a full gallop.

Little Rock leveled his revolver and fired.

The three riders drew and shot from the saddle, never slowing their gallop.

Three chunks of lead slammed into Little Rock. The boy contorted and twisted as he tumbled from the wagon, blood trailing as he fell across the dead mules.

Callahan returned fire but hit nothing.

One of the riders wheeled his horse around to Callahan's side of the wagon. A lean, mean-looking little man. He squeezed off three shots. Dust kicked up around Callahan's feet. He fell back, dropped to the ground, and rolled under the chuckwagon.

The two other riders hopped aboard the lead wagon. Callahan couldn't see what they were doing under the wagon's cover, but he fired blind, hoping to hit something. He crawled out from under the chuckwagon and crept forward, pistol up and ready. He heard horses galloping away and ran forward to see two riders departing rapidly, each holding one end of a wooden chest, carrying it between them.

The man who'd shot at him stopped, horse rearing. He threw something. It arced over Callahan, trailing fire. It hit the wagon behind him and burst into flames. The wagon was a roaring inferno in seconds, and it sent Callahan reeling back, the heat suddenly intense.

Callahan started to run but stopped. He scooped up Little Rock's body and retreated back toward the other wagons.

The chuckwagon mules bucked and panicked at the flames. Billy had the reins and was doing his best to get the team to back up. It took some coaxing, but he finally managed.

Callahan noticed that the rifle fire from the hilltops had stopped.

A dozen men with shovels rushed forward and began shoveling dirt at the fire, but it was no use.

"Everybody get back!" Callahan shouted. "Nothing to do but let it burn!"

He laid Little Rock on the ground, knelt next to him, and checked for a pulse.

Cookie Mayfield came galloping up like the wind, reining in his horse abruptly in a cloud of dust next to Callahan. "Good Lord! What in thunderation—" His eyes fell to the boy on the ground. "Is he . . . ?"

Callahan stood and shook his head. "He's gone."

CHAPTER 19

His name had been Ralph Bascomb. Callahan hadn't even known because everyone had called him Little Rock. Billy Thorndyke had supplied the kid's real name, so Callahan could say a few words over the grave. Ralph Bascomb—Little Rock—had fallen in love with the bigness of the world all around him, the soaring mountains and the endless prairie. Now his world was a six-by-three hole in the ground, covered over with dirt and rock.

It was a bad trade, but everyone made it sooner or later. Too soon for some.

Most everyone had come to pay respects. They drifted away now. Billy Thorndyke stood there looking at the fresh mound, hat held to his chest.

Callahan paused next to him. "That wagon out of the way?" They'd let the wagon burn, and when it had finally cooled, Callahan had ordered that the remains and the dead mules be moved to the side.

"Yessir," Billy said. "The way's clear."

"You okay?"

Billy didn't look up, and a moment passed. "I didn't

fire a shot. I just jumped in the back of the wagon and hid. Like some dang coward. I should have . . . done something."

Callahan put a hand on Billy's shoulder. "And then we'd dig a hole for you right next to Little Rock's. Sometimes you fight, and sometimes you duck."

"How do you know when to do which?" Billy asked.

"It's a guess every time, and all you can do is hope you're right," Callahan said. "Come on. Time to go."

Billy put his hat back on and snugged it down low. "Right."

Cookie came up to Callahan and handed him his droopy gray hat. "Found this."

"Thanks." Callahan stuck a finger through the fresh bullet hole. "Another inch."

Cookie's eyes went to Little Rock's grave, then back to Callahan. "Some's lucky. Some ain't."

"Let's get moving, Cookie," Callahan said. "We've basically lost a day, but I want to get out of this tight place at least. I hate it here. Let's get somewhere we can circle the wagons. Then you and me need to have a talk."

As soon as the wagon had gone up, Roy Benson had nudged Vincent and said, "Let's go."

Vincent grunted, which Benson took for agreement.

The ride from Benson's side of the defile to the abandoned farmhouse was shorter than it would be for the others, which was exactly according to Benson's plan. They made their way down the other side of the hill, mounted up, and galloped a straight line to a wooded valley where the farmhouse nestled next to a crooked, shallow stream.

They passed fallow fields. Benson couldn't say what might have been planted there once upon a time. Farming wasn't his line of work. They dismounted in front of the little house. It was in good shape, considering nobody was around to take care of it—solid roof, shutters on the windows, no holes in the clapboard. Adequate shelter for a short stay.

Benson nodded toward the stream and took a double-barreled twelve-gauge from his saddle sheath. "Water the horses. I'll make sure the house is clear."

Vincent grunted again and led the horses toward the water.

Benson pushed the front door, and it creaked open on rusty hinges. Bare floor and walls. A couple of rickety chairs and a narrow table. A small fireplace made of river rock. A layer of dust on everything. A sink under the window across the room. He went through the little door to the left. A small bedroom. Empty. Nothing had changed since he'd been here the last time.

He crossed back through the main room to the back door, opened it, and went out. A large pile of firewood stacked against the back of the house. He went back inside.

Vincent was just coming through the front door.

"How are the horses?" Benson asked.

"Watered," Vincent said. "Tied up out front."

"You take off the saddles?"

"No."

"We'll do it later. Help me get some firewood."

Vincent frowned. "I ain't cold."

Benson rolled his eyes. "Don't you think a hot meal would be nice?"

Another grunt, which Benson again interpreted as agreement. He held the back door open and allowed Vincent to exit first.

Vincent bent over the pile to gather an armload of firewood.

Benson drew his six-shooter, thumbed back the hammer, and shot Vincent between the shoulder blades. Vincent twitched once and fell across the pile, scattering logs. Benson thumbed the hammer back again and trained the revolver on the corpse on the off chance there was any life left in him. When Vincent didn't move or make a sound, Benson eased the hammer down and returned the gun to its holster.

He went back inside, closing the door behind him.

He went out front to the horses and considered removing the saddles, but he wasn't sure he had time. The others would be along shortly. He took his saddlebags inside and set them on the table. He took out a bottle of whiskey, pulled the cork, and took a slug. He smacked his lips and drank again, then set the bottle aside.

Now to prepare. Benson went back into the saddlebags and came out with a hammer and nails and strips of cloth he'd cut earlier. The last thing he took out was a little .32 rimfire revolver. An extra gun was never a bad idea.

He crawled under the table, grunting and feeling it in his back. Lordie, he wasn't that old, was he? He hammered the strips of cloth to the underside of the table, creating two little slings. Benson stood and slipped the barrel of the shotgun through the cloth loops under the table. Then he went back out the front door and walked inside, looking at the table to see if the shotgun was visible or not. If somebody bent down to gander under the table, they'd see it plain as day, but if anyone walked in normal, it wasn't visible.

Good enough.

Benson took another slug of whiskey.

Then he dragged two chairs around to the other side of the table, so he could sit facing the front door. He put the .32 revolver on the seat of one of the chairs where he could reach it.

More whiskey. Not too much. There was still work to do.

He wondered how much time had passed while he'd been rigging the shotgun. The others should be along any time.

Benson went back out front but didn't see anyone coming. The day had gone still, not even a breath of wind, so he cocked his head and listened. Nothing interesting.

He took the saddles off the horses and the bits out of their mouths.

Still no sign of Hawkins and his men. Had they run into trouble?

No, Benson realized. The answer was obvious. They'd stopped to open the chest, and when all the promised money wasn't there, they had a little chinwag about what to do next. This development was not unforeseen, but it would make Benson's job more difficult.

He went back inside and sat at the table. He had another drink. They wouldn't come in shooting, he told himself. They'd want to know. There'd be questions asked very loudly, and they'd want answers, and when Benson didn't have good answers . . .

Two minutes later he heard the horses.

They approached, then arrived, and Benson could hear the men dismount and their low muttering. He couldn't make out the words, but the tone was clear, an odd mix of hostile and businesslike. He thought about drawing his six-shooter, but better to play it innocent for as long as possible until he could get the setup he wanted.

The door slammed open, and one of Hawkins's men burst into the little farmhouse, revolver pointed right at Benson's chest. "Don't even twitch."

Benson frowned and put his hands up. "What is this?"

"Shut up."

Benson could glimpse two more outside. He needed them to come in. He needn't have worried.

"Clark, Frank, get in here!" said the one with the gun.

Benson knew little of these men and certainly hadn't bothered to learn their names.

The other two men entered, carrying a wooden chest between them. Obviously the one they'd taken from the wagon train. It looked heavy. Was it possible there was actually gold inside. Benson almost laughed at the thought but stopped himself. It wasn't a time to laugh.

The two men went into the corner and set the chest

down. That was no good. Benson needed them in front of the table.

The one holding the gun nodded toward the door across the room. "Clark, check it."

"Right."

The one called Clark opened the door and stuck his head in. "Empty."

"Okay." The one with the gun on Benson thumbed the hammer back for emphasis. "Now let's talk."

"Where's Hawkins?" Benson asked.

"Never mind that. You're talking to me now."

Benson frowned. That was curious. Had they had some kind of falling out. Did they blame Hawkins for signing them onto a bad job?

"Fine," Benson said. "What's the meaning of this?"

"That's what we're going to find out. I'm going to ask you all about it, and depending on your answers, maybe I fill your face full of lead or maybe I don't. It's a fun game because I win either way. First things first. Take that six-shooter out and set it on the table. Nice and slow by the thumb and forefinger."

Benson did as he was told, taking the revolver by the grip between thumb and forefinger and slowly lifting it from the holster, then setting it gently on the table. The .32 revolver was out of sight on the seat next to Benson. He could reach it easily and start shooting, but the setup was all wrong. Clark still stood over by the bedroom door, and the other one was on the opposite side of the room next to the chest in the corner.

"Look, my gun's on the table, now what's all this about?" Benson demanded.

"Like you don't know. Who told you there'd be money?"

"Like I said, that information is confidential," Benson said.

"No, no, forget all that. It was rotten information, so it don't get to be confidential no more."

"Where's Hawkins?"

"Shut up about Hawkins. I said you're talking to me now."

"I don't believe there was no money," Benson said. "I think you killed Hawkins to take the money for yourself."

"Why you son of a—" The man puffed, face going red with anger. "There wasn't a plug nickel in that chest. No money at all!"

"I don't believe it!"

"You calling me a liar?"

"Show me then," Benson insisted.

"Boys, bring it over."

The one near the bedroom door rejoined his partner in the corner, and together they lifted the chest and brought it over to the table. They flipped open the latch and tilted the chest on its side, the contents spilling out—hammer, saw, chisel, hand drill, horseshoes, nails, and a myriad of other such similar objects.

Benson's eyes grew wide. "What is the meaning of this?" He didn't consider himself much of an actor, but his mock shock helped cover the fact he'd let his right hand drop below the surface of the table, where it gripped the shotgun. All three men now stood in a neat row in front of him.

"No money. A bunch of tools," said the one with

the pistol. "So what have you got to say for yourself, Benson?"

Roy Benson smiled. "Just this."

He squeezed both the shotgun's triggers, and twelve-gauge thunder shook the tiny farmhouse.

Buckshot ripped across their bellies and thighs. They screamed, stumbling back. The one who'd held the pistol on Benson got off a shot, but it went wide. Two of the men went down, hitting the floor hard, clutching their bloody guts and writhing in pain, their moans and screams filling the room.

The one called Clark had been standing a little to the side, and the shotgun's spread wasn't wide enough to put him down. He caught a few pellets down the side of one leg, grunting in pain as he staggered back. He drew his six-shooter and fired, but Benson was already ducking to one side, grabbing the .32 as he dove for the floor.

Benson stood and shot Clark in the shoulder.

Clark shouted, dropped his revolver, backed against the far wall, and slid down into a sitting position, eyes wide, knowing he was about to be killed.

"Sorry." Benson lifted the .32, took careful aim at Clark's heart, and thumbed back the hammer.

"Don't." A voice behind him.

Benson froze.

"Put that little .32 on the table next to your other gun." Hawkins's voice.

Benson cursed inwardly. The racket of guns blazing in the little farmhouse had covered the sound of Hawkins coming in the back door. He set the gun on the table as instructed and waited.

All three of Hawkins's men had been shot, Clark

moaning in the corner and the two shotgunned men rolling around on the floor, keening like animals and holding their guts in. Benson had shot them up pretty good, and he doubted Hawkins was too happy about it.

Hawkins came around to where Benson could see him, still pointing his six-gun.

"He suckered us." Clark held his wounded shoulder, blood seeping between his fingers.

"I see." Hawkins swung his six-shooter from Benson to Clark and pulled the trigger.

The shot hit Clark in the center of the forehead, knocking his head against the wall. He sat dead, eyes wide-open, blood trickling from the hole in his head. Hawkins circled around to the men full of buckshot and still moaning and groaning on the floor. He shot one, then the other.

The sudden silence struck Benson almost like a physical force.

The smell still lingered heavily—blood and gun smoke. And someone's bowels had loosened.

Hawkins turned his revolver back on Benson. "I saw Vincent on the woodpile out back. Tipped me off right away."

"I didn't think I'd have time to lure him out somewhere," Benson said. "Anyway, I figured you'd all come through the front."

"Sit down."

Benson sat. His eyes darted to the guns on the table, and he calculated his chances. As a man who earned his living with guns, he was faster than average, but Hawkins earned his living the same way. Benson kept his hands away from the revolvers.

"There never was no money, was there?"

Benson shook his head. "No."

"That was a cover for something else."

Benson nodded. "Yes."

"Something for which you're being paid a lot of money."

Benson hesitated only a moment. "Yes."

Hawkins pulled a chair up to the other side of the table and sat. He thought a moment and then set his six-gun on the table. Benson understood he was seeing a tentative show of trust. It didn't go both ways, not by a long shot, but for the moment he elected to listen.

"So," Hawkins said. "Let's you and me discuss the details of our new partnership."

CHAPTER 20

"Pete Johansen's my guess," Cookie Mayfield said.

Callahan and Cookie rode side by side next to the chuckwagon. The ground had become hillier as the day progressed, and soon the wagon train would be in the mountains, where their daily progress would be significantly reduced.

This wasn't the first time they'd discussed this. Somebody in the wagon train was committing sabotage, maybe even trying to murder Callahan. It was hard to believe, but the sawed wagon wheel spokes couldn't be denied, and some gang had attacked the wagon train for no apparent reason. Poor Little Rock had been killed, but there could have been many more deaths with so much lead flying around.

Now, as they rode along, they discussed who might be the rat in their midst.

"How do you figure Pete?" Callahan asked.

"He's cranky as all get out for one thing," Cookie said.

Callahan shook his head. "Cranky don't mean villain."

"Well, you're right about that, I guess," Cookie admitted. "Some people's just naturally unpleasant. But consider this. Most everyone in the wagon train had signed on *before* the wager with the railroad. Pete Johansen signed on late. Does that make him automatically guilty? Well, no, but if the railroad tried to sneak somebody in on us, then it just goes to figure it would be a latecomer. And he stays off to himself. Why's that? So nobody can see what he's up to sneaking around? I'm just saying the man bears watching."

"You made your point," Callahan said. "But that goes for anyone who signed up after the wager. We'll need to keep our eyes and ears open."

They traveled the rest of the day without incident and circled the wagons as usual that night. Callahan told Billy and Clancy to keep their eyes peeled as they made the rounds. He didn't need to tell them why. They'd seen the sabotage to the wagon wheels with their own eyes.

"When we pass Fort Hall, I'll tell the marshal." Callahan considered riding ahead himself to inform the law about what had happened, but he didn't want to leave the wagon train any more shorthanded than it already was. "We have to pass Fort Hall, anyway, to get to the Snake River ford, yes?"

"That's right," Cookie said. "Unless we want to avoid the mountain pass coming up . . . in which case we could go way south, take one of the alternate paths."

"Why would we do that?"

"If the weather's bad, or if it's late in the season and we don't want to risk getting snowed in," Cookie said. "But there ain't a cloud in the sky. There's been freak blizzards before at high elevation, but I would have smelled it before now."

"Then we're not going to lose a lot of time going south," Callahan decided. "Take us over the mountains, Cookie."

The Henry's Lake Mountains weren't the biggest Callahan had ever seen, but they were plenty big enough to slow down a wagon train, and the column of Conestogas was reduced to crawl as they zigzagged up the narrow switchback trail to Jericho Pass.

Callahan nudged his horse alongside Clancy's. "Ride up to the top and back. Let us know if it's clear."

If a tree had fallen across the path or if some other obstacle blocked the way, then better to send the boys ahead to clear it rather than bring the whole wagon train to a halt. Despite the slow progress, Cookie insisted the route through Jericho Pass would save them half a day over the next closest trail.

Clancy trotted ahead, and Callahan steered his horse alongside the next wagon in line, which happened to belong to the Grainger family.

Matt Grainger had looked better. His skin was pallid, he had dark circles under his eyes, and his hair was mussed.

"How you holding up, Mr. Grainger?" Callahan asked.

"Let me tell you something, Mr. Callahan," Grainger said. "This is a long way to travel with three kids. This wagon gets smaller and smaller every mile that goes by."

Callahan pretended to scratch his nose to hide his grin behind his hand. "Don't you fret, Mr. Grainger. We'll be to Salem before you know it."

Grainger shook his head wearily. "Lord, I hope so."

Callahan slowed his horse and allowed the Grainger wagon to move ahead. Pete Johansen's came next.

Callahan recalled Cookie's suspicions about the man and decided to have a word.

"Everything okay with you, Mr. Johansen?"

A grunt and a shrug. "Every day's pretty much like the last."

Callahan nodded. Johansen seemed to take pretty much everything in stride. Cookie had a good point about the man joining the wagon train so late, but that didn't mean he was guilty.

But he wasn't necessarily innocent, either.

The simple fact was Callahan had no idea what to think of the man or of any of them. Callahan had generally taken people exactly as they presented themselves, considering them to be law-abiding decent folk up to and until they displayed something different. He wanted to believe people were exactly as good as they seemed.

But of course, any criminal with half a brain would pretend to be just that—good and decent and law-abiding. No outlaw he'd ever heard of walked around announcing, "I am here to do villainy."

Callahan slowly let each wagon pass, calling out greetings or striking up conversations with each family. There was a general fatigue among the settlers—not surprising, considering how many miles they'd put behind them—but also there was a feeling of optimism. Callahan found himself in a good mood by the time Becky's wagon passed.

Lizzy sat up front with her mother, clutching her doll to her chest.

"Hello, Miss Lizzy!" Callahan called out. "Is your mom talking to me today?"

"Hey, Mr. Callahan, I'll ask." Lizzy turned to her mother. "Mom, you talking to Mr. Callahan?"

"Please tell Mr. Callahan that I don't know what he means," Becky told Lizzy. "I am happy to talk to him about wagon train business whenever he feels the need."

Lizzy grinned and leaned out of the wagon. "Mom says come around and visit tonight, Mr. Callahan!"

"Lizzy!"

The little girl squealed with laughter and vanished into the back of the covered wagon.

Becky glanced at Callahan, looking embarrassed. She recovered quickly, stuck her nose in the air, and said, "Good day to you, Mr. Callahan."

Callahan laughed and let her be on her way.

Slowly, the wagon train rolled by until finally Callahan found himself riding alongside Anna Masters's wagon.

"Sniff out any juicy stories lately, Miss Masters?" Callahan asked.

"Extra, extra, read all about it," Masters said bitterly. "My butt hurts, and I hate this wagon!"

Callahan laughed.

"Glad I could provide you with some entertainment, Tomahawk," she said. "How long are we going to be climbing this blasted mountain?"

"If we don't have a problem, we'll be up and through the pass and down the other side before nightfall," Callahan told her. "Cookie says there's an open space on the other side suitable for circling the wagons."

"And when can I send another telegram?"

"Fort Hall."

Masters shook her head. "I never heard of half these places. Don't we pass any actual cities?"

Callahan smiled. "You looking for a hot bath and a fine meal in a bistro?"

"Yes, frankly."

"Boise maybe," he said. "Cookie tells me we circle the wagons pretty close to town."

"Boise. So that's what passes for an actual town in these parts." She rolled her eyes. "How far?"

"Three weeks give or take," Callahan said. "Maybe a bit more with this terrain."

She groaned. "Good grief. Did I really volunteer for this? I need to have my head examined."

"Stay strong, Miss Masters. We'll get you there."

Just as her wagon pulled away, Clancy came riding from the head of the column, and Ike Thorndyke approached from the other direction, both trying to talk to Callahan at once.

He held up a hand. "One at a time. Ike, how we doing?"

"The sheepherders keep falling behind," Ike reported. "And since the cattlemen are behind them . . ."

"They're behind, too. Right. Ike, tell them if they can't keep up, I can't guarantee their safety, and if they insist on going slow, they need to move aside and let the cattle through."

Ike frowned. "Mr. Schultz ain't gonna like that."

"That's what I'm counting on," Callahan said. "Might light a fire under his backside."

Ike grinned. "Right." He turned his horse and rode back toward the sheepherders.

Callahan turned to Clancy Davenport. "Well?"

"The road's been washed out up near the pass," Clancy told him.

Callahan's eyes shot wide. "The road's gone?"

"Well, no, it's not that bad," Clancy said. "But it's crazy narrow. We'll have to take it real slow, and I mean *slow*."

If we move any slower, we'll be going backward.

"Is Cookie up front?" Callahan asked.

Clancy nodded. "I told him already."

"Then pass the word as we near that spot," Callahan ordered. "Tell everyone to keep tight control of their mules. One wrong step, and it's a long ways down."

Roy Benson and Zeke Hawkins paralleled the wagon train, keeping out of sight on the other side of some low hills.

When the hills started turning themselves into mountains, Hawkins said, "Let's have a look."

They urged their horses up a low rise, pausing at the top in the shadow of some tall evergreens, looking down at the wagon train below as it jogged slightly north. They sat in silence for maybe ten minutes and just watched.

"Jericho Pass," Hawkins said.

"What's that?" Benson had been lost in his own thoughts and felt he'd missed something.

"The way they're going," Hawkins said. "It's the only thing that makes sense. They'll come out near Fort Hall. There's good fords there. The river."

"Right."

"What are you thinking?"

"Can we get up to the pass ahead of them?" Benson asked.

"Two men on fast horses against a slow-as-molasses wagon train?" Hawkins said. "You tell me."

Benson pondered his options.

Hawkins sat quietly, waiting.

The two men had struck an uneasy bargain. Hawkins wanted in on the big payday Benson had described, and Benson had reluctantly let Hawkins convince him they'd be better off working together. Benson couldn't really do it alone, which was why he'd hired Hawkins's gang in the first place. All of Hawkins's talk about loyalty to his men and how many years they'd ridden together was just that. Talk. Benson was simultaneously encouraged and concerned by the notion. On the one hand, he was glad Hawkins wasn't some sentimental simpleton. On the other hand, that they found each other useful wasn't exactly the same as trust. They could have shot each other in the back a dozen times since leaving the little farmhouse.

Benson's instinct told him it might come to that, but not yet. There was still work to do.

"Let's get up there then," Benson said. "I want to get there ahead of them and find a good spot."

Hawkins raised an eyebrow. "You got something in mind?"

Benson smiled. "I do indeed."

CHAPTER 21

The road was just as bad as Clancy had described it.

Callahan dismounted and walked the bad stretch, Clancy pointing out where the road narrowed severely. It would be tight. The road was like a groove gouged into the side of the mountain. The slope continued both up and down at a steep angle. Callahan stood at the edge of the road and looked down. Anyone going over the side would tumble a long time before slamming up against a boulder or a tree trunk. The dirt crumbled and gave way under Callahan's boot, and he stepped back quickly.

"The wagons will have to hug the side of the mountain all the way," Callahan said. "Not a lot of room to spare on the left side. How far is it like this?"

"Fifty or sixty yards," Clancy said. "At least it's level here. Mostly. As soon as you're through the bad patch, it starts downhill."

Callahan sighed. "I hate to go any slower than we're already going, but we'll need to bring the wagons through one at a time. The weight of multiple wagons all bunched up together is not a risk I'm willing to take. That road crumbling away is the last thing we need."

"Now what, boss?"

"I want you to scout all the way down to the other side," Callahan told Clancy. "I don't want any other surprises. I'll go back and organize things with Cookie to start bringing the wagons through."

They mounted their horses, Clancy taking off one way, Callahan the other.

Callahan found Cookie at the head of the column and explained what they were going to do.

"One at a time, huh?" Cookie frowned. "That'll take forever and a day."

"It's just not safe any other way."

"There's no place to turn around, anyway," Cookie said. "Not like we're going to get fifty mule teams to go backwards all the way back down the mountain without a heap of trouble."

"Then the sooner we start the better."

Cookie nodded. "Right."

"Cookie, why do they call it Jericho Pass?"

Cookie shrugged. "No idea."

Roy Benson and Zeke Hawkins tied their horses to a skinny spruce well above the pass. They each pulled rifles from their saddle sheaths and then slowly picked their way closer for a better look, sliding at times as gravel and loose soil shifted beneath their boots.

They squatted behind a fallen log and watched the wagon train crawl along below.

Hawkins sighted along his rifle barrel at the wagons below. "We could pick off a dozen of them and be gone before they even figured out what was happening."

Benson stopped himself from rolling his eyes. "I told you it can't seem intentional. That'll undermine the whole point. When we hit them the first time it can be explained as random bandits looking for a score. If we just keep bushwhacking them over and over again, it'll be obvious somebody has it out for this wagon train specifically."

Hawkins scowled. "Then why'd we bother bringing the rifles?"

"Habit."

"So what then?" Hawkins asked.

"If they lose a certain number of wagons, then the whole wagon train is considered to have failed. I explained this," Benson said. "It's why I was hoping you'd set more wagons aflame when you and your boys grabbed the chest."

"Well, I didn't know, did I?" Hawkins said irritably. "One was enough to block them chasing after us."

"Now we both know the whole story, so let's concentrate on how we can get the job done." Benson turned his head one way and then the other, looking around for an opportunity. Finally, he saw one and pointed. "Over there."

Hawkins looked. "Over there what?"

"That big boulder," Benson said. "The one teetering precarious like."

Hawkins craned his neck trying to get a better look without revealing himself. They were pretty far up the mountain, and the two men doubted they'd be seen even if one of the settlers did happen to glance up, but there was no sense in taking chances.

"I don't know," Hawkins said. "Is there a clear path? If it hits a tree or gets stuck, all we might accomplish is letting them know somebody's up here."

"Let's get a closer look," Benson suggested.

They crouch-walked to the boulder and ducked behind it, leaning this way and that to eyeball the path down the steep slope of the mountain. The boulder was almost as tall as Benson and just as wide. It sat in a shallow divot, leaning forward, as if it would only take one good shove to send it rolling.

"If you can just avoid that tree. The big one." Hawkins pointed.

Benson nodded. "Right."

Hawkins looked down at the column of wagons. "They ain't stupid. Spacing the wagons far apart. I was hoping we might get two, but no chance. Unless we find more boulders."

"We can't do more," Benson said. "One boulder is an act of God. A bunch more and they'll know it's intentional."

Hawkins blew out a frustrated sigh. "Fine. If we can only do one, then it's got to be just right. Time it wrong, and you'll roll it right between two wagons, and then we've wasted our shot."

"I know."

"You've got to time it," Hawkins said.

"I *know*."

They watched awhile, getting the rhythm of the wagons passing below them. Benson counted slowly, measuring the seconds between wagons. He tried to imagine the boulder rolling and tumbling down the slope.

Hawkins frowned. "Well?"

"Don't rush me."

Benson focused his attention on the next wagon. According to his estimate, he'd need to get the boulder rolling well before the wagon came into line with the boulder's path.

He took a deep breath and counted . . . one . . . two . . . *THREE*!

Benson rushed forward, shoving with both hands. The boulder rocked in place but didn't begin its roll down the mountainside. It wasn't budging as easily as Benson had hoped.

"Help me!"

Hawkins rushed to Benson's side and put his shoulder against the boulder. It eased forward, both men grunting and shoving for all they were worth. Beads of sweat broke out across Benson's forehead. And then the boulder . . .

. . . went over.

End over end, once, twice . . . three times. It looked for a moment like it might get stuck, but then it gained momentum, bouncing and rolling and making a catastrophic racket through the underbrush, snapping small saplings, dislodging other small rocks and loose gravel, a sort of mini avalanche accompanying the boulder down-down-down the mountainside, picking up speed as it went.

Benson watched, holding his breath. The extra split second it took to get the boulder rolling might have spoiled his aim. The wagon might make it all the way past before the giant rock reached its target, instead passing harmlessly through the gap between wagons.

The boulder headed straight for the thick trunk of the tree Hawkins had been worried about earlier. Benson cursed. If it slammed to a halt up against that tree, then the effort would have been for nothing. It took a jog at the last second and did hit the tree but only a glancing blow, a loud crack, bark flying.

But even the slight glancing blow was enough to alter the trajectory. As best as Benson could tell, the boulder would pass harmlessly three feet behind the wagon he'd been aiming for.

He spat a string of inventive curses that would have made a saloon gal blush.

Then the boulder hit an uneven patch of ground and bounced the other way. There was a chance now. The boulder might just catch the back of the wagon.

"This is going to be close," Hawkins said.

Callahan leaned low in the saddle, watching the wagon come or, more specifically, watching how close the wheels on one side of the wagon came to the edge of the road and the perilous drop-off.

The wheel barely had three inches to spare.

"Over more!" Callahan waved left. "Get over!"

If one side of the wagon scraped rocks and overhanging tree branches, then so be it. Better than the alternative.

"Okay, good. Come on." He gestured them forward. "Take your time but don't *stop*."

It had been slow, nervous work, but one by one, Callahan and his crew were getting them across.

"Billy, come here and take over!" Callahan called.

Callahan traded places with Billy Thorndyke and rode back to the next wagon in line. He wanted to get a view of this one from behind. Billy would instruct them from the front. So far, there hadn't been any mishaps.

"Looks like it's our turn." Matt Grainger was sweating, hands tight on the reins of his mule team.

"Hug the right," Callahan told him. "It looks narrow, but trust me, you've got room. Just go slow."

Grainger licked his lips. "Right." He flicked the reins, and the team lurched forward.

Callahan gave the Grainger wagon a head start, then nudged his horse in behind them, keeping a close eye on the wheels near the road's edge. A bit of dirt and rock crumbled and fell away, the wagon wheels right on the verge of going over.

Callahan opened his mouth to yell a warning.

But Billy Thorndyke beat him to it.

"Get over, Mr. Grainger!" Billy shouted. "Get them over!"

Grainger jerked the reins, and the wagon went right, scraping past low-hanging evergreen branches.

Callahan breathed a sigh of relief.

This will work. We'll get them across. We just need to be patient and—

A deafening racket drew Callahan's attention. He craned his neck and looked up the mountainside. An enormous boulder came banging down, bouncing and smashing through the underbrush and snapping tree limbs. It smacked against a tree trunk and bounced one way, then hit an uneven patch of ground and bounced the other way. It only took Callahan a second to assess the situation. The boulder was going to come perilously close to smashing into the back of Grainger's wagon.

"Mr. Grainger, look out!" Callahan shouted.

It had been exactly the wrong thing to do. If Grainger had kept going, there was a chance the boulder might have missed.

But as soon as Grainger heard Callahan shout, he jerked back on the reins. "Whoa!"

The wagon stopped.

Callahan's eyes went back to the boulder, the scene for a split second unfolding in excruciating slow motion. The boulder hit another rock and launched, came tumbling through the air, arcing toward . . .

Callahan's eyes widened. *Son of a—*

Everything sped up again.

The boulder slammed into the back end of the wagon, demolishing the rear wheel in a tumult of splintering and cracked wood. The impact knocked the wagon over. Children within screamed. The wagon landed hard and slid off the side of the road and down, dragging the mules with it.

In a flash, Callahan leapt from his horse and crossed the space in a sprint, grabbing the mules by the harness. Billy appeared at his side, doing the same thing.

"They'll get dragged over," Callahan yelled.

"I'll unhitch them," Billy said frantically.

"No!" The mules were the only thing keeping the wagon and the Grainger family from tumbling down the side of the mountain. "Hang on!"

The weight of the wagon dragged the mule team

across the road. The animals dug in their hooves, and Callahan and Billy hung on for all they were worth, but their boots gouged ruts in the soil as they were slowly dragged along.

Pete Johansen came running from his wagon. He knelt at the edge of the road, looked down at the wagon, then over at Callahan. "Come help me!"

Callahan locked eyes with Billy. "You hang onto these mules."

Billy looked scared but set his jaw. "Yes, sir."

Callahan rushed to Johansen's side. The wagon was poised to slide down the hill, and only the mules prevented it, but not for long.

Johansen reached out. "Take my hand. Don't let go."

Callahan took his hand.

Johansen leaned over the roadside, reaching toward the front opening of the overturned wagon. "Grainger!"

Grainger handed up a little girl through the front of the wagon. She was maybe seven years old and crying. "Take the children first."

Johansen scooped her in one hand and handed her up to Callahan, who helped the girl scramble out of the way.

A boy, maybe twelve, climbed up past his father.

"Jacob!" Grainger called after him.

"It's okay, Pa," Jacob said. "I can climb out. Help the others."

The boy climbed up past Callahan, nimble and surefooted.

Callahan allowed himself a glance back. Three more men had come from the wagons to help Billy hold the mules, but the animals were frightened and fidgety, still being dragged back toward the precipice.

Johansen handed up another little girl, five years old, crying and bewildered.

"Come on, Grainger!" Johansen shouted.

"My wife," Grainger shouted back, on the verge of panic. "Take her first!"

"Hurry!"

Grainger's wife was fortunately a slight woman, eyes wide but in control of herself. Men reached passed Callahan to help lift her to the road.

Only Matt Grainger himself remained to be rescued.

The mules slid across the road right up to the edge, their strength giving out. The wagon dropped another two feet.

"Better hurry, boss," Billy shouted.

Grainger started climbing out. He looked terrified as the wagon rocked under him.

Callahan's hand had gone sweaty, and he had to squeeze so hard to maintain his grip on Johansen's hand he was afraid he might hurt the man. "Sorry."

"Break the fingers if you have to," Johansen said. "Just don't you let go."

Grainger had climbed out on the wagon and reached up for Johansen's other hand, outstretched as far as it could go. Just a couple inches short.

The animals brayed panic.

"We're losing the mules," Billy shouted.

"Everyone listen to me," Callahan shouted. "I'm counting to three. Billy, on three, cut them mules loose from the rig. Grainger, you jump up and grab Johansen."

"Wait! Hold on!" Grainger said, alarmed.

"No time to discuss it!" Callahan told him.

"Just grab me and don't let go," Johansen told Grainger.

Callahan shouted, "One . . . two . . ."

The mule's rear hoofs slid off the edge of the road. The wagon shook. The whole kit and caboodle was going to plunge over the side. Nobody in the world had ever looked as frightened as Matt Grainger because he knew one simple, irrevocable fact.

He was going to die.

"Three!"

Grainger jumped just as Billy cut the mules loose from the rig.

The wagon fell away beneath Grainger, sliding, then tumbling down the mountainside. It broke apart as it rolled, the Grainger family possessions leaving a trail down the slope. Wheels flew off and went bouncing in every direction until the battered remains of the Conestoga wagon slammed to a halt against two thick evergreens in a final calamitous din.

Grainger had grabbed hold of Johansen's hand. The weight pulled Johansen over, in turn yanking Callahan over the edge. All three men would have gone over the side if Billy Thorndyke hadn't grabbed Callahan around the waist from behind.

They all backed up together, dragging Grainger up and over, and then all of them collapsed to the ground, panting and sweating. The men behind them slapped each other on the backs, congratulating each other on holding the mules or helping in other ways. Nothing bonded men like successful teamwork.

Callahan, Johansen, and Grainger stood slowly, dusting themselves off.

Grainger looked at Johansen. "Mister, I guess I had you figured wrong. You saved my life, and I'll never forget that."

Johansen shifted awkwardly. It didn't surprise Callahan at all that a gruff man like Johansen wasn't used to compliments and kind words.

"Well . . . I guess we did get off on the wrong foot." Johansen offered his hand.

But that wasn't good enough for Grainger, who stepped past the hand to throw his arms around Johansen in a huge bear hug. Suddenly, Grainger's wife was there and then his kids, the whole family surrounding Johansen and gathering him into a group embrace. Callahan had to turn away so the cranky Johansen—suddenly alarmed by the outpouring of affection—wouldn't see him laugh.

Johansen broke away from the hug and went back to the edge of the road, pointing to the left. "Well, it's not so steep over there. It might be we could make our way down there and salvage what we can. Not quite as steep over yonder."

It struck Callahan suddenly that Jericho Pass would cost them at least half a day now, maybe more. He looked back up the hill. Just dumb luck a rockslide happened when it did.

Suddenly, Cookie Mayfield was standing next to him. "What in thunderation happened here?"

Callahan related the mishap. "Cookie, I think I know why they call it Jericho Pass now."

Cookie raised an eyebrow. "Oh?"

"Isn't Jericho where the walls came tumbling down?"

CHAPTER 22

The railroad handcar sped along the track, two laborers working it furiously—up-down-up-down—and sweating profusely as Kent Arbuckle and his new foreman Kelso held on with one hand and kept their hats on their heads with the other as the wind whipped past their ears.

"Pump your arms off, you sluggards!" Kelso shouted at the men. "Mr. Arbuckle has places to be."

A few miles later, they slowed and finally came to a stop at the tent village. The tents housed the workers, and the camp was struck, moved farther up the line, and set up again every three or four days. Additionally, there was a cookhouse tent, a shower tent, a mercantile tent, and a big tent set up like a saloon. Arbuckle had been given to understand the saloon tent sold cheap whiskey to the railroad workers in exchange for the scrip they were paid, and, in this way, recovered a good bit of the money the workers might have otherwise sent home to loved ones.

Arbuckle couldn't quite decide if that was a dirty trick or not, but it was none of his business.

Kelso ordered the handcar to be loaded with tools

that were needed up the line and then sent the men back the way they'd come. Arbuckle and Kelso headed for the saloon.

It was a large tent but somehow claustrophobic at the same time, a multitude of mismatched chairs and tables and a wide plank across two barrels for a bar. A man in a plaid vest stood behind the makeshift bar, wiping glasses with a hand towel and then stacking them in a pyramid.

Kelso snapped his fingers for the man's attention. "A bottle and two glasses. And not that cheap rotgut. I know you have at least one good bottle back there."

"Right away, Mr. Kelso."

Arbuckle and Kelso sat at a table off to the side. The bottle arrived just as Mycroft Jones entered and joined the other two men.

"I'll bring a third glass," the barkeep said.

"Never mind," Jones said. "I'm not thirsty."

The barkeep left, and the three men got down to business. Jones spread a map out on the table, and the other two men leaned in to look at it. The purpose of the map was obvious. It showed the progress from Salem going east and the amount of track from Hansen's Bend going west, with a gap in the middle where the tracks would eventually meet.

"How long until those two tracks join?" Arbuckle asked.

"Four to six weeks," Jones told him. "There's just no way to predict if we might hit some snag or not."

"If anything gets snagged on my end, you better believe I'll get it unsnagged right quick," Kelso said. "I can't speak for the other crew."

Arbuckle threw back his whiskey, then examined the map, brow furrowed in thought. He could look at the map until the end of the world and not get any answers.

Although there was really only one question he wanted an answer to, he'd asked it over and over again. "Will we get there first?"

Jones sighed. "I just don't know, sir. The race is basically neck and neck. Some good luck here or some bad luck there could make all the difference."

Arbuckle turned to the foreman. "Mr. Kelso, I'm sure you've got important matters to attend to. Please don't let us keep you."

Kelso frowned but stood. He wasn't the sort of man who liked to be casually dismissed, but he was also well aware of his place in the pecking order. He tossed back his whiskey, then set the empty glass on the table. "If you need me, you know where to find me."

Arbuckle waited for Kelso to leave the tent before turning back to Jones. "You've heard from him?"

Jones took the telegram from his shirt pocket and slid it across the table to Arbuckle. "From Fort Hall."

The railroad man unfolded the telegram and read it. A progress report from Benson.

Or rather, a *lack* of progress report.

It was clear now to Arbuckle that he *might* be able to win a straightforward race with Callahan's wagon train, but the outcome was far from guaranteed. And Arbuckle was way past feeling sportsmanlike about it. If Arbuckle couldn't lick Tomahawk Callahan one way, then he'd do it another.

It was no longer about winning a race. It was about making sure Callahan didn't cross the finish line with enough wagons or people to constitute a win. It meant doubling down on playing dirty.

Arbuckle had two operatives at his disposal. Roy Benson, but also his undercover person in the wagon train itself. So far, Benson had torched one wagon and had destroyed another at someplace called Jericho Pass. Arbuckle had never heard of it. Not that it mattered.

He decided he needed to get more out of the undercover operative.

"I need you to send two telegrams," Arbuckle said. "Is Benson still at Fort Hall?"

Jones nodded. "I instructed him to wait for a reply."

"Tell him this." Arbuckle related what he wanted done, basically upping the ante on what was already happening.

"What about our other operative?" Arbuckle asked.

"Problematic . . . but I'll try."

"Make it happen," Arbuckle told his assistant. "I want results, not excuses."

Fort Hall was a fairly busy trading post. Roy Benson walked out of the mercantile—the back corner of which was taken up with the telegraph desk—and stood on the front porch, surveying the small cluster of buildings, which included a livery stable, a saloon, and the army outpost. There was also a small house where a man lived who purported to be a doctor and a dentist and a barber all wrapped up into one.

Benson considered Kent Arbuckle's reply telegram.

It was terse and spoke in code, but Benson understood plain enough.

Wagons.

Destroy them.

But Benson was stuck with the same old problem. Plausible deniability. The railroad couldn't be implicated. Bandits burn one wagon. Sure. A random rockslide sends an unfortunate boulder rolling down a mountain slope. It happens.

So . . . something else. Something plausible. Nothing to do with Arbuckle or the railroad.

Zeke Hawkins emerged from the mercantile behind him, lighting the nickel cigar he'd just purchased. He puffed, shook out the match, then tossed it aside and asked, "Now what?"

"Now I gotta think," Benson said. "I think better with whiskey."

They walked over to the saloon, a dank place called the Saber for the cavalry sword that hung on the wall behind the bar. They ordered a bottle and claimed a table. It was late afternoon, drifting into evening, and those finished with their day were beginning to wander in. Benson figured the place would soon be shoulder to shoulder, so they'd need to keep their voices down.

Benson recapped the situation for Hawkins.

"I get it," Hawkins said impatiently. "Destroy wagons, but make it look accidental . . . or at least like it's got nothing to do with the railroad."

"Right."

"Okay then," Hawkins said. "So how?"

"That's what we're trying to figure out." Benson filled the shot glasses.

They drank.

And thought.

The saloon filled up.

A half dozen horse soldiers entered, U.S. Cavalry, enlisted men. They squeezed in at the bar and had the look of men who'd come a long way, slumped shoulders and road dust. Weary men, saddle sore and thirsty.

Next, an officer walked in, a burly sergeant at his side. They stood a moment, looking at the crowd, probably not liking their chances of snagging a table. The beginnings of a possible idea began knocking around inside Benson's head. He'd heard rumors recently and wanted to have them confirmed or denied, and the young officer might just be able to accommodate him.

Benson stood and waved the two men over. "Lieutenant, over here."

"What are you doing?" Hawkins said in a low voice.

"Just play along."

The two men crossed the room and arrived at Benson's table.

"Join us," Benson said. "Chairs are a bit hard to come by this time in the evening. The least we can do for our men in uniform."

"Obliged, sir," the young officer said. "I'm called Foster. This is Sergeant Isaiah Parks."

Benson introduced himself and Hawkins.

The bartender brought over two more glasses, and Benson filled everyone up.

"I infer you and your men have been out in the field," Benson said.

"For quite longer than I care to be, if I'm being honest," Foster said. "Six weeks out of Fort Keogh."

"That's a far piece from here," Hawkins commented.

"I was obliged to give chase to a bunch of Indians." Foster finished his whiskey and set the empty glass back on the table. "My orders were to keep after them as long as the trail didn't go cold. Sadly, it looks like we may be at the end of our chase with little to show for it."

Benson's ears perked up. This was exactly the topic for which he'd hoped to attain further details. He filled the lieutenant's glass again. "I thought the Indian uprisings had been quashed in this region and everything was relatively quiet."

"Quashed in an official way, yes," Foster said. "But some outcasts from various tribes have found each other and have been causing trouble. A dozen or so. Fifteen at the most. Really, they're just another bandit gang who only *happen* to be Indians. As far as the actual tribes are concerned, everything's peaceful."

"A distressing thing to hear," Benson said. "My partner and I have a long journey ahead of us. I'd hate to think we'll ride smack into a gang of Indian bandits. Whereabouts are they?"

"The *whereabouts* are exactly the problem," Foster admitted. "They're a sneaky lot, even for Indians. Every time we think we have them, they melt away, scatter. Then they rob somebody or hit a farmhouse, and we pick up the trail again. But this time . . ." Foster shook his head and sighed. "Well, maybe the trail's just too cold now. They've been laying low, probably somewhere . . ." Foster turned to the other man. "Where did Slow River say they were headed, Sergeant?"

"They're between here and Boise," Isaiah Parks said. "Slow River thinks they might turn south. That's what the lieutenant and me and the rest of the troops are doing here. Just waiting to see if Slow River and his boys can pick up the trail."

"Slow River?" Benson asked.

"Our Indian scout," Foster said. "He can track a gnat through a thunderstorm, but Tall Elk's been giving him trouble."

"I take it this Tall Elk is the leader of the Indian bandits?" Hawkins said.

"You take it correctly," Foster confirmed. "And a crafty one, let me tell you. He was behind bars, waiting to swing from a rope, but he broke out of his cell and took five other captive Indians with him. Killed a guard in the process. I guess he lulled us into a false sense of security by behaving so well those months he was in custody."

Hawkins shook his head. "Should have hanged the skunk right away. Why wait?"

"He got himself wounded when we went out to grab him. The U.S. government prefers a man to be healthy when he's hanged," Foster said. "Anyway, I guess Tall Elk got more than he bargained for when he went up against Tomahawk Callahan."

"Tomahawk Callahan?" Benson had been caught by surprise and inwardly chastised himself for blurting the name.

Foster laughed. "I'm not surprised you've heard of him. All the newspapers have been talking about that crazy race with the railroad."

Relief flooded Benson. Of course. The newspaper stories were how Benson had heard of Callahan. Just like anyone else.

Still . . .

This might be a good time to get some additional information from people who actually knew the man.

"This Callahan fellow must be quite a character," Benson said.

"I was surprised to hear he'd be part of a wager like this," Foster said. "He doesn't strike me as the type. Sergeant, you know him better than I do."

Parks shrugged. "I tend to agree with you, Lieutenant, but I will say this. He's not the sort of man to shrink from a challenge. It might not be the sort of thing he'd usually do, but if he had a good reason, he'd see it through and do his best. He's tough and courageous but quiet about it. Callahan's no braggart."

Benson let that information sink in. If he should ever have the need to go up against Callahan face-to-face, maybe it would be useful. They engaged in small talk for another half hour or so, and Benson got a little more information out of them concerning where Tall Elk and his band might be headed. In Benson's estimation, the sergeant's information was probably more reliable than the lieutenant's, but between the two of them, Benson gleaned enough information to help him begin his search.

Benson bid the two cavalrymen a good evening, then

left the saloon with Hawkins in tow. There was no hotel, but Foster suggested a boarding house on the edge of town where a widow woman rented rooms.

The sun had gone down. The night was warm but not oppressively so.

"Now what?" Hawkins asked.

"Too late to head out now," Benson said. "Let's see if the widow has rooms. Then in the morning we'll get to work."

Hawkins' eyes narrowed. "Get to work how? Did we come up with a plan, and I missed it?"

"Isn't it obvious," Benson asked. "We're going to arrange an Indian attack."

CHAPTER 23

Callahan leaned over the cookfire, squinting into an iron pot full of beans. He tossed in a chunk of bacon. Usually, he was more than happy to leave meal preparation to Cookie Mayfield, but the old wagon train veteran had yet to return from escorting Anna Masters to Fort Hall and back so she could telegraph the latest update to her newspaper. Callahan wondered if the near-death of the entire Grainger family, their wagon smashed to kindling down a mountainside, would excite her readers.

He spooned beans onto a tin plate and began to eat. He was halfway through his meal when Cookie showed up with Anna Masters riding his horse.

"I was beginning to wonder," Callahan said. "It's past dark."

Masters dismounted and rubbed her backside. "Thanks for lending me your horse. Sorry we're late, but I interviewed a couple of cavalry soldiers."

"Oh? What outfit?"

Masters frowned. "I didn't think to ask that, but they're out of Fort Keogh."

Callahan sat up at the mention of Fort Keogh. "Who

was the officer in charge? Clark or a green kid named Foster?"

"I only talked to a couple of troopers," she said. "Didn't ask about the officers."

Now Callahan wished he'd gone to the fort with them. It would have been good to share a drink with Isaiah Parks. Of course, the sergeant might not even be with them. For a brief moment, he considered riding to the fort to see. His horse was still saddled.

Callahan discarded the idea immediately. Even if he rode directly to the fort and back again without dallying, it would get him back late, and wagon trains were an early morning business.

"Did the soldiers have anything interesting to say?" Callahan asked.

"They've been chasing some Indian called Tall Elk."

Callahan's eyes shot wide. "Tall Elk?"

"You've heard of him?"

Callahan hunched over his plate of beans. "Yeah. I guess you could say that."

Anna Masters narrowed her eyes. "There's more, isn't there?"

"Nope."

"Tomahawk Callahan," she said sternly. "You're a rotten liar."

Cookie laughed and took his and Callahan's horses by the reins. "I'll take the saddles off and get these nags put up for the night. I can see you two have a lot to talk about."

Callahan scowled at him. "Thanks."

When Cookie had gone, Anna Masters sat down and scooted in close to Callahan. "Okay. Dish."

"Look, I'm not that interesting."

"The hell you aren't," she said. "Or if you weren't before, you better believe you are now. My newspaper keeps getting letters wanting to know more about Tomahawk Callahan."

Callahan rolled his eyes and groaned.

"They want to know more about the hero who jumped into a raging river to save a little girl," Masters insisted. "And they *really* want to know how a man earned a nickname like Tomahawk."

"A lot of it is just being in the right place at the right time," Callahan said. "Trust me. There's nothing more heroic about me than there is any other man in the same situation."

Anna Masters leaned in and lowered her voice. "But we're not talking about any other man, are we? We're talking about you. Maybe my readers won't even care. Maybe I'm just asking all these questions for my own curiosity. Because I'm a nosy woman, and I want to know."

Callahan was acutely aware of how close she was, her body language, with her leaning in, eyelids heavy, and frankly, she didn't smell half bad, and all he'd have to do is lean back, meet her halfway, and . . .

He stood abruptly, cleared his throat, and went to the fire. "Beans are good. Want a plate of beans?" He scooped another spoonful onto his plate.

She grinned, shook her head, and produced a pencil and a pad of paper. "Readers don't care about beans, Callahan. Tall Elk. Talk."

Callahan briefly related the story of his duel with Tall Elk and the Indian's capture, downplaying anything the newspaperwoman might interpret as heroics. It wasn't in his nature to talk about himself.

"What I want to know is why Tall Elk isn't behind bars where he's supposed to be," Callahan said.

Masters told Callahan everything she'd heard from the soldiers, how the Indian had escaped and now led a gang of bandits and was somewhere in the area.

It bothered Callahan how hard he'd worked to capture Tall Elk, even taking an arrow in the shoulder, only to hear he'd escaped again. It bothered him even more to hear that Tall Elk now roamed the area, posing a threat to unsuspecting travelers.

Callahan made the decision to get up earlier than usual the next morning and try to find the troopers. Anything he might be able to find out about Tall Elk's plans could be the tidbit of information that would keep the wagon train safe.

"If you've no more questions, Miss Masters, I should make the rounds," Callahan said. "And then I need to get some shut-eye."

"I'll let you off the hook for now, Tomahawk," Masters said. "But it's still a long way to Salem, and I'll have more questions. My readers want to know all about you."

She started walking away but paused to glance back and shoot him a sly smile. "And so do I."

Callahan took a leisurely stroll around the circle of wagons, nodded to those still awake or exchanged a pleasant word, knowing he'd eventually arrive at the one place he'd intended to go all along.

Becky was cleaning up after dinner. She looked tired, as many did after each long day. Her hair was pulled back. A few strands had broken loose, falling in front of her face. A smudge of ash was on her left cheek from the cookfire.

She looked up, suddenly seeing him. "Oh. Luke."

"Lizzy told me to come around for a visit." He smiled, trying to look charming or at least friendly. He probably just looked like some darn fool.

"Well, Lizzy's asleep," Becky said, her tone neutral. "I'll tell her you stopped by."

"I get the feeling I'm not as welcome around here as I used to be."

"I don't know what you mean," Becky said. "Now if you don't mind, I've got to clean up and get to sleep."

"I thought we could take a walk."

"Why don't you walk with Anna Masters?" Becky suggested. "She's got legs."

"Becky."

"Or you can share a bottle and trade jokes and laugh and have a big old time."

"That was nothing," Callahan said. "She's a news-paperwoman. She was just trying to get friendly with me and Cookie to find out things she could write about in her paper."

"Uh-huh." Becky gathered her dishes and took them to the back of her wagon. "Well, you seemed pretty friendly."

"And what's that to you?"

"Nothing. Why would it be anything to me?" Becky said. "You know, she came to talk to me, too, to ask about my reasons for coming on this trip and how I felt when Lizzy almost drowned, stuff she thought her readers might be interested in . . . but she didn't bring me no bottle of whiskey."

"Was she mean to you or rude?" Callahan asked. "Is that why you dislike her?"

Becky put the dishes in the wagon, then slowly shook her head. "She wasn't rude. That's not why I dislike her. I dislike her because she's . . . nice."

Callahan wasn't sure he'd heard right.

Becky blew out a tired sigh. "She asked me questions. She was interested and respectful the whole time. And I know she's educated. And pretty. And . . . well, what man wouldn't want . . . I mean, of course, it's only natural you would . . ."

Callahan took Becky by the shoulders and pulled her close. He didn't even know what he was doing. Some instinct had taken hold of him, and the next thing he knew he was leaning down, and her head was tilted up, and then their lips met.

A hesitation, almost nothing, so brief it couldn't be measured by anything but an eye blink or a heartbeat, but then she was kissing him back—hard—her arms going around him, holding him tight.

They eased apart, and she put her head against his chest. She was crying softly.

"What's wrong?"

She nestled into him, and he put his arms around her, rocking gently.

"I don't know," she said. "Nothing."

Callahan didn't say anything. It was a lesson he'd learned long ago. If you don't know what to say, keep your fool mouth shut.

"I don't know what you expect," Becky told him.

"What you think I am. What do you see when you look at me? Some painted up . . . somebody I'm trying not to be anymore maybe. I don't know what you want. It worries me."

Callahan lifted her chin with a finger so they were looking in each other's eyes.

"I see a girl in pigtails all grown up," he told her. "A woman brave enough to do what she had to do for her child. And tough enough to go halfway across the country for a better life, dragging a sewing machine along with her."

She put her head back against his chest, letting out a long sigh, her breath warm, tears wetting his shirt.

"I'd still be there," she said. "If you hadn't walked into that saloon, I'd still be right there wishing I was somewhere else but not doing a darn thing about it. And then I saw you and remembered a whole life I used to live, a whole different person I used to be."

They stayed like that for a bit, not speaking, holding on to one another and swaying with the breeze.

"This probably looks kind of funny without the music," Callahan said.

"Shush," she said. "Don't talk. Just let it be nice a minute."

Callahan shut up and let it be nice.

CHAPTER 24

Callahan saddled his horse and was on his way to Fort Hall while the rest of the wagon train was just waking up and brewing coffee. A cool morning and moist. It would warm soon enough as the sun climbed into the sky.

People went about their morning routines in and around the fort. Callahan asked around and soon learned he'd just missed the cavalrymen by a little more than an hour. He considered riding hard to catch up with them, but the folks around Fort Hall had offered Callahan conflicting reports on which way the horse soldiers might be headed. Some said they'd given up looking for Tall Elk and were headed back to Fort Keogh. Others said they'd gone west to meet up with their Indian scouts. Callahan couldn't find anyone who'd heard this from the soldiers directly. It was always someone who'd gotten the news from somebody else. At least nobody had claimed the troopers had taken off north or south for unknown reasons.

There was no point in chasing them back toward Fort Keogh, Callahan decided. If he chose wrong, then he'd be going out of his way. If he headed west and didn't find them, he'd at least be going in the same direction as his wagon train and could catch up sooner.

He left Fort Hall at a gallop, the sun still rising behind him.

A couple hours later, he walked the horse, letting it rest. Still no sign of the cavalrymen, and Callahan was beginning to think he'd guessed wrong and the troopers were on their way back to Fort Keogh, after all.

He paused and drank from a canteen. The day had grown hot. He took off his borrowed hat and wiped the sweat from his forehead. He'd rest the horse a little longer, then mount up again and angle himself back toward the wagon train. Hopefully, they hadn't gotten into trouble without him.

He grabbed the saddle horn and was about to heave himself up again when movement caught his eye. He eased his hands down, slowly, not letting on anything was wrong. He pretended to adjust the saddle straps, then eased around to the other side of the animal, glancing side-eyed into the woods off the road.

Whatever he'd seen before wasn't there now or, more likely, had ducked out of sight. His instinct told him the movement had been human, not some animal. He took the horse by the reins and began walking again, keeping the animal between him and the person he supposed was hiding in the woods. He thought about riding away fast, but knew he'd make a pretty target sitting tall in the saddle. Better to head on down the road a bit and then mount up and ride away to—

Another flash of movement, this time on the other side of the road. Callahan felt sure he'd seen buckskin.

That could mean an Indian, although Callahan was wearing buckskin himself. It could be anybody. If there were two of them, then there might be more he hadn't spotted yet. He wondered how long they'd watch him before striking. Whatever he was going to do, Callahan thought he'd better make it quick.

He thought about mounting up again. If he leaned low and rode fast, he wouldn't be so much of a target.

But that was no guarantee, and even if he escaped, he'd still be left with the mystery of who'd been stalking him.

He walked a bit more, sizing up the situation, catching an occasional glimpse of movement but nothing definitive. The one on the left side of the road was ahead of him, the one on the right lagging behind. Callahan formed a plan.

Not a *great* plan, but it would do on short notice.

He veered toward the right side of the road. Not fast, nothing sudden, just as if he were idly drifting. He wanted a spot where the trees and undergrowth grew a little more thickly. A few seconds later, he found a good spot.

Callahan slowed down as if he was going to look at something on the ground, then suddenly dashed into the woods to his right, leading his horse by the reins. He scrambled through the underbrush, took his Henry rifle from its sheath, and gave his horse a light slap on the rump. The horse took off deeper into the woods. It was a good animal, and Callahan knew it wouldn't go far. He ducked into a thicket.

If his plan worked, those stalking him would think he'd ridden off with the horse. If his plan didn't work, then Callahan would be a sitting duck with no way to escape.

The one ahead of him on the left side of the road hesitated only a moment before crossing and following his horse into the brush, a young Indian brave in buckskin and moccasins, carrying a Winchester crossways against his chest. Callahan stayed hidden and let him pass.

The one behind came along a few seconds later at a brisk jog. No longer trying to stay concealed. He looked similar to the other brave but maybe even a year or two younger.

Callahan lifted the Henry and took aim, the barrel of the rifle tracking the brave as he jogged.

He hesitated, some instinct telling him not to squeeze the trigger, not just yet.

Then Callahan felt the cold barrel of a gun pressed to his flesh just behind his left ear. He froze.

"Please don't shoot my nephew," said the man behind him.

Callahan smiled, recognizing the voice. "You sure can move quiet when you want to, Slow River."

Callahan felt the rifle barrel removed. He stood and turned, and both men clasped arms.

"It is good to see you again, friend Callahan," Slow River said. "We are both far from home, yes?"

Callahan felt it was true, even more so since he wasn't exactly sure where *home* was these days. Back in Kansas City? Fort Keogh? Maybe the trail was his home now. The West itself. A dumb romantic notion, maybe.

The other brave—the one Slow River had referred

to as his nephew—came to stand with them, looking embarrassed.

"The faster you move, the less you see, Bright Moon," Slow River said, chastising his nephew. "Tomahawk Callahan is craftier than the average white man. He fooled you with an easy trick."

Callahan laughed. "But not crafty enough for you, Slow River."

The old Indian shrugged. "When you've seen as many winters as I have . . ."

The other brave returned, leading Callahan's horse.

"My grandson. He is called Black Feather," Slow River said. "Both boys have potential but have much still to learn."

The two braves exchanged chagrined looks.

"I heard Tall Elk escaped," Callahan said. "I guess you're out here trying to find him for Lieutenant Foster."

"We've found him." Slow River said. "Come see if you have the time."

"I'll make the time," Callahan told him.

"We must climb to the top of that ridge." Slow River gestured northward. "Then we shall see."

He set a brisk pace for a man his age. Callahan followed, leading his horse, Bright Moon and Black Feather right behind. They climbed steadily and paused near the top.

"Bright Moon and Black Feather will wait here with your horse," Slow River said. "Come with me and stay low."

They reached the top, going to their bellies to look over the side without being seen.

A small camp below. Indians. Ten or twelve of them,

some coming and going, others milling about a cookfire. He thought he saw horses in a stand of trees. None of the Indians looked familiar. Certainly, none of them were Tall Elk.

"This is Tall Elk's band," Slow River said.

"Will you send for Lieutenant Foster and his men?" Callahan asked.

"This is the question I have asked myself," Slow River told him. "The horse soldiers are a large group of men. They use the road and can be seen coming from far away. Tall Elk's bandits flee as a group or scatter, and Foster cannot get close. For two days, I have watched, hoping to catch sight of Tall Elk, but I have not seen him. My thought was that if I could kill or capture Tall Elk, it would be enough. The rest of the band would disperse without Tall Elk's leadership. There would be no need to bring Foster and the horse soldiers."

"Is Tall Elk hiding?" Callahan asked.

Slow River shook his head. "He would not think to hide, for he does not know he is being watched. My nephew and grandson were clumsy with you because you are a white man, and so they underestimated you. Not so with Tall Elk and his band. We have been careful and have stayed concealed."

"If he's not hiding, then where is he?"

"I fear he is scouting his next victim," Slow River said. "Perhaps a stagecoach. Or possibly he will raid a farmhouse. I have not enough men to both watch this camp and search for Tall Elk."

"I wish I could help," Callahan said. "But I don't work for the army anymore."

"We have heard this," Slow River said. "I wish good

luck to you and your wagon train. You should not fear Tall Elk. He only attacks the weak and the few. Many wagons means many people and many guns. Have a safe journey." A sly grin. "It would make my heart glad if you were to embarrass the iron horse people."

Callahan chuckled. "I'll do my best. But what about you? What's next?"

"We will wait a little longer," Slow River said. "Perhaps he will show himself, although the spirits whisper that I shall go back empty-handed. I will not bring Foster and the soldiers. It would not do any good. Tall Elk will be someone else's problem."

"I wish you well."

"Be well, friend Callahan."

Slow River escorted Callahan back to the road and wished him good travels once more before vanishing back into the woods.

Callahan caught up with the wagon train a couple hours later.

Cookie Mayfield brought his horse alongside Callahan's. "Accomplish anything?"

Callahan shrugged. "Not sure."

He told Cookie about his encounter with Slow River and the news about Tall Elk.

Cookie's brow furrowed with concern. "This Indian gonna cause us trouble?"

"I don't think so," Callahan assured him. "Slow River told me that Tall Elk likes easy pickings. A wagon train this size might be a bit much for him."

"That's a relief," Cookie said. "The last thing we need is Indian trouble."

They rode until nightfall, circled the wagons, and made camp.

Callahan made the rounds. People were friendly and seemed in a decent mood.

These are good folks, Callahan thought. *They deserve to get to Salem without any more bother.*

Callahan was determined to get them there.

He was heading to Becky's wagon when a surprise stopped him short. "Mr. Johansen?"

Pete Johansen looked up and offered Callahan a curt nod. "Callahan."

Callahan blinked. "Mr. Johansen, what are you doing here?"

"Huh?" Johansen looked confused at first, then figured out what Callahan was asking. "Oh. Well . . . yeah."

They'd all gotten used to the cranky old Pete Johansen making camp off by himself every night. Seeing his wagon in the circle along with the others was more of a shock to Callahan than hearing Tall Elk had escaped from the army.

A little girl stuck her head out of the back of Johansen's wagon and waved. "A good evening to you, Mr. Callahan!"

Callahan immediately recognized one of the Grainger children. "Uh . . . Mr. Johansen . . ."

Matt Grainger's son arrived at that moment with an armload of firewood. "I'll stoke the cookfire, Mr. Johansen."

Callahan grinned at Johansen.

The older man shuffled awkwardly. "Well, I'm just one man and had this wagon all to myself, and with

Grainger's wagon in pieces down the mountainside . . ."
A shrug.

Pete Johansen and Matt Grainger had picked their
way down that mountainside, gathering whatever they
could salvage of the Grainger family belongings. The
men who'd been more than happy to trade blows weeks
ago at the beginning were now comrades. The people of
the wagon train knew they were all in this together.

Callahan was proud of them.

"Anyway . . . well, I don't need that much room,
really," Johansen said. "No problem to squeeze in a few
more."

The man clearly felt awkward, as if embarrassed to
be caught doing a good deed.

Callahan leaned in and whispered, "Don't worry, Mr.
Johansen. I won't tell anyone you're really a nice man."

Johansen turned away, rolling his eyes.

Callahan chuckled and walked on.

He found Becky's wagon. She spotted him and
brightened, coming to him, her steps light. She tilted her
head up, obviously inviting a kiss.

He obliged her, brushing his lips against her. A nice
kiss, nothing lurid.

That didn't stop Lizzy from giggling as she spied on
them from the back of the wagon. "Naughty!"

"Lizzy!" Becky scolded, but there was no heat in it.

The girl giggled again and vanished into the depths
of the Conestoga wagon.

"Have you eaten?" she asked.

"Cookie's whipping up something," he said. "I'm
making the rounds."

"Come eat with us tomorrow night."

"I will," he promised.

They talked for a few minutes, nothing important, just pleasantries.

Finally, Callahan said, "I'd better get to bed. Tomorrow—"

"Comes early," Becky finished for him. "Just like yesterday.

"And the day before that."

He kissed her again, then went back to his own cookfire and ate dinner with Cookie.

Callahan unloaded his Peacemaker and cleaned it. The gun wasn't especially dirty, but Callahan felt like having something to do with his hands. A monotonous chore was often good for sitting quietly and thinking. He remembered the derringer he'd taken off one of the men who had attacked Cookie Mayfield. He hadn't thought much about the little gun, but he carried it in his front right pocket now out of habit. He took out the .41 short round and cleaned the derringer. He cleaned the Henry rifle, too. Everything shipshape.

He closed his eyes that night, feeling for the first time in a long time that everything was going to be okay. The world wouldn't come down around their ears. Salem waited.

Callahan fell asleep almost immediately and enjoyed a long and undisturbed slumber.

CHAPTER 25

The three Indians stepped out of the woods surprisingly close and startled Roy Benson.

Zeke Hawkins reached for his six-shooter.

"Don't," Benson warned. "I think they want to talk."

The two men waited for the Indians to approach.

They reined in their horses and the lead Indian—an older man, now that Benson got a good look at him—did the talking.

"We are scouts for the army," the Indian said. "I must warn you that there might be danger ahead."

Benson raised an eyebrow. "Oh, really."

"There is a gang of Indian bandits in the area," the old Indian told them. "Two men traveling would be an attractive target for them."

"This would be Tall Elk then."

The Indian looked only slightly surprised. "Then you have heard."

"We talked to soldiers at Fort Hall."

"You spoke with Lieutenant Foster?"

Benson nodded. "That's right."

"Please, sir, can you tell me if the soldiers have gone back to Fort Keogh?"

Benson shook his head. "Sorry. They were still at Fort Hall when we left. They might still be there. Or maybe they moved out. I couldn't say."

The Indian looked disappointed. "I suppose we shall catch up with them sooner or later."

"Can you tell us exactly where Tall Elk and his band are?" Benson asked. "So we can make sure to avoid them."

The Indian explained where Tall Elk's camp was hidden. "The road forks a few miles from here. If you take the northern route, you should be able to avoid Tall Elk and his braves."

Benson thanked the Indians, then he and Hawkins watched them ride back east.

"Now what?" Hawkins asked.

"What do you think?" Benson replied. "We go see Tall Elk."

"The two of us ride right into the middle of a band of Indians?"

"Afraid?"

"Not wanting to get scalped isn't being afraid," Hawkins said. "It's simple prudence."

"This isn't some tribal war," Benson explained. "They're just bandits who happen to be Indians. And what do bandits want?"

"Money?"

"Right," Benson said. "They want a good score just like the rest of us. We just need to explain to them there's a way for them to get a lot more than they would get robbing us."

"If we get the chance to make our pitch," Hawkins said. "It's hard to explain anything to them if we're full of arrows."

"Nobody promised there wouldn't be risk."

"Fine. Lead on."

They soon reached the fork but didn't take the northern route. It didn't take long before they realized they were being watched.

"Off to the left," Hawkins said.

Benson nodded. "I see him."

Bird calls flew back and forth across the road. *Not bad*, Benson thought. They almost sounded real. It was soon clear that the Indians were all around them.

The two men reined in their horses and waited.

A few minutes later, three Indians stepped out into the road ahead of them. Another four behind.

"Just for the record, I'm the one that said this was a bad idea," Hawkins reminded him.

"We're here to talk to Tall Elk," Benson called.

The three in front of them put their heads together and jabbered back and forth for a few seconds. Then one ran back into the woods.

"Just keep your hand away from your gun," Benson said.

Hawkins frowned. "I know."

They waited.

The one who'd run off returned, bringing another Indian with him.

"I am Dances in the Rain," the newcomer said. "I speak the white man's tongue."

"I am Benson, and this is my associate Hawkins," Benson told the Indian. "We come with an offer for Tall Elk."

"Tell me," Dances in the Rain said. "I will decide if it is something that might interest Tall Elk or not."

Benson shook his head. "Sorry, friend. Our words are only for Tall Elk's ears."

"Perhaps we will simply kill you now," Dances in the Rain said. "Then the words from your forked tongue need never trouble anyone's ears ever again."

"Then you will have deprived Tall Elk of a great opportunity," Benson warned him. "If you kill us, then what have you gained? Our horses, guns, money? This is a small reward compared with what we wish to offer Tall Elk. We are not like the other white men. We're not with the blue coats or others who wish to bring you to justice. It's not our justice, but theirs. We're like you. We seek opportunities for reward, and my offer will benefit us as well as you. But Tall Elk must hear my words and decide for himself."

Dances in the Rain looked back at his brethren, and they exchanged words. Benson could only guess what they were saying, and he hoped Hawkins wasn't right about the situation after all. Some of the Indians carried bows and arrows, but he saw at least three rifles. He was reasonably fast on the draw, and he began thinking which man he'd go after first.

"We will bring you to Tall Elk," Dances in the Rain said.

Benson breathed a sigh of relief.

"You must dismount," the Indian told them. "And hand over your guns."

Hawkins muttered a curse.

"We have not come to threaten you," Benson assured him.

"You will hand over your guns," he said. "Or we will kill you and take the guns. Decide now."

"Fine," Benson said. "Just take it easy."

Benson and Hawkins dismounted and handed over their six-shooters. He didn't mention the .32 revolver, and they didn't search him, so he decided to keep it just in case. An Indian led their horses several paces behind, and Dances in the Rain led them into the woods. Armed Indians walked on all sides of them in case either Benson or Hawkins took it into his head to make a run for it. They were committed now, their fates in the hands of Tall Elk.

Hawkins bent his head toward Benson and whispered, "I figured they'd blindfold us."

"Why?"

"So we can't tell anyone where their camp is."

"Think it through," Benson said. "Either we strike a deal with Tall Elk or they'll make sure we never tell anyone anything ever again."

Hawkins mumbled another curse. "Well, then you'd better talk fast and pretty and convince him to take our deal."

"That's the plan."

They entered a clearing where another half dozen Indians standing around a fire turned their heads to gawk at the white men. They crossed the clearing to where a man sat on a rock against the wide trunk of a red cedar tree.

This had to be Tall Elk, Benson figured. He sat with his back straight, chin up, an arrogant expression on his face.

Benson took an immediate dislike to the man. Under other circumstances, he would have liked to smack that smug expression right off his face. But this wasn't other circumstances. They were surrounded by Indians. Benson's fate was completely in Tall Elk's hands.

"Wait here," Dances in the Rain said.

He went to Tall Elk and bent to talk into his ear. Tall Elk's hard eyes turned on Benson and Hawkins, the Indian's expression twisting with contempt.

It occurred again to Benson that he'd made a terrible mistake. He had no idea what sort of man Tall Elk was. Benson had concocted his scheme thinking the same things that motivated him would also be what motivated the Indian. For all Benson knew, Tall Elk might be some bloodthirsty maniac who was more interested in collecting scalps than turning a profit.

If push came to shove, he could try to shoot his way out with the .32. If he could reach a horse, he might have a chance.

A moment later, Dances in the Rain waved them over. Tall Elk appraised the two white men, a sneer on his face.

"So you think to tempt me with some offer," Tall Elk said. "Or perhaps it is a trick to lure me to someplace where the blue coats can put me into chains again."

"This is no trick," Benson assured him. "I want to make a bargain. One which will benefit us both."

"What bargain?" Tall Elk demanded. "Speak quickly.

I have little patience for the white man and his forked tongue."

"Our employer—my *chief*, so to speak—is a great man. A rich man," Benson said. "His name must be kept secret, and for that I apologize. We have a task for the mighty Tall Elk, and for the successful completion of this task, my chief promises gold."

Tall Elk shook his head, frowning. "You are not off to a good start, paleface. A mysterious, unnamed man and his unseen gold. Go on then and spin the rest of your tale. I am curious how much dung you expect me to swallow."

"I know how it sounds," Benson said. "The old saying goes that if something sounds too good to be true, then it probably is. But not in this case."

"Keep talking," Tall Elk told him. "I will be the one to decide what sounds good and what seems true."

"We want you and your men to attack a wagon train," Benson said. "There is one passing through this area even now. My chief has his reasons. All that should matter to you is the gold."

"This task does not appeal to me," Tall Elk said. "Many people in a wagon train. Many guns."

Benson had been afraid Tall Elk might feel that way. Lieutenant Foster had told him that Tall Elk mostly raided small parties or people traveling alone or farmhouses with small families. For all of Tall Elk's posturing as a big man, he didn't quite seem to have the guts for a big risk.

Although Benson doubted it would do any good to put it that way.

"We don't need the entire wagon train defeated," Benson said. "A quick raid should do it. We want you to destroy wagons. Set them on fire or do anything you like. As many as possible, but five or six would be enough to earn your gold. If you raid quickly, you can destroy the wagons and be away before those in the wagon train can get organized and do you any harm."

"What is accomplished by destroying the wagons?" Tall Elk asked.

"If a certain number of wagons are destroyed, then the wagon train will be considered a failure," Benson explained. "This will please my chief."

"Why?"

"Suffice it to say that the people running the wagon train are the enemies of my chief," Benson said.

"But I want to understand why."

"It's enough that you understand the gold," Benson said.

"If your chief has so much gold, then he can hire men to do this," Tall Elk pointed out.

"The blame cannot be laid at the feet of my chief," Benson said. "You and your men are already known to be raiding in the area. It will simply be seen as bad luck for the wagon train."

Tall Elk sat back against the tree trunk, scratching his chin as he thought. Finally, he shook his head and said, "No. I will have no part of this foolishness."

"But the gold," Benson said quickly. "I promise the amount will be—"

"Your promises are words on the wind," Tall Elk said. "A chief wants wagons burned for no reason. These are not even good lies. You must think me a fool. Or you won't tell me the reasons because you think I cannot understand. In which case, you think me a child. This is a blue coat trick."

"It's no trick!" Benson insisted.

"Take these men and kill them," Tall Elk told the other Indians. "Take whatever they have of value. Then strip them and leave their bodies for the carrion eaters."

Benson almost went for his .32 revolver, but he was grabbed roughly from behind, two big Indians, each holding an arm.

The same thing was happening to Hawkins. He managed to wriggle free and throw a punch, catching one of the Indians across the jaw, but three more Indians crowded him, raining down blows with their fists and knocking him to the ground.

Hawkins looked up at Benson with hate in his eyes, a trickle of blood from one corner of his mouth. "Curse you, Benson! I told you this was a dumb idea. We could have gotten at Callahan some other way."

Tall Elk stood, holding up a hand. "Stop!"

The Indians holding Benson stopped dragging him away. The ones hovering over Hawkins ceased their pummeling.

Tall Elk walked to Benson, stopping a foot from him, curiosity in his eyes, but something else smoldered there as well.

"Did he say Callahan?" Tall Elk asked.

Benson nodded. "He leads the wagon train. He is the enemy of my chief."

"*Tomahawk* Callahan?"

"That's him," Benson said.

Tall Elk crossed his arms. Benson could tell something was going on inside the man's head.

"In that case," Tall Elk said. "Let us talk of gold."

CHAPTER 26

The terrain was about to get difficult again, moving through another mountain pass, the road narrowing with no convenient place to circle the wagons, so Cookie Mayfield suggested stopping early.

"If we start through now, we won't get to the other side before dark," Cookie said. "Better to stop now, give everybody some extra rest, and then make a run at it bright and early."

Callahan didn't like wasting daylight, but he yielded to the older man's experience. They found a spot wide and flat enough. Callahan called a halt and passed the word to circle the wagons as usual. As far as morale was concerned, it turned out to be a good decision. For weeks, the routine had been the same. Stuck in a wagon all day, sunup to sundown. Then just enough time to make a meal or tend to the animals before falling exhausted into sleep. Callahan had seen haunted looks in many of the men and women as he rode up and down the column of wagons each day, people in a daze, hypnotized by the relentless monotony.

Now, stopping for the day with a few extra hours of

sunshine remaining, many of the wagon train folks were transformed. Children ran through the long grass, bright-eyed and giggling. Adults chatted idly with those in neighboring wagons.

Callahan wasn't immune. He took the saddle off his horse, wiped the animal down, and took a leisurely stroll, knowing where he'd end up.

He found Becky stacking wood for her cookfire.

"A little early for dinner," Callahan said.

She smiled at him. "Habit, I guess."

"How about a walk?"

"Okay."

"Bring Lizzy," he suggested.

"Come on, Lizzy," Becky called. "We're going to stretch our legs."

They walked through the grass in no particular hurry toward a line of trees. Lizzy ran ahead of them, stooping occasionally to pluck a wildflower, purple-blue camas by the look of them, although Callahan was no expert on flowers. Soon Lizzy had a fistful of them.

Becky's slender hand slipped into Callahan's. Her hands were soft in places and callused in others. They probably hadn't been rough like that back at the saloon where she'd worked. Velvet had been softer. Callahan liked Becky's hands better. They were honest hands. He squeezed, and she squeezed back.

They stopped short of the woods, lingering near the tree line.

"I wonder what sort of bird that is," Becky said. "Did you hear it?"

He hadn't. His own thoughts were louder than the world around him.

"There it is again."

Callahan went rigid, and he had to stop himself from reaching for his Peacemaker. He relaxed his posture, eyes slowly moving across the tree line in front of him.

"I wish I could see it," Becky said. "I just love birds with brightly colored feathers."

The bird called again, and from deeper in the woods another answered.

Callahan casually draped an arm around Becky's shoulders, drew her close, and leaned in as if he were going to give her a peck on the cheek. Instead, he whispered, "I need you to take Lizzy back to the wagons. Hurry, but don't *look* like you're hurrying."

Becky tensed. "Luke, is something wrong? What's—"

"Just act normally."

Becky let out a long breath. "Okay."

"Go on then," Callahan said. "Take Lizzy back."

"Lizzy, honey, let's go," Becky called.

"But I'm picking more of these flowers."

"Lizzy."

The little girl must have sensed something in her mother's voice. Lizzy immediately stopped picking flowers and went to her mother, taking her hand.

"We'll see Mr. Callahan later," Becky assured the little girl.

Lizzy turned and gave Callahan a wave. "See you later, Mr. Callahan."

Callahan smiled and nodded. "See you later."

He watched them go for a few moments. Becky did exactly as instructed, walking a straight line back toward the wagon train but proceeding at a normal pace, no hint that anything was awry.

Callahan turned and took a couple of slow steps back toward the tree line. He bent and picked up a couple of dead branches, then continued along the edge of the woods, head down as if looking for more firewood but eyes up and scanning the woods. He heard the so-called bird calls a few more times but made a point not to react to them. He caught a few glimpses. He thought there were at least three of them, but there could have been a hundred for all he knew if they were staying hidden.

When his arms were full of firewood, he turned and walked slowly back toward the circle of wagons. This was the moment he was most nervous. He guessed his broad back made an inviting target. He braced himself for the hiss of an arrow cutting through the air or the crack of a rifle shot.

Nothing happened.

He reached the wagons and passed Pete Johansen.

"Mr. Johansen, can you find Matt Grainger and bring him to the chuckwagon? I'd like a word."

Johansen raised an eyebrow. "Trouble?"

"Maybe."

Callahan found Cookie at the chuckwagon, getting his pots and pans ready. Billy Thorndyke leaned against the wagon, filling Cookie's ears with a story about a girl he once knew.

Callahan dropped the firewood. "Billy, round up the boys, will you? We might have a problem."

"Sure thing, boss." Billy jogged away to find the others.

"You got bad news, don't you?" Cookie said.

"Indians." Callahan explained what he'd seen and heard near the woods.

"Huh." Cookie scratched behind one ear. "Could be they don't want any trouble. Maybe just having a look-see at the wagon train."

"Maybe," Callahan said. "But I've got a lot more experience with Indians than I do wagon trains. The way they were birdcalling each other gave me a bad feeling."

Billy Thorndyke returned with his brother Ike and Clancy Davenport just as Johansen arrived with Matt Grainger.

Callahan explained about the Indians.

Grainger's eyes popped wide. "Shouldn't we get out of here?"

"Tell me how fast you think these wagons can move, Mr. Grainger," Callahan chided.

"Sorry." Grainger looked embarrassed. "It's just . . . well . . . my wife and kids."

"It's a lot of wives and kids, Mr. Grainger. I understand," Callahan told him. "My job is to protect all of us, and that's why I need your help."

"Just tell us what to do, Callahan," Johansen said.

"Get everyone inside the circle of wagons," Callahan said. "Nothing panicked or rushed. Don't let on like anything's out of the ordinary. Have your womenfolk start on supper just like everything's normal. Then any man with a rifle needs to line up on the north side, but tell them to stay hidden. They're hoping to surprise us, but we'll turn the tables."

"Just the north side?" Clancy asked. "What if they surround us, hit us from every direction?"

"If there's enough of them to surround us, then it might not matter what we do," Callahan said gravely. "But I've got some ideas on that. Billy, get word to the sheepherders and the cattlemen. They can come inside the wagons and take cover if they like, but I suspect they'll want to protect their livestock. Okay, everyone. You know what to do. Get to it."

They all left in a hurry. Callahan could tell they were nervous. They'd all heard stories about Indian raids.

"I've been back and forth on the Oregon Trail more times than I can count. Never been attacked by Indians even once," Cookie said. "Guess it was bound to happen sooner or later."

"We might get lucky yet," Callahan told him. "Maybe it's like you said. They're just curious about the wagon train and want a look-see."

But in Callahan's gut, he knew it wasn't true.

Tall Elk watched Dances in the Rain emerge from the woods and walk toward the new camp the Indians had set up to be near the wagon train. Depending on what Dances in the Rain had to report, they would attack soon. The white man Benson had promised an astonishing amount of gold, so much so that Tall Elk again suspected it was some kind of trick.

Not that it mattered. Tall Elk and the rest of the band were in hiding and waiting for Dances in the Rain and the other scouts to report.

This was Tall Elk's chance for vengeance. It was because of Tomahawk Callahan that Tall Elk had been captured by the blue coats. It was Callahan's fault that Tall Elk had been banished from his own tribe and now lived as an outlaw. Tall Elk fully intended to collect his gold from Benson, and woe unto the man if it was, in fact, some sort of trick.

But above all else, Tomahawk Callahan had to die.

"What did you see?" Tall Elk asked.

"The wagons have circled," Dances in the Rain said. "They make camp."

"So early?"

"I think they do not want to try going through the pass so late in the day. The sun would set before they could make it to the other side."

"This makes sense," Tall Elk said. "Were you seen?"

"No," Dances in the Rain told him. "They go about their business. They cook food and tend their animals. If we attack, we will take them completely by surprise. I left two braves to keep watch. They will tell us if anything changes."

"And did you see . . . him?"

"Perhaps," Dances in the Rain said. "I have never seen the man before, so I cannot be certain. But the man I saw had a tomahawk stuck in his belt. He had the bearing of a leader."

Tall Elk considered this. He knew of no other white man who carried a tomahawk. Surely, this was Callahan. It *had* to be him. Tall Elk had fourteen braves in his band. The settlers in the wagon train had them outnumbered and outgunned. Surprise was key. The men would look to their women and children. That would divide their attention.

"Tell half the braves to prepare fire arrows," Tall Elk said. "They will torch as many wagons as possible while the rest keep the settlers pinned down with rifle fire. We will strike fast and be away before they can get organized."

"It shall be done," Dances in the Rain said.

"One more thing," Tall Elk said seriously. "No one is to touch the man with the tomahawk. Callahan is mine."

"The cattlemen and sheepherders want to guard their animals, just like you thought, boss," Billy Thorndyke reported. "But they appreciate the warning. They've got their rifles ready, and they're hidden. If the Indians try for the livestock instead of hitting the wagons, they'll be as ready as they can be."

Callahan wasn't surprised. Those men didn't bring those animals halfway across the country just to have them slaughtered or stolen by an Indian raiding party.

"Okay," Callahan said. "Get your brother and Clancy and get back here double-quick. I've got a job for you boys."

"Back soon, boss!" Billy took off running.

Pete Johansen passed him coming the other way.

"Are the men in place?" Callahan asked him.

"Situated as best we can manage," Johansen replied.

"How are they fixed?"

"A half dozen with good repeaters," Johansen said. "Winchesters. Or Henrys like yours. I'm surprised how many have army surplus trapdoor Springfields. They got 'em cheap, I reckon."

"Those are single shot," Callahan said with concern.

"You don't have to tell me."

"Tell them to hold fire until I give the signal," Callahan told Johansen. "We have to make that first volley count."

"So you're certain they're coming?" Johansen asked.

"The only thing that's certain is we'll be kicking ourselves if they do come and we're not prepared."

Callahan inspected the preparations. The men all faced the tree line where Callahan had heard and glimpsed the Indians earlier. Some had crawled under their wagons and had gone to their bellies. Others knelt behind wagon wheels. They waited nervously for an attack they hoped wasn't coming.

Billy Thorndyke caught up with Callahan. His Winchester leaned on his shoulder. He handed Callahan his Henry. "Thought you might need this, boss."

"Thanks." Callahan checked the rifle's load.

Ike had a Winchester like his brother, and Clancy carried a Spencer.

"I've got a job for you boys," Callahan said.

"You just tell us what you need, boss," Billy said.

All three boys looked nervous but ready. Callahan thought of them as boys, but of course, they were men even if they were young, and there was nothing a young man wanted to do more than prove himself.

"I want you boys to wait in the middle of the wagons," Callahan said.

The boys frowned at each other.

"Probably not going to get a clear shot from here," Billy said.

"Clancy's comment earlier made me think we need to take precautions," Callahan told them. "I still doubt there's enough of them to surround us, but when they come charging and we let loose with that first volley, they're likely to break one way or another, circling the camp to the left or the right, in which case some of them might come at us from another direction," Callahan explained. "Your job is to plug the holes. You're protecting our backs."

They nodded, jaws set. Callahan could see in their eyes that they thought the task important. They had no intention of letting him down.

"Now pick your spots, and keep those rifles low," Callahan said.

He crossed the circle, heading toward Becky's wagon. The women of the wagon train went about the business of tending fires or washing clothes, sewing or minding the children, or any of a dozen other ordinary tasks. From a distance, it would look exactly like they were going about their normal routine.

But Callahan could see worry in their eyes as he passed. They'd probably heard stories about Indian raids and what happened to the womenfolk. Anyone would be unnerved with such a fate staring them in the face, but these women were doing their part, playacting like everything was okay. Real courage was being afraid but doing what you had to do, anyway.

And these women had as much courage as anyone.

Callahan found Becky hanging wet clothes on a line strung between wagons. "Why don't you and Lizzy get in back of the wagon and keep out of sight?" They were on the opposite side of the wagon circle from where they expected the attack. Hiding in the wagon would give her and the little girl decent cover.

"Luke Callahan," Becky said, her voice firm. "That's not what you told us to do. You said to act normal."

Callahan shifted awkwardly and pushed his hat back on his head. "I know what I said . . . now do what I say."

"Are you saying I'm not as brave as these other women?" Becky asked.

"You know I wouldn't say anything like—"

She crossed her arms. "Or are you trying to tell me you're the only one in this wagon train who cares about his woman?"

My woman?

Callahan hadn't heard it put so bluntly before. He didn't mind.

He drew his Peacemaker, spun it around in his hand, and handed it to her butt first. "Can you use this?"

She took the revolver and held it in two hands, looking down at it. "Cock it back with my thumb, point it at whatever I want dead, then squeeze the trigger. Except . . . well, I'm probably not a very good shot."

"Only use it if one of them gets close," Callahan said. "So close you can't miss. So close you've got no other choice."

"Okay." She dropped the gun into the pocket of her apron.

"It holds six rounds. If you use up five . . . well . . . number six . . . ."

"Luke Callahan, don't give me any frontier horse pucky about saving the last two bullets for Lizzy and me," Becky said. "I'm only going to shoot Indians or, preferably, I won't fire the dang thing at all."

Right.

"What about Lizzy?" Callahan asked. "Hide her at least."

"She's playing with the Grainger girls," Becky told him. "She knows to come right back here when things start. You worry about protecting your own skin, Luke.

I was just beginning to warm up to you. Don't get killed now."

He was about to try once more to convince her to hide in the wagon but stopped himself.

Instead, he leaned in and gave her a quick kiss on the lips. "I'll be right back."

He jogged back to the other side of the wagon circle, the lack of the Peacemaker's weight in its holster noticeable and disconcerting but he still had his Henry.

Callahan knelt behind a wagon wheel a few feet from Cookie Mayfield. "Anything?"

Cookie shook his head. "No sign of 'em. Maybe they went home."

"Suits me."

They waited.

And waited some more.

In two hours, the sun would go down. Callahan didn't think the Indians would attack at night. Some of them were superstitious about fighting in darkness. Callahan didn't pretend to understand, and anyway, he could be wrong. He didn't like the idea of them coming at night.

Another half hour passed. Callahan caught himself nodding off.

Hoots.

Then yells. The thunder of hooves.

Cookie Mayfield cocked his rifle. "Here they come."

CHAPTER 27

Tall Elk rode hard and fast, his horse tearing up turf as it galloped. He sat astride the animal, back straight, one hand lifting his rifle over his head as he screeched a war cry. Seven of them rode in a line, all brandishing rifles and ready to lay down fire when they got closer. Those riding behind were ready to loose fire arrows at the wagons.

Looking beyond the wagons, Tall Elk could see the women at their chores. And why wouldn't they be? There was no reason to suspect peril loomed a short distance away.

Surprise was everything. There would be confusion at first. The men would run for their guns, but then they'd hesitate, thinking of their women and children. The brave men would, of course, fight immediately, but others would hide.

The Indian braves would let loose with their fire arrows before the settlers fully realized what was happening. The fire would cause additional confusion. Smoke. Men and women alike would shrink from the flames. By the time the settlers organized themselves, Tall Elk and his braves would be well away.

Except . . .

Tall Elk had business of his own. If the opportunity presented itself, Tall Elk would have his revenge on Tomahawk Callahan.

He saw the women running now, breaking for the other side of the wagon circle as if a few more feet between Tall Elk and his charging braves would matter at all. Many of the women gathered up children as they ran. The men . . .

Tall Elk frowned. He couldn't see any of the men.

Then came puffs of smoke and flashes simultaneous with the rapid-fire cracks of multiple rifles. The hiss of invisible death streaking through the air, spanning the distance between the wagon circle and Tall Elk's braves in less than a heartbeat.

The meaty *thups* of lead hitting flesh.

The braves riding on either side of him tumbled from their horses, screaming and trailing blood.

Tall Elk looked to either side of him, fearing the unexpected volley might rattle and scatter his braves.

But they held true, all still riding hard for the wagons.

Tall Elk held his rifle high.

And shouted the order to unleash fire.

Callahan levered another shell into the Henry's chamber, spitting curses the whole time. When he'd given the order to fire, they'd caught the Indians by surprise, as expected, but evidently many of the men in the wagon train were out of practice with their rifles.

Callahan had dropped the Indian he'd been aiming for, and three others went down as well, but all of the other shots had been off the mark, scattering lead all over Idaho.

I should have let them get closer, Callahan thought, chastising himself.

"Fire at will!" he shouted.

The men with repeaters began firing immediately. A more ragged volley followed from the men with the single-shot rifles. Two more Indians went down. They'd spaced themselves differently now, riding evasively.

Callahan lifted the Henry and took a bead on the closest Indian, leading him. He held his breath, finger about to squeeze the trigger and—

A half dozen streaks of fire drew Callahan's attention. He watched them arc through the air, then descend.

And strike the wagons on other side of him.

Fire arrows!

Flames rapidly spread across the thick, doubly-ply cotton bonnet of each wagon. Soon the smoke was thick, the wind blowing it back into their faces. Some men continued to shoot at the Indians, others backed away in confusion, hands up to fend off the sudden heat.

Callahan grabbed Cookie by the shoulder. "Get buckets and any of the women not looking after children. Take water from the barrels." Most of the wagons had a water barrel lashed to the side. "Start dousing those bonnets!"

Cookie ran away to do as bidden.

Callahan coughed and stepped back from the billowing smoke, his eyes watering. The Indians had broken left, circling around the wagons as expected.

Scattered rifle shots. Men yelling.

Some of them dropped their guns to fight the fire. Three wagons burned.

Only half the bonnet burned on one wagon. A settler hurriedly unfastened the bonnet from the other side, even as the flames crawled toward him. He yanked hard, trying to get the burning wagon cover away from the rest of the wagon. He pulled it free but had to go outside the wagon's protective circle to drag it out of the way.

A rifle shot spit the air, and the settler jerked, arching his back, an explosion of blood between his shoulder blades. Even as he fell, Callahan was lifting his Henry, taking dead aim at the Indian who'd fired the shot. He squeezed the trigger.

The Henry bucked in Callahan's hands, and a splash of red bloomed across the Indian's chest. He tumbled backward off his pony and hit the ground hard.

A scream.

Callahan turned, levering another shell into the rifle's chamber.

A trio of Indians had come through a gap in the wagons, horses rearing as women fled before them. The lead Indian took aim at a running woman.

Callahan lifted his Henry, but he never got the chance to shoot.

Just as they'd been told to do, Billy, his brother Ike, and Clancy saw the three Indians break through. They rushed forward, feverishly working the levers of their rifles, blasting hot lead at them.

The three braves jerked and twitched as the slugs

slammed into them, and they went down in a spray of blood.

Callahan turned back to the burning wagons. Cookie and his bucket brigade had done a good job of dousing some of them, but at least two others burned out of control, and a third might also be unsavable, even with Cookie and his helpers tossing water like mad.

The gunfire had let off and dwindled to nothing. Callahan glimpsed a pair of Indians riding east and another one heading north. He wasn't sure how many had been killed and how many now fled, but the plan to take the Indians by surprise had worked. The Indians hadn't expected the wagon train to be ready for them.

But the fires remained to be fought. He set aside his rifle and ran for Cookie and the others fighting the fires, looking for a bucket so he could help.

The wind shifted, and suddenly Callahan was engulfed in smoke, his vision momentarily shrinking to nothing.

The shrill, high-pitched whinny of a horse. Shouts. A single rifle shot. A rider and his mount suddenly came barging through the smoke. The horse slammed into Callahan, knocking him to the ground. He hit face-first and came up spitting dirt. He scrambled to one knee and saw the Indian riding across the inside of the wagon circle. Callahan's eyes went wide.

Tall Elk!

His hand fell to his Peacemaker, but there was only an empty holster.

Callahan got to his feet, cursing a blue streak, and ran after Tall Elk.

Men and woman scattered as the Indian screamed his

war cry, riding his horse like a maniac and heading straight for—

Oh no!

Lizzy was out of the wagon. Perhaps she'd thought it safe when the shooting stopped. Tall Elk was riding right at her. Lizzy froze, obviously terrified, eyes as wide as dinner plates.

Becky emerged from the back of the wagon. "Lizzy!"

She frantically pulled Callahan's revolver from her apron pocket. Her hands shook. She thumbed back the hammer and fired.

The shot missed by a mile. Becky repeated the process, the second shot no closer to hitting Tall Elk than the first.

She'll end up shooting somebody else by accident if she doesn't stop. Callahan ran toward the scene at a full sprint.

And then, suddenly, Callahan thought he might be wrong. Tall Elk began to tilt off the back of the horse as if he'd been hit. Had one of Becky's wild shots actually hit the mark?

With alarm, Callahan saw he'd misinterpreted the situation. The Indian hadn't been shot off his horse at all. Tall Elk leaned low, one arm outstretched, the horse still carrying him along at a full gallop.

He grabbed Lizzy around the waist as he passed, hauling the small child up to sit on the horse in front of him.

She screamed and screamed and screamed, high-pitched and terrified.

"Lizzy!" Becky frantically cocked the revolver again and lifted it.

"Don't!" Callahan shouted. "You'll hit her!"

Becky hesitated.

Now others within the wagon circle saw what was happening. The Thorndyke brothers brought up their rifles, but they, too, held fire, fearing they might hit the girl.

"Fight me, Callahan!" Tall Elk shouted. "Do you have honor, or are you a coward! Come fight me if you want to see this little girl alive ever again!"

"Lizzy!" Becky hopped down from the wagon and ran toward Tall Elk, the weight of Callahan's Peacemaker dragging her hands down.

But Tall Elk had already turned his horse and was galloping away with the little girl.

Callahan didn't even pause to think.

He grabbed the nearest horse—an Indian pony, its former owner shot by Billy Thorndyke—and leapt onto its back. It had been a long time since Callahan had ridden bareback, but there was no time to be picky. He took off after Tall Elk at full speed, leaning low, the wind whipping past his ears as he tried to get all possible speed out of the horse.

Callahan cursed, realizing that in his haste not to let Tall Elk out of his sight, he'd ridden off like a fool with neither his Peacemaker nor his Henry. Turning back to collect his weapons was out of the question. He'd lose track of Tall Elk.

And Lizzy.

They streaked across the field of wildflowers, and Callahan felt a stab of panic as they entered the trees and he lost sight of them.

Callahan crossed the tree line into the woods and was

forced to slow, low branches slapping him across the face and chest. He thought he caught a glimpse of them off to the left and turned his Indian pony in that direction. Callahan heard running water. Was there a river nearby?

He came out of the thick woods into a small clearing.

Tall Elk waited for him on the other side. Behind him, the ground fell away sharply down to fast-flowing water, probably a tributary to a larger river.

The Indian had dismounted and let the horse wander away, a clear indication Tall Elk didn't intend to run. He held Lizzy firmly by the neck. The girl was white with fear, eyes red, face sticky with tears. Tall Elk held a long knife to her throat. His rifle leaned against a tree trunk two feet away.

"Get off that horse," Tall Elk said. "Get down and fight me. We have unfinished business, you and I."

"Just let the girl go," Callahan said. "I don't want to fight you. You think I've wronged you? Do you blame me for getting arrested by the blue coats? Then shoot me if you want revenge, but leave children out of it. This little girl's done nothing to you."

"Shoot you?" Tall Elk shook his head, a cruel smile curling his lips. "And have it be said I killed you in cold blood, that I was too afraid to face you man-to-man?"

"Who would even know?" Callahan pointed out.

"*I* would know," the Indian said heatedly.

"We've done this already," Callahan pointed out.

"We're doing it again!" Tall Elk shouted, eyes wild with rage. "But this time the outcome will be different. It will end as it should have the first time."

Callahan had seen men like this before, out of their

minds with hate, laboring under the illusion the world had dealt them a bad hand somehow. They'd get it into their heads that they were the victims of something unfair, some great injustice, and they just couldn't rest until things were set right.

Tall Elk had no interest in letting Callahan talk sense into him. All the Indian wanted was blood.

Callahan just had to make sure it wasn't Lizzy's.

"Nobody's going to call you brave for harming a little girl," Callahan said. "Your rifle's right there. Get your revenge already. Don't drag this out."

"No!" Tall Elk shouted.

He let go of Lizzy for a moment and grabbed the rifle. He worked the lever repeatedly until all the shells had been ejected and then flung the rifle away.

"No easy death for either of us, Callahan," Tall Elk said. "We will embrace in honorable battle, one of us tasting death, the other life."

Callahan didn't share this particular Indian's sense of honor. Honor had gone out the window when he'd grabbed Lizzy. If Callahan had his Peacemaker, he would have drawn it and shot him. That simple. Instead, he was forced to humor this madman's warped sense of justice.

Suddenly, Tall Elk lifted Lizzy into the air. She made a startled bleating sound.

"Grab that branch," Tall Elk commanded. "Climb into the tree. Go on!"

Lizzy pulled herself up, climbing until she was a dozen feet off the ground. She clung to a thick branch, trembling with fear.

Tall Elk stood between Callahan and the tree. "She stays up there until one of us is dead. You want to climb up and get her? Then come through me."

Callahan climbed down from the horse. He gave the animal a light slap on the haunch to send it on its way. He drew the tomahawk from his belt.

"I'll say it one more time, Tall Elk. Forget this nonsense," Callahan told him. "Pick up your rifle and fetch your horse and ride away free. I won't tell the blue coats where you went. Go live your life whatever way you think best."

"You'd like that, wouldn't you?" Tall Elk scoffed. "Do you think I could stomach that, you telling everyone that *you* spared my life, that *you* gave me my freedom?"

Callahan shook his head. "Not everything's about trying to look good."

"Enough talk!"

Callahan's grip tightened on the Tomahawk. "For once, we agree."

Callahan launched himself at Tall Elk, extending his arm for a full swing.

Tall Elk barely had time to stumble back, the tomahawk coming within an inch of his nose. He came back with the knife.

Callahan dodged the thrust and raised the tomahawk. He was angry now and wanted nothing more than to split Tall Elk's skull in two.

But instead of backing away, Tall Elk moved in fast, one hand going up to grab Callahan by the wrist, preventing the tomahawk from falling and delivering the killing blow. Tall Elk stabbed, going for the other man's ribs, but now it was Callahan's turn to grab Tall Elk by the wrist, thwarting the Indian's knife thrust. They stayed locked like that, each holding the other and unable to bring their weapons to bear, pulling and pushing and trying to get leverage.

They moved toward the drop-off, the sound of the rushing river growing louder. They spun in an awkward circle, boots and moccasins sliding in the dust as each man wrestled for control.

Tall Elk twisted at the waist and brought his knee up hard into Callahan's ribs.

Callahan grunted, pain flaring up and down one side of his body. Still, both men hung onto each other, faces locked in dire grimaces, sweat pouring off them. Tall Elk brought his knee up again but couldn't get the height this time. Instead of another blow to Callahan's ribs, the Indian's knee caught Callahan square in the crotch.

Pain exploded. Callahan felt a wave of nausea wash over him as his knees went watery. He wilted to the ground, dropping his tomahawk. By some miracle, he held onto Tall Elk's wrist with his other hand, knowing he was dead if he didn't keep the Indian's knife at bay. He went down, pulling Tall Elk along with him.

The Indian landed hard on top of him, knocking most of the air from Callahan's lungs. Still, he desperately held off Tall Elk's knife. Tall Elk bore down, putting all his weight into bringing the edge of the knife blade to Callahan's throat. Callahan tried to buck the Indian off him, but it was no use. He was still weak and dizzy from the blow to his crotch.

Tall Elk grunted, gritting his teeth, sweat running down his face.

"And now, you will die, Callahan," Tall Elk said through clenched teeth. "The blade will sink into the soft flesh of your throat. I will feel your warm blood on my hand. The light in your eyes will dim as death takes you."

Callahan tried to punch with his free hand, but the arm was mostly trapped by Tall Elk's weight. He couldn't get an angle. The blows he landed to the Indian's ribs might as well have come from a child.

Instead, Callahan felt along his side, fingers finding his gun belt, but his knife was on the other side. Again, he lamented his empty holster. His fingers felt lower, felt the lump in his front pocket. He reached in, hand closing around the cold grip.

A loud and sudden *pop*.

Tall Elk screamed. The pressure bringing the knife down vanished.

Callahan pushed the Indian off him.

The two men crawled away from one another. Callahan sucked in breaths, trying to banish the sick feeling, forcing the pain to the edge of his consciousness. He looked down at the single-shot derringer in his fist, gray-blue smoke oozing from the barrel. Then his eyes shifted to the Indian.

Tall Elk crawled away from him, dragging one leg, his hand over the wound in his upper thigh, syrupy red blood oozing between his fingers.

Callahan stood and dropped the derringer. He cast about for his tomahawk, saw it nestled nearby in the grass, and staggered toward it. The pain in his crotch was fading but only a little. He bent and retrieved the tomahawk.

Then he turned back to Tall Elk.

The Indian had gone ashen, whimpering in pain as he scrambled away. He got to his feet, wincing. There was no fight in him now. He only wanted to get away from Callahan and his avenging tomahawk. There was fear in his eyes even more than there was pain.

Callahan lifted the tomahawk. *Time to make sure you never trouble anyone ever again.* He advanced on the Indian.

Tall Elk turned to run. His bad leg gave out immediately, and he fell and tumbled . . .

. . . over the side of the drop-off.

Callahan ran to the edge just in time to see Tall Elk roll down the hill and splash into the raging river. The Indian disappeared under the foaming, racing water. Callahan watched for him to come up again, his eyes going downstream, anticipating where Tall Elk might surface.

But he didn't surface. Callahan watched for another moment to be sure.

Tall Elk was gone.

"Mr. Callahan!"

Lizzy still clung to the tree branch.

Callahan hobbled over, positioned himself directly beneath her, and stretched out his arms. "Come on. I'll catch you. I promise."

She let go of the branch, and Callahan caught her. Lizzy flung her arms around Callahan's neck, buried her face in his chest. Her whole body wracked with sobs, fat tears wetting his shirt.

"Nobody's going to hurt you, not now, not while I'm around." Callahan held her, gave her a gentle pat on the back. "Not ever."

CHAPTER 28

The man who'd risked his life to pull the burning bonnet off one of the wagons was named Irwin Fishburn. An Indian brave had shot him for his troubles. Irwin Fishburn had been traveling west with his younger brother Gerald. They'd planned to open a haberdashery. Irwin's quick actions had saved all the samples and cloth and accessories they had in the wagon.

At the cost of his own life.

Gerald said a few heartfelt words, tears in his eyes, and then they covered his brother with dirt and rocks.

Then the people of the wagon train turned to the next two graves.

Harris and Emily Farnsworth were newlyweds, their new life in Oregon snuffed out before it ever got started. They'd burned to death in one of the wagons. Another young couple who'd made friends with them said the words over their graves.

All Callahan could do was stand there, hat in his hands, feeling sick and exhausted.

They concluded the funerals, and everyone drifted back to their wagons. There was no hurry. Callahan had already declared a day of rest. The Indian attack had rattled everyone, and they'd spent a long night nervous that the raiders might return.

But the Indians hadn't returned.

Three people dead. Two wagons burned to ash. The fire had damaged three other wagons but not badly. They could make it the rest of the way to Salem. All things considered, it could have been a lot worse.

And yet it was still a catastrophe. At least that's how it seemed to Callahan. Three people that would never breathe again, never step foot in Oregon.

So they all needed a day off. To heal bodies and spirits. To repair damage. Never mind that he'd lose a day against the railroad. Ten thousand dollars was a lot, but Aunt Clara's livelihood, the business her husband and Luke's father had started, was worth plenty.

If only what? If Callahan had taken a different route and never run afoul of the raiding party? If they'd all shot straighter and faster and never given those Indians a chance to loose their fire arrows? Lots of *ifs* and *maybes*. A man could go mad thinking of everything he might've done different.

"Luke!"

Callahan paused and let Becky catch up to him. Her hand slipped into his.

"I guess I need to thank you . . . again," she said.

"How's Lizzy?"

"Off with the Grainger girls like always," Becky told him. "Laughing and playing like nothing ever happened. I guess kids are made of sterner stuff than we think. Sterner stuff than we are maybe."

"Keep an eye on her," Callahan suggested. "See how she sleeps."

"I will."

They stood a moment.

Then Becky squeezed his hand. "Hey."

"Hey what?"

"Anyone asked how *you* are doing?"

A wan smile from Callahan. "Ask if you want."

"How are you doing?"

"Never better."

Becky frowned. "You already won me over, Luke Callahan. You don't got to impress me with what a big strong man you are, looking out for everyone. Who's looking out for you?"

He put an arm around her. "You want the job?"

"That's not for me to say. I haven't heard no proposals."

Callahan let that go.

"I'm not kidding," Becky said. "You can get worn out just like anyone else, and then where would we all be without you?"

"I'll make the rounds, check on everybody," Callahan said. "Then who knows? Maybe I'll grab a nap."

Becky kissed him on the cheek, then Callahan went from wagon to wagon, offering a kind word and just generally making sure everything was okay.

He made a point to check in with both Bart Schultz and Ace Franklin to see how they and their animals had faired during the raid. Both men were happy to report that not a single cow or sheep had been harmed or taken. In fact, the Indians had shown no interest in the livestock at all.

Callahan told both men he was glad they hadn't had any trouble, but as he walked away, the notion troubled him. Indians raided because they wanted something—horses or cattle or guns or whiskey or even women. The idea that they'd attacked the wagon train just so Tall Elk could take revenge on Callahan seemed farfetched.

He looked up and found he'd been walking back toward the woods without even realizing it. Soon he found the spot where he and Tall Elk had fought. He stood at the edge of the drop-off and looked down at the river, half-expecting Tall Elk to suddenly surface from the fast-moving water, knowing it was a silly thought. The familiar weight of the Peacemaker back in its holster was a comfort.

The bank was steep, and he had better things to do, but he found himself picking his way down. He walked along the edge of the river a ways, careful with his footing. The current was fast, and he was in no mood for a swim. Callahan wasn't sure what he expected to find. Tall Elk's body washed up on the bank downstream? Tracks in the soft mud leading away? Maybe Tall Elk had drowned, or maybe he'd managed to swim to the other side and escape.

Maybe anything.

Callahan didn't like loose ends, but he simply had no time to dwell on Tall Elk's fate.

He had a wagon train to run.

When he got back to the wagons, he ran into Anna Masters.

"You've got an exciting story for your next telegram, I reckon," Callahan told her.

"I suppose."

Callahan detected a distinct lack of excitement. "Had enough of newspaper reporting?"

"Had enough of wagon trains," she said. "Those funerals didn't sit well on my stomach."

"Your readers don't like funerals?" Callahan hadn't meant it as a dig, but it was obvious she'd taken it that way.

"You think I have no feelings?" Masters shot back. "You think the thought of that newlywed couple doesn't make me . . ." She looked away and shook her head. "I just telegram the raw facts. Some man sitting safe at his desk will type it up all exciting. It'll all just be a story to him, names and places. He won't know the smell of that burning wagon and the people inside or how the ice went down my back when I heard those Indians whooping, the way the ground shook when the horses thundered toward us. I'll tell you something, Tomahawk Callahan, I hope this really is the last wagon train. I hope people from now on come west in safety and comfort. Let them ride a train instead of going for weeks and weeks until their brains are numbed by boredom only to suddenly be frightened out of their wits by a flood or an avalanche or a pack of savages looking to take a scalp. There's only so much emotion a person can stand."

Callahan sighed and let her harsh words hang there a moment. "When you say it like that, I guess it's hard to disagree. Sometimes I wonder why anyone would make a journey like this."

"That's exactly what I said to the Hendersons," Masters told him.

The name rang a bell. It took Callahan a moment to

remember. "That's the old couple who was burned out of one of the wagons."

"They're with me now."

"With *you*?"

Masters frowned. "Don't act so surprised. I can be just as generous as anyone, you know. And no, it's not just because I want to put them in a story. Anyway, it's just me in a wagon all by myself. Seemed the right thing to do."

First Pete Johansen and now Anna Masters. Callahan wasn't usually keen on surprises, but this was the sort that struck him just right and came just when needed. He supposed no matter how cantankerous or mercenary or self-serving, nearly anyone had good in them if they were given a chance to show it.

"Miss Masters, that's good of you," Callahan said. "If in the past I might have said anything . . . that is if I've cast any aspersions on you or your motives . . . the point is, you're okay in my book."

Masters rolled her eyes. "Don't go all soft and sweet on me, Callahan. Just get me to Boise in one piece and we'll call it even. I need a meal cooked by somebody other than myself, a soft bed, and another bottle of whiskey."

All those things sounded good to Callahan, too.

Boise. The town had grown large in everyone's hopes and expectations over the last week. Cookie said there was a wide-open space right next to town that could easily accommodate the wagon train. People could shop and replenish supplies, and those with the means were welcome to take advantage of whatever entertainment the town had to offer.

"I'll get us to Boise, Miss Masters," Callahan promised. "First drink's on me."

Callahan finished making the rounds. The settlers were understandably glum after the deaths, but there was still a general feeling that the wagon train's occasional episodes of bad luck were the exception and not the rule. There were dangers that came with the Oregon Trail. It was as simple as that, and it would be foolish to think otherwise.

Callahan wasn't so sure.

Yes, some of the mishaps could be put down to the normal perils of Oregon Trail. Nobody had arranged for wolves to steal Bart Shultz's sheep just to sabotage the wagon train. That was just the Oregon Trail having a go at them. But somebody taking a shot at him? Maybe an accident or maybe not. And the flood? Nobody controlled the river or the weather.

But sawing the spokes of wagon wheels was deliberate.

So what was Callahan to make of these Indian attacks?

These thoughts played heavy on Callahan's mind as he ate a plate of beans in stony silence with Cookie. He went to visit Becky and Lizzy before turning in for the night. It was clear to Becky something was on Callahan's mind.

"I'd say penny for your thoughts," she said. "But I'm saving all my money for when I get to Salem."

Callahan forced a laugh. "They're not worth a penny. I'm just thinking about tomorrow. We've got to get this wagon train moving again."

Becky didn't believe him, but she pretended to, and Callahan appreciated her for it. He wandered back to his campfire and sat looking into the flames, thinking the same thoughts around in a circle. Cookie Mayfield had already turned in, head on his saddle and hat over his face as he snored lightly.

Callahan took a folded piece of paper from his back pocket. He hadn't looked at it once since leaving Kansas City, but he'd carried it with him every step of the way as a reminder. He unfolded the paper now and squinted at it by the flickering light of the campfire.

The terms of the wagon train's wager with the railroad man Arbuckle had been all over the newspapers, but this copy was one his Aunt Clara had scribbled out for him in her neat scrawl, copied from Uncle Howard's copy that had been signed by both him and Arbuckle. It was the specifics of the exact terms that now interested Callahan. He had a good memory but wanted to make sure.

He scanned through the agreement until he came to the part he wanted, the section that covered what it meant for the wagon train to arrive in Salem "whole and intact." When he'd first looked at the thing weeks and weeks ago, this part had struck him as a bunch of fancy lawyer double-talk. Now it seemed crucially important.

He read it five times just to make sure he understood what he thought he was understanding.

Kent Arbuckle had insisted that the entire wagon train and all of its people must all arrive together in Salem for the wagon train to be considered successful. But Uncle Howard was no fool. The Oregon Trail was a journey with potential danger around every corner. People and wagons were often lost.

So Uncle Howard and the railroad man had dickered back and forth until they'd arrived at the magic number.

Ten percent.

If the wagon train lost ten percent of its wagons or ten percent of its people, it would no longer be considered *whole and intact* as far as the wager was concerned.

They'd left Kansas City with fifty-one wagons and one hundred and fifty-nine people.

Except that wasn't exactly true. If you added the chuckwagon and the other wagon that belonged to the outfitter in with the others, it brought the total to fifty-three wagons. Did they count? Callahan checked the wording of the agreement again. It said all wagons and people associated with the wagon train and did not differentiate between the settlers' wagons and those belonging to the outfitter.

Likewise, the hundred fifty-nine people swelled to a hundred and sixty-five once Callahan and his crew were included.

Callahan had never been strong at math, but these numbers were simple enough to work in his head. They'd sadly lost four people since leaving Missouri— Little Rock, Irwin Fishburn, and the newlyweds. A tragedy, yes, but not even close to ten percent of the wagon train's population.

The wagons . . . well, that was something different.

They'd lost four wagons—one burned by bandits, another down the side of a mountain, and two set ablaze during the Indian attack.

Ten percent of fifty-three wagons was five and a

little bit more. There was nothing in the paperwork about rounding up or down, but Callahan suspected the math in this case was pretty simple.

Losing one more wagon would also mean losing the bet.

CHAPTER 29

They watched the wagon train emerge from the pass from a safe distance atop a nearby mountain.

"Start counting," Roy Benson said.

Zeke Hawkins frowned. "Why me? You don't know how to count?"

"I *am* counting," Benson shot back. "You count, too. Then we'll compare. It's called being sure."

Hawkins grumbled but started counting.

The wagons came down from the pass at a snail's pace. The afternoon waned. The wagon train was likely trying to make a large clearing a few miles away while they still had daylight.

The last wagon came through. The two men waited a moment to make sure.

"Forty-eight," Hawkins said.

Benson nodded. "That's what I got too."

He grinned. Kent Arbuckle had told him the wagon train had left Kansas City with fifty-three wagons. Forty-eight wasn't enough. Tomahawk Callahan had just lost his bet.

"I guess them Indians did the trick," Hawkins said.

Benson's grin fell at the thought of Tall Elk and his Indian bandits. "I wonder why they didn't come tell us the job was done. Don't they want to get paid?"

"Who can tell with injuns?" Hawkins said. "Maybe they're looking for us right now. It's not like we're trying so hard to not be found, and we don't got any gold for them, anyway."

Benson had planned to wire Arbuckle for gold to pay the Indians, but he wanted to wait and see if they'd earned it first. He decided it was up to Tall Elk to come find him if he wanted to get paid. Benson wasn't going to wait around all day.

"Our work's done," Benson said. "Let's get to Boise. I'm sick of the wilderness. I want clean sheets and a bottle of whiskey."

"Now you're talking my language," Hawkins said. "How long, you figure?"

"A few nights if we don't dawdle. We'll get there well ahead of those jokers." Benson nodded at the wagon train.

"Then let's go," Hawkins said. "Time's a-wasting."

They turned their horses and headed for Boise.

"The wheel went in a deep rut and twisted bad," Clancy Davenport said. "That's four cracked spokes."

Callahan stood next to Clancy, looking at the wagon and the troublesome wheel. "Can it last until we stop for the night?"

"Probably not," Clancy told him.

Anna Masters stuck her head out of the wagon. "Is this going to take all day?"

Callahan shook his head, muttering to himself. Anna Masters's wagon was last in line. How every other wagon had missed the deep rut, he couldn't guess. One more wagon and they'd be on their way. But no, Masters had to steer right for it.

"I don't suppose you have a spare wheel in there?" he asked.

"Nope."

"Then this might take a while." Callahan turned back to Clancy. "Ride back to the column. Scrounge us a wheel."

"Right." He mounted his horse and rode away at a gallop.

Callahan looked around. They were nearing the mouth of the pass, and the path had widened significantly.

"Get the wagon over to the side as far as you can," Callahan told her. "Let the cattle and sheep pass."

Masters scooted the wagon over, and soon the stink-filled dust cloud of animals moved past. Clancy arrived sometime later with a new wheel and a few men to help change it. By the time they caught up with the rest of the wagon train, the sun had set and the other settlers were going about their nightly routine.

Cookie had already built a fire. He handed Callahan a plate of beans.

"Thanks." Callahan spooned beans into his mouth. He was famished. "When we get to Boise, we need to find a wheelwright. I want to buy some extra wheels. The way we're going through them . . ." He spooned in another mouthful of beans.

Cookie nodded. "Right. I should make a list. Boise's

a good place to get whatever we need. Then we make the final run to Salem."

The final run to Salem. Cookie made it sound like a short hop, skip, and jump, but it was easily another three or four weeks. And there were the Cascades to get through, too. How did people like his Uncle Howard and his father make this trip over and over again, taking a new group of settlers each year?

Once was more than enough for Callahan.

His thoughts drifted to his Aunt Clara. Even if they won the bet, would she keep the outfitters going without Uncle Howard? Did she expect Callahan to stay on and take his place?

And, of course, if they lost the wager, it wouldn't matter. The outfitters would no longer be Clara's business to worry about.

Callahan decided to put it out of his mind. Clara was a strong, determined woman and could take care of herself. Callahan needed to remain focused on his current concern: the Oregon Trail. One day at a time. One mile at a time. And then one day he'd look up and there would be Salem right in front of him.

"Put some groceries on that list," Callahan said.

"You have something particular in mind?" Cookie asked.

"Anything but beans."

Kent Arbuckle relaxed in his private train car as the locomotive chugged and belched smoke and streaked toward Boise.

He was in a very good mood. Benson's telegram

from Boise had been clear. Enough wagons had been destroyed to invalidate the wagon train. There was now nothing Tomahawk could do to win the bet. He could arrive a day ahead of the railroad or a year, and it simply wouldn't matter. The terms were clear, spelled out in black and white.

Tomahawk Callahan had lost too many wagons.

Okay, well, yes, Arbuckle had to admit that a legal technicality wasn't the most dramatic way to win a bet, not like everyone breaking their necks to be the first over the finish line. That's what Arbuckle would have preferred.

But a win was a win. Gladstone Railways would not suffer the embarrassment of having to fork out ten thousand dollars to some two-bit wagon train outfitter. The loss of the wagons would highlight the dangers of journeying to the West Coast by such an antiquated method and reemphasize the relative comfort and safety of rail travel. The Gladstone brothers would not terminate his employment.

And yet . . .

Arbuckle couldn't quite keep himself from feeling just a little disappointed. He wanted to beat Callahan soundly in a straight-up race, not skate by on a disqualification.

Never mind. Arbuckle would not be punished for his brash wager. That's what counted.

Benson had contacted Arbuckle not simply to brag but also to arrange payment. He'd told Benson that he would meet him in Boise, but it would be a couple of days since Arbuckle still intended to complete the new rail line as quickly as possible. As a matter of efficiency, yes, but also because he still had hope to defeat Callahan in a straight-up contest. Arbuckle wanted to make sure all of the work crews were still clicking along at full speed.

Satisfied that all the crews were laboring at full steam, Arbuckle finally set course for Boise. He'd pay Benson, then send the criminal on his way.

And then Arbuckle could get on with the business of railroads.

"Mycroft!"

Mycroft Jones scurried into the compartment. "What can I do for you, Mr. Arbuckle?"

"I think something of a celebration is in order," Arbuckle told his underling. "As soon as the train pulls into Boise, I want you to get a suite of rooms at the best hotel and make dining reservations at the best place to eat. You'll join me, of course. You've been indispensable on this little escapade."

"Most generous, sir."

"And see if you can arrange . . . ah. How can I put this?" Arbuckle considered his words. He and Jones were both men of the world. At the same time, Arbuckle was reluctant to appear crass. "I think some female companionship is in order, but . . . uh . . . let's not be too obvious."

Jones nodded, understanding what his employer was driving at. "I think it's very nice you'd like to spend some quality time with your lovely young . . . nieces?"

Arbuckle grinned. "Nieces. I like that. See to the arrangements."

Jones made a slight bow. "Sir, do you have any preference when it comes to . . . nieces?"

Arbuckle thought about it. "Redheads."

Arbuckle sat back, put his feet on his desk. They'd arrive in Boise the next day. Arbuckle would see to Benson's payment as well as some additional payment for an assistant Benson had apparently hired. All quite expensive. No matter. Money well spent. Then the outlaw would be on his way, and Arbuckle could return to the legitimate business of running a railroad.

But it could all wait until Arbuckle had rewarded himself.

He couldn't wait to meet his nieces.

Benson read the telegram, nodding with satisfaction. He'd decided he didn't like Kent Arbuckle. The railroad man pretended to be made of tougher stuff than he actually was, but there was no doubt his money was good.

He walked out of the telegraph office, the late afternoon sun slapping him in the face. He squinted up and down the street. Saloons were plentiful in Boise, and it took Benson a moment to remember where Hawkins said he would be. He folded the telegram, put it in his shirt pocket, and headed down the street.

The Copper Kettle was less than a block away, marked—unsurprisingly—by a large, pitted copper kettle hanging over the open doorway. Benson entered, stopped just inside, and looked around. There wasn't much to the place, and Benson suspected Hawkins had picked the place simply because it was close. There were only a few patrons, so Hawkins was easy to spot, across the room at the far end of a pine bar.

Benson joined him.

Hawkins was working on a bottle, still mostly full. He pushed it toward Benson. "Help yourself."

Benson waved the bartender over and asked for another glass. He filled it, drank, smacked his lips, and drank another. He began to feel warm and pleasant all over. The job was done.

Or close enough, anyway.

"Well?" Hawkins asked.

"He has our money," Benson said. "Wants to meet at a defunct silver mine out of town. Secluded but easy to find." Benson described where it was.

Hawkins frowned. "That's an hour's ride out of town. And another hour back."

"I told you," Benson said. "A man like him doesn't want to be seen with the likes of us."

"Rude."

Benson rolled his eyes. "Don't make me laugh. You know who we are and what we do. Would you want to be seen with us if you were a legit citizen?"

Hawkins shrugged. "I guess it's just the money that counts."

"Now you're right in the head," Benson told him. "We don't get paid any more or any less by being offended. Now let's mount up and go get our money."

Hawkins hesitated. "This your idea to meet at the mine? Or his?"

"His. You think I want to ride all the way out there?"

"Huh."

Benson could tell Hawkins didn't like it. This hadn't been unexpected. Hawkins would, of course, be suspicious, expecting some kind of trick or double cross. Benson had to give him something.

"If you don't feel like it, I can ride out myself," Benson offered. "He'd probably feel more comfortable dealing with just one of us, anyway. I'll go, and give you your share when I get back."

"Oh, no, you don't." Hawkins wagged a finger at him. "You go get both shares and then I never see you again is what will happen. We'll ride out together."

Benson grinned like a kid who's been caught with a hand in the cookie jar. Hawkins had suspected chicanery, and now Benson was letting him think he'd found it out. Hawkins was obviously more comfortable now, thinking himself one step ahead of Benson.

"It's okay if you don't trust me. Like I said, I don't get paid any extra by being offended." Benson took one more shot of whiskey, then slid off his barstool. "Let's go get our money."

They rode together north of Boise, eventually branching off onto a lesser-used road and climbing up into some low hills.

"There was a big strike here, and the mining company rushed to set up an operation," Benson explained. "Then two years later it went bust all of a sudden, like there'd never been any silver here at all. The point being, it's well away from prying eyes."

They rounded a bend in the road, and the woods opened into a clearing, the abandoned mine visible ahead, built into the side of a rocky hill. A narrow-gauge rail for ore carts went into the low opening of the mine. There were dilapidated shacks and a sluice operation and a lot of rusty tools and spare axles for the ore carts.

Hawkins's eyes raked the scene. "We must be here first."

"He said he'd be in that big shack out front." Benson dismounted. "I'll have a look. Wait here."

"I don't think so." Hawkins climbed down from his horse also. "I think I'll go in first." He drew his revolver.

The sight of the long-abandoned mine must have renewed Hawkins' suspicions. Benson hadn't anticipated this situation, but he should have. He was too used to thinking of himself as smarter than Hawkins, and, true or not, it was never a good idea to underestimate somebody you intended to kill or who might kill you.

The fact was that Benson had gotten lazy. He hadn't wanted to kill Hawkins back in town and then have to wrap up his body and drag it all the way out here and risk being seen hauling around a corpse. At the time he was hatching this scheme, it had seemed easier to lure the man to the edge of a mine shaft, shoot him in the back far from witnesses, and then drop him into a dark hole, never to be seen again.

Now it had gotten just a little trickier.

"Go ahead," Benson said. "Go first. Makes no difference to me."

Benson let Hawkins get ahead of him, then followed more slowly. Hawkins reached the shack's door, pushed it open with caution, and entered slowly. Benson headed in after him, drawing his own gun. Best to do it now. Hawkins would see the shack was empty, that nobody was waiting to ambush him, and he'd let his guard down again, not a lot, but enough.

Do it now. No more waiting around. Do it before he wises up.

Benson pushed the door open, rushing into the shack, lifting his pistol to—

An explosion of pain.

Stars went off in his eyes, his vision blinded by the flashing colors. His pistol flew out of his hand and landed somewhere out in the great unknown. He felt something hot and wet over his lips, tasted salt. Blood from his flattened nose. Benson knew immediately what had happened. Hawkins had entered the shack, moved to the side of the door, and waited for Benson to enter. Then Hawkins had slammed his pistol into Benson's face. It had been that simple, but there was no time for Benson to do anything about it at that precise moment.

Because he was too busy falling.

The world tilted and dumped Benson on his head. He writhed in the dirt, trying in vain to rediscover which way was up.

Hawkings cocked his revolver's hammer back. "No more messing around. I'm owed some money and I aim to get it. The only reason you ain't dead is because I figure that railroad man might not talk to me directly. So get up, dust your sorry self off, and—"

Benson grabbed a fistful of dirt and flung it back into Hawkins's face. A lucky toss, the dirt blinding both eyes.

Hawkins cursed and shot, but Benson was already moving, zigging one way and zagging the other as Hawkins cocked the hammer back and shot again and then a third time, lead flying past Benson's head.

Benson dove behind an ore cart, hand going to his nose. He winced at the contact, touching more gingerly to assess the damage. Not broken but bashed good, his face a bloody, throbbing mess. He blinked to clear the stars from his eyes. Benson was alive by dumb luck. Hawkins had him dead to rights.

He reached into his jacket and pulled out the .32, thumbing back the hammer.

Hawkins spat a stream of curses at him, postulating unflattering things about Benson's lineage.

Benson didn't like his chances with the .32. It was a small caliber with a short barrel and lousy for any target more than ten feet away, and in order to shoot, he'd have to expose himself and let Hawkins blaze away at him with his six-shooter. He tried to remember if Hawkins had fired twice or three times.

"Come out from behind there with your hands up," Hawkins called. "You can still save your own life. I want that railroad man's gold. You're gonna get it for me."

Benson pictured where the horses were. He could make a run for the rifle in his saddle sheath, but that would give Hawkins a wide-open shot. No, he'd have to make his play with the .32. He'd pop up and squeeze one off fast, then duck down again before Hawkins had a chance to respond.

"You hear me, Benson?" Hawkins was shouting again. "Your six-gun's on the ground and your rifle's on your saddle. Maybe you got another shooting iron squirreled away, and maybe you don't. But you won't like it if I have to come get you. Better to surrender now and—"

Benson stood, aimed, and squeezed the trigger. A sharp *pop* from the .32, and Hawkins howled as a splotch of blood erupted from the thickest part of his thigh. Benson had been aiming for his chest.

Hawkins was faster than Benson had expected and shot from the hip. The slug tore a chunk of wood out of the ore cart just as Benson ducked again, his heart hammering in his chest. He heard Hawkins groaning and grumbling and muttering curses.

Benson mumbled a few choice words of his own. Hitting Hawkins in the meaty part of the thigh wouldn't put him down. Hurt and infuriate him, yes, but not put him out of action. And now Hawkins knew he was armed. The man would be more careful. Benson wasn't sure if he'd improved his situation or not. He no longer heard Hawkins's moans and groans.

He needed another look, but Hawkins was likely expecting Benson to pop his head up again. Instead, Benson went to his hands and knees and crawled to the edge of the ore cart and took a peek around the corner. He didn't see Hawkins, and that worried him. The door to the shack stood open. Benson saw no movement there or in the windows flanking the doorway. He watched a moment, not liking it.

Benson glanced through the doorway at the horses. They'd moved off several feet, shying away from the gunfire, but they were both good animals. They hadn't bolted.

He thought about making a run for the horses. He could either get his rifle or simply take the horses and go, but that would leave Hawkins alive and a dangerous loose end. He looked around again. Still no sign of

Hawkins. He had to be inside the shack, either licking his wounds or preparing his next move against Benson.

The horses were farther than he liked, but it was doable. There was a water trough halfway, not the best cover but better than nothing. Benson sucked in a breath, then let it out slowly, readying himself.

Run fast, idiot.

Benson sprang to his feet and ran, arms and legs pumping for all he was worth.

Hawkins immediately appeared in the window to the right, fanning his six-gun, lead flying as Benson dove behind the water trough. The man had obviously reloaded. A pause in the gunfire. Was he reloading again?

Benson got his answer as Hawkins began shooting up the water trough, wood chips flying, holes blasting through the thin wood barely an inch from Benson's face. The water trough was even worse cover than Benson had thought. He counted four shots.

Then five.

Six.

Benson jumped up and sprinted for the shack, bursting through the front door, turning toward the right window, .32 revolver up and ready.

Hawkins's head came up, eyes going wide. He sat below the window, spent brass on the floor around him as he reloaded his six-shooter.

Not that Benson was going to give him a chance.

He fired the .32 and hit Hawkins in the belly. The man flinched and toppled over, fresh shells falling out of his hand and rolling across the shack's uneven floor.

Hawkins looked up with pain and hate in his eyes. "You dirty son of a—"

Benson fired until the .32 clicked empty, Hawkins twitching with each shot. The inside of the shack, suddenly quiet now, smelled like fresh blood and gunpowder. Benson went to the corpse and nudged it with the toe of his boot.

Zeke Hawkins was no more.

Benson stashed the .32 away, empty. He made a note to buy more ammo for it when he was back in town. He retrieved his six-shooter and put it back in the holster. He searched the dead body. Hawkins had eleven dollars on him and a pretty nice watch. Benson took the money and left the watch. There was always a chance someone would recognize it. The same for Hawkins's six-gun, which had the dead man's initials carved in the grip.

He took Hawkins by the ankles and dragged him to the mine and tossed him down the shaft. It must have been a long way down because it took a few seconds for Benson to hear the body hit bottom.

Benson went back to the horses and looked through Hawkins's saddlebags. There was little of use or interest in the dead man's possessions, so they went down the shaft also. He kept Hawkins's rifle, which was a good weapon but looked like any other and wouldn't be recognized. Saddle and bridle went down the shaft.

The horse was a good animal, but anyone with an eye for horseflesh might know it had belonged to Hawkins. He gave it a slap on the rump and sent it prancing away. It could fend for itself until someone found it and gave it a home.

Benson took off his hat and wiped the sweat from his brow. Killing a man and then erasing him from existence was hot work. He drank from his canteen.

He took a last look around. He was finished here. He climbed onto his horse and took out the telegram from Arbuckle. The railroad man would arrive in Boise tomorrow.

And then Benson would collect both his money and Hawkins's and be on his way.

CHAPTER 30

The wagon train arrived on the outskirts of Boise without incident. The feeling among both the settlers and Callahan's crew was that the place was something just short of heaven. It was all from built-up expectations, of course, everyone ready to visit town, replenish supplies, or even—as Callahan and Cookie Mayfield intended—grab a beer in one of the town's many saloons.

Callahan assigned the Thorndyke brothers the task of getting the wagons circled. They'd been disappointed to learn they were not going into Boise but understood someone needed to stay behind to keep an eye on things . . . especially when some unknown villain was sabotaging wagons. The brothers, along with Clancy Davenport, would take turns patrolling the camp.

The boys brightened somewhat when Callahan promised they'd all get a saloon night on their way home after the job was done. Callahan would even buy the first bottle.

Anna Masters appeared in the same dress Callahan had seen her wearing all those weeks ago on the outskirts of Kansas City when she'd arrived last to join the wagon train.

"I want to get to the telegraph office before it closes so I can file my next story," she told Callahan.

"I don't remember you looking so fancy when you went to the telegraph office before," Callahan said.

Masters smiled warmly. "I appreciate the compliment. I'm also definitely not coming back tonight. I'm going to find a place to eat and drink until I bust and then find a feather bed in the best hotel Boise has to offer."

"Sounds mighty fine," Callahan said. "But my old saddle under my head is all I can afford. The drink doesn't sound bad. If you can give me half an hour, Cookie and I will ride in with you."

"Don't keep me waiting," she said with mock severity. "A half hour and not one second longer. I need to get into town before I go wagon-crazy."

Callahan felt like he might be going a little wagon-crazy himself and assured her he'd be along shortly.

He found Becky and Lizzy unloading their cook pot.

"Lizzy, go find us some firewood," Becky told the little girl.

"I thought you might like to come into town with me," Callahan said. "A lot of the folks are going in to hit the mercantile, load up on supplies, that sort of thing."

"Well, I don't have any money to buy anything, so that's a wasted trip for me," Becky said. "I have everything I need here."

"Oh. Okay." Callahan shuffled awkwardly. "Well, I'll stay, too. I'll stay here with you."

Becky threw back her head and brayed laughter.

"Luke Callahan, if you aren't the sorriest, most hangdog thing I've seen in a pair of boots. I'm a grown woman. Go on with Cookie Mayfield and have a few beers."

Callahan brightened. "You know I'd rather be with you."

"Liar. Go have fun. Just don't get all full of whiskey and fall for that newspaperwoman's tricks." Becky batted her eyes and affected a back East accent. "Oh, Mister Callahan, you're so big and strong. Could a Vassar girl like me ever turn your head?"

Callahan didn't know what a Vassar girl was, but he grabbed Becky and gave her a quick kiss. "Nobody's turning my head but you." He kissed her again. "See you later."

"You don't have to be *so* happy," she said.

He grinned. "I miss you already." He blew her a kiss as he jogged away.

Anna Masters borrowed Clancy Davenport's horse, and she, Callahan, and Cookie Mayfield rode into town.

They tied their horses to the hitching post in front of the first saloon they came to, a respectable-enough-looking place, although not *too* respectable. Cookie licked his lips and was practically dancing at the thought of a cold beer and a shot of whiskey.

"Get us a table, boys," Masters said. "I'll send off my report, then come join you."

Callahan and Cookie exchanged looks.

Masters frowned. "I know what you're thinking. Only one sort of girl frequents a place like this. Well, you can put that sort of thinking right out of your head. I didn't survive wolf attacks, a bandit holdup, and an Indian raid just to be kept out of a saloon like this. Now get a table and a glass for me. I'll be right back."

Callahan and Cookie looked at each other again, shrugged, and went inside.

The saloon was called Brady's and boasted a friendly atmosphere. Men stood at the bar. Others played cards at a nearby table. There was an upright piano against the far wall, but nobody played it at the moment. Maybe later. Callahan wouldn't mind some music. Callahan saw a woman in a low-cut dress leading a cowboy up a flight of steps to indulge in the sort of activity that usually went on in the upstairs part of a saloon.

Callahan thought briefly of Becky, then stopped himself.

That's not Becky I'm thinking of. It's Velvet, and Velvet don't exist no more.

Cookie grabbed a table in the corner. Callahan went to the bar and came back with two mugs of beer, a bottle of whiskey, and three glasses. They each tossed back a shot of whiskey, relishing the burn, then sipped their beers more slowly.

"I'd forgotten what life was like on the trail," Cookie said. "Makes a man really appreciate something as simple as a cold beer."

Callahan couldn't disagree.

Anna Masters entered a few minutes later and paused just inside the door to let her eyes adjust.

Heads turned, probably wondering if this proper young lady was lost.

She saw Callahan and Cookie in the corner, waved, and walked straight for them. The bartender watched her walk past, then shrugged and went back to his business, as did the rest of the saloon's patrons.

Masters sat, grabbed the bottle, filled her empty shot glass, and gulped it down. "I needed that."

"Did you take care of your correspondence?" Cookie asked.

"I did," she replied. "I needn't have hurried. The telegraph office is in back of the mercantile, and they're both open late tonight for some reason. I didn't ask why."

She refilled her glass and lifted it. "To the last wagon train."

Sure, Callahan thought. *Why not?* He and Cookie lifted their glasses.

"To the last wagon train."

The Imperial Hotel was the finest accommodation Boise had to offer, so, of course, that was where Kent Arbuckle took a suite of rooms. The place was truly opulent. One could not swing a cat without hitting something velvet or crystal or trimmed in gold. Not that anyone would ever do anything as crass as swing a cat in the Imperial. Carpets were thick. Servants scurried when summoned. The manager dutifully looked the other way when women from the Dancing Grizzly Saloon were smuggled up the back stairway.

The manager was a man of the world, after all, and understood the appetites of other men of the world.

Mycroft Jones had enjoyed the best meal he'd ever eaten, the best wine he'd ever drunk, in the hotel's restaurant, where the service bordered on the obsequious.

After Jones had enjoyed a sumptuous dessert, the aforementioned worldly manager of the Imperial had told him in a hushed tone with a wink and a nod that the Dancing Grizzly was likely the best place to round up a couple of quality—*ahem*—nieces.

The Dancing Grizzly's proprietor was a smarmy, greasy man with a lascivious grin, and he smelled money when he talked to Mycroft Jones. Jones made his needs clear. Young. Fresh. At least one redhead. They should be freshly bathed.

Jones had been impressed with the two women who'd been selected. Clear white skin. Good teeth. The redhead was especially buxom, had sparkling green eyes, and freckles that gave her a playful quality. He escorted the fetching young things back to Arbuckle's suite at the Imperial, where he learned much to his chagrin that *both* of the nieces had been earmarked for Arbuckle's entertainment.

Mycroft Jones had been treated to a sumptuous dinner, and apparently, Arbuckle's hospitality stopped there when it came to extracurricular activities. Jones played it off beautifully, excusing himself as if he'd known all along that he would not be included in what would doubtlessly be a thoroughly enjoyable evening.

Mycroft walked the streets of Boise, hands in pockets, wondering what to do with himself, wondering when it might be safe to return to the suite, and wondering why his employer had not simply booked him a separate room.

He paused on the wooden sidewalk, looked up, and saw he was at a place called Brady's. He figured he might as well get another drink.

Mycroft Jones turned to enter.

And almost walked straight into Tomahawk Callahan.

Kent Arbuckle sat on the plush sofa of his parlor, one of three rooms in his suite at the Imperial. The gorgeous redhead sat next to him, one leg thrown over his. She sipped champagne from a flute. Arbuckle had taken off his jacket and pulled his tie loose.

The leggy brunette crossed the room, brought Arbuckle a freshly filled flute, and handed it to him, her smile wide and dazzling. Mycroft Jones had done a fine job of rounding up a couple of quality nieces to keep Arbuckle company.

"Drink up, ladies," Arbuckle said. "I'll send down for more champagne if we run out."

The girls cooed and made various noises about his generosity and so on. And how good-looking he was. And my, oh my, how fascinating it was to be a railroad man. Arbuckle didn't quite listen but rather nodded along to the lilt and gentle rhythm of their voices.

They had nice voices. Feminine and soft. A pleasant change from barking railroad foremen and gruff laborers.

A knock at the door.

Arbuckle's eyes narrowed with curiosity. Who could that be? Had he already sent down for more champagne and forgotten? It was a possibility. He'd had a good bit to drink already, starting with a lovely cabernet over dinner with Mycroft.

Mycroft. The fellow had been a good sport to excuse himself. Arbuckle needed quality time with his nieces.

The knock again.

Oh, that's right. Somebody's at the door.

Arbuckle stood, giving the red head a friendly slap on the thigh. "Don't go anywhere. I'll be right back."

The girls giggled and assured him they'd be waiting.

Arbuckle crossed the parlor and opened the door. He blinked at the man standing there. It took him an extra moment to recognize Roy Benson.

"Benson, I was going to look you up tomorrow," Arbuckle said. "Never mind. Come in."

Benson entered, casting an appreciative eye at the ladies. "It seems I've come at an awkward time."

"Nonsense." Arbuckle's mood was too good to be spoiled by an unexpected visitor. "Have a quick drink." He poured champagne for Benson. "Allow me to introduce . . . you know, I'm sorry, ladies, but I've forgotten your names."

"Esmerelda," the redhead said.

"Victoria," the brunette told him.

"Roy has done me a good job of work," Arbuckle told the ladies. "I'm sure he'd like the money he's owed. He's certainly earned it. Ladies, I won't be a moment. Come with me, Roy. Your money's in the hotel safe."

The two men walked downstairs together, and Arbuckle asked, "You told me you had a sidekick. He's not with you?"

"I'll take him his share," Benson said. "He wants to remain anonymous. I also figured he's not the sort you really want to be seen associating with."

"Ah, that's good thinking," Arbuckle said. "And the wagons? You're sure?"

"We both counted and compared numbers. They've

lost one too many," Benson assured him. "You have somebody on the inside, yes? Double-check if you like." "

"I've already sent my operative a message for just that purpose, and I've bribed the telegraph man to work late tonight in case I get a reply" Benson said. "A mere formality. I'm sure your information is sound, old boy. Also, I've told my railroad crews to keep the pressure on. I still intend to beat Callahan to Salem, but it's a relief to know the bet's already won."

They arrived at the front desk, and the manager was more than happy to retrieve a pair of saddlebags from the safe. He set them on the front counter with the telltale *clink* of coins. Benson had preferred to be paid in gold. It was all the same to Arbuckle, so he was happy to oblige the man.

Benson slung the saddlebags over his shoulder. "A pleasure doing business with you."

"Don't you want to count it?" Arbuckle asked.

Benson shook his head. "I'm sure a businessman of your stature would not do anything so crass as to short the hired help."

That made Arbuckle chuckle.

"I think a few nights rest and relaxation would do me good. Do you happen to have any available rooms?" Benson asked the hotel manager.

"One, yes, sir," the manager said. "But I'm afraid it's only a single."

"That will do nicely." Benson turned back to Arbuckle. "Should you need me to do anything else, I'll be here the next few days."

"I'll take it under advisement," Arbuckle said. "Now

if you'll excuse me, I think my nieces must miss their uncle terribly."

Mycroft Jones had never met Tomahawk Callahan, but he recognized his description from the newspapers—tall, rugged good looks, and a lean and hungry way about him. Also, the man Jones had nearly walked smack into on his way into Brady's Saloon had what was clearly an Indian tomahawk tucked into his belt.

But what clinched it for Jones that this was indeed *the* Tomahawk Callahan was the fancy lady on Callahan's arm who said, "Tomahawk Callahan, will you watch where you're going? You nearly knocked this poor man right over."

Callahan grinned and doffed his hat. "My pardon, sir."

Jones smiled. "No harm done. Have a good night, you two."

He stepped aside and allowed the couple to pass. They were followed by an older bandy-legged gentleman. The trio turned the way Jones had come, laughing and talking as they strolled.

Jones considered what to do. He'd been given to understand the wagon train was near Boise, but apparently they were making good time and had already arrived. According to Jones's employer, Kent Arbuckle, the matter was settled. Callahan and his crew had lost too many wagons.

On the other hand, Callahan and his friends didn't act like people who'd just lost a big bet. They were drinking and laughing and clearly having a fine time.

Something didn't fit.

Jones followed the trio, keeping his distance but not letting them out of his sight.

Callahan suspected he'd done exactly what Becky had warned him not to do, which was drink just a little too much, making himself susceptible to Anna Masters's charms. The simple fact was that the woman *was* charming and funny and easy on the eyes. She clung to his arm. Laughing at his dumb jokes as they walked down the streets of Boise.

Not that he'd fall for the woman. He wasn't that drunk or that stupid. Still, she was pleasant company. They'd all needed the saloon time.

And, anyway, Cookie Mayfield was there to chaperone.

"Well, I'll see you two later," Cookie said. "If Miss Masters is right, then the mercantile is still open, and I can pick up a few things we need before heading back."

"Oh, uh . . . yeah," Callahan said, suddenly feeling awkward. "I should probably go with you. Help you carry the stuff."

Masters held tight to his arm and pulled him closer. "Mr. Callahan, you disappoint me. Are you really going to let a lady walk the streets of a cutthroat town like Boise, Idaho, without an escort?"

Callahan went red.

Cookie chuckled. "You two young people don't need me. I'll get the supplies and meet you back at the wagons." He was still chuckling as he ambled away.

"Come on," she said and tugged on his arm. "Just walk me to my hotel, and then I'll let you off the hook."

Callahan let out a relieved sigh. Surely, there was nothing wrong with simply making sure she made it safely to her hotel.

"Lead on!" Callahan said.

They walked a few more minutes until Masters indicated they'd arrived, a hotel called the Golden Slipper.

"It was either here or the Imperial across the street," Masters said. "Both came highly recommended."

"They look fancy enough," Callahan said. "I'm sure you'll be comfortable."

"I'm told the beds are very soft, the sheets clean and white." She stepped close to him, put the palm of her slender hand against his chest. "Now doesn't that sound much more comfortable that the cold, hard ground and a saddle for a pillow?"

Callahan swallowed hard.

"You'd be surprised at the various . . . amenities . . . this hotel has to offer." A smile slowly spread itself across her face, eyelids going heavy.

Callahan took a step back. "I . . . uh . . . I should probably catch up with Cookie and help him or . . . where'd he say he went? The mercantile?"

Anna Masters threw back her head and laughed. "Oh, Tomahawk, you're a hoot, you know that? I guess our young Miss Becky has nothing to worry about. Lucky girl."

Callahan's nervousness eased somewhat. "I guess I'm the lucky one. Not that I wouldn't . . . I mean . . . not that I haven't thought . . . Look, you're a beautiful woman, and I'm not blind. So don't take offense if I'm not . . . if I don't . . ."

"Oh, stop your stammering, Tomahawk," she said. "I think you know I'm the kind of woman that does what she wants. I made my pitch, and you didn't bite." A shrug. "So what? I'm a big girl. And the soft bed and clean sheets are still waiting." She went up on tiptoes and gave him a sisterly peck on the cheek. "You have a good night."

He watched her go inside the hotel, then turned abruptly and headed back for his horse at a fast walk. He was impressed by his own willpower.

But not enough to risk a look back.

CHAPTER 31

A pounding, loud and insistent.

At first Kent Arbuckle thought it was inside his head. He'd had a lot of champagne last night. Then he thought the pounding might be at the door.

He sat up and realized it was both. He held his head in both hands, groaned, and said, "Lay off the door, will you? What could be so important?"

"Mr. Arbuckle, I need to talk to you. It's *very* important." The voice of Mycroft Jones.

Arbuckle glanced around the bedroom. His nieces weren't there. Judging by the harsh sun slanting in through the window, it was late morning, maybe even noon. He'd slept a good part of the day away. He heaved himself to his feet, crossed the room, and opened the door. Jones stood there looking eager and impatient. Behind him, the hotel manager waited in the doorway leading to the outer hall.

"I tried knocking on the outer door several times," Jones said. "I finally prevailed upon the manager to let me in."

"Good Lord, Mycroft, where did you sleep last night?" Arbuckle asked.

"I took a room at the place down the street," Jones said. "It seemed indelicate to disturb your quality time with your, uh, nieces, but that's not really the point at the moment. I've found out—"

Arbuckle looked past Jones to the hotel manager. "Sorry for the trouble. We've got it sorted now."

The manager bowed before leaving. "Please let me know if I can be of further assistance."

"Sorry, Mycroft," Arbuckle said. "Of course, I'll reimburse you for the hotel room."

"No, sir. I mean, yes, thank you, sir. That's most kind, but not really the point at the moment."

"What is the point then?" Arbuckle asked. "Breakfast? I could murder a plate of bacon and eggs, although I suppose it's closer to lunchtime."

"Sir, Tomahawk Callahan was in Boise last night," Jones told him. "The wagon train was camped just on the edge of town."

"Really?" Arbuckle was genuinely surprised. The wagon train was making better time than he'd thought. "Well, that's no worry, is it? We know they've already lost the wager."

"Sir, that might not actually be true."

Arbuckle blinked at Jones, replaying that last sentence in his head. Surely, he wasn't understanding the man correctly.

"Mycroft," Arbuckle said. "I think you're confused."

Jones looked halfway between embarrassed and chagrined. "Would that it were true, sir."

"Say what you said again," Arbuckle told him. "Maybe I didn't hear it right."

"It's possible, sir, that you have not, in fact, won the wager," Jones said carefully. "It would seem that the outcome of the wager is yet to be determined . . . if I'm understanding my facts correctly."

"Then let us examine these facts together," Arbuckle said. "To determine where you may have gone wrong."

"I saw Tomahawk Callahan coming out of a saloon," Jones related. "He was with people. They were laughing and drinking and . . . well, not acting like people who'd just lost a significant amount of money on a wager."

"You understand, Mycroft, that such behavior, while understandably suspicious, proves nothing," Arbuckle said blithely.

Jones nodded vigorously. "I quite concur. However, spurred by his suspicious demeanor, I took it upon myself to follow him."

Arbuckle could already tell he wasn't going to like this.

"I followed him back to his camp, where all the wagons were arranged in a circle."

"And?" Arbuckle was growing impatient. He wanted his assistant to hurry up and get to the part where he got it wrong so Arbuckle could go back to thinking about bacon and eggs.

"And I counted the wagons."

Arbuckle went cold. He felt absolutely certain he was going to completely hate what Jones was about to tell him, and yet Arbuckle so desperately wanted to cling to hope. "You counted the wagons and . . . confirmed they've lost too many?"

"I'm afraid not, sir."

Arbuckle unleashed a stinging string of expletives.

"I wasn't sure I'd counted correctly, so I counted again," Jones said. "Knowing you'd be displeased with the outcome, I counted a third time."

Arbuckle groaned.

"The wagon train is still viable," Jones said. "The wager is still on."

Arbuckle crossed the parlor to a sideboard, pulled the plug on a crystal decanter, and filled a tumbler halfway with brandy. He gulped it down. At first, the liquor inflamed his hangover, his head pounding, his churning gut threatening to give it back. Then the hair of the dog did its job, easing his muscles. He drank some more, then let out a long sigh.

"Although an unpleasant surprise and bitterly disappointing, setbacks are inevitable." He tried to sound determined and businesslike, even if he didn't feel it, not quite yet. He gulped more brandy. "Time to get to work, Mycroft. Roy Benson is staying at this hotel. Find him. Check at the front desk to see if there are any new telegrams. It would be nice if our undercover operative in the wagon train can confirm or deny what you've found out . . . No, no, I'm not criticizing, Mycroft. I'm sure you counted correctly, but confirmation never hurts."

"Right away, sir. Anything else?"

"Send telegrams to each railway crew foreman," Arbuckle ordered. "Tell them not to let up. We haven't won our wager yet."

"I'll see to it, sir."

"And Mycroft?"

"Sir?"

"Run down the valet and tell him I need a hot bath right away," Arbuckle said. "I can't solve the world's problems smelling like champagne sweat and saloon vixens."

Roy Benson was not sure how everything had gotten so messed up. Closing his eyes, he pictured the wagon train coming out of the pass. He and that fool Hawkins had counted right, hadn't they?

Maybe not.

Kent Arbuckle looked down at him from the back of his private train car like some two-bit politician scrounging votes at a whistle-stop. Benson had not been invited up to join him. Arbuckle was understandably irked that he'd laid out quite a bit of gold, only to find out Benson hadn't delivered as promised.

"And the money is still in the hotel safe?" Arbuckle asked.

"Yes." Benson had been obliged to return the money, even if only temporarily. Under the circumstances, he couldn't really object. He cursed himself for not lighting out the previous evening, but a comfortable night at the fancy hotel had been irresistible.

"Then that's where it should stay," Arbuckle said. "When you've truly earned it, you can come back and fetch it. For now, I need you to finish the job you started. Where's this sidekick of yours?"

Dead as dead can be. "I'll catch up with him on the

way out of town. Don't worry. I'll make your wishes clear. Uh . . . what are your wishes again?"

"Must I spell it out for you?" Arbuckle sounded exasperated. "As before. Only finish the job this time." He leaned down and lowered his voice. "If you get the chance . . . if you can somehow make it look like an accident . . . I wouldn't mind terribly if you killed Tomahawk Callahan."

Benson's eyes widened slightly with surprise. Killing a man didn't put him off. Indeed, he'd done it before for a variety of reasons. No, Benson didn't balk at the thought of killing a man. It was just that Benson couldn't quite see how that would help the situation. The death of one man would not be sufficient to invalidate the wagon train. Was Callahan's leadership so valuable that the wagon train would fail if he suddenly disappeared?

Possibly.

But Benson doubted it.

He supposed it didn't matter. Arbuckle was the one paying the bills. If he wanted Callahan dead, so be it. There was a chance Arbuckle simply wanted the man dead on general principles. Callahan had caused Arbuckle a good deal of anxiety.

"Just remember, nothing can be linked to me or the railroad," Arbuckle said.

"I know."

A hiss of steam, and the locomotive made its initial lurch forward.

"I'm off." Arbuckle waved as the train pulled away. "You know what to do."

Benson returned the wave. "Leave it to me."

He stood and watched as the train picked up speed, heading west, dwindling into the distance, and then finally vanishing from sight altogether. In spite of Arbuckle's urgency, Benson felt no need to hurry. The wagon train was a slow-moving animal, and Benson would catch up easily enough. The question was what to do when that happened. He'd need to spend some time devising a plan, and, as always, he did his best thinking with a bottle of whiskey next to him. So the first order of business was obvious. Find a comfortable place to drink and think . . . and perhaps pay a visit to Arbuckle's lovely nieces. Man cannot, after all, live by bread alone.

Benson considered the money in the safe. He could simply ride away without it. He hated to part with so much gold, but he was starting to wonder if working for that pain in the neck Arbuckle was worth it.

There was, perhaps, another option.

Yes, he definitely needed some whiskey. There was much to think about.

There was a feeling of optimism as the wagon train left Idaho behind and finally, at long last, rolled into Oregon. There was still a solid month of travel ahead of them to get to Salem, maybe a little less if they could get across the Cascades without too much trouble.

The wagons rolled across the sagebrush prairie of eastern Oregon, junipers dotting the landscape. Callahan rode out in front, savoring the landscape. It was a fine day and not too hot.

A few hours later, Billy Thorndyke nudged his horse alongside Callahan's. "Spell you?"

"Thanks, Billy," Callahan said. "I'll ride back and see how everyone's doing."

Callahan headed back down the column of wagons, offering friendly nods and waves as each wagon passed. Pete Johansen returned Callahan's greeting with a respectful nod but abandoned all pretense of dignity when the Grainger girls stuck their heads out on either side of him, shouting boisterous *hellos* at Callahan.

Callahan laughed and rode on.

He turned his horse and walked alongside Becky's wagon for a few minutes.

"A good day to you, Mr. Callahan." Becky smiled sweetly.

Callahan grinned and touched the brim of his hat. "And a good day to you, Miss Griffith."

"Will you be coming around tonight, Mr. Callahan?"

He shrugged. "Is it official wagon train business?"

Her smile widened. "I'm sure I can think of something."

"You two aren't fooling anybody, you know!" Lizzy called from within the wagon.

Callahan and Becky both laughed. He told her he'd see her later and continued his tour back down the column.

He came to the final wagon and saw Old Man Henderson holding the reins. Maybe Anna Masters was having a nap in the back. He wondered how she was getting along with the old couple. They seemed nice enough, but the newspaperwoman struck Callahan as the sort of person who insisted on having a certain amount of elbow room. Maybe her night in a comfortable Boise hotel room would be enough to carry her through to Salem. He offered Henderson a quick wave and kept moving.

The smell and sound of the two herds hit him at once. Callahan paid quick visits to Bart Shultz and Ace Franklin. Both men reported nothing amiss. Since the wolf attack earlier in their trek, nothing had molested either the cattle or the sheep.

On the way back, Callahan saw Anna Masters hanging out the back of her wagon.

"What's the good word, Tomahawk?" she called.

"The sky is blue and Salem inches closer," he called back.

"Where can I send off my next missive?"

Callahan didn't even need to think about it. He'd memorized the map a hundred times and knew every stop along the way. Not that he'd *been* to every stop, but as a first-timer on a wagon train, he'd been more nervous than a cat in a room full of rocking chairs. Studying the map and preparing as best he could helped ease those nerves.

"Pendelton," he said. "They have a telegraph."

"How many days?"

"Ten if we're lucky," Callahan told her. "More like two weeks if something bogs us down."

She groaned and rolled her eyes. "What am I sup- posed to do for two weeks?"

"Talk to people," Callahan said. "Aren't you getting their stories for your book?"

"I've talked to everyone fifty times," Masters told

him. "And that includes Myrna Linkletter's story about how her dog can play checkers."

Callahan shook his head. He didn't believe for one minute a dog could play checkers. "I'm sure you'll figure some way to amuse yourself, Miss Masters."

He spurred his horse and headed back up the column.

He paused when he saw a man astride a horse about a hundred yards to the right of the wagon train. He looked again and saw it was Clancy Davenport.

What in the world is the kid doing out there?

Callahan tugged on the reins and headed for Davenport at a trot.

He eased the horse to a halt next to Davenport and asked, "Seeing the sights?"

"Sorry, boss. I promise I'm not shirking," Davenport said. "It's just that I saw . . . well . . . are those what I think they are?" The boy pointed.

Callahan squinted. "Let's get closer."

They approached a length of raised ground—maybe two feet up from the rest of the prairie—that ran parallel to the wagon train's course. When they got there, Callahan shook his head. Davenport had been right.

"Train tracks."

"Are these the ones we're racing against?" Davenport asked.

Callahan twisted his head one way, then the other, picturing the rail line on a map. If the line came down from the northeast at Hansen's Bend, then straightened out to head west to Salem . . .

"Yeah, that's it," Callahan said. "That's the new line. New steel."

Davenport's gaze drifted west. "I wonder how far they've gotten."

Callahan had been wondering the same thing. "When we get to Pendleton, that's the first thing I'm going to find out."

CHAPTER 32

The wagon train crossed sagebrush lands and climbed into the Blue Mountains, where the passes were wide and easy. They had ten solid days of good weather and no mishaps. If the saboteur was still intent on foiling the wagon train, then he was taking a good long break. Callahan wasn't sure if he should be thankful or even more cautious and suspicious than usual.

Don't they say it's calmest right before the storm? He shrugged. *They also say don't look a gift horse in the mouth.*

On the eleventh day, Cookie Mayfield said, "I reckon we'll make Pendleton tomorrow."

Callahan raised an eyebrow. "Already?" Callahan had thought they were still two or three days away.

"If we get an early start and push hard . . . yeah, I reckon so."

That night, Callahan cleaned his guns around the fire again, even though they didn't need it. He was doing some thinking.

"I guess Miss Masters will want to go into town to send her telegram to the newspaper," Callahan said.

Cookie leaned over the cookfire and gave the pot of beans a stir. "'Spose so."

"Stay here if you like," Callahan said. "I'll ride in with her."

Cookie looked up from the cook pot, frowning. "No. I mean . . . I'd rather do it." He suddenly looked embarrassed. "To tell the truth, she ain't exactly terrible to look at, and I sort of like having her to myself for a bit. I know an old codger like me won't turn her head, but it's still a pleasant way to spend some time."

Callahan laughed. "Okay, then, but I'm riding along. I need to ask around, dig up some news on that rail line. I'm in a race, and I have no idea if I'm winning or losing."

"The three of us will ride in together." Cookie grinned suddenly. "Too dangerous for you to be alone with her, anyway."

Callahan felt his ears go red. "I know you're funning with me, but just don't talk like that if Becky's within earshot, okay?"

Cookie laughed, shaking his head.

The next morning, they roused the wagon train just a little earlier than usual and set the pace just a little faster. Callahan kept pushing. Now that his curiosity had been roused about the rail line, he didn't like the thought of having to wait another day. He kept the wagon train moving.

Just as the sun was beginning to set, Pendleton came into view. Callahan tasked the Thorndyke brothers and Clancy Davenport with circling the wagons and setting the watch. He assured them he'd be back as soon as possible.

But not before finding out the information he wanted.

He saddled up and rode into town with Cookie and Anna Masters. On the way in, he noticed the railroad tracks, which made a straight line right into Pendleton.

Pendleton wasn't big but it was lively. A crew of laborers worked hard on a new building right next to the tracks, and Callahan guessed it must be a new railroad station. That would be the perfect place to start asking his questions.

"Cookie, take Miss Masters to find the telegraph," Callahan said. "I'll meet you later."

Callahan approached the construction. Men swarmed over a wooden frame with hammers and saws. The sun had gone down, and a number of lanterns had been hung around the site. A skinny, middle-aged man stood a few feet back from the scene, hat back on his head, a pipe in his mouth, shirtsleeves rolled up. To Callahan's thinking, the man had foreman written all over him.

Callahan ambled up next to him. "Your crew?"

"That's right," he said. "A train station for the new line. She'll be a beauty—raised platform, ticket counter, waiting area, a place to load freight."

"Sounds like a good job of work."

The foreman blew out a sigh. "You said it, brother. That's why we have these lanterns up, working extra hours. The tracks are not quite connected yet, but they want this station ready, anyway. The company wants to park their shiny new locomotive here to gin up some attention. It's all a big to-do."

Callahan's ears perked up when the foreman mentioned the tracks. "What do you mean not connected?"

"Haven't you been following it in the newspapers?"

The foreman seemed genuinely surprised. "The big wager!"

Brother, I don't have to read it in the papers. I've been living it.

"Two crews laying track," the foreman continued. "One from Salem heading east. The other from Hansen's Bend going west. More track in the same amount of time. Not quite a new strategy, but not what they usually do for these branch lines. I guess this was a special situation."

Callahan bit off a curse. It seemed unfair. On the other hand, there was nothing in the rules against it. Kent Arbuckle had the resources of the entire railroad company at his fingertips. Of course, he'd use them.

"Not that any of that has anything to do with me," the foreman said. "I just do stations and water towers and the like. I don't do track. Another two weeks and I'll be off working on some other line."

"Two weeks?" Callahan asked. "Is that when the track will be complete?"

"That's the estimate. Maybe sooner. Do you know they're laying three miles of track a day? Four, some days." The foreman whistled. "They must be working them boys into the grave."

Two weeks. That was just about the same time Callahan would get the wagon train to Salem. Give or take. He could still win this bet.

And he could still lose it.

"Thanks," Callahan said. "Good luck getting your station built."

"Take care now."

Callahan shuffled back toward the telegraph office,

hands in pockets, deep in thought. It was going to be a close thing. One bump in the road and he'd lose the bet, maybe only by a day or by a few hours.

Or maybe it didn't matter. Maybe he never really had a chance.

"Tomahawk!"

He looked up to see Anna Masters approaching. "You send off your newspaper story?"

"All done," she said. "Is Pendleton really the last place I can send a telegram until Salem?"

"As far as I know," Callahan said. "We can double-check with Cookie."

Masters frowned. "Drat."

"You can send your last story from Salem," Callahan told her. "That's the big finale, anyway. Win or lose."

"I suppose."

Callahan looked around. "Where is Cookie, by the way?"

"I lost track of him," Masters said. "I assumed he'd be with you."

Callahan looked past her and saw Cookie emerge from the telegraph office. "Here he comes."

"What were you doing in there?" Masters asked.

"Looking for you," Cookie said. "I guess we somehow missed each other." He turned to Callahan. "Get the information you was looking for?"

Callahan related what the foreman had told him.

"Wow," Masters said. "It's going to be close, isn't it?"

"I reckon that'll make a good story for your readers," Callahan said. "I don't know what'll happen, but maybe . . ."

Callahan trailed off, the sight of a man across the street distracting him. He was struck with the absolute certainty that he knew the man, but he couldn't place the face. Callahan watched as the man entered a saloon called Custer's Mustache.

"You see a ghost?" Cookie asked.

"Maybe," Callahan replied. "Cookie, escort Miss Masters back to camp. I'll be along directly. I need to check on something first."

Callahan walked across the street and entered Custer's Mustache.

The interior was like any of a hundred other saloons Callahan had ever been in, the one difference being the huge portrait of George Armstrong Custer behind the bar. He headed for the bar, casually casting about to catch sight of the man he was following. He spotted him at the far end of the bar. Callahan took a spot at the other end and ordered a beer, sipping and trying to remember.

He was halfway through the beer when the memory came flooding back. It was the beard that had thrown him—or rather, the lack of a beard. The man was clean-shaven now but dressed the same as when Callahan had first met him back at Shakey's Place. He wore a dark suit with a red waistcoat, a tight pattern in the fabric. A gold chain disappeared into the waistcoat pocket. Gold cufflinks. Bowler hat cocked at a jaunty angle.

Callahan eased down the bar toward him, making sure not to appear in a hurry or look threatening in any way. He leaned against the bar, sipping his beer.

"They sure are hammering up a storm out there,"

Callahan said by way of casual conversation. "I'm told it's going to be a new train station."

"I wouldn't know," the other man said without looking up.

"Say, don't I know you?" Callahan worked to keep his tone affable without pouring it on too thick.

A bored glance from the other man. "Sorry. You must be thinking of somebody else."

The man drank the rest of his whiskey, set the glass on the bar, and turned to walk away.

"I think we do know each other," Callahan called after him. "In fact, I think you owe me a cigar, Ronald Parsons."

The man broke into a run, and Callahan gave chase. Everyone in the saloon turned to look, but nobody intervened. They knew better than to insert themselves in a dispute between men. If one of them had been a marshal, he might have stuck his nose in, but nobody was.

Parsons exploded out the saloon's back door into a narrow alley with Callahan right on his heels. The man started to sprint away. Callahan leapt. He grabbed Parsons around the knees, and both men went down into the mud.

Callahan got to his feet first. He grabbed Parsons by the lapels, hauled him up, and slammed him against a wall.

Parsons put his hands up. "There's been a terrible misunderstanding."

"Don't make me laugh." Callahan's first impulse was to beat the man within an inch of his life. After all, Parsons had hit Callahan in the back of the head, stolen his poker winnings, and left him facedown in the mud.

But the flash of anger faded. Callahan could throw fists when he had to, but to simply beat a man who wasn't fighting back wasn't his style. Better to just turn the man over to the law. Callahan wouldn't be a bit surprised to learn there were bounties out for this slicker.

And yet . . .

An idea began to take shape in Callahan's brain.

"I am, of course, terribly sorry for that unfortunate business back at Fort Keogh," Parsons said. "I think it will please you to know that I do have your money *plus* interest. I never really considered that I was *robbing* you. More like . . . uh . . . a loan by force with *every* intent to pay you back. I know this all sounds a bit farfetched, but—"

"Maybe shut up."

Parsons shut up.

"Now," Callahan said, "for the moment, remain calm and hear me out."

"Okay."

"You can choose from the following," Callahan said. "First, I can beat the living tar out of you, take your money, and leave you in an alley the same way you've done me."

"I'm hoping the next choice is better," Parsons said. "I bruise easily."

"Choice number two is I take you to the law, tell them everything I know, and they put you in jail."

"Better, but still not ideal."

"The third choice is that I don't beat you. I don't take you to the law, and you keep your money," Callahan said. "In addition, I'll pay you an additional five hundred dollars."

"I assume choice number three includes some favor I do for you," Parsons said. "Some onerous task I doubt I'll enjoy."

"Whether or not you enjoy it is beside the point," Callahan told him. "And the five hundred dollars comes later. You'll understand if I don't quite trust you. Run out on me, and not only will you not get the five hundred dollars, but I'll also hunt you to the ends of the earth and then you *will* get a beating."

"Then I suppose I'd better hear the details of this favor."

Callahan explained the sort of thing he had in mind.

Parsons grinned. "You know, that actually sounds like fun."

"Then we're in agreement?"

"We are."

"One more thing," Callahan told the slicker.

"Uh-oh."

Callahan fixed Parsons with a hard look to show he was serious. "You still owe me a cigar."

Callahan dragged into camp and found Cookie next to the campfire.

"What kept you?" Cookie asked.

"Long story."

"Listen, it's been a while since we talked about . . . you know," Cookie said, lowering his voice. "That we've got someone inside the wagon train trying to mess us up. It's been so long since we've had a mishap that I sort of just let it go, but we're in the home stretch to Salem now. This rat might want to take one last shot."

Callahan had been thinking something similar. The wagon train still had a chance to win the wager if they got to Salem first. Or maybe the train would get their first. But losing fair and square was one thing. Losing because some mystery saboteur helped the railroad cheat would stick in Callahan's craw.

"We'll just have to be extra vigilant, I guess." Callahan sprawled on his back and put his head on his saddle.

Cookie leaned toward Callahan and lowered his voice yet again. "What if I was to say maybe I know who it is?"

Callahan sat bolt upright. "What's his name?"

"Not his name," Cookie said. "Her name."

CHAPTER 33

The wagon train left Pendleton behind early the next morning. Callahan had passed the word among the settlers that they would be pushing hard for Salem in these final days. Even an extra mile each day might make the difference. Everyone seemed to understand what was at stake and seemed eager to do their part.

It's going to be close, Callahan kept telling himself. *Dang, but it's going to be close.*

As for the saboteur, Callahan both liked and disliked Cookie Mayfield's plan.

He liked it because at least they were *doing* something. Having the matter settled would be a load off Callahan's mind.

But Callahan disliked it because he hated to accuse someone and then find out he was wrong, especially if that someone was Anna Masters.

"She sneaks away from camp," Cookie Mayfield had told him the previous night in hushed tones. "And she's always sending off telegrams. Sure, they could be to the newspaper, but maybe she sends another after that informing what we're doing to the railroad people.

I know this ain't exactly hard proof, but she's had the opportunity all the way along the trail to send information to the people against us."

Callahan hadn't been happy to hear it, but it had made a certain kind of sense. "And she sneaks away every night?"

"No, not every night," Cookie had told him. "But too many."

Callahan considered what he knew about Anna Masters. She was headstrong, ambitious, and didn't seem to care what anyone thought of her. None of those things meant she was a villain, but Callahan had known men like that, and not all of them had been good. Masters could be just as greedy and self-serving as any of them.

She'd probably only shown amorous interest in Callahan to keep him distracted. He could have kicked himself. What a fool he'd been.

Callahan decided to make a few preparations of his own. They had to get this right. Sooner or later, Anna Masters would take one of her secret midnight strolls, and then . . .

Well, then they'd see what they would see.

They made camp that night as usual. Callahan cut his visit with Becky short, telling her he had to attend to some wagon train business. He waited for Cookie near the cookfire.

Cookie appeared sometime later and shook his head. Not tonight.

They repeated the process the next day. Callahan was even more nervous than before. He wanted this over with.

This time when Cookie came back, he was grinning. "Tonight's the night."

Callahan grabbed his Henry rifle. "Let's go."

Cookie led Callahan away from the wagon train and into a patch of nearby woods. Cookie felt confident he remembered the direction she'd been heading.

"She wouldn't have gone so far just to relieve herself," Cookie said. "And she ain't no soft-stepping Indian. Just keep your ears open and you'll hear her crashing about."

And a few seconds later they did hear the rustling sound of somebody pushing their way through the underbrush.

Callahan kept a tight grip on the Henry. Maybe Anna Masters was only out here to pass along information to a single confederate. Or maybe she was meeting a gang of cutthroats she intended to set loose on the wagon train. Nothing would surprise Callahan anymore.

Masters suddenly burst through the bushes. She saw Cookie and Callahan, and her eyes went wide. "Oh!"

Callahan lifted his rifle, not quite pointing it at her. "Hold on, Miss Masters. I'm afraid we need to know what you're doing out here in the middle of the night."

"Are you crazy?" Masters looked appalled. "Cookie asked me to meet him out here. He said something was going on that would make a great newspaper story."

"And it would've made a great story. Too bad nobody's ever going to read it." Cookie cocked his rifle and turned it on Callahan. "Drop that Henry."

Callahan cursed himself, hesitating only a moment before letting his rifle fall to the ground.

"What in heaven's name is going on?" Masters demanded.

"Isn't it obvious?" Cookie asked. "No? Then I'll explain it to you. I'll explain it the same way I'm going to explain it to all those settlers back at the wagon train. Anna Masters snuck in among us to do the railroad's dirty work. Our big hero leader Tomahawk Callahan tried to confront her about it, but she shot him. I shot her, trying to save my friend Tomahawk, but I was too late. Ain't that a darn shame? As second-in-command, I'll need to take control of the wagon train. I'll slow us down because somebody might get hurt with all this rushing around. I guess we'll lose the bet with the railroad, but the safety of the settlers comes first."

Callahan raised his voice. "You hear that, boys?"

"Yes, sir," came a voice from the darkness, followed by the sound of a shell being levered into a chamber.

Another cocking sound came from the other side.

"The Thorndyke brothers don't quite move like soft-stepping Indians, either, but they can be quiet enough when they need to," Callahan said. "Your turn to drop the rifle, Cookie."

Cookie hesitated, eyes darting this way and that as if he could discover the Thorndyke boys somewhere in the night. Finally, he gave up and dropped his rifle.

"I got to thinking," Callahan said. "You went with Anna Masters whenever she sent those telegrams, so you had plenty of opportunity to send your own to anyone you wanted to. Or pick up any telegrams sent to you. You had more than enough know-how about wagons to cut those spokes back at the flood, thinking that was a good opportunity to put some wagons out of commission. I can't prove it was you that took a shot at me during the wolf hunt, but I wouldn't be surprised."

Cookie scowled. "Think you're so smart, don't you?"

"And it was *your* idea to change course and go through that narrow defile, but you didn't suggest that until *after* you and Miss Masters came back from sending telegrams in Fort Fetterman, so it couldn't have been her that leaked the information."

"Then in Pendleton," Masters said. "You came out of the telegraph office. You said you'd been looking for us, but you could have been picking up a message. Maybe getting your instructions to kill Callahan and pin it on me."

"It was the money that first made me wonder," Callahan said. "Aunt Clara said you never saved money, and five hundred dollars was a nice round number. You were bragging about it in the saloon, all right. That's why those robbers came for you, but it wasn't no life savings they were after. It was payoff money from Arbuckle."

Cookie shook his head, laughing bitterly. "But none of that was good enough, was it? You needed me to say it."

"That's right, Cookie. For all I knew, the saboteur *was* Miss Masters," Callahan said. "I didn't want to believe it, but I had to know. I had to be sure. I had to let this play out and see which one of you was the villain. You want to know something? Either way, I wasn't going to feel good about it. I didn't want to think either of you would betray me and the wagon train. I'm sick about all this, but here we are."

"And now what?" Cookie asked. "Hogtie me and take me to the marshal?"

"I suppose if you play nice, there's no need to hogtie anyone," Callahan said.

"And I'm supposed to be grateful for that, I guess." Cookie shook his head, let his shoulders slump. "Well, there's no point dragging this out any—"

With surprising speed for a man his age, Cookie lurched to the side, latching onto Masters's arm and pulling her to him. In an eyeblink, he had a knife at her throat.

"Don't shoot!" Callahan called to the Thorndyke brothers. "You might hit Miss Masters."

"Don't figure I'm keen to let you take me to the law," Cookie said. "So I'm just going to take Miss Masters for a little walk. No shooting. Nobody gets hurt. She don't have to taste this knife if everyone plays nice."

"Then what?" Callahan asked.

"Then I don't go to prison," Cookie said. "I'll pick a direction and keep going and start over somewhere they don't know me or anything— *Yeeaaaoow!*"

Anna Masters had sunk her teeth into the thumb of Cookie's knife hand and held on like an enraged wolverine. Blood spilled down Cookie's arm. He tried to jerk his hand away, but Masters was into him too deep. Still screaming in pain, he finally shoved her away.

Ridding himself of his shield at the same time.

Cookie saw Callahan go for his pistol and went for his own.

The Peacemaker spat fire before Cookie's gun had

cleared the holster. He took the shot high in the shoulder, staggered back, hurt but still trying to pull his six-shooter.

Callahan fanned the Peacemaker's hammer three times, three holes exploding red across Cookie's chest. He staggered back again, then tried to right himself but pitched forward, going to the ground with a hard thud. Callahan went to one knee next to Cookie and flipped him over, looking for signs of life.

Cookie Mayfield was dead.

Callahan called Billy and Ike out of the darkness. "Take Cookie's body back. Explain what happened. Tell them I'll be along if they have any questions."

The boys took Cookie away.

Callahan helped Anna Masters to her feet. "You okay?"

"I'm fine." But she hung onto his arm to steady herself. She turned her head and spit. "I need something to get the taste of his blood out."

"I'll walk you back to your wagon."

"I told you I'm fine." But she didn't let go of him.

Back at her wagon, Masters reached into the jockey box. She came out with a half-full bottle of whiskey. She took a slug, swirled it around inside her mouth, then spit. She swallowed the next mouthful, then offered the bottle to Callahan.

"No thanks. You keep it."

She took another swig. "You really thought I might have been working for the railroad?

"I didn't want to think it," Callahan said. "I had to allow it was a possibility."

"And you were sure it was Cookie?"

"More sure than I was it might be you," Callahan said. "But not all the way sure."

"What a night." She drank again. "Now what?"

"Now we finish the race," Callahan said. "But without worrying that we have a traitor in our midst."

"There's still a thousand things that could go wrong," she reminded him. "Bad weather. Another Indian attack. We could all suddenly get smallpox. Heck, that wheel you put on my wagon has been creaking something awful. A thousand things."

That got a weak smile from Callahan. "Well, a thousand is better than a thousand and one. You going to be all right?"

"Yeah. Thanks, Tomahawk."

"Get some sleep then. We're doing it all again tomorrow."

A pall hung over the wagon train the next few days. Cookie Mayfield had been popular. It was a blow to morale to hear not only he was dead but also that he'd betrayed the entire wagon train.

A week went by, mercifully uneventful. The routine of the journey was its own sort of balm—travel all day, circle the wagons, cook a meal, slip into exhausted slumber, rise with the dawn, gobble a quick breakfast, then head out again.

Repeat until you got there.

More days passed.

As they drew ever closer to Salem, the mood of the wagon train took a turn for the better. Their destination was within reach, and soon their long journey would be over. There must have been times the settlers thought they'd never get there.

About two hours before sundown, Billy Thorndyke reined in his horse next to Callahan's. "Uh, boss, me and the boys been talking, and, well . . ."

"You want to know how close."

Billy shrugged as if he'd been caught asking an embarrassing question.

Not that Callahan blamed the kid. He'd been doing the math in his head all day. If Cookie Mayfield had still been with him, he'd look at a tree and a bird and a cloud and spit out the answer. The man had been a veteran, and he'd known the Oregon Trail backward and forward.

The rest of them were greener than snot.

No, that's not true. These boys have proven them-selves. Maybe I have, too. It's just this last little bit. We haven't done it before. We think we know, but we don't want to be wrong.

For the hundredth time, Callahan pictured the map in his head. Again, he did the math.

"Tomorrow," Callahan said. "Unless there's some unforeseen problem, we should get to Salem tomorrow."

Billy's face blazed with a sudden grin. "Tomorrow. I can hardly believe it."

"Believe it," Callahan said. "You helped make it happen."

A new expression washed across Billy's face. Pride, Callahan realized. Sure. Why not? The boy had earned it.

Callahan twisted in the saddle, looking back the way they had come, all the long miles, as if he might actually be able to see all the way back to Missouri.

Something caught his eye. They'd been paralleling the railroad tracks the last two days, using them as a guide into Salem. Something came along the tracks now, coming from behind, gliding smoothly over the rough terrain. Too small to be a locomotive.

A handcar, Callahan realized. Not nearly as fast as a locomotive.

But faster than a covered wagon.

"Come on," Callahan said. "I want to talk to these fellas."

They set an intercept course and headed for a spot on the track where they thought they might catch the handcar. They'd guessed well and arrived just as the handcar passed. Callahan waved for the two men working the handcar to stop.

They didn't.

"Can't stop and lose momentum," one of the men shouted from the handcar as he pumped furiously. "Got a schedule to keep!"

Callahan spurred his horse after the handcar, matching speeds with an easy gallop. "Did they finish the tracks?"

"Yesterday!" the man called back.

Callahan's heart sank.

"The Pendleton-Salem Direct they're calling this stretch. Leaves tomorrow morning at six. Every seat sold," the man shouted. "They'll make Salem about noon."

Callahan didn't need to do the math this time.

The wagon train was going to lose.

CHAPTER 34

He wanted to look the part and went over his wardrobe while sipping a cup of coffee in his shabby hotel room. The black suit and matching vest would do nicely. It was the same suit he wore when he occasionally posed as a preacher, but he eschewed the string tie in favor of a bow tie. He donned a bank clerk's visor and stuck a pencil behind his ear. Then he put on a pair of wire-rim spectacles. The so-called lenses were nothing more than flat glass. The spectacles had come from an optician's sample display.

Ah, but the crowning glory to his disguise was the badge.

When Tomahawk Callahan had told him what he wanted, Ronald Parson's wheels had started to turn. He did so relish a good scheme. He could usually make a fine living at cards, but on that rare occasion when lady luck turned against him, he often supplemented his income with a clever confidence trick.

Actually hitting a man in the back of the head and taking his money—as Parsons had with Callahan—was always an ugly and unfortunate last resort. It was an artless way to earn a buck and required little thought or skill.

But Callahan had offered Parsons a chance to redeem himself. Parsons had quickly concocted a scheme and was immediately off to the local tinsmith. The man had come through for him in spades. The tin badge was artfully crafted, slightly smaller than a fireman's badge Parsons had seen once back East. It pictured a well-wrought locomotive. The words RAILROAD COMMISSION above and INSPECTOR #24601 below.

Parsons pinned it to his lapel, then looked at himself in the mirror.

Perfect.

He took his coffee cup to the window and looked at the new train station across the street. The sun was just rising. The locomotive was there, already getting warmed up, three passenger cars and a freight car attached, the passengers slowly starting to board. There was a festive feeling in the air. A new line. A big wager. There was the notion that this inaugural train ride would be something historic, and people wanted to be part of it.

Parsons finished his last sip of coffee and set the cup aside.

Now to go ruin everyone's good time.

He went downstairs, crossed the street, and walked right up to the locomotive. It was ten minutes to six, and the big engine was already letting off steam, raring to go like some great prehistoric animal that wanted meat and refused to be held back. He climbed the steps up to the cab as if he owned the place.

The engineer blinked at him. He was a ruddy-faced man with a drooping gray mustache and had the look of somebody not to be trifled with. The expression on his face made it clear Parsons was no more welcome in his cab than a rabid skunk.

"I think you're in the wrong place, mister," the engineer said.

"Don't worry, I'll be out of your hair soon." Parsons thumbed the badge on his lapel. "Routine check."

The engineer squinted at the badge. "Say what now?"

"Paperwork and so on," Parsons said. "I'm sure you know what it's like."

"Mister, this train leaves the station in ten minutes, and I need you to vacate this here locomotive right now."

Parsons laughed affably. "My good, sir, I do not intend to delay you. Quite the contrary, a strict adherence to schedule makes the world go around in this inspector's humble opinion."

A lanky man with a vacant expression arrived and stood next to the engineer, slack-jawed and covered to the elbows in coal dust. Obviously, the locomotive's fireman.

"Who's this?" the fireman asked.

The engineer shook his head as if he didn't have time for such nonsense. "Some kind of inspector, he says."

"Arnold Gross," Parsons said. "Inspector number two-four-six-zero-one."

"What's he want?" asked the fireman.

The engineer scowled at Parsons. "What *do* you want?"

"I just need to see your firebox certificate," Parsons said. "Then I'll be out of your way."

"Firebox *what*?"

"Certificate."

"Well, I don't have it," the engineer said.

Parsons *tsked*. "Well, you're supposed to keep it in the cab, so it can be produced upon demand. Never mind. Go fetch it, wherever it is. If you hurry, you can still leave on time."

The engineer's face had gone red. He was close to puffing as much steam as his locomotive. "Mister, I don't know what the blazes you're talking about!"

Parsons eyes widened. "Are you saying you don't have a firebox certificate *at all*?"

"I don't even know what that is!"

"The stays, man. The stays," Parsons said heatedly. "Do you want a crack in the stays to compromise the integrity of the entire firebox? Good lord, man. Just last week there was an explosion that killed the engineer." Parsons turned his gaze onto the slack-jawed idiot. "*And* the fireman."

The fireman's eyes went wide.

Parsons groaned, whipped his fake spectacles off his face, pinching the bridge of his nose between thumb and forefinger. "Well, there's no help for it now. I'll have to do an inspection. I can't do it hot, of course. The inspection has to be done cold."

"Cold?" raged the engineer. "Cold? Do you know how long it will take . . . are you even aware . . . you can't just . . ." The engineer was in danger of a full-blown conniption fit. "That'll take hours!"

"Well, it's not my fault you don't have your firebox certificate."

"I've got a better idea," the engineer said. "I toss your scrawny butt off my train and get going."

"Now listen here, my good man. If you want to risk violating Article Seven of the state of Oregon's railroad codes—fully backed by the United States Railroad

Commission—with a fine of one hundred dollars and up to six months in jail, then be my guest." Parsons blustered with the bureaucratic outrage common to all petty dignitaries everywhere. "I'll wire the appropriate authorities in Salem, where I assure you that you shall be arrested upon arrival."

The engineer's face had gone to the next shade of red. He looked helplessly at his fireman.

"I can't lose no hundred dollars," he said. "My wife'll kill me."

The engineer threw up his hands. "Fine! Shut her down!"

"I'm glad you've seen reason," Parsons said. "Come get me in the hotel across the street when the firebox has cooled enough for inspection."

Parson turned to go, hiding a wicked grin.

Kent Arbuckle sat at his desk aboard his private train car, feet up, tie pulled loose, with a glass of expensive brandy in one hand and a fat cigar in the other.

Life was good.

It had been a blow to hear that Callahan still had enough wagons to legitimately win the bet, but as soon as Arbuckle had received word that the tracks were complete, his spirits had lifted. His mood had improved even further when spotters had reported the wagon train's position.

They wouldn't make it.

Close? Yes, Arbuckle had to admit Callahan had put up a good fight. He would magnanimously mention that to the newspaper reporters when they interviewed him about his historic victory. But everyone had agreed that even if the wagons really pushed it, they would arrive—at best—a few hours behind the train.

Arbuckle had hoped to be aboard the train when it pulled into Salem. Alas, he couldn't get to Pendleton in time for that to happen. The Pendleton-Salem Direct needed to be on its way to reach its destination on time.

Never mind. Arbuckle would follow in his private train and join the celebration when he arrived.

Mycroft Jones entered the car, looking flustered.

"Mycroft, you look ill," Arbuckle said. "Have a drink and relax."

"Mr. Arbuckle, we might have a problem," Jones said.

Arbuckle sighed. "Out with it then."

"We're approaching Pendleton, sir," Jones told him. "And the Pendleton-Salem Direct is still in the station."

"What?"

Arbuckle leapt up, spilling his brandy across his desk. Even as he rushed to the window, he could feel the train decelerating.

He stuck his head out the window, looking ahead. They were pulling into the station, or as close as they could get since—as Mycroft had pointed out—the Pendleton-Salem Direct was still at the platform.

Arbuckle's string of expletives were so loud and obscene, they almost shattered the glass in the train car's windows.

He grabbed his coat and headed for the door. "Come on, Mycroft. We'll get to the bottom of this!"

He pushed his way through the grumbling crowd that milled about the station, realizing as he went that they were the passengers, all wondering why they weren't on the train and on their way to Salem.

Arbuckle reached the locomotive just as two men were coming down from the cab, presumably the engineer and fireman by the look of them.

"Why isn't this train on its way to Salem?" Arbuckle demanded.

The engineer frowned. "And just who in the world are you supposed to be?"

"I'm Kent Arbuckle, you fool."

The engineer obviously recognized the name, for his demeanor changed immediately. "Now, Mr. Arbuckle, sir, this ain't my fault. The inspector was here and said we didn't have our firebox certificate. It took four hours to cool down so he could inspect it proper. I was just on my way to fetch him."

"Firebox certificate?" Arbuckle shouted. "What are you talking about?"

The engineer shrugged. "That's what I said!"

They quickly exchanged words, and Arbuckle ascertained that this so-called inspector waited in the hotel across the street. Arbuckle stomped toward the hotel, with Mycroft, the engineer, and the fireman in tow.

He flung open the doors and stormed into the hotel's small lobby and shouted, "Where's Arnold Gross?"

A man sat in an armchair across the lobby, reading a newspaper. He lowered it and regarded Arbuckle with a cool, unruffled expression. "I'm Gross. What's all the fuss?"

"Fuss?" Arbuckle strode across the lobby and stuck a finger in the man's face. "My train is four hours behind schedule because of *you*!"

"Not because of me," the man called Gross said. "They should have been up-to-date with their firebox certificate."

"There's no such thing!"

Gross narrowed his eyes. "I assure you there is."

"I'm Kent Arbuckle of Gladstone Railways," he shouted. "Don't you think I'd know?"

Gross stood, looking very put out. "I can settle this right now. I have a copy of the updated edition of the state of Oregon's railway rules and regulations, *including* the supplement from the federal commission in Washington, DC. I can fetch it right now and show you the page and the paragraph."

"Do it!" Arbuckle snapped. "I'll be right here."

"Very well." Gross spun haughtily on his heel and walked down the hall to his room.

Arbuckle jammed his hands into his trouser pockets and paced with a manic energy. "We'll just see, Mycroft. We'll get to the bottom of this."

Arbuckle waited for Gross's return.

And waited.

He was starting to get a bad feeling.

Mycroft stood at the lobby's front window, peering out. "There he goes."

"What?"

Arbuckle rushed out the front door. He stood and watched as the railroad inspector galloped out of town as fast as he could make the horse go.

Arbuckle swallowed hard. "Mycroft."

"Sir?"

"I think we've been had."

CHAPTER 35

The temptation to sleep an extra hour and take it easy that final day was strong.

But no. That struck Callahan as unprofessional. The wagon train rose early and got underway as usual.

They'd reach Salem by the end of the day.

Which meant that sooner or later the Pendleton-Salem Direct would come roaring by, hissing steam and belching smoke, and leave them in the dust.

So close. Callahan shook his head and slouched in the saddle.

Callahan kept looking over his shoulder, expecting to see the locomotive puffing after them.

Later, Callahan saw something in the distance coming toward them, gliding along the railroad tracks. It was obviously the handcar coming back from the other direction, and it looked like it was slowing down.

Callahan nudged his horse toward the tracks.

The two men aboard the handcar waved just as it came to a stop.

"Not in so much of a hurry this time," Callahan said.

"We had to get the line inspected before the first passengers came through," he said. "No big hurry to get back. Anyway, you was curious about the Pendleton-Salem Direct, so we thought you might be interested to hear the latest."

Callahan shrugged. "Can't hurt, I guess."

"Some kind of trouble," said the man on the handcar. "They're running late."

Callahan blinked. "Late?"

"Real late. I don't know the details. I figure they'll tell us when we get back."

Callahan blinked again, face blank. "Late?"

"Yep."

Callahan sat in his saddle a moment, digesting what he'd been told.

Then suddenly, his eyes went wide. "Parsons!"

"Say what now?" asked the man on the handcar.

Callahan wheeled his horse around. "Thanks, fellas!" he called over his shoulder.

He galloped back for the column, leaning low in the saddle, riding for all he was worth.

"Billy!" he shouted as he neared the wagons.

Billy Thorndyke rode out to meet him. "Trouble, boss?"

"The Pendleton-Salem Direct is late," Callahan said. "Real late."

It took Billy a moment, and then he suddenly sat up straight in his saddle. "Does that mean . . . ? Can we still . . . ?"

"Pass the word," Callahan told him. "Let's get this wagon train moving."

In no time the wagon train buzzed with the news. The settlers would not get one red cent of the ten-thousand-dollar wager, but they got those mules moving faster for Tomahawk Callahan, who'd risked life and limb to bring them nearly two thousand miles to a new life.

These are good people, Callahan thought. *I'm lucky to know them.*

The settlers had urged their mules into sort of a sad half trot. The animals had good endurance and could pull wagons a long distance, which is why mules or oxen were best for this task.

But mules weren't built for speed.

The settlers would urge the animals faster for a while, then let them rest, then hurry them again. It wasn't what anyone would describe as *fast*, but it was faster than usual. The faster pace wouldn't be comfortable for the settlers, the cumbersome Conestogas swaying and bumping and rattling more than usual.

Callahan kept looking over his shoulder, desperately hoping *not* to see the train bearing down on them.

Then late into the afternoon, it happened. Salem's vague shape humped up from the horizon. The railroad tracks were only fifty feet to the left, like a steel guide. It seemed impossible that the town would finally be in sight, right in front of them, real. Callahan took one more look back, but still saw no train. It was happening. They were going to do it!

Callahan urged his horse out front, raised his arm, and motioned forward. "Let's go!"

The settlers flicked the reins of their mule teams, urging them into their clumsy half gallop.

Callahan spotted a rider coming toward them. He came into focus as he got closer, a middle-aged man with a tin star pinned to his vest. He passed Callahan, wheeled his horse around, and then reined in alongside.

"Tomahawk Callahan?"

"That's me," Callahan said.

"Sheriff Conway," he said, motioning ahead toward Salem. "Follow me in!"

Callahan frowned. "Am I in trouble?"

Conway grinned, shaking his head. "I'm your escort. Don't go to the usual area on the edge of town. I'm taking you right to Main Street!"

"Main Street?"

"We've been planning this for weeks!" Sheriff Conway told him. "Now follow me!"

The sheriff spurred his horse ahead, and Callahan followed. He looked back, the wagons rattling and swaying and bouncing along as the mules huffed and puffed, the whole column kicking up a magnificent cloud of dust.

Callahan looked ahead. Empty railroad tracks led to a brand-new train station on the left. He saw Main Street, the entrance to Salem. The street had been cleared, and the sidewalks on either side were crowded with the townsfolk, all gawking and waiting to see history being made.

They'd stretched a wide red ribbon across the width of Main Street.

The finish line!

At the last second, Sheriff Conway veered away.

Tomahawk Callahan rode through the red ribbon at a full gallop. It caught on his chest and streamed behind him like the cape of some ancient, Greek hero.

A cheer went up from the crowd, so loud that Callahan felt it vibrate down his spine.

A brass band suddenly played a rousing march, all blaring horns and drums.

Callahan jerked the reins, his horse skidding to a halt. He leapt from the saddle and slapped the horse on the rump to send it out of harm's way.

"Billy Thorndyke, front and center!" he shouted.

Billy reined in his horse next to Callahan and dismounted as people crowded around.

"Keep waving those wagons down the street," Callahan told him. "Don't let them bunch up!"

"Right, boss!" Billy scrambled to obey.

The wagons came rumbling through, with Billy waving them on to the end of Main Street, dust kicking up, everyone still cheering like mad. The brass band gave it everything they had.

People crowded around Callahan, everyone wanting a turn to slap him on the back. A man in a fine suit pushed his way through the crowd, top hat perched on his head, a white flower in his lapel, gray sideburns. He held a brass key a foot long in his hands.

"You Callahan?"

"That's right." Callahan kept trying to look past the crowd at the wagons coming in.

He caught a glance of Pete Johansen and the Graingers speeding past, Johansen's face hard as stone, a white-knuckle grip on the reins.

"I'm Mayor Elwood Meriweather," said the man with the key. "And for your victorious and historic . . . uh . . . victory." It was clear he'd forgotten his memorized speech in all the excitement. "Well. I have this key to the city for you!"

Callahan still watched the wagons come in. He saw Becky go by, Lizzy peeking over her shoulder and grinning like crazy.

How many? Had Billy Thorndyke remembered to count?

The mayor was still talking. "And, well, the people of Salem want to welcome—"

"Sorry, Mr. Mayor," Callahan said. "There's still work to do!" Callahan pushed through the crowd toward the wagons.

"But wait!" the mayor called after him.

Callahan found Billy. "How many?" He had to raise his voice to be heard over the band.

Billy shook his head. "I don't know! I've just been waving them on!"

Callahan ran back down the line of wagons.

The last one came through, and Callahan stood on the edge of town, looking back into the dust floating in the air. That was all, surely. Right?

He saw Clancy Davenport and waved him over. "Go count the wagons!"

"You got it, boss!" Davenport turned his horse and galloped back toward the wagons.

Suddenly, the mayor was there again, looking a little red-faced and sweaty. "I got this key to the city for you, Callahan. They're waiting to take our picture over by the bank."

But Callahan wasn't listening. He peered into the dust. Something was coming through.

Sheep.

In the next ten seconds, an entire herd of sheep swarmed around Callahan and the mayor, bleating and not smelling too good.

Bart Schultz waded through his sheep and went straight up to Callahan.

"Miss Masters wanted me to relay a message," Schultz said. "She said that she told you that dang wagon wheel was no good."

Callahan's eyes bugged wide. "What?"

"She's broke down about two miles back," Shultz said. "Okay, I told you. I better get these sheep out of the way now."

Callahan felt sick. *Noooooo, no, no, no, no.*

"Look, Callahan, do you want this blasted key or not?" Mayor Meriweather asked.

"I hate to break it to you, Mayor, but this race ain't over," Callahan told him. "We've still got a wagon out there."

"What?"

Callahan looked around frantically, trying to figure out what to do.

Parked in back of the new train station, out of the way of the Main Street traffic, an enormous man sat on the bench seat of an empty freight wagon with a team of horses attached.

Callahan ran for it, the mayor still yelling about the key and the photograph behind him.

Callahan arrived at the empty freight wagon and looked at the man sitting there. He was at least a foot taller than Callahan and had shoulders as wide as the West but also a friendly open face.

"Mister, you busy?" Callahan asked.

"Nope," he said. "Just finished unloading the wagon

and decided this was a good spot to sit and watch the excitement."

"I'm in a fix and could use a favor," Callahan said.

"Sorry. I'm supposed to get this wagon back."

"Look, my name is Tomahawk Callahan and—"

"Tomahawk Callahan?" The big man's face lit up. "No foolin'?"

"No foolin'."

"Congrats on your big win." He stuck out his hand. "I'm Delbert Cole."

Callahan shook his hand. "Well, Delbert, it's good to meet you, but I've got some bad news. I haven't won anything yet. I got one more wagon stuck out there. I need to borrow you. And your horses."

"Well . . . I mean I'd like to help . . . but . . ."

"Please help me," Callahan said. "Help me, and I'd be proud to share a bottle of whiskey with you later."

"Get on."

Callahan climbed aboard the wagon. Delbert flicked the reins and snapped his whip, and the horses took off.

They passed Ace Franklin and his cattle on the way.

Callahan hung on, the horses galloping for all they were worth. Soon the broken-down wagon came into view.

Anna Masters stood there with hands on hips, looking angrier than a bunch of riled hornets.

"I told you about that wheel!" she said crossly as Delbert reined in the horses.

"Not now!" Callahan jumped down to take a look at the wheel.

Busted. The wagon leaned alarming to one side.

Callahan circled to the rear of the wagon and looked inside. The Hendersons looked shaken but otherwise unhurt.

Callahan turned back to the big man. "Delbert, I hate to ask, but what are the odds I can have one of the wheels off your freight wagon?"

Delbert shrugged. "Why not? I'm probably already fired, anyway. I've got tools and a big lever in the bed of the wagon."

"Miss Masters, unhitch those mules, will you?" Callahan asked.

A confused look on her face. "What for?"

"Please hurry."

She did as told.

Delbert shoved the lever under the freight wagon and lifted it. Callahan worked the wheel off and set it aside. Both men were sweating buckets.

"Okay, now to get the bad wheel off this Conestoga," Callahan said. "I'll get the old folks out to lighten the load."

"Leave 'em."

Delbert stuck the lever beneath the Conestoga and pulled down, lifting the Conestoga, grunting, face going red. Callahan tugged the broken wheel off the axle.

He went to the freight wagon, grabbed the good wheel, and rolled it over.

Callahan paused, stood straight. "Did you hear that?"

"I didn't hear nothing."

Callahan waited, listened. There it was again. The unmistakable sound of a forlorn train whistle in the distance.

Oh no. Callahan felt a stab of panic.

"Uh, Mr. Callahan?" Sweat dripped from Delbert's nose, his face as red as a tomato. His muscles bulged and threatened to burst from his shirt. "I wouldn't exactly hate it if you hurried."

Callahan shoved the new wheel into place and hammered it home with a mallet. Delbert let the wagon drop, panting for air.

"The horses!" Callahan shouted.

The shrill shriek of the train whistle sounded alarmingly close now.

Callahan, Delbert, and Anna Masters rushed to hitch Delbert's horses.

They finished the job quickly, and Callahan told Masters to climb into the back of the wagon. "I'll take us in."

"No, chance, Tomahawk!" Masters leapt onto the wagon and grabbed the reins. "I've got the perfect ending to my last installment, and I'm the star!" She flicked the reins hard. "Yah!"

Callahan barely had time to jump onto the side of the wagon, where he hung on for dear life as the wagon sped forward, the horses pulling it faster than mules ever could. It was a rough ride, jostling and rattling, Callahan clinging until his muscles hurt.

He looked back.

The train was visible now, billowing smoke and coming fast.

A mile sped by.

The train had gained and was still coming.

Callahan looked ahead and saw that someone had stretched the red ribbon across Main Street again. The mayor had apparently ordered a do-over.

When Callahan looked back again, the train was so close he could see the expression on the engineer's face as he leaned out of the cab. The hissing locomotive bore down on them like some hungry beast, getting closer and closer, no intention of braking for the upcoming station, now pulling even with the rear axle of the wagon, edging forward—

The horses ran through the ribbon as Anna Masters urged them on like a woman gone mad. The crowd cheered even louder than before.

The train rumbled through the station and kept going on down the line.

The wagon hit a bump in the road, and Callahan was knocked off. He rolled through the dirt, came to a stop, and slowly sat up. He saw that Anna Masters had managed to finally rein in the horses. The entire town had crowded around her wagon, and a moment later, they had her up on their shoulders, parading her around.

The band didn't play any better, but somehow, they managed to play louder.

Callahan tried to stand, his knees going watery, and he gave up and just sat in the middle of the road.

The mayor walked over, looked down at him. A moment later, he sat next to Callahan in the dirt. He offered the big brass key again. "You gonna take this now?"

Callahan threw back his head and laughed loud and long.

Winning felt good.

EPILOGUE

The next two days were a blur for Tomahawk Callahan.

Kent Arbuckle handed ten thousand dollars in gold to Callahan in front of a gaggle of reporters. The men shook hands, both pretending to be good sports. Callahan had never liked the man and never would. The feeling, he guessed, was mutual.

He sent a telegram to his Aunt Clara: "We won!"

She sent a telegram back the next day: "Half the money yours. Well done."

Callahan talked to Delbert's boss. Delbert didn't get fired.

Everyone wanted to buy Callahan a drink. A sort of festival atmosphere reigned in Salem for the next few days. The race, with its exciting finish, was the biggest thing to happen to the town in a long time.

Eventually, things settled down. A few members of the wagon train still camped on the edge of town. Others had gone off to join family members or start their new lives on a piece of property somewhere or . . . well, it wasn't any of Callahan's business. He'd gotten them this far. He wished them luck.

Callahan walked down a Salem sidewalk, holding Becky's hand. It was good to have a simple, quiet moment with his girl after all the nonstop excitement.

"Where's Lizzy?" he asked.

"Saying good-bye to the Grainger girls," Becky said. "They're moving on tomorrow."

"That'll be sad for Lizzy."

"She'll make new friends."

They strolled a bit and then stopped in front of a small, two-story building a block over from Main Street. The big front window was empty except for a small sign that said FOR SALE.

"Hey, have you thought about opening a shop?"

"I hadn't thought much past making it to Oregon alive," she admitted.

"No, really," Callahan said. "Hang up some pretty dresses in the window, sewing machine in back." He craned his neck, looking up. "Probably some comfortable rooms to live in up there."

"Uh-huh. Right now, I'm living just fine in my palatial covered wagon."

A man appeared inside the window. He gave the couple a friendly wave, then put a sign that said SOLD right next to the other sign.

"See?" she said. "It's gone, anyway."

"Yeah," Callahan said as they started walking again. "Somebody bought it. Probably some lucky fool that just came into a bunch of money."

"Yeah," Becky said.

She stopped walking, abruptly, and looked up at him. "Luke, what did you do?"

"Do?" Mock innocence on his face.

"Luke, did you . . . ? I mean, are you really . . . ? You can't just . . ."

He took her by the hand again and gently pulled her along. "I can do whatever I want. I'm Tomahawk Callahan."

Kent Arbuckle had found it exhausting pretending to be magnanimous.

Eventually, the newspaper reporters had left him alone.

After the telegram arrived telling Arbuckle that his employment with Gladstone Railways had been terminated, Mycroft Jones had taken charge of the private train and had left Salem that morning. Arbuckle took a hotel room and bent his thoughts toward what he planned to do next. It was difficult to think past his hatred for Tomahawk Callahan.

He ate dinner alone, walked slowly back to his hotel, went up to his room, and closed the door.

He heard the unmistakable sound of a revolver being cocked and froze. He turned slowly to see who'd gotten the drop on him.

Roy Benson sat at the table near the window, a bottle of whiskey and a glass in front of him, a revolver in one hand pointing at Arbuckle's chest.

Arbuckle was too disgruntled by recent events to be alarmed by Benson's presence. "Where have you been? I might still have won that bet if you'd done your job."

"This is my job now." He took a piece of paper from his jacket pocket and placed it on the table.

Arbuckle crossed the room, took the paper, and read it. A telegram from the Gladstones.

"Have arranged for assets in Imperial Hotel safe to be released to you in exchange for final removal of liability."

"So I'm a liability now, am I? I guess Woodrow had the final word," Arbuckle said. "Is that how you get your money?"

A shrug from Benson. "Seemed easier."

Arbuckle took a glass from the sideboard and sat at the table across from Benson. "You wouldn't begrudge a man a final drink."

"Go on then."

Arbuckle filled the glass and took a sip. "I worked for the railroad company a decade."

"So what?"

"So I took quite a bit of my pay in stock," Arbuckle said. "If I liquidate, I'll be a wealthy man."

Benson raised an eyebrow. Arbuckle's words had clearly caught his interest. "You want to buy your life?"

"No." Arbuckle tossed back the rest of the whiskey. "I want to hire you again. At a good rate. More than is in the safe at the Imperial, I assure you."

"I see." Benson eased the hammer down on his six-shooter. "Hire me for what?"

A smile spread slowly across Arbuckle's face. "Revenge."

TURN THE PAGE
FOR A GUT-BUSTIN' PREVIEW!

**JOHNSTONE COUNTRY.
HOMESTYLE JUSTICE WITH A SIDE OF
SLAUGHTER.**

**In this explosive new series, Western legend
Luke Jensen teams up with chuckwagon cook
Dewey "Mac" McKenzie to dish out
a steaming plate of hot-blooded justice.
But in a corrupt town like Hangman's Hill,
revenge is a dish best served cold . . .**

**BEANS, BOURBON, AND BLOOD:
A RECIPE FOR DISASTER**

The sight of a rotting corpse hanging from a noose
is enough to stop any man in his tracks—
and Luke Jensen is no exception.
Sure, he could just keep riding through.
He's got a prisoner to deliver, after all. But when a
group of men show up with another prisoner for
another hanging, Luke can't turn his back—
especially when the condemned man
keeps swearing he's innocent.
Right up to the moment
he's hanged by the neck till he's dead . . .

Welcome to Hannigan's Hill, Wyoming.
Better known as Hangman's Hill.

Luke's pretty shaken up by what he's seen but decides
to stay the night, get some rest, and grab some grub.
The town marshal agrees to lock up Luke's prisoner
while Luke heads to a local saloon, Mac's Place.
According to the pub's owner—a former chuckwagon
cook named Dewey "Mac" McKenzie—it serves up a
bellyful of chow and an earful of gossip. According to
Mac, the whole stinking town is run by corrupt
cattle baron Ezra Hannigan. Ezra owns practically
everything, including the town marshal. And anyone
who gets in his way ends up swinging from a rope . . .

Mac might be just an excellent cook. But he's also
got a ferocious appetite for justice—and a fearsome
new friend in Luke Jensen. Together, they could end
Hannigan's reign of terror. But when Hannigan calls
in his hired guns, it'll be their necks on the line . . .
or dancing from the end of a rope.

National Bestselling Authors
William W. Johnstone
and J.A. Johnstone

BEANS, BOURBON, AND BLOOD
A Luke Jensen–Dewey McKenzie Western

On sale now, wherever Pinnacle Books are sold.

Live Free. Read Hard.
www.williamjohnstone.net
Visit us at www.kensingtonbooks.com

CHAPTER 1

Luke Jensen reined his horse to a halt and looked up at the hanged man. The corpse swung back and forth in the cold wind sweeping across the Wyoming plains.

From behind Luke, Ethan Stallings said, "I don't like the looks of that. No, sir, I don't like it one bit."

"Shut up, Stallings," Luke said without taking his gaze off the dead man dangling from a hangrope attached to the crossbar of a sturdy-looking gallows. "In case you haven't figured it out already, I don't care what you like."

Luke rested both hands on his saddle horn and leaned forward to ease muscles made weary by the long ride to the town of Hannigan's Hill. He had never been here before, but he'd heard that the place was sometimes called Hangman's Hill. He could see why. Not every settlement had a gallows on a hill overlooking it just outside of town.

And not every gallows had a corpse hanging from it that looked to have been there for at least a week, based on the amount of damage buzzards had done to it. This poor varmint's eyes were gone, and not much remained of his nose and lips and ears, either. Buzzards went for the easiest bits first.

Luke was a middle-aged man who still had an air of vitality about him despite his years and the rough life he had led. His face was too craggy to be called handsome, but the features held a rugged appeal. The thick, dark hair under his black hat was threaded with gray, as was the mustache under his prominent nose. His boots, trousers, and shirt were black to match his hat. He wore a sheepskin jacket to ward off the chill of the gray autumn day.

He rode a rangy buckskin horse, as unlovely but as strong as its rider. A rope stretched back from the saddle to the bridle of the other horse, a chestnut gelding, so that it had to follow. The hands of the man riding that horse were tied to the saddle horn.

He sat with his narrow shoulders hunched against the cold. The brown tweed suit he wore wasn't heavy enough to keep him warm. His face under the brim of a bowler hat was thin, fox-like. Thick, reddish-brown side whiskers crept down to the angular line of his jaw.

"I'm not sure we should stay here," he said. "Doesn't appear to be a very welcoming place."

"It has a jail and a telegraph office," Luke said. "That'll serve our purposes."

"Your purposes," Ethan Stallings said. "Not mine."

"Yours don't matter anymore. Haven't since you became my prisoner."

Stallings sighed. A great deal of dejection was packed into the sound.

Luke frowned as he studied the hanged man more closely. The man wore town clothes: wool trousers, a white shirt, a simple vest. His hands were tied behind his back. As bad a shape as he was in, it was hard to make an accurate guess about his age, other than the fact that he hadn't been old. His hair was a little thin but still sandy brown with no sign of gray or white.

Luke had witnessed quite a few hangings. Most fellows who wound up dancing on air were sent to eternity with black hoods over their heads. Usually, the hoods were left in place until after the corpse had been cut down and carted off to the undertaker. Most people enjoyed the spectacle of a hanging, but they didn't necessarily want to see the end result.

The fact that this man no longer wore a hood—if, in fact, he ever had—and was still here on the gallows a week later could mean only one thing.

Whoever had strung him up wanted folks to be able to see him. Wanted to send a message with that grisly sight.

Stallings couldn't keep from talking for very long. He had been that way ever since Luke had captured him. He said, "This is sure making me nervous."

"No reason for it to. You're just a con artist, Stallings. You're not a killer or a rustler or a horse thief. The chances of you winding up on a gallows are pretty slim. You'll just spend the next few years behind bars, that's all."

Stallings muttered something Luke couldn't make out, then said in a louder, more excited voice, "Look! Somebody's coming."

The town of Hannigan's Hill was about half a mile away, a decent-sized settlement with a main street three blocks long lined by businesses and close to a hundred houses total on the side streets. The railroad hadn't come through here, but as Luke had mentioned, there was a telegraph line. East, south, and north—the direction he and Stallings had come from—lay rangeland. Some low but rugged mountains bulked to the west. The town owed its existence mostly to the ranches that surrounded it on three sides, but Luke knew there was some mining in the mountains, too.

A group of riders had just left the settlement and were heading toward the hill. Bunched up the way they were, Luke couldn't tell exactly how many. Six or eight, he estimated. They moved at a brisk pace as if they didn't want to waste any time.

On a raw, bleak day like today, nobody could blame them for feeling that way.

Something about one of them struck Luke as odd, and as they came closer, he figured out what it was. Two men rode slightly ahead of the others, and one of them had his arms pulled behind him. His hands had been tied together behind his back. His head hung forward as he rode as if he lacked the strength or the spirit to lift it.

Stallings had seen the same thing. "Oh, hell," the confidence man said. His voice held a hollow note. "They're bringing somebody else up here to hang him."

That certainly appeared to be the case. Luke spotted a badge pinned to the shirt of the other man in the lead, under his open coat. More than likely, that was the local sheriff or marshal.

"Whatever they're doing, it's none of our business," Luke said.

"They shouldn't have left that other fella dangling there like that. It . . . it's inhumane!"

Luke couldn't argue with that sentiment, but again, it was none of his affair how they handled their law-breakers here in Hannigan's Hill. Or Hangman's Hill, as some people called it, he reminded himself.

"You don't have to worry about that," he told Stallings again. "All I'm going to do is lock you up and send a wire to Senator Creed to find out what he wants me to do with you. I expect he'll tell me to take you on to Laramie or Cheyenne and turn you over to the law there. Eventually, you'll wind up on a train back to Ohio to stand trial for swindling the senator, and you'll go to jail. It's not the end of the world."

"For you it's not."

The riders were a couple of hundred yards away now. The lawman in the lead made a curt motion with his hand. Two of the other men spurred their horses ahead, swung around the lawman and the prisoner, and headed toward Luke and Stallings at a faster pace.

"They've seen us," Stallings said.

"Take it easy. We haven't done anything wrong. Well, I haven't, anyway. You're the one who decided it would be a good idea to swindle a United States Senator out of ten thousand dollars."

The two riders pounded up the slope and reined in about twenty feet away. They looked hard at Luke and Stallings, and one of them asked in a harsh voice, "What's your business here?"

Luke had been a bounty hunter for a lot of years. He recognized hardcases when he saw them. But these two men wore deputy badges. That wasn't all that unusual.

This was the frontier. Plenty of lawmen had ridden the owlhoot trail at one time or another in their lives. The reverse was true, too.

Luke turned his head and gestured toward Stallings with his chin. "Got a prisoner back there, and I'm looking for a place to lock him up, probably for no more than a day or two. That's my only business here, friend."

"I don't see no badge. You a bounty hunter?"

"That's right. Name's Jensen."

The name didn't appear to mean anything to the men. If Luke had said that his brother was Smoke Jensen, the famous gunfighter who was now a successful rancher down in Colorado, that would have drawn more notice. Most folks west of the Mississippi had heard of Smoke. Plenty east of the big river had, too. But Luke never traded on family connections. In fact, for a lot of years, for a variety of reasons, he had called himself Luke Smith instead of using the Jensen name.

The two deputies still seemed suspicious. "You don't know that hombre Marshal Bowen is bringin' up here?"

"I don't even know Marshal Bowen," Luke answered honestly. "I never set eyes on any of you boys until today."

"The marshal told us to make sure you wasn't plannin' on interferin'. This here is a legal hangin' we're fixin' to carry out."

Luke gave a little wave of his left hand. "Go right ahead. I always cooperate with the law."

That wasn't strictly true—he'd been known to bend the law from time to time when he thought it was the right thing to do—but these deputies didn't need to know that.

The other deputy spoke up for the first time. "Who's your prisoner?"

"Name's Ethan Stallings. Strictly small-time. Nobody who'd interest you fellas."

"That's right," Stallings muttered. "I'm nobody."

The rest of the group was close now. The marshal raised his left hand in a signal for them to stop. As they reined in, Luke looked the men over and judged them to be cut from the same cloth as the first two deputies. They wore law badges, but they were no better than they had to be.

The prisoner was young, maybe twenty-five, a stocky redhead who wore range clothes. He didn't look like a forty-a-month-and-found puncher. Maybe a little better than that. He might own a small spread of his own, a greasy sack outfit he worked with little or no help.

When he finally raised his head, he looked absolutely terrified, too. He looked straight at Luke and said, "For God's sake, mister, you've got to help me. They're gonna hang me, and I didn't do anything wrong. I swear it!"

CHAPTER 2

The marshal turned in his saddle, leaned over, and swung a backhanded blow that cracked viciously across the prisoner's face. The man might have toppled off his horse if one of the other deputies hadn't ridden up beside him and grasped his arm to steady him.

"Shut up, Crawford," the lawman said. "Nobody wants to listen to your lies. Take what you've got coming and leave these strangers out of it."

The prisoner's face flamed red where the marshal had struck it. He started to cry, letting out wrenching sobs full of terror and desperation.

Even without knowing the facts of the case, Luke felt a pang of sympathy for the young man. He didn't particularly want to, but he felt it anyway.

"I'm Verne Bowen. Marshal of Hannigan's Hill. We're about to carry out a legally rendered sentence on this man. You have any objection?"

Luke shook his head. "Like I told your deputies, Marshal, this is none of my business, and I don't have the faintest idea what's going on here. So I'm not going to interfere."

Bowen jerked his head in a nod and said, "Good."

He was about the same age as Luke, a thick-bodied man with graying fair hair under a pushed-back brown hat. He had a drooping mustache and a close-cropped beard. He wore a brown suit over a fancy vest and a butternut shirt with no cravat. A pair of walnut-butted revolvers rode in holsters on his hips. He looked plenty tough and probably was.

Bowen waved a hand at the deputies and ordered, "Get on with it."

Two of them dismounted and moved in on either side of the prisoner, Crawford. He continued to sob as they pulled him off his horse and marched him toward the gallows steps, one on either side of him.

"Just out of curiosity," Luke asked, "what did this hombre do?"

Bowen glared at him. "You said that was none of your business."

"And it's not. Just curious, that's all."

"It doesn't pay to be too curious around here, mister . . . ?"

"Jensen. Luke Jensen."

Bowen nodded toward Stallings. "I see you have a prisoner, too. You a bounty hunter?"

"That's right. I was hoping you'd allow me to stash him in your jail for a day or two."

"Badman, is he?"

"A foolish man," Luke said, "who made some bad choices. But he didn't do anything around here."

Luke allowed his voice to harden slightly. "Not in your jurisdiction."

Bowen looked levelly at him for a couple of seconds, then nodded. "Fair enough."

By now the deputies were forcing Crawford up the steps. He twisted and jerked and writhed, but their grips were too strong for him to pull free. It wouldn't have done him any good if he had. He would have just fallen down the steps and they would have picked him up again.

Bowen said, "I don't suppose it'll hurt anything to satisfy your curiosity, Jensen. Just don't get in the habit of poking your nose in where it's not wanted. Crawford there is a murderer. He got drunk and killed a soiled dove."

"That's not true!" Crawford cried. "I never hurt that girl. Somebody slipped me something that knocked me out. I never even laid eyes on the girl until I came to in her room and she was . . . was layin' there with her eyes bugged out and her tongue sticking out and those terrible bruises on her throat—"

"Choked her to death, the little weasel did," Bowen interrupted. "Claims he doesn't remember it, but he's a lying, no-account killer."

The deputies and the prisoner had reached the top of the steps. The deputies wrestled Crawford out onto the platform. Another star packer trotted up the steps after them, moving with a jaunty bounce, and pulled a knife from a sheath at his waist. He reached out, grasped the dead man's belt, and pulled him close enough that he could reach up and cut the rope. When he let go, the body fell through the open trap and landed with a soggy thud on the ground below. Even from where Luke was, he could smell the stench that rose from it. He didn't envy whoever got the job of burying the man.

"How about him? What did he do?"

"A thief," Bowen said. "Embezzled some money from the man he worked for, one of our leading citizens."

Luke frowned. "You hang a man for embezzlement around here?"

"When he was caught, he went loco and tried to shoot his way out of it," Bowen replied with a shrug. "He could have killed somebody. That's attempted murder. The judge decided to make an example of him. I don't hand down the sentences, Jensen. I just carry 'em out."

"I suppose leaving him up here to rot was part of making an example."

Bowen leaned forward, glared, and said, "For somebody who keeps claiming this is none of his business, you are taking an almighty keen interest in all of this, mister. You might want to take your prisoner and ride on down to town. Ask anybody, they can tell you where my office and the jail are. I'll be down directly, and we can lock that fella up." The marshal paused, then added, "Got a good bounty on him, does he?"

"Good enough," Luke said. He was beginning to get the impression that instead of waiting, he ought to ride on with Stallings and not stop over in Hannigan's Hill at all. Bowen and those hardcase deputies might have their eyes on the reward Senator Jonas Creed had offered for Stallings's capture.

But their horses were just about played out and really needed a night's rest. They were low on provisions, too. It would be difficult to push on to Laramie without replenishing their supplies here.

As soon as he had Stallings locked up, he would send a wire to Senator Creed. Once he'd established that he was the one who had captured the fugitive, Bowen wouldn't be able to claim the reward for himself. Luke figured he could stay alive long enough to do that.

He sure as blazes wasn't going to let his guard down while he was in these parts, though.

He reached back to tug on the lead rope attached to Stallings' horse. "Come on."

The deputies had closed the trapdoor on the gallows and positioned Crawford on it. One of them tossed a new hangrope over the crossbar. Another deputy caught it and closed in to fit the noose over the prisoner's head.

"Reckon we ought to tie his feet together?" one of the men asked.

"Naw," another answered with a grin. "If it so happens that his neck don't break right off, it'll be a heap more entertainin' if he can kick good while he's chokin' to death."

"Please, mister, please!" Crawford cried. "Don't just ride off and let them do this to me! I never killed that whore. They did it and framed me for it! They're only doing this because Ezra Hannigan wants my ranch!"

That claim made Luke pause. Bowen must have noticed Luke's reaction because he snapped at the deputies, "Shut him up. I'm not gonna stand by and let him spew those filthy lies about Mr. Hannigan."

"Please—" Crawford started to shriek, but then one of the deputies stepped behind him and slammed a gun butt against the back of his head. Crawford sagged forward, only half-conscious as the other deputies held him up by the arms.

Luke glanced at the four deputies who were still mounted nearby. Each rested a hand on the butt of a holstered revolver. Luke knew gun-wolves like that wouldn't hesitate to yank their hoglegs out and start blasting. He had faced long odds plenty of times in his life and wasn't afraid, but he didn't feel like getting shot to doll rags today, either, and likely that was what would happen if he tried to interfere.

With a sour taste in his mouth, he lifted his reins, nudged the buckskin into motion, and turned the horse to ride around the group of lawmen toward the settlement. He heard the prisoner groan from the gallows, but Crawford had been knocked too senseless to protest coherently anymore.

A moment later, with an unmistakable sound, the trapdoor dropped and so did the prisoner. In the thin, cold air, Luke distinctly heard the crack of Crawford's neck breaking.

He wasn't looking back, but Stallings must have been. The confidence man cursed and then said, "They didn't even put a hood over his head before they hung him! That's just indecent, Jensen."

"I'm not arguing with you."

"And you know good and well he was innocent. He

was telling the truth about them framing him for that dove's murder."

"You don't have any way of knowing that," Luke pointed out. "We don't know anything about these people."

"Who's Ezra Hannigan?"

Luke took a deep breath. "Well, considering that the town's called Hannigan's Hill, I expect he's an important man around here. Probably owns some of the businesses. Maybe most of them. Maybe a big ranch outside of town. I think I've heard the name before, but I can't recall for sure."

"The fella who was hanging there when we rode up, the one they cut down, that marshal said he stole money from one of the leading citizens. You want to bet it was Ezra Hannigan he stole from?"

"I don't want to bet with you about anything, Stallings. I just want to get you where you're going and collect my money. Whatever's going on in this town, I don't want any part of it."

Stallings was silent for a moment, then said, "I suppose there wouldn't be anything you could do, anyway. Not against a marshal and that many deputies, and all of them looking like they know how to handle a gun. Funny that a town this size would need that many deputies, though . . . unless their actual job isn't keeping the peace but doing whatever Ezra Hannigan wants done. Like hanging the owner of a spread Hannigan's got his eye on."

"You've flapped that jaw enough," Luke told him. "I don't want to hear any more out of you."

"Whether you hear it or not won't change the truth of the matter."

Stallings couldn't see it, but Luke grimaced. He knew that Stallings was likely right about what was happening around here. Luke had seen it more than once: some rich man ruling a town and the surrounding area with an iron fist, bringing in hired guns, running roughshod over anybody who dared to stand up to him. It was a common story on the frontier.

But it wasn't his job to set things right in Hannigan's Hill, even assuming that Stallings was right about Ezra Hannigan. Smoke might not stand for such things, but Smoke had a reckless streak in him sometimes. Luke's hard life had made him more practical. He would have wound up dead if he had tried to interfere with that hanging. Bowen would have been more than happy to seize the excuse to kill him and claim his prisoner and the reward.

Luke knew all that, knew it good and well, but as he and Stallings reached the edge of town, something made him turn his head and look back anyway. Some unwanted force drew his gaze like a magnet to the top of the nearby hill. Bowen and the deputies had started riding back toward the settlement, leaving the young man called Crawford dangling limp and lifeless from that hangrope. Leaving him there to rot . . .

"Well," a female voice broke sharply into Luke's thoughts, "I hope you're proud of yourself."

Visit our website at
KensingtonBooks.com
to sign up for our newsletters, read
more from your favorite authors, see
books by series, view reading group
guides, and more!

Become a Part of Our
Between the Chapters Book Club
Community and Join the Conversation

Betweenthechapters.net